TALKING DIRTY WITH THE BILLIONAIRE BOSS

by

SERENITY WOODS

CONTENTS

Chapter One

Sidnie

People employed in intelligence agencies must have balls of steel. They put themselves in danger every day, donning disguises to infiltrate top-secret locations. They risk being shot or tortured or locked away in terrible foreign prisons. How do they manage to do it without hyperventilating into a paper bag?

I'm not in disguise, unless you count the green coveralls that Shine Professional Cleaning and Maintenance Services give me to wear. And this location isn't exactly a top-secret government office. But my palms are still sweating, and I'm close to throwing up.

Relax, I scold myself, taking deep breaths as I slot my battered old Toyota into a space in the car park out the front of Koru Technology. Nobody has a clue that I'm doing anything suspicious. I've been working for Shine for four months, and I quickly established myself as a reliable and trustworthy employee, always on time for my shift. Plus, it's nearly seven p.m., and the other offices I clean are normally empty by this time. Most office workers are out of the door soon after their official hours, unless it's a law firm, when they might hang around a bit longer. But this is a technology company, so I would imagine most of the employees have headed home by now.

I get out and check the pockets of my coveralls, finding my phone, a lip salve, a pair of sunglasses, a poem I scribbled on a serviette an hour ago in the coffee shop, three fifty-cent coins, a tissue, and finally my Shine ID card. After locking the car, I walk across to the security guard sitting in a small office by the barrier.

"Evening," I say, proud that my voice doesn't waver. "I'm from Shine Cleaning."

The guard—a good-looking Maori guy—slides his gaze over me and says, "Can I see your ID please?"

I push the Shine ID card across to him, and he scans it into his computer. "Haven't seen you here before," he says conversationally.

"I'm covering for Pippa. She's off sick."

"Oh, right. Okay, all cleared. Have a good evening."

"Thanks." I pocket the ID, give him a wave, and head toward the main office block.

It's an impressive building. Constructed entirely on one level, it's a pretty blue from the lamps nestled in the neatly trimmed grass strip in front of it. The setting sun has lit the large windows that make up most of the front wall, and it glows like a jewel in the evening air.

It's quiet here, despite Grafton being a busy part of Auckland, New Zealand. Auckland City Hospital is just down the road, and so is the main University of Auckland campus. It's a stone's throw from the CBD—the central business district, with its shops and entertainment—and a short walk to the beautiful Albert Park. Talk about prime real estate. But it's relatively quiet here, the main road far enough away to muffle the sound of the never-ending traffic.

I walk up to the Shine van parked out the front of the building. Dodie has already started unpacking the cleaning carts with two other members of her staff, and she nods at me as I approach. In her forties with salt-and-pepper hair tied back in a ponytail and not a scrap of makeup, she's brusque but friendly, with the air of someone who takes pride in her work. She told me at my interview that she's been Head Maintenance Attendant for twenty years. I silently begged the heavens to shoot me if I'm still cleaning when I'm forty-two.

"Hey, Sid," she says, turning to face me. She chuckles. "Have trouble with your hair tonight?"

"Lost the battle, but I'm hoping to win the war." My shoulder-length hair is a mass of messy blonde curls. I've had so many women tell me they wish they had hair like mine, but I'd kill to have limp, straight locks. Unfortunately, my hair straightener has given up the ghost, and I can't afford another one, so I'm stuck with the mop. Tonight, I tried to wrestle it into a bun, but, as Dodie's noticed, I wasn't a hundred percent successful.

"Thanks for doing this at the last minute," she adds, pulling out another cart.

I move forward to help her. "No worries. How is Pippa?"

"Feeling better, apparently, but I told her to stay at home. I don't want anyone else coming down with her bug. We're short-staffed as it is with Chris on vacation and Lou off on maternity leave."

I take one of the carts and only then notice that my hands are shaking. I'm certain Pippa was paid to say she was sick. Does she feel as uneasy about lying as I do?

"It's pretty quiet around here," I say. "I'm guessing everyone's gone home?"

"The general office staff will have done, yeah." Dodie shuts the back of the van and locks it. "Let's get a move on."

Pushing my cart, I follow her and the other two cleaners to the main entrance. Another security officer checks our IDs again before pressing the button to open the doors.

We enter a large lobby with an impressive reception desk to one side, now empty, a waiting area with a large coffee machine and water cooler, and in the center a ring of soft cream leather seats around an enormous Christmas tree decorated with silver and black tinsel and decorations—the colors from the Koru Tech logo. Huge paintings hang on the walls—unusual art that looks abstract, but on closer inspection contains details of the inside of a computer—zoomed-in fans, motherboards, and video cards. There's a sense of opulence without it being ostentatious.

"Wow." I follow Dodie across the tiled floor, looking around with wide eyes.

"I know, it's very classy, isn't it? Must be a cool place to work." She stops by the door. One of the cleaners has already started washing the lobby floor. The other turns toward the right wing and pushes his cart along the corridor.

"This way," Dodie tells me. "You'll be doing Pippa's section—the management offices. If you need me, send me a text—I'm off to the hall that contains the supercomputer. They don't let just anyone in with Marise."

"Marise?"

She grins. "That's what the computer's called. I don't know why." She looks ahead and stops walking. "Hang on a minute."

The huge main office in front of us is open plan, so we can see right through the building. Four people are walking toward us, talking and laughing. All of them are wearing suits and carrying laptop cases. One is a woman, in her thirties maybe. One guy is Japanese, slender and good looking; the one next to him has striking ginger hair and the typical pale, freckly skin that accompanies it.

But it's the last man who grabs my attention. He's very tall, and big like a rugby player, but he carries his height well, not stooping the way a lot of tall men do. His dark hair is cut in a fashionable short fade, and he's clean shaven with light-brown skin. He's wearing a dark-navy suit, and even from this distance I can guess it must be bespoke, because it fits him like a dream. A white shirt and light-blue tie complete his outfit.

A Cocker Spaniel trots at his side, keeping pace with him better than the others, because he's walking fast. It's a beautiful golden color, and young, probably only a year or eighteen months, still growing into its paws, which are almost too big for its body as it runs with a distinctive beautiful floppy gait.

It's hard to say who's the most gorgeous—the man or the puppy.

"He walks as if he owns the place," I comment, a little envious of the guy's confident stride and the slight roll of his shoulders. A man like that clearly has no trouble with self-esteem.

"He does own the place," Dodie says, amused. "He's the Chairman and CEO of Koru Tech."

My jaw drops. "That's Mack Hart?"

If Dodie's surprised that I know his name, she doesn't say so. "Yep. In the rather sexy flesh." She grins.

"But… he's so young." I'm genuinely shocked. I'd expected a guy in his fifties, graying and bearded with a paunch. Or at most, an aging forty-something with an orange tan, a penis-extension sports car, and a wife half his age.

"Twenty-seven, I believe. And a genius, by all accounts—I read an article about him. He has an IQ of 172. Invented some kind of super-fast computer processor in his early twenties. A self-made man. Now he's worth several billion."

"Sorry… billion?"

"Nine zeroes. Can you imagine having that kind of money? God knows what he spends it on. I've done the six a.m. and late-night shifts here, and he's nearly always in his office working. It's unusual for him to leave this early."

The other three are struggling to keep up with Mack, who's striding out as if his arse is on fire. He reaches the doors leading out of the offices, which only just manage to slide apart in time to let him through, then glances over at us and flicks us a smile.

"Hey Dodie," he says, his voice deep and gravelly. He knows the name of his cleaner? Usually we're invisible to top management.

"Hey Dr. Hart," she calls back.

He looks at me, and I find myself suddenly breathless and panicky. So much for being invisible.

His gaze lifts to my hair. The corners of his mouth curve up just a little as his eyes drop back to mine.

Then he's gone, through the next set of doors into the lobby, the other three scurrying along behind him as he stalks across the tiles toward the main entrance.

My face burns. Cheeky bastard, smirking at my hair. Self-consciously, I lift a hand to smooth back a loose strand, only to discover I have about twenty sticking out from my bun like springs through an old mattress. I scowl, glad now that I've been sent to spy on him. Serves him right for being so smug. Nobody should be that self-assured.

"Weird having a dog in the office," I say.

"That's Gus. He never leaves his side. But I guess if you own the place, you can do whatever you want."

"Yeah, I suppose. You called him *Dr.* Hart?"

"Yeah. Not a medical doctor—he has a PhD. Not bad for a twenty-seven-year-old, eh? Smart fella. Anyway, you're going to clean those six offices, please." Dodie directs me to the individual rooms beyond the main office. "At least you won't have him watching you now. See you back here at seven, then we'll get going on the main room, okay?"

I nod my assent, and Dodie pushes her cart off along the corridor. At the end, I can see two white double doors that must lead through to the aircraft hanger-sized hall beyond the building that I spotted as I drove in. I guess that's where the supercomputer is. I wonder why it's called Marise?

It's no good putting it off anymore—I have to get this done. I take the cart along to the first office and go inside.

I work as quickly as I can to give myself as much time as possible in Mack's office at the end. As I dust, polish, and clean the glass surfaces, I look for any documents that might be lying around. Everywhere is surprisingly neat and tidy compared to other offices I've cleaned, where piles of Manila folders, reports, and printouts often litter the desks. I check the bins too, but it soon becomes clear they must shred anything important. There are no computers, so I'm guessing the occupants use laptops which they've all taken home.

I get to the large boardroom in the middle of the offices. The long wooden table seats sixteen, fronted by a huge interactive whiteboard, with a projector set in the ceiling that can be linked into a laptop to display presentations. The windows overlook the gardens at the side, lit now by lights set into the numerous bushes and trees. A business lunch must have taken place here today—all the crockery and cups have been removed, but crumbs and smudges litter the table, and the bins are full of leftovers and paper wrappings. I sweep up the crumbs, empty the bins, and polish the table until it shines, too proud to rush the job, even though I want to get it over with.

In the penultimate office, the nameplate that's turned to face visitors states the desk belongs to Mrs. Nadine Cooper, who must be Hart's PA. The desk bears a framed photo of a smartly dressed woman with neat brown hair and creases at the corners of her eyes, standing with a gray-haired man and two children who look to be in their late teens or early twenties. Presumably Nadine is therefore in her forties. I grudgingly give Hart a little kudos for not hiring a young blonde bombshell to have at his beck and call.

A coffee machine rests on a table underneath the window, along with a box containing a dozen different capsules, ten types of herbal tea, and hot chocolate. A fridge next to it holds fresh milk, bottles of water, diet sodas, three varieties of fruit juices, and what looks like a plate of leftovers from the business lunch—neatly cut club sandwiches, asparagus rolls, a selection of small quiches, and beautiful little cakes, all covered with plastic wrap.

Her desk is also neat and free of folders and papers. A diary sits on the left of her chair; I open it and discover Hart's appointments written in her tidy cursive script. Today was busy; Nadine has listed a financial meeting this morning at 10:00 a.m., a HR meeting at 11:30 a.m., a visit from Norman Cunningham from a company called Redford & Bloom at 12:30 p.m., lunch with the senior management team in the board room at 1:30 p.m., a Zoom call with Julia Peterson from Squires Appointments at 4:00 p.m., then another meeting with Andrew Pierce of Trinity Engineering at 5:00 p.m. I can't imagine any of this being useful or enlightening, but I pull out my phone and take a photo of the page anyway, and of the few days before and ahead too.

The drawers in Nadine's desk are locked, and so are all the filing cabinets. I'm not going to find anything else here.

I pick up her rubbish bin and take it over to the cart. As I tip the plastic sandwich container, broken pencil, and other insignificant items into the black plastic bag, I spot an unopened envelope.

I take it out of the bin. It feels as if there's a card inside. A Christmas card? The front is addressed to Mack Hart, c/o Koru Technology, and it lists the Auckland address. The postmark reveals it was posted in Edinburgh, Scotland. It's unopened. Presumably Nadine threw this away as it's in her bin. Why didn't she give it to Mack?

I hesitate. My stomach twists. I close my eyes for a moment, turning the card over in my hands. She threw this away for a reason. This isn't just spying—this is snooping and invading his privacy. I've never hated myself as much as I do now. But I don't have any choice.

Opening my eyes, I turn the envelope over, slide a finger beneath the flap, tear it open, and remove the card.

The front says, 'Happy Birthday'. It has a picture of a dog wearing a tartan scarf. It looks like the kind of card you buy off a rack in a petrol station for someone you don't really care about.

I open it up. The card bears only two handwritten words: From Iona. There's no kiss at the bottom.

Iona—I know that's the name of an island in the Inner Hebrides in Scotland. And I also know the name Mack is of Scottish origin. So is Iona a relative of his?

Sister? Aunt? Mother? Grandmother? Ex-wife?

If so, why didn't Nadine give him the card?

I feel a stab of guilt, followed swiftly by a wave of nausea. This is awful. I'm intruding into this man's private life in the worst way possible. This isn't why I came here.

Furious with myself, I stuff the card and the envelope in the black bag on my cart along with all the other rubbish.

With twenty minutes to go, I finally push open the door at the end, next to the neat nameplate that declares the office belongs to 'Dr. Mack Hart, Chairman and CEO, Koru Technology.'

Not surprisingly it's the largest office in this section. As I walk in, I can smell the faint, pleasant scent of his aftershave.

Situated in the corner of the building, the windows on two sides look out onto the lawns. On one side, unusually for an office, is a set of sliding glass doors that lead out onto a fenced deck, nice and private, with a smart outdoor table and chairs where I'm guessing he works on nice days, or maybe takes visitors to chat over coffee. I have the sudden, irrational thought that maybe he sunbathes there nude in the summer. Hurriedly, I turn my attention back to the inside.

The carpets here are light gray, and the walls are eggshell white. Two big paintings hang on one wall—one is a painted portrait of a Māori warrior with a *tā moko* or traditional full-face tattoo. Another is a contemporary piece signed by someone called Ra Wihongi that blends Māori symbols with what I realize when I move back to look at it from a distance is actually a computer motherboard—that's clever. I bet he commissioned this and the other paintings in the lobby.

At the end of the room, I nearly miss a door that's cleverly set into the decor so it looks like part of a bookcase. Tentatively, I try the handle, and I'm surprised to find it open. I go inside cautiously. Wow—it's a whole separate apartment that's bigger than the house I live in. It contains a bedroom with a king-size bed, a sofa and a TV, a kitchen, a bathroom, and a gym with a treadmill, an exercise bike, a rowing machine, and weights. Going into the bedroom, I open the wardrobe and find half a dozen suits, neatly folded shirts, a selection of ties, and a few pairs of what look like handmade leather shoes, as well as tees and shorts, and running shoes. The bathroom smells of his body spray. I can't imagine he lives here all the time, surely? Dodie says he often works very late; maybe then he just crashes here to save going home.

It's one thing to poke around someone's office, and another to invade their private living space. Dodie didn't say anything about cleaning here, so hastily I go out of the room and close the door behind me.

I cross the room to his desk, which is made of a pale wood with a charcoal-colored surface. I pick up a framed photo and study it. A young guy dressed in a vest, shorts, and running shoes beams at the camera, holding up a trophy in his right hand and a medal in his left. He's a lot younger, maybe mid-teens, but it's obviously Mack Hart. Next to him, an older Māori guy—his father?—stands with his arm around him, pride written all over his face. So, Mack's a sprinter? Maybe that explains why he walks so fast.

It's the only photo in the room. No pictures of a sweetheart or children. And nothing else to tell me anything about the man himself.

Behind the desk is a series of artsy shelves on different levels. They contain a variety of ornaments, including the trophy he's holding in the photo. I can see the inscription on it now—'1st place 100m 2010 Under 17 New Zealand Athletics Championships'. It's quite a feat for a young kid.

How did he end up here?

Conscious that time is running out, I scan the rest of the ornaments. Most of them are pieces of technology, some of which I know— several motherboards, video cards, a RAM stick—other bits I don't recognize, maybe parts he or his company have invented, displayed on wooden stands, highly polished and gleaming. I pull out my phone and take photos of them, but I presume they must be outdated and defunct, and can't imagine they're going to be of any use.

With growing frustration, I try all the drawers in his desk, but I already know they're going to be locked. There are no filing cabinets in here. The glass table by the window bears only a small vase of fresh flowers. There's no computer on the table, and I remember that he was carrying a laptop case.

Defeated, I quickly polish the desk and the photo in its frame. Then I pick up the bins tucked next to the desk—one for recycling, one for general rubbish.

Feeling about an inch high, I go through the contents of the general bin. There are two banana skins, an apple core, two KitKat wrappers— the four-fingered ones, not the two-fingered—the packaging from two boxes of sandwiches, and an empty chip packet. And presumably he attended the business lunch as well. Jesus, how much does this guy eat?

The recycling bin contains three empty water bottles and a few pieces of white cardboard without anything written on it. There are a couple of torn sheets of A4 bearing a typical guy's handwriting— angular, untidy, written fast as if his hand couldn't keep up with his brain. Most of it looks nonsense—doodles of clouds filled with strange words like 'petaflops barrier' and 'LINPACK benchmark,' nothing specific enough to be of use, I'm sure, considering they're in the recycling bin. Still, I fit the pieces together as best I can and take photos of them.

There's also a piece of card, torn into four pieces and then scrunched up for good measure. I retrieve the pieces, lay them on the table, and push them together. At the top is a logo in the shape of a koru—the spiral shape of the curled-up silver fern that is an important

Māori symbol. It's from the Royal Society Te Apārangi—I think it's a society that promotes research into science and technology. It states that Dr. Mack Hart has been nominated for the MacDiarmid Award, and it invites him to attend the Research Honours Awards Ceremony on January sixth.

Interesting. Why has he ripped up the invitation and thrown it away?

Unable to solve the puzzle, I take a photograph of it, then put the pieces in the black bag. There's nothing else of interest here. I pull up the few photos I've taken, hesitate for a second, then grit my teeth and send them.

My stomach churning, I polish the glass table, clean the shelves, and make sure the rest of the place is spotless.

I push the cart out of the room and down to where I'm supposed to meet Dodie. I'm filled with conflicting emotions, including relief that I've finished, and guilt at poking my nose into Mack Hart's personal life. I can't even comfort myself with the thought that I found anything useful. This whole debacle has been nothing but a huge waste of time.

I walk along the corridor with a sinking heart, desperate for the day to be over, so I can go home, get into bed, pull the covers over my head, and shut out the horrible world.

Chapter Two

Mack

On the morning of Wednesday 21ˢᵗ December, Jamie, my chauffeur, draws up out the front of Koru Tech at seven a.m. as usual, leaving the engine running.

"I'll be back around ten," he says.

"Okay. See you later." I get out, let Gus out of the back, and walk across to the front entrance, Gus at my heels, as Jamie pulls away.

"Morning, Dr. Hart," the security guy says as I approach. He bends to pet Gus, who licks his hand.

I don't really want to stand and chat, but equally I don't want to be rude. "Hey, Wiremu," I say. "How's Maia doing?"

"She's good thanks, Dr. Hart. Recovering nicely. And she says thank you for the flowers. She's got them by her bed at home."

"Oh, I'm glad. Don't forget, don't hesitate to say if you need extra time off."

"I will, sir, thank you."

I nod and go inside. "Morning, Rachel," I call to the woman on reception.

"Morning, Dr. Hart!"

"Hey, Steve," I say to the janitor, who's up a ladder fixing a bulb in the ceiling.

"Morning, Dr. Hart—beautiful day, isn't it?"

"Gorgeous. Going to be a nice Christmas, by the look of it."

Steve grins, and I head through the sliding doors into the main office.

I breathe a sigh of relief as the doors close behind me. The rest of the building is empty and quiet. My shoes and Gus's paws make next to no noise as we cross the carpeted floor. I love this time of day. The place smells of polish and glass cleaner, and everywhere is tidy and peaceful. It's the summer solstice today, so the sun has already filled the building with bright lemon-colored sunshine. Soon the place will be buzzing with people, but for now it's all mine.

Nadine won't be in until eight thirty. I cross to the fridge and investigate the contents, then pull out a plate of club sandwiches leftover from yesterday's business lunch, take it through into my office, and place it on my desk with my briefcase and the coffee I bought on my way in.

I love this office. It's my haven, the place I'd rather be than anywhere else in the world. Later, it'll be bustling with various members of staff and customers all wanting a piece of my time, but right now it's as quiet and beautiful as a desert island. Like the main room, it smells of polish and glass cleaner.

Through the windows, the leaves on the trees and bushes are all painted with the golden sun. Picking up my coffee, I go over and open the sliding doors, letting in the song from the two *tauhou* birds sitting in the trees outside, distinctive with their olive-green heads and silver-rimmed eyes.

This morning, I woke up agitated, remembering as soon as I opened my eyes that it was my birthday. Sipping my coffee, though, and looking out at the beauty of the scene, I begin to feel calmer. Luckily, nobody knows it's my birthday except Arjun, the head of HR, and Nadine, and they're both sworn to secrecy. Arjun won't remember anyway because he's a guy, and the only thing Nadine will do is probably make me some of her chocolate cookies, which will touch me and irritate me in equal measure.

I've got a lot to do, and I wish I didn't have any plans today so I could just immerse myself in the work. But tonight there's a Christmas party at my business club, Huxley's. I don't like crowds and I don't generally go to parties, but I promised Oliver Huxley himself that I'd go, and I don't want to let him down.

I also said I'd bring a date, but I haven't organized anything. I run through my mental little black book, bringing up and then discarding names. I don't want a second date with anyone. Second dates tend to make women believe there'll be a third date, and I don't have the time or patience for that.

Nope, looks like I'll be flying solo tonight. Maybe I'll be able to sneak off early, if nobody notices.

Turning from the window, I walk across to my desk and sit in the leather chair. Opening my case, I take out my laptop, then retrieve a pile of folders and put them to one side. Taking out my keys, I unlock my side drawers and retrieve a notepad and pen, and a couple of other files I was working on yesterday.

"Hey, you," I say as Gus comes up for some fuss. "Want a treat?" I dig a hand into the packet in my desk drawer and toss one up in the air. He catches it deftly. "Good boy. Another?" I toss a second. This time it bounces off his nose at an angle and tumbles to the floor. I roll my eyes. "Not quite ready for the circus, are you?"

He follows it over to the shelves behind me, and I turn in my chair and watch him snuffle for it. I've had several dogs in my time, but he's possibly the gentlest, content just to be by my side.

He's still snuffling, and it's then that I spot what he's seen—a piece of paper on the floor, tucked in a small space between two of the shelves.

"Hey, leave that." I pick up the dropped treat and lure him away, then bend to collect the piece of paper, only to discover that it's not paper—it's a serviette with writing on it. Turning the chair back to my desk, I put the crumpled serviette on the surface and smooth it out.

It contains a poem. It's not Nadine's writing. It's written—I'm sure—by a young woman, judging by the loops in the 'g's and 'y's, the flowers that take the place of dots over the 'i's, and the love hearts doodled around the edge. It looks like a work in progress, some words crossed out and replaced by others written above.

I read it through, and gradually my eyes widen and my eyebrows rise.

Obsession
I touch myself as I think of you.
The nape of your neck, your clean-shaven jaw,
Your lips claiming mine the way you like to do,
Demanding, taking, sugar-sweet,
Your tongue, sliding against mine in its beautiful dance,
Your hands, stroking my skin, cupping my breasts,
Your hot mouth on my nipples,
Sucking, fingers plucking.
My fingers slide through my swollen folds,
I'm so wet for you, baby,

Aching for that feeling when you enter me,
I want you inside me,
Now,
Stretch me, fill me up, to the brim,
Ride me hard and fast…
Oh God…
I'm coming…
And it's all for you…

I turn the paper over. The other side is blank.

I turn it back and read it again. Then I lean back in my chair and stare at it.

Holy fuck. I think that's possibly the hottest thing I've ever read. I don't know why. Maybe because it's handwritten, and she's clearly thought about every word. It's sexy without being crude. I can almost imagine this young woman lying there, sliding her fingers beneath the elastic of her pretty lace underwear, and touching herself as her eyelids flutter shut.

My lips curve up. Well. That has drastically improved my mood.

Happy birthday, Mack.

Chuckling, I fold the serviette in half and tuck it into my top pocket. Then I open my laptop and fire it up.

Nadine arrives about eight thirty as usual, by which time I've been working for an hour and a half, and I'm ready for a break.

"Morning," I say, going into her office.

She hangs up her coat on the stand behind the door, then turns and smiles. "Morning, Dr. Hart." She always calls me Dr. Hart, no matter how many times I've told her to call me Mack. I kind of like that, although I'd never admit it.

I lean on the door jamb with my hands in my pockets. "Did you have a nice evening?" She told me she was going to the theater last night.

"Yes, thank you. The play was great, Alan loved it. And Jill brought her new boyfriend to meet us."

"Oh, what's he like?"

She walks over to the table with the coffee machine and begins making us both a cup. "A lovely young man, actually. Works in finance, so I think he has plenty of money. I know it's not the most important thing in life, but I'm pleased for Kim. It's no fun being poor."

"No," I say with feeling, "it's not."

Nadine has been my PA since I founded Koru Tech six years ago. I interviewed a couple of dozen applicants, because it was important to me to find the right person. PAs fulfill a strange role, often knowing intimate details about their boss as they organize both their business and private calendars. I suspect sometimes they understand a boss better than a wife. Nadine was thirty-five at the time, with superb secretarial qualifications and excellent references. She was smart, funny, and very happily married, and we got on immediately.

Over the years, we've often spent time together alone in the car or on flights and got chatting. She knows I don't come from money and has admitted to me too that she and her husband struggled a lot financially when they were first married, so I understand her wanting the best for her daughter.

She bends to get some milk out of the fridge and laughs. "Been at the leftovers, have we?"

"Might have."

"I'll never understand how you manage to eat so much and stay so trim." She pours milk into the jug and begins steaming it. "I have one chocolate bar and it goes straight to my hips."

I chuckle. Then I clear my throat. "I have a bit of a strange question. Do you know if anyone's been in my office?"

She looks over her shoulder at me, eyebrows raised. "Not that I know of. Why?"

"I found something… a note someone dropped by mistake, I think. It… interests me. I'd like to track down the owner."

Pondering on it as she pours the milk over the espresso, she eventually says, "It wouldn't have been Steven?"

"I sincerely hope not," I say with feeling, accepting the cup as she brings it over.

She gives me an amused look. "Then… what about the cleaner? Someone from Shine will have done the offices last night."

"Oh, of course." I think about when I was on my way out. I saw Dodie, and with her was… hmm… oh yes. The girl with the hair.

"Can you do me a favor and get Dodie Banks from Shine on the phone for me?" I ask.

"Sure. You want to take it in your office?"

"Yeah, thanks."

I carry my cup through and sit back at my desk. Was it Dodie who dropped the note? If it was, that'll be the end of the puzzle. She's friendly, and she works hard, but my interest ends there.

If it was the blonde, though…

My phone buzzes, and I pick up the receiver. "Dodie Banks for you," Nadine says.

"Thanks." I wait for her to put her through. "Hello?"

"Good morning, Dr. Hart," Dodie says.

"Hey, Dodie. Sorry to bother you."

"That's okay. What can I do for you?"

"I was just wondering about last night. Did you clean my office?"

"Of course, we always make it a priority."

"You personally, I mean?"

"Oh, no, sorry. I cleaned Marise's room as normal. Usually Pippa does the management offices but she was off sick yesterday, so we had another girl fill in. Is there a problem?"

"No. Not at all. Was it the girl with the hair?"

She chuckles. "That's her. Her name's Sidnie, not like the city, but S-I-D-N-I-E. We all call her Sid."

"Is she returning tonight?"

"No, Pippa's back today."

"Hmm. Do you know anything about her? Sidnie, I mean?"

"A little." She sounds cautious, maybe wary of revealing any personal details about an employee to someone she hardly knows.

"I don't want you to betray any confidences," I tell her. "She left something in my office, by mistake, I think, and I was hoping to return it to her. In person."

"I see." She's smiling now. "If you're asking if she's single, the answer is yes, as far as I know."

I give a short laugh. "Okay."

"Would you like me to send her in?"

"Yes please."

"Let me contact her. I know she works during the day as a copywriter, I think. She cleans for us in the evenings. She probably has a lunch hour though. Would that work for you?"

"Yeah, I can make space around one, if she's available."

"Let me get back to you."

We say goodbye and end the call.

In less than a minute, Nadine puts her through again.

"One o'clock," Dodie says. "She's terrified."

"Why?" I ask, amused.

"If you need to ask that, Dr. Hart, there's no hope for you at all. Good luck!"

"Thanks." I end the call, a little puzzled. Terrified was an odd word to use. Still, maybe she's read about me somewhere. Some people find wealth and power intimidating, and I admit I have more than my fair share of both.

It's only nine, so I still have four hours to wait.

I take my empty coffee cup back into Nadine's office and say, "Can you call the SMT and move them to two p.m.? I'm meeting with someone, and she can only come during her lunch hour."

"Want me to organize a light lunch for you both?"

"Mmm, that would be nice, thank you."

"Is it with Dodie?"

"No. Her name's Sidnie."

"Surname?"

"No idea. She was the cleaner here last night. She's coming to pick up the item she left."

"Are you sure you don't just want me to drop it off to her?"

"No…"

She smiles.

"Don't start," I scold.

"I didn't say a word."

I roll my eyes. She's always telling me I need to find a nice girl and settle down. She was very disappointed when I said Felicity wouldn't be calling in anymore—until Felicity threw her coffee machine through her window, and then I think she was rather relieved.

"Can you collect her from reception when she arrives at one?" I ask.

"Of course." She's still smiling. "Was she pretty?"

I think about the brief glimpse I had of Dodie's assistant. She'd been dressed in thick green coveralls and flat boots—hardly the sexiest of clothing. Her curly hair had been crazy wild. She hadn't been wearing makeup, from what I could see from across the room. She was totally the opposite of all the women I meet every day in the city, with their groomed, sophisticated appearance, designer clothes, and expensive accessories.

"Stunning," I say.

Nadine's smile widens. Then she says, "I got a morning snack for you." She opens her drawer and retrieves a single chocolate cupcake with a swirl of rich frosting, the nearest thing she can risk to a birthday cake. "And this is for you," she says to Gus, who's come to see what all the fuss is about, and presents him with a chew.

"Thank you," I say wryly. I take it back to my office, sit back, and bite into the sweet cake.

Your lips claiming mine the way you like to do,
Demanding, taking, sugar-sweet.

I sigh. The next four hours are going to feel like a fortnight.

*

It turns out to be a hectic, somewhat stressful morning, and in the end I don't have much time to think about my lunch appointment. I have back-to-back meetings with each of my senior management teams to discuss the progression of our latest research, and by the time one o'clock comes, I'm relieved to leave the board room and return to my office.

"Rachel just called from reception," Nadine says, popping her head in. "Sidnie's here. I'm off to get her."

"Okay, thanks."

She leaves, and I walk over to the glass table near the window. Two platters sit on the table containing small sandwiches, tiny quiches and other savory pastries, carrot sticks with hummus, sushi, fruit, and tiny cakes, all bite-sized, along with cold bottles of water and two glasses.

I look out at the garden, wondering whether I'll have time to take a quick walk before my two-p.m. appointment. I've been sitting down for most of the morning, and I could do with stretching my legs. I guess it depends how it goes with Sidnie.

It's an unusual name for a girl, but oddly I quite like it.

There's a knock on the door, and I turn to see Nadine in the doorway. "Dr. Hart? Sidnie's here to see you."

She appears behind Nadine, glances at the PA, then sidles into my office. Nadine smiles, then closes the door behind her.

Gus trots across to discover this new visitor, but I don't think she even sees him as we study each other across the room. Jesus, the poor girl looks absolutely terrified. Her face is white as a sheet, and she's clutching her purse with both hands before her as if she's ready to wield it as a weapon.

"Come in," I say.

She takes a few steps forward, then stops. She's wearing a white shirt and gray pants, traditional office wear, apart from her Converses. It's not a bad look. She's had a bit more success with her hair today, most of which is pulled back into a ponytail, leaving only half a dozen strands bouncing around her face. She has a touch of gray eyeshadow and mascara, and a slick of lip gloss. The look is simple and understated. Once again, she looks stunning.

"I know this is your lunch hour," I say, "so Nadine got us a light lunch, if you'd like to join me." I gesture at the table.

She stares at it. Then she stares at me.

"What?" she says.

"You know why you're here?" I'm conscious she's probably embarrassed about the poem.

She nods and looks at her feet. Christ, she's actually shaking.

I walk forward so we're only a couple of feet apart, and duck my head to try to catch her eye. "Honestly, it wasn't that bad. I found it funny more than anything."

"Funny…" She looks up at me then. Her eyes are the color of the summer sky outside—a vivid blue. "I… don't understand."

"It was just a poem. Okay, it was a bit risqué, but even so…"

"A poem?" She looks completely bewildered.

I reach into my top pocket and hand it to her. "It was stuck between two shelves behind my desk. Gus nearly ate it."

She takes it from me and opens it up. Her expression is so comical it would have made me laugh in any other situation—her jaw drops, and her eyes widen as if I've just told her the King's coming to visit.

She lifts her gaze to mine then, and her face turns the color of the baby tomatoes on the platter. "Holy fuck."

That makes me laugh. "You look surprised. Why did you think I called you here?"

"I thought…" She swallows hard and glances around. "I wasn't sure. I thought maybe I'd broken something last night."

"Please, come and sit down before you fall down." I put a hand under her elbow to guide her to the table by the window, mainly because I want to touch her.

Reluctantly, she walks forward to one of the chairs and perches on the edge. She nods when I gesture at a water bottle, and I open it and pour it into one of the glasses before doing the same for myself. "Help yourself," I say, taking one of the sandwiches and eating it in one go.

She doesn't. Instead, she glances at the piece of paper in her hand, then stuffs it into the pocket of her trousers. "I must have dropped it when I took my phone out," she mumbles. "I'm so sorry."

"Don't apologize." I eat another sandwich. "It made my day."

Her lips twitch, but she puts a hand up to her face, covering her eyes for a moment. "I can't believe I did that… What must you have thought?"

"I was just worried the janitor wrote it. He's sixty-four, bald as a coot, and missing his two front teeth."

She laughs at that and lowers her hand. "I think I owe you an explanation."

"You don't have to explain anything. But I have to say I'm very interested to hear what you have to say."

Her eyes meet mine again, and she gives a mischievous, shy smile. Wow, she really is something.

Chapter Three

Sidnie

My terror is just starting to die down.

I nearly didn't come to the office. I was on the verge of buying a ticket to Alaska and leaving on the first plane.

Even though Dodie reassured me that apparently the CEO wanted to return something I'd dropped last night, I checked my pockets and couldn't think of anything that was missing—I'd completely forgotten about the poem. I was convinced he was going to say he'd checked the security cameras and caught me snooping. I half expected to find the police waiting for me, ready to whisk me down to the station.

Instead, I find myself having lunch alone with this young billionaire.

We're sitting at the glass table by the sliding doors, which are open, letting in the summer sunshine. Gus comes over to me, and I bend to fuss him for a moment as I gather my wits. He's a beautiful-looking dog with his soft strawberry-blond hair, and his big brown eyes are to die for. As I stroke his ears, he lays down, then rolls over onto his back and puts his feet in the air.

"I'm guessing you have that effect on a lot of men," Mack says, leaning back in his chair with a smile.

"Not quite," I reply honestly. I have a hopeless track record where guys are concerned. But I'm not about to admit that to him.

I sit back in my seat, and Gus gets up and wanders out onto the deck, where he flops onto his side with a big sigh.

I return my attention to Mack, and we study each other for a moment. Today he's wearing a dark-gray suit, a white shirt with a stylish black-and-silver-striped tie, and black Oxford shoes. His haircut is so sharp I could cut myself on it, as if he visited the barber five minutes ago. His jaw looks as if he's shaved with a cutthroat razor, it's so smooth. His hands are big, his nails short and neat. As he leans forward to take another sausage roll, I smell the scent of his aftershave, warmed through by his body. When he leans back, he sits in the typically male fashion with his legs wide open, and it's all I can do not to stare at the way his pants are pulled tightly across his impressive thighs.

Instead, I find myself staring at his eyes. They're sky blue, but one has patches of light brown and a touch of green, like our blue planet as seen from above.

"It's called heterochromia," he says, lifting a hand to point from one eye to the other as he sees me looking at them.

"It's very unusual," I murmur.

"Yeah. My optician offered me colored lenses, but I thought what the hell, I'm flawed, I might as well flaunt it." He smiles.

"It would be a crying shame to cover them up. I've never seen anything like it."

His smile stays. I think he likes the compliment.

I swallow hard. What the hell am I doing? I should excuse myself and run a mile. Every second I'm here, I run the risk of him discovering what I did and calling the police.

Or am I being foolish? Even if he has cameras in here, I'm guessing nobody was watching them, or he would definitely not be as friendly as he is right now. I don't think he has a clue what I did in here last night. I think he called me in only because he found the poem.

Oh yes, the poem. Fuck.

I drop my gaze to the platters, full of beautiful bite-sized pieces of food, vegetables, dips, fruit, and cake. I'm starving, and I've got to be back at work soon.

"Go on," he says. "Or I'll have to eat it all and run a few extra miles to burn it all off."

"I'm vegetarian," I say. "I'm just wondering which bits don't contain meat."

"None of it does," he says. "I'm vegetarian too."

"Oh! Even the sausage rolls?"

"Yep. Sweet potato and kidney beans are the main ingredients, I think."

I take one and try it. It's really nice.

"The baby quiches are great, too," he says, "and so's the sushi. Fill your plate, please."

I take a few pieces, then have a sip of water. This feels so surreal. I know I should run, but this guy fascinates me. He's so big and… well-scrubbed. His nails are neat and clean. I bet he has a manicurist. His teeth are white and perfectly straight. Energy and power radiate from him as if he's the sun. I'm not surprised he eats a lot; something must feed the furnace.

"You left your motor running," I say, gesturing at his knee, which is constantly on the move as he bounces his foot.

He chuckles. "I find it hard to sit still. Neurodivergence for the win."

"You have ADHD?"

He nods, taking another veggie roll. "Great for energy levels at times. Lousy for sleep."

"The hyper focus must be good for a guy in your position. My brother has it," I explain at his querying look.

"Oh yeah. Fourteen-hour days or more are normal around here. I'll work flat out for a fortnight, then crash and sleep for a whole day." He clears his throat. "Anyway, enough about me. Tell me about you. What's your surname, by the way?"

I hesitate, and as he meets my eyes, my lips curve up.

"What?" he says.

"I don't want to tell you."

"Why?"

"After the poem, it's not going to help my case."

He dips a carrot stick in the hummus and takes a bite. "Well now you absolutely have to tell me."

"It's Beaver."

That makes him laugh out loud. "Sorry," he says as I give him a wry look. "You did set me up for the joke, though."

"Yeah, I guess I did."

He grins.

"Dodie told me you're a doctor," I say.

"Of computer science engineering, yeah. I got it earlier this year."

"That's pretty cool."

"I think so."

"I thought you couldn't get one until eight years after finishing a degree."

"I went to university at seventeen," he says.

"Really?"

"Graduated at twenty. Finished my MA by the time I was twenty-two. They made an exception for me with the doctorate and granted it a year early. Now I can purchase stuff off Amazon, and when it arrives, I can say 'that's just what the doctor ordered.'"

That makes me laugh. He's self-deprecating, I like that. But it doesn't detract from the fact that his achievements are seriously impressive. Smart fella, as Dodie said.

Then he blows out a breath and looks out at the sunshine. "Do you mind if I take off my jacket? It's warm in here."

"It's your office."

"Yes, but you're a woman, and we're alone, and you don't know me, and I want to make sure you're comfortable with it." His gaze is direct.

"I don't mind," I say softly.

He stands, flicks open the buttons, shrugs it off, and hangs it over the back of his chair. As he sits, he takes out his cufflinks, then folds back his shirt sleeves. An intriguing Māori tattoo curls up his lower right arm from his wrist to his elbow.

"Nice *tā moko*," I say. "Does it represent your *whakapapa*?" I know that Māori tattoos often portray a person's *whakapapa* or genealogy.

He looks at it, clenching his fist, then releasing it, so the movement of his muscles brings it to life. "Yeah."

"It's beautiful."

"Thank you." He places a finger on one of the swirls and follows it across his arm. "This represents my journey to New Zealand."

"You weren't born here?"

"No. I was born in Scotland."

I think about the birthday card. I'm even more intrigued now, despite still being terrified.

"I came here when I was twelve," he continues. He traces a koru, the spiral shape of a curled-up silver fern. "This represents my new life with my father."

"Is he the guy in the photo on your desk?"

He returns his gaze to me, surprised. "Yeah."

"I saw it when I was cleaning."

He looks back at his tattoo, and his lips twist.

"What?" I ask.

He takes a sandwich and studies it for a moment. "I haven't told anyone about that. And here I am, blurting out my life history ten minutes after meeting you."

"I have that kind of face. It makes people think they can talk to me."

"People tell you their secrets?"

Again, I think of the fact that I sneaked around his office and took photos, and I have to fight not to wince.

"I have one as well," I say, pulling up my sleeve to reveal the tattoo of a pile of books, the top ones lifting up with open pages, growing smaller until they look like flying birds.

"That's cool," he says, bending to look at it. His warm breath whispers lightly across my skin, and I shiver. He straightens, and his eyes gleam—I think he noticed. "You like books and reading?"

I smile at the understatement. "Yeah, I have an English degree."

"Nice. Dodie said you're a copywriter in your day job?"

"Yeah. And I suppose now you want to know where."

"Uh… I guess."

"At a lubrication firm."

His eyebrows lift.

"Machine lubrication," I clarify. "Oils and grease and stuff. Unfortunately, or the free samples would have been more useful."

He laughs. I look down at the platter and help myself to one of the small chocolate tarts.

"How long have you worked for Shine?" he asks as I bite into it.

I remove a couple of crumbs from my bottom lip, not missing the way his gaze drops to watch. "Four months." I study the other half of the tart. "It's not the most impressive job, I know, but I need the money."

"Nothing wrong with good honest work. I waited tables as a teen."

I finish the tart. "Really?"

"Yeah. I'm a mean barista too."

"Ooh. I love coffee. Now you've got my interest."

And… I'm flirting. I can't help myself. He mesmerizes me.

My fingers are sticky. Knowing he's going to watch, I insert them one by one in my mouth and suck the crumbs off. He does watch, and then his eyes return to mine, hot and interested.

Suddenly flustered under his intense gaze, I say, "So… Dodie told me you were only twenty-one when you made a really fast microprocessor."

"Yep."

"How fast?"

"One-point-eight times faster than the latest eight-core PC laptop chip, but it used only seventy percent of the power."

"And you still make them? I bet they're faster now."

"The fastest in New Zealand at just over ten PetaFLOPS."

I laugh. "Peta-what? You're making it up now."

He chuckles. "A PetaFLOPS is equal to one quadrillion floating point operations per second, which is the way we measure computer speed. Imagine every person on Earth—all seven-point-eight billion of them—doing a million calculations per person every second. That would be the equivalent of around eight PetaFLOPS of computing power. Marise rated ten PetaFLOPS on the LINPACK benchmark."

"I'm guessing that's pretty fast."

He smiles. "It's not bad. The fastest computer in the world, Frontier, reaches 1102 PetaFLOPS. But we've just snuck into the top twenty supercomputers in the world, which is cool."

"The top twenty?" I know very little about supercomputers, but even I can tell how impressive that is when he's obviously competing against the U.S., Japan, and China.

"Yeah. We're quite proud of that."

I dip a carrot stick into the hummus. "My laptop's got sixteen gigabytes of RAM. Not sure where that fits on the LINPACK benchmark."

He chuckles.

"Why did you call the computer Marise?" I ask, curious.

"Through the fifties and sixties, Marise Chamberlain was the fastest New Zealand woman over eight hundred meters. She won seventeen national titles."

"Oh, of course. You're a sprinter, aren't you?"

"I was. Slowed a bit in my old age." He grins.

"In the photo, you're what, fifteen, sixteen?"

"Sixteen."

"But you didn't pursue it?"

"I was heavily into science too by then. My coach told me I needed to choose between sprinting or computers. I chose computers. Mainly because I knew I wouldn't make much money from sprinting." He gives me a 'well-at-least-I'm-honest' look.

We fall quiet for a moment. Eventually his lips curve up. "Come on then. You said you were going to give me an explanation for the poem."

"And you said I don't have to."

"True. But I'd love to hear. It was very…" He thinks about how to finish the sentence.

"Dirty?" I suggest.

He laughs. "I was going to say sensual, but your word works too."

I like his description. I study my hands for a moment, wondering whether to confide in him.

"I won't tell anyone," he says eventually.

"It's not that." I bite my lip.

He tips his head to the side. "What?"

"People tend to make fun of it," I say softly. "And I don't want you to mock me." My face warms at the admission. I don't know why it's important to me that he doesn't.

A frown flickers on his brow. "I won't, I promise."

I sigh. In for a penny… I'll probably never see him again after this anyway. "Okay. Well, I read mainly romance novels. I like them because they're feel-good. You know they've always got a happy ending."

"Fair enough."

"The ones I like are… um… quite… um… racy."

"You're a *Fifty Shades* fan?" He doesn't say it with the scorn that so many people do.

"Yeah, I mean, I'm not particularly into the S&M part, but I like the hotter stories." Jesus, am I really talking about bondage with this guy I've just met?

But he just nods. "Fiction can be a good way of exploring fantasies, I guess."

"Yes." I feel a bit more enthusiastic because he's not making fun of it. "Anyway, I've always enjoyed creative writing, and so I thought I'd have a go at some stories myself. So I wrote a couple of shorts and let some of my friends read them." My face flushes more at the memory. "They thought they were great, and one of them asked if she could give the stories to someone else she knew. And then somehow everyone was reading them. And that's when the mocking started. I loved my stories and I was proud of them, but people kept saying I wrote porn. I've nothing against it, but I don't believe that's what my stories are. There's a big difference, in my opinion, between a romance that features intimate love scenes, and porn that's meant purely to get you off."

That does make him smile, but he says, "Of course. I'm sure your stories are sensual and romantic. And sex is a healthy part of life and relationships, right? I'm sure writing and reading about it is a great way for women, especially, to share ideas and to learn from each other."

"I think so." I warm through at the thought that he understands. Okay, so now to admit the next part. "Well, after that, some of the girls said I should do some videos on social media. I thought it sounded fun, so I recorded some—not of me, but with text on a background, with poems and tips. And one small series went viral."

"Really?"

"Yeah."

"What was it about?"

I purse my lips. "Talking dirty."

Now he's smiling. "I see."

"It gave people suggestions for how to talk dirty with their loved ones. I did three videos—beginner, intermediate, and advanced—with a guide on how to start, suggestions of what to say, that kind of thing. They've had over a million views. I still do a few videos each week. I'm constantly jotting down ideas. Like the poem you found. And now I'm writing a book."

His eyebrows rise. "A book?"

"Yeah. A romance novel. I'm about halfway through. I want to write for a living. I'm doing as much as I can in my spare time, but what with the day job and cleaning in the evening, I don't get as much time as I'd like." I sigh.

"I bet your friends and family are impressed with that," he says.

I give a little shrug. "My folks would be embarrassed. My friends would probably make fun of me. I haven't told anyone. Except you. I have no idea why."

"I guess I have that kind of face."

We both smile.

He has a long drink of water, then sits back in his chair, legs stretched out, hands linked in his lap. "I'm intrigued as to what the difference is between the three levels of talking dirty."

"If you watch my video, you'll find out."

"I might just do that. Is it under your real name?"

"God, no. I go by Whisper2Me on all my social media."

He smiles. There's a strange look in his eyes that gives me goose bumps.

"What does your boyfriend think about your business?" he asks.

"That wasn't very subtle," I scold.

"Points for trying?"

I laugh. "I'm single. And in answer to your question, I don't usually tell guys about it. It tends to scare them off."

"Really? I'd have thought they'd be all over a girl who was an expert in… ah… textual relations."

"Oh I like that. I'm definitely writing that down."

"You're very unusual."

"I get told that a lot. I think it's the hair."

"Your hair is… unique, shall we say?"

I touch it self-consciously. "It's like a wild dog. It refuses to be tamed."

As if on cue, Gus comes back into the office and presses his sun-warmed body against me. "Not you," I say. "I bet you're a good boy."

Gus lies down and almost immediately starts snoring.

"You like dogs?" he asks.

"I adore them. I'd love to get one, but I work all day so it wouldn't be fair, and anyway my landlord doesn't allow pets."

Mack's quiet for a moment. Then he says, "It's not just the hair. The rest of you is also pretty exceptional."

A bubble of laughter rises up in me and bursts forth before I can stifle it. "Sorry," I say at his amused look. "You're a billionaire genius with an IQ of 172 and I'm a cleaner. It strikes me as kind of funny to hear you say I'm exceptional."

"Nevertheless, that's how I see you."

He's serious. "Oh," I whisper, flummoxed. "Um, thank you."

He studies me for a long while. It seems to be his way, while he thinks about what to say. I help myself to another chocolate tart. He watches me eat, a slight smile on his lips.

"What are you doing tonight?" he asks eventually.

I look at him in surprise. "Um… cleaning. At another office block."

"If I were to have a word with Dodie, would you like to come to a party with me?"

I stare at him. "A party?"

"Yeah. It's at my business club, Huxley's, on the other side of Albert Park. The owners are good friends of mine and I promised I'd go. But I don't have a date."

"Really? Why not?"

"What do you mean?"

"Why don't you have a date?" I'm genuinely puzzled. "You must have women falling over themselves to get to you."

"You'd be surprised. I don't get out much."

"I don't believe that," I scoff. "You don't strike me as the sort of guy who lives like a monk."

He grins. "No, I couldn't claim that."

"But you're single?"

"I am."

"Not married?"

He laughs. "No." He manages to make it sound as if it's a crazy question.

"And… you're really asking me to go with you?"

"Yeah."

"I'm not your type," I inform him.

"How do you know what my type is?"

"Mack, come on. You're a billionaire businessman. I'm… me. I can't even afford to get a new hair straightener."

"Believe me, that's a good thing."

I blush. "I'm a cleaner, for fuck's sake. Why on earth would you be interested in me?"

"I like your hair." He smiles.

It makes no sense. Unless… something occurs to me. "The poem wasn't about you," I say, wondering if he thought I'd written it after seeing him last night.

His lips quirk up. "I didn't think it was."

"It was about my perfect guy. I mean, you do fit the bill, but…" FFS, why won't my mouth stop talking?

He gives a short laugh, his eyes filled with humor.

I really like this guy. For a moment, hope and excitement swell inside me. It's been a while since I've been out on a date, and ages since I've met someone who makes my heart race like this. We seem to have lots in common: we're both vegetarians; we have a similar sense of humor; we both like dogs. And sex, apparently. That's probably about it. But I'd be lying if I said the idea of going out with a gorgeous rich guy didn't ring my bell.

His reaction to me asking if he's married suggests he's not looking for anything long-term. With his money, he probably dates a different girl every night. In fact, it wouldn't surprise me if he was expecting to get me into bed tonight.

Ride me hard and fast…

I feel a bit dizzy. There are worse things than having a one-night stand with a billionaire.

But I need to be honest. Well, semi-honest. I'm not yet ready to admit why I was really in his office last night.

"Mack… the poem, and my writing… you should know it's all talk. I mean, I'm not a virgin, but I wouldn't want you to think I'm an expert. I'm far from it. You can see from my face that I get embarrassed saying those things in real life." I point to my flushed cheeks.

"Maybe, but you like saying what's on your mind, don't you?"

"*Caveat emptor*, that's all. Buyer beware. Not that you'd be paying for it." Jesus. Could I screw this up any more than I already am?

But it just seems to be making him laugh. "Sidnie," he says, "if you're trying to put me off, it's really not working. In my line of business, we get excited by something that has a lot of potential. And anyway, a man in my position is used to getting his own way." His eyes gleam.

I look into them—those beautiful, mismatched planets. I wish I could be totally honest and tell him the reason why I cleaned his office last night, but I can't. The thought of doing so makes me curl up inside like a spider. But even though I feel ill at the thought of the deception I've carried out, I could no more pass up this chance to be with him than fly to the moon.

His smile fades. I've waited too long to reply.

"You don't have to—" he begins.

"Yes," I interrupt, and give him a shy smile. "I'd love to."

His expression fills with relief, which I find surprisingly sweet since he could almost certainly pull any woman on Earth. "Oh! Okay. I thought your poem was a cool birthday present, but this is even better."

I go cold as I remember the birthday card I read, but I force a smile onto my face. "It's your birthday? Today?"

"Ah…" His lips twist. "Yeah. But I'd rather you kept that to yourself." He doesn't elaborate and pulls out what looks like a brand-new, top-level iPhone with a huge screen. "Let's exchange numbers, just in case."

A little embarrassed, I take out my old, battered phone with the cracked screen. He glances at it, flicks his gaze up to me, but doesn't say anything. He reads out his number, I program it into my phone, and then he does the same with my number.

"Where do you live?" he asks. I tell him my address. "I'll be there at seven," he says, "and I'll ring Dodie and cancel tonight for you."

"Please apologize for me. I don't like to let her down."

"I'll make it worth her while, don't worry."

We stand, and he follows me over to the door. Gosh, he's tall—he towers over me, and he's big—big hands, big shoulders, big… feet.

"What should I wear?" I ask.

"It's semi-formal."

"Okay." I have no idea what that means. Hopefully Caro and Hana will give me some clues. "Thank you for lunch."

"You're welcome."

I bend to say goodbye to Gus, then straighten. Mack has closed the distance between us, and he's close enough now that if I were to reach onto my tiptoes, I'd be able to kiss his jaw. He smells amazing. And he's so gorgeous.

It's such a shame I'm the worst human being on Earth.

"Goodbye," I murmur, and before he can say anything else, I slip out of the door and walk fast toward the exit.

Once I'm out of the building, I scurry over to my car, heart banging. I've just got inside when my mobile buzzes, announcing a call. Is it him already?

It's not.

The screen informs me the caller is Socrates. I don't think it's his real name.

I'm tempted to ignore it, or just end the call, but I know better than to push this guy's buttons.

I answer it, "Hello?"

"Why did he call you into his office?" he asks.

"How did you know that?" I demand.

"Just answer the question. Did he find out about last night?"

I swallow hard. "No. I dropped a… piece of paper, and he wanted to give it back to me."

"What was on the paper?"

"Something private," I say sharply. "Not connected to you in any way."

"Was that it? Why didn't he send it over in a cab?"

I study my fingernails. It takes all my willpower not to tell him to fuck off. "He wanted to meet me."

"And?"

I close my eyes. "He's asked me to a party tonight."

"At Huxley's?"

I know there's no point in asking how he knows. "Yes."

"Perfect," he says. "He has a suite there, and he often stays the night. He usually takes his briefcase and leaves it there. Get him to take you back to the room and see if you can get into the briefcase."

My heart, which had previously soared, sinks to the ground like a popped balloon. I lean forward and put my forehead on the steering wheel. My eyes sting.

"I don't want to," I whisper.

"Really? Have you forgotten what's at stake?"

I bite my bottom lip hard. "No."

"If you get the information, you get the money. If you don't… I'll tell Mack why you were at his office last night."

I go cold. I can only imagine what Mack's reaction would be. He'd be furious. He might even phone the police.

I don't have a choice. I started this. I have nobody to blame but myself.

"All right," I say dully.

"I'll call tomorrow morning, eight a.m.," he says. "Good luck tonight. Enjoy yourself." And he chuckles before ending the call. Fucking bastard.

I sit there for a moment.

I want to bawl my eyes out. I've never hated anyone as much as I hate him right now.

But there's nothing I can do about it. I've just got to get on with it, and finish this.

My throat tightens. A little part of me is sure there could have been something between me and Mack. But I'll never be able to explore that, because I've ruined our relationship before it's even begun.

I start the engine and head to the main road, trying not to think about Mack and his beautiful, planet-filled eyes.

Chapter Four

Sidnie

Just after five-thirty, I pull up outside the house I share with Caro and Hana and park a few cars down. When we finished university, I assumed that the two of them, being a couple, would want their own place at last, but they were keen to split the rent on a house, and that's why the three of us still share. It's a tiny two-bedroom house with a garden the size of a postage stamp just ten minutes out of the city not far from the preschool where Caro teaches, but it's relatively quiet, and we're quite comfortable here.

I let myself in the front door and go in, calling, "Hello?"

"We're in the kitchen."

I go through and find them in the process of making pizzas. Caro, or Caroline, is average height and pretty with long dark-brown hair she mostly wears in a braid over one shoulder. She's been my best friend since high school. She told me she was gay when she was sixteen, although I'd already guessed. She's gentle, funny, and brilliant with young children, and in her element now she's qualified as an Early Childhood Teacher.

Hana's parents are Korean, but she was born in New Zealand, and she's very striking, with short black hair and flashing eyes. She was in my English class at uni, and I knew Caro would be both shocked and entranced by her mischievous and quirky nature. As soon as I discovered she was gay too, I introduced them, and as I expected, they hit it off immediately. It was only a few months later that Hana moved in.

"We're making you a roast veggie pizza," Hana says as I plonk myself down in one of the chairs at the table.

"And we've bought a giant packet of Maltesers and splashed out on two bottles of Pinot Gris that were on special," Caro adds, "so we're all set for the evening."

"Actually, I'll have to take a rain check," I tell them. "I have a date."

They both stare at me, eyebrows rising. "What?" Caro grins. "Simon finally asked you out, did he?" He's a trainee at Lubricanz and the only guy there who's less than fifty years old, with a face like the pizza they're making, and a brace.

"Nope." I chew my bottom lip. "His name's Mack Hart. And he's a billionaire."

Comically, their jaws drop together. "Right," Caro says, pulling up a chair. "Tell us everything."

I don't, of course, leaving out the bit about how I ended up covering for Pippa, and how I was spying on him. Neither Caro nor Hana know anything about the pickle I've got myself into, and I intend to keep it that way. But I tell them everything else, and when I explain how he found the dirty poem I'd written, they both collapse into helpless laughter.

I make it seem as if I'm scared witless because I'm so out of my depth, which actually isn't far from the truth either.

"What was his name again?" Hana's pulled out her phone. I tell her, and she Googles him. "Fucking hell." She shows me his photo to confirm she's got the right person, and when I nod, shows it to Caro.

"Sid!" she exclaims. "Oh my God. He's gorgeous."

"I know." I pull a face. "That's why I'm terrified."

"Aw!" Hana gives me a pitying look. "He's still an ordinary guy beneath all the money."

"He used to work as a waiter and a barista," I confirm. "But even so, now he's so rich he could have any woman he wants. Why does he want me?"

"Because you're unique," Caro says with a smile.

"Weirdly, that's the word he used. He said he likes my hair."

They both laugh. "He's got a Wikipedia page," Hana says, and scans it. "It's quite short. He was born in Scotland."

"Does it say what his parents' names are?"

"No. He came to New Zealand when he was twelve," Hana continues. "That's all it says about his childhood. At school he excelled in athletics."

"Yeah, he's a sprinter. There was a trophy in his office—when he was sixteen, he won first place in the hundred meters in the New Zealand Athletics Championships."

"Wow," Caro says.

Hana scans the rest of the article. "He invented a super-fast computer processor in his early twenties and sold it to Intel for a million dollars. He received job offers from Intel, Apple, and most of the other major computer technology firms, but he chose to set up his own company, and his net wealth is now estimated to be several billion dollars. Holy fuck. Billions, Sid. Has that sunk in?"

"Not really. He's got weird eyes, too. One blue, one sort of Earth-like. What else does it say?"

"A section about supercomputers." She makes a gesture that implies it's going over her head. "Blah blah blah… It says he was the keynote speaker at last year's virtual International Conference on Supercomputing. That's pretty impressive when you think who he'd be up against. He also does a lot of work in New Zealand schools and universities apparently, giving talks to up-and-coming talent in the industry. Do you think this guy ever sleeps?"

"Probably not," I say, thinking about the untouched bed in his office.

"Does it say if he's married?" Caro asks.

Hana shakes her head. "The personal section just says he's been linked with various famous Kiwi models, the latest being Felicity Scarlett-Rose, daughter of the CEO of Archangel Media Corp."

I've seen the model in Kiwi women's magazines. She has short red hair and she's very beautiful. Now I'm intimidated.

"Wow. So where's he taking you?" Hana asks.

"To a party at a business club—Huxley's. He said it's semi-formal. I have no idea what to wear."

"Semi-formal is kind of in between business suit and cocktail dress," Caro says.

"I've got jeans or miniskirts," I reply. "Do either of them count?"

"We'll find something," Hana says firmly. "When's he picking you up?"

"Seven."

"Right. Just under an hour. Let's go."

Caro pours us all a glass of wine, mainly because I'm shaking like a leaf, and we take them into my room. I have a few large gulps, desperately hoping the alcohol will calm me down.

"What sort of look do you want to go for?" Hana asks. "Understated? Or do you want to knock his socks off?"

"It's always better to be under- than overdressed," Caro says helpfully.

It's true, but I'm not going tonight with the intention of providing the kind of first impression that will keep him coming back for more. I know I'll never see him again after this date. I don't want to see him again knowing what I've done to him. After tonight, I'm going to walk away as fast as I can and never look back.

But what I do need to do is get him to take me up to his room.

"I want to knock his socks off," I reply. "Make me look amazing."

"Easy," Hana says. "Come on, Caro."

They start by going through my wardrobe and taking out any outfit they consider appropriate for the evening. Then the two of them go to their room to raid their own wardrobes. I'm taller than both of them, so everything's going to be too short, but we're all roughly the same weight, so I occasionally borrow from their wardrobes.

I finish off my glass of wine and pour myself another. What the hell. No way am I going to be able to get through this sober.

I've just taken my first sip when my phone vibrates. Hoping it doesn't say Socrates, I check the screen. It's a text from Mack.

Just watched one of your videos, he says. *I'm impressed.* He ends with the face-with-tongue emoji.

My lips curve up. I chew my bottom lip as I consider what to say. Then, smiling, I type back.

Thanks! I hope you learned something. I add a hot face to the end. And it goes from there.

Him: *Definitely! This should be on the school curriculum.*

Me: *I think the PTAs would take issue with that.*

Him: *Probably LOL. I'm still confused about the difference between the three levels.*

Me: *In what way?*

Him: *I wondered if you could give me some examples?*

Heat rushes through me. There are plenty of examples in the videos. He wants me to do it personally. He wants to play.

I start to hyperventilate, and put my head between my knees.

Why on earth is this guy interested in me?

But of course, I know why.

He doesn't do relationships, he told me that. To achieve everything that he has, he must be very single-minded, and that doesn't leave much room for fun. So when he saw my poem, he just thought it was a way to have a fun evening and probably a one-night stand.

If I assume I'm going into this for sex, I don't have to worry about anything except getting him into bed. Then at the end, I'll check his briefcase and run out the door. I know he's a sprinter, but he's not going to be able to see me for dust.

I look back at my phone. Sadness blooms inside me, because I like him, and it would be nice to believe there could be more between us. But hey-ho. Sex is good too. I'm just going to push the thought of the post-sex task to the back of my mind and enjoy myself.

I have another mouthful of wine and text back.

Me: *At the beginning, I suggest starting gently until you get to know your partner, as not everyone is comfortable with frank or crude descriptions.*

Him: *It's okay, I never swear.*

Me: *Yeah, right! So I suggest starting with a compliment, something like… I love your beautiful eyes.*

Him: *Thanks! They've been known to freak people out.*

Me: *I thought they were amazing. I've never seen anything like them.*

Him: *Okay. How about… I love that you're tall. The perfect height for kissing.* He adds the lips emoji to the end.

I warm through at the thought of getting up close to him. Having his lips on mine. Mmm.

Me: *Oh, you're good at this.*

Him: *I have a good teacher.*

Me: *:-)*

Him: *Here's another one. I love your crazy hair. I'd like to sink my hands into it while I kiss you.*

I feel a surge of naughtiness.

Me: *I like that you're clean shaven. Less bristle burn…*

Him: *Oh, are we progressing to intermediate now?*

Me: *Hehe. Don't think I've got time for that. I need to get ready. I have a date, you know.*

Him: *I'm sure you don't need long. You're already gorgeous.*

Me: *I need three hours just to tame my hair.*

Him: *Wear it down. I want to see it in all its glory.*

Me: *You don't know what you're saying. I look like Princess Merida on steroids.*

As soon as I press send, I wince as I have a feeling he doesn't like being reminded of his Scottish heritage.

But he just returns with: *LOL. Now you've definitely got to do it. I want to see that.*

Me: *All right… you have been warned…*

"Okay," Caro says, coming back in. "These are our options." She looks at the phone in my hand and grins. "Is that him?"

"We're sexting. Beginner style. He wants me to teach him."

"About time you put it into practice," Hana says, following her in.

"He wants me to wear my hair down."

Caro raises an eyebrow. "Really? Is he nuts?"

"I did warn him. I don't think he fully realizes what he's let himself in for."

"Okay. Well, in that case, I think you need a more subtle outfit so it doesn't compete with The Hair." She takes away some of the more colorful choices.

"What look do you want to go for?" Hana holds up a standard little black dress she wore to her graduation. "Look how cute I am, I could be wild, but you won't know until you get me into bed?"

"Too boring," Caro says. "We need something more suggestive."

Hana exchanges it for a dusky pink dress with butterfly sleeves and a plunging neckline. "I'm hot and confident, look at how gorgeous my boobs are?"

"It's too short," I reply. "On me it'll barely cover my knickers."

"That's a bad thing?"

"It's at a business club. I don't want to look like an escort he's hired for the evening."

"Fair enough." She puts down the pink dress and holds up a light-blue dress covered with layers of tulle. "Treat me like a virgin and you might be in for a treat?"

I purse my lips. "I'm not sure."

"Ask him," Caro says, eyes sparkling.

Giving her a mischievous smile, I send him a text, while the two of them look over my shoulder to read his response.

Me: *I'm trying to decide what kind of look to go for. Virginal?*
Him: *Nope.*

We all giggle. "So innocence doesn't turn him on," Caro teases.

"Bit of luck," Hana comments.

"Ha-ha," I say sarcastically. I text again. *Slutty?*

Him: *If we were on our own, definitely. But maybe something in between?*

I grin at the other two.

Me: *Okay. But just so you know… I won't be wearing any underwear…*

They laugh, and we all wait for his reply.

Him: *Ah… good girl…*

We all inhale and exchange a look.

"I think he's ready for the intermediate class," Hana says.

I knock back the rest of my wine. "I need something sexy but not slutty. What else have you got?"

We settle on a silvery-gray sheath dress that's calf-length on Hana but reaches to just above my knees. It has spaghetti straps and it's covered with a layer of gray lace that extends up from the bodice to around the neckline, and down the arms to the elbows.

"It's perfect," I say happily. "Right. I think I'll take a quick shower."

Afterward, I spend five minutes making sure I'm hairless where it counts and slather on some body lotion from my neck to my toes. While I'm doing that a text pings up, and I read it with a smile.

Him: *What are you doing right now?*

Me: *Making myself smooth for you.*

Him: *Oh… you know how to say all the right things.*

Me: *Just don't squeeze me too hard or I'll slip through your hands like a peeled avocado.*

Him: *LOL. Do you recommend using humor in your videos?*

I cringe. *Actually, no, sorry, I forgot I was supposed to be in seduction mode. I'm spoiling the mood.*

Him: *Not at all. I love your sense of humor. Now, tell me more about this seduction mode.*

I laugh and start applying some makeup in the mirror in between texts. Definitely time for some smoky eyes.

Me: *I'll get better as the evening goes on. I tell jokes when I'm nervous.*

Him: *You're nervous?*

Me: *Well, yeah. It's not every day a girl gets to date such a gorgeous, perfect guy.*

Him: *If you're expecting perfection, you're going to be very disappointed.*

Me: *I sincerely doubt it.*

Him: *I just walked into the rubber plant in the lobby and knocked it over. Now Steven has to sweep up the earth I spilled all over the floor. I need to give that guy a raise.*

That makes me laugh out loud. *You need to look where you're going!*

Him: *I would, but some sexy girl keeps sexting me.*

Me: *And we're still in beginner mode. What are you going to be like when we move to intermediate?*

Chuckling as I think of him knocking over the plant, I apply some mascara. Now it's time to attack The Hair. I've washed it, heaped on the conditioner, applied some anti-frizz product, and now I set to drying it with the diffuser. When I'm about fifty percent done, I leave the rest to dry naturally and check my phone again.

Him: *So have I passed the beginner exam?*

Me: *You're ready to move on to intermediate?*

Him: *What do you think?*

Me: *I think the good girl comment was enough to get you to pass on its own.*

Him: *Oh, you liked that?*

Me: *Every girl likes that.*

Him: *Noted.*

Me: *Like you didn't already know that. Don't think I don't understand who's the teacher and who's the student here.*

Him: *Even experts need to be open to new data.*

Me: *Trust you to have a computer analogy.*

Him: *Heh. You still haven't explained what intermediate includes.*

I decide to leave him waiting. Wearing a towel, I go into my bedroom and close the door. Dropping the towel, I look at myself in the full-length mirror on the inside of my wardrobe. I don't have a bad figure—a little straight, B cup and slim-hipped, and sometimes I've wished it were more hourglass. But we get what we're given, and it could be a lot worse.

I promised him I wouldn't wear underwear, so it's time to go commando. Luckily we don't have much of an underground train system in New Zealand so I don't have to worry about doing a Marilyn Monroe impression.

I pull the dress on carefully and smooth it down over my hips. Then I slide my feet into the one pair of flesh-colored pretty sandals I own. They have a two-inch heel, but Mack's tall enough that I can get away with it.

My hair is still damp, and it looks as if I've stuck my fingers in the electric socket. But it is striking, I have to admit. And there's nothing I can do about it now.

I grab the matching purse with a chain strap that Hana has left on the bed, stuff a few things in it, and then sit on the bed. Ten minutes to go.

I look at the phone. He's still waiting for an answer to the definition of intermediate. Maybe it's time to ramp things up a little. Luckily, the alcohol is threading through my system, and I'm getting a grip on my nerves.

Me: *I don't think we're ready for intermediate yet. Maybe Beginner Plus.*

Him: *Ha, okay. Explain.*

Me: *It means turning the conversation more intimate. Suggesting what might happen later. Turning up the heat a little.*

Him: *Something like… where would you like me to touch you first?*

Me: *Oh yes, that's great. Should I say good boy?*

Him: *I'll warn you now, I wouldn't make a great sub.*

I shiver at the thought of him being dominating in bed. Oh my.

Me: *What a shock.*

Him: *LOL. So, your answer?*

Me: *Oh, I'm not going to tell you just yet. But I will say that waiting to see you is unbearable.*

Him: *So anticipation is important?*

Me: *You like to analyze, don't you?*

Him: *It's my job. But yeah. When something works, I want to know why. I take it apart. Look at the individual pieces and how they interact.*

Me: *That makes sense. And in answer to your question, yes, at Whisper2Me I talk a lot about anticipation. I think it's one of the easiest and most powerful ways for people to improve their love lives.*

Him: *Okay. So let me say this. I've been thinking about you all afternoon. In all my meetings. I can't get you out of my head. I think I'm a little bit obsessed. And I can't wait to see you.*

His words make me glow.

Me: *What a lovely thing to say. Are you still at work?*

Him: *No, I've just pulled up outside your house. And I'm about to knock on your door, so you'd better be ready.*

"Eek!" I jump up and scurry out. Hana and Caro are in the kitchen, finishing off their pizzas. "He's here," I say breathlessly. "Do I look okay?"

"Absolutely amazing," Hana states.

Caro smiles. "You're going to knock his socks off. Now go back in the bedroom and we'll let him in."

Hana has already gone over to the window, and she peers out, then turns, jaw dropping. "Holy fuck. He's got an Aston."

"A what?"

"An Aston Martin! James Bond's car. Wow. I've never seen one in real life. Oh, the passenger door's opening and a guy is getting out. Is that him?"

I look over her shoulder, my heart banging as I watch him close the door and walk around the car. "Yeah."

"He has a fucking chauffeur! I don't believe it."

Caro runs over to look. We all stare at him silently for a moment as he opens the small gate. Then Caro looks over at me with glittering eyes. "Sid… he's gorgeous."

"I know," I say faintly.

"Go on," she insists. "Into your room."

I run away as fast as my heels will allow me, duck into my room, pull the door almost closed, and put my ear to the crack.

Mack rings the bell, and a few seconds later the door opens.

"Hello," he says. "I'm looking for Sidnie."

"She's just finishing getting ready," Caro replies. "Come in, please. I'm Caro, and this is Hana."

"Pleased to meet you." His deep voice sends a shiver running down my spine. "I'm sorry I'm early."

"No, she's ready, I think she's just looking for her purse," Caro says.

I grab the purse, take a deep breath, and go out. Mack is standing by the door, towering over Caro and Hana. He must be about six-foot-two. He's wearing beige trousers, a navy jacket, and a blue-and-white-striped shirt with a navy tie. He looks young, handsome, smart, wealthy, and so sexy I'd have pushed him onto the carpet and done him there and then if we'd been alone in the house.

"Hello," I say breathlessly.

He glances over, and his gaze brushes up me, taking in my outfit before ending at my hair. He gives me an impish smile.

"I did try to warn you," I say.

"I love it."

I try not to blush and cross the carpet to stand beside him. Even with my heels on, he's much taller than me. Oh… how I love that.

"Back before midnight or you'll turn into a pumpkin," Caro says.

"It wasn't Cinderella who turned into the pumpkin," I remind her.

"Behave yourself," Hana says. She looks at Mack. "I'm sure she will. She's a good girl."

Caro elbows her hard. I close my eyes for a moment. When I open them, Mack's giving us all a wry look as opens the door and holds out his hand to me. "Shall we?"

I slide mine into his, throw them a glare, and follow him out to the car.

He walks me around to the back passenger door and opens it for me. That's enough to melt my heart, and the evening hasn't even started yet.

I let go of his hand reluctantly, get in, try as elegantly as I can to swing my legs in, then watch him stalk around to the other side.

Then, for the first time, I look at the driver. "Oh, hello."

"Evening." He smiles at me in the rear-view mirror. "I'm Jamie."

"Sidnie." I reach a hand over his shoulder. He laughs and shakes it as Mack slides in next to me.

"I was just introducing myself," I say.

My heart is racing. I'm terrified and excited and ecstatic and sad all rolled into one. I like him so much. Now I just have to wait and see if the evening plays out the way I'm hoping.

Chapter Five

Mack

Jamie drives the car to the end of Sidnie's street to join the traffic heading into the city.

It's a little after seven, and the sun is setting on top of the tall buildings of the CBD to the west. The city glows orange, and shadows lie across the street like fallen trees.

I haven't slept much the last few nights, caught up in my latest research project. Tonight, the strange buzz that accompanies being overtired has kicked in, and I feel wired, too afraid to sit still in case I fall asleep.

I glance across at her. The silver-gray dress she's wearing has ridden up to reveal her long, slender legs that I'm sure, after her comment about applying body lotion, are going to be soft and silky smooth. She said she wasn't going to wear any underwear—was that just a line, or is she really going commando?

Back at the house, I noticed that she's wearing high-heeled sandals, and she's painted her toenails a sexy cherry red. This girl knows how to ring every bell I possess.

She's released her hair from its clip, and it looks freshly washed, cascading down past her shoulders in a mass of glorious golden curls. She's going to turn every head at Huxley's tonight. And she's with me. I know I'm wealthy, but right now I could be penniless and I'd still feel a million dollars with her on my arm.

She looks nervous, though, her spine stiff, her hands clasped in her lap.

"So," I say. "You let your friends read my texts? I should put you across my knee for that."

She glances at Jamie, who I can see is hiding a laugh, then back at me, maybe not sure whether I'm joking. "I'm so sorry," she says. "They didn't read all of them. They happened to be standing there when you made the good girl comment."

"I don't care—I'm teasing you because you look nervous."

Her blue eyes are large and alluring with their smoky-gray eyeshadow. "Sorry, it's my default setting. I've had a couple glasses of wine, though, and that's helping." She clears her throat. "So Gus isn't coming with us this evening?"

"No, he's at home with Jamie's girlfriend. He doesn't like parties."

"Gus or Jamie?"

Jamie grins at us in the rear-view mirror. "Both," he says.

She runs her fingers along the wooden inlay of the Aston. "This car is beautiful."

"She is," I reply. "She drives like a dream, too."

"She's big, powerful, and sleek. A bit like you." She wrinkles her nose at me.

I chuckle. "Thank you."

She leans forward and whispers in my ear. "Do you purr like her, too?" Her eyes are sultry, interested.

My body stirs with pleasure at her flirting. "You'll have to find out, won't you?"

She smiles.

"Here we are."

The Italianate-style quarry-stone building rears before us, the red and green leaves of the Virginia Creeper that cloaks the walls glowing in the last rays of the summer sun. Jamie pulls up outside and leaves the engine idling.

"Ready?" I ask.

Sidnie swallows hard, then nods.

"You look amazing," I tell her. "I can't wait to introduce you to everyone."

The comment pleases her—she smiles and blows out a long breath. "I'm ready."

"Come on, then."

"Text me if you want me to pick you up," Jamie says.

"Will do." We get out, and we make our way toward the club.

"So why's it called Huxley's?" she asks, gesturing at the name above the door.

"After Oliver Huxley, the owner." I open it and we go inside.

We find ourselves in a foyer that leads to a series of function rooms. I place a hand in the small of Sidnie's back and guide her over to the elevators. I stroke down her back with my thumb. Definitely no bra, and I can't feel any other underwear either. Nice.

A carriage is waiting, so we go in, I press the button, and the doors close.

Sidnie stands facing the door, her hands linked in front of her. I don't touch her, but it's not a huge carriage, and I'm only standing six inches away. I can smell her perfume, an evening scent, different from the citrus perfume she wore earlier today. This is smoky and spicy, stirring my senses.

She's staring ahead, but she knows I'm looking at her. Her pale cheeks bear a touch of rose pink. The pulse in her neck is beating fast, inviting me to lean forward and press my lips to it.

I don't. But I want to.

She clears her throat. "So… what is a business club, exactly? I mean, I guess it's a club where you do business, but…"

"Huxley's is a place for top executives to meet and make connections."

"Like yourself?"

"Yeah. CEOs, entrepreneurs, judges, politicians. It's very exclusive. There are several restaurants, lounges, and bars."

The doors open, and we walk out. The lobby is all polished wood and leather. Her hand sneaks into mine. I can see how she might find it intimidating if she's not used to mixing in these circles.

I tighten my hand on hers, enjoying just touching her. "Huxley and I went to high school together. He opened the club a year ago." I lead her across the lobby to the woman on the front desk. She's in her thirties, dressed in a light-gray pantsuit and white blouse, her dark hair twisted up into a sophisticated chignon. "Evening, Gail."

She smiles warmly. "Good evening, Dr. Hart."

"This is my guest, Sidnie."

"Very pleased to meet you, Ms…?"

"Sidnie's fine," she says, glancing at me as I try not to laugh.

Gail smiles. "Pleased to meet you, Sidnie."

"Where's Huxley?" I ask.

"In the Chess Room with Victoria."

"Thanks." I lead Sidnie toward the double doors on the right.

"I'm guessing you don't play chess there," Sidnie says.

"Some people do, but that's not why it's called the Chess Room. You'll see why it's called that in a minute." I nod at the bouncer on the door. "Evening, Ed."

"Good evening, Dr. Hart." He opens the door and smiles at Sidnie.

She glances at me as the doors swing shut behind us. "Do you know everyone's name?"

"I was brought up to believe it's important to know the names of all the people you meet on the way up, because you never know when you might need them on the way down."

I lead her along the corridor, past the main dining room, toward the sound of the music. A few tables are filled, but most of the club's members will be going to the party tonight. Sidnie looks at the polished wooden tables, the leather chairs, the chandeliers, and her eyes widen.

"The club is a place to meet people," I explain. "And to work, too. There are lots of meeting rooms and places to work. A gym. And private rooms for hire, like motel rooms, only a bit more upmarket."

"You like it here, I can tell."

"I do. It's busy, and modern. I get to meet interesting people. Huxley owns the club. Victoria is his partner."

"Are they married?"

"No, she's his business partner. She does the day-to-day stuff. She's very good at her job. She reads people well, and knows what they need before they ask for it."

"You're fond of her."

"The three of us are old friends—we all went to school together."

She gives me a curious look. "Were you and Victoria an item?"

I smile. "No." I don't elaborate and offer her my arm, and she slides her hand into the crook of my elbow.

We walk into the Chess Room. The central dance floor consists of large black and white squares, hence its nickname. The bar runs all the way along one wall, manned by three bartenders who are all busy serving drinks to the members. Tables and chairs line two of the other walls. A popular Kiwi band is performing one of its songs on the stage at the front of the room.

"It's Paua of One," Sidnie says, surprised. "I love them!"

She has to lean forward to say it in my ear because the music is quite loud. Her breath whispers across my skin. When I turn my head, my lips are only inches from hers. Jesus, I want to kiss this woman.

But there's no time, because someone says, "Mack!" and I turn to see Victoria standing there, beaming at me.

"Hey." I accept her kiss on my cheek. "Looks like it's going well."

"It's fantastic," she says. "Everyone turned up, I'm so thrilled."

She looks amazing tonight, in an extremely sharp black three-piece pantsuit, a white blouse with a frill down the front, and black high heeled sandals that take her already tall frame up to a good six foot. Her dark hair is pinned up in a bun and studded with what are almost certainly diamond pins. Her makeup, as always, is immaculate.

"And who's this?" she asks, turning to Sidnie.

"Vic, this is my friend, Sidnie. Sidnie, meet Victoria Brown."

"Very pleased to meet you." Victoria shakes her hand.

"Likewise," Sidnie says. "Mack tells me he went to school with you and... do I call him Oliver or Huxley?"

"Oh, everyone calls him Huxley or Hux. We were all besties through some tough times at Oakland Grammar, weren't we, Mack?"

I nod and glance at Sidnie to see if she got the reference. Oakland Grammar is, and always has been, a boys' school. Victoria sometimes mentions it if she wants to let someone know she's a transgender woman.

Sidnie frowns for a moment, obviously puzzled. Then the penny drops, and her expression clears. She smiles. "I have to say, I love your suit. You look amazing. It's so hard when you're a tall woman to get suits to fit, I find."

Victoria grins. "It is. And by the way, your hair is absolutely divine. I adore it."

"Thank you! It's Mack's fault. I was going to restrain it, but he insisted I let it go free-range."

Victoria looks at me, her smile warm. "I love her," she says. "Hang on to this one, Mack."

She's already turning away as a member of her staff calls her over to the bar and misses my exasperated look. "Oh," she says, "I'm so sorry, please excuse me for a moment." She moves away toward the bar.

I look down at Sidnie. She lifts her gaze to me. "What?"

I absolutely adore this woman. Lowering my head, I press my lips to hers.

It's only a peck, but it's enough to send my blood racing around my body, and I feel her inhale sharply, too.

When I lift my head, her eyes are wide and sparkling. "What was that for?"

"Vic's important to me. I'm pleased you like each other."

"She's gorgeous. And I'm so impressed. It's good to see women running businesses like this."

I want to kiss her again, but the club's busy and people are knocking into us, so in the end I just rest my hand in the middle of her back again—keen to touch her somewhere—and guide her toward the bar. "What can I get you?"

"G&T please. Diet tonic, if they have it."

I attract the attention of the bartender, and he comes over with a smile. "Good evening, Dr. Hart."

"Hey, Simon. Can we have two gin and diet tonics, please."

"Any particular gin, sir?"

I look at Sidnie, who purses her lips.

"We'll have the Scapegrace Gold, please," I say.

"Yes, sir." He goes off to get the bottle.

"Sorry, I just normally get whatever's on special," Sidnie admits to me.

"Fair enough. They're all quite different, though. We'll have to do a taste test."

"Now you're talking."

Simon brings our drinks back and passes them to us with a smile before going off to serve someone else.

"Don't you have to pay?" Sidnie asks.

"He'll put them on my tab."

She sips the G&T, her eyes dancing over the rim of the glass. "Imagine having a tab at a club like this. Ooh, that's nice."

It is—the taste of tangerine pops on my tongue. "It's navy strength," I warn her. "Fifty-seven percent."

"Wow." She licks her lips. "I've always wondered why it's called that."

I try not to stare at her mouth. "In the British Navy, gin and rum were stored next to the gunpowder. If the barrels split and the gin mixed with the gunpowder, it would still explode with the higher alcohol content."

She laughs. "I never knew that."

"I'm a font of useless information."

"Technically, it's fount."

"Oh really?"

"From fountain. But it's interchangeable nowadays. See? I know plenty of useless information, too."

I lean on the bar and sip the gin as I study her. Her cheeks are a little flushed. Her wild hair gleams in the flashing lights.

"You're absolutely stunning," I say.

She licks her lips. "You're not so bad yourself."

God, I want this girl. I want to push her up against the bar and kiss her senseless. I want to feel her soft body against mine, and pull her close against me so she can feel how turned on I am.

I look at my gin glass. I should probably have something to eat.

"Mack!"

I turn and see my closest friends approaching. Not surprisingly, they're all staring at Sidnie. It's been a while since I brought a date here.

"Hello." I put my arm around Sidnie again, resting my hand in the spot at the base of her spine that I'm quickly beginning to feel belongs to me, and introduce her to my friends. "Sidnie, this is Oliver Huxley."

Huxley is the same height as me, and a big guy too, with dark hair. He's affable, charming, and charismatic, and it's not a cover—he's genuinely one of the good guys.

She shakes hands with him. "Pleased to meet you. I love your club."

"Thanks," he says. "I'm glad you managed to drag Dr. All-work-and-no-play here tonight."

"It wasn't easy. I had to physically pull his laptop out of his hands."

He laughs, and I grin. "This is Elizabeth Tremblay," I continue, gesturing to the woman in the middle. She's as small as Victoria is tall, and even though she tends to wear three-inch heels, she still doesn't reach any of our shoulders. She has dark-brown hair she wears in a chic long bob, and big dark eyes. "She owns MediTechNZ."

They shake hands. "I love your hair," Elizabeth says to Sidnie, leaning close to make herself heard. "It's gorgeous."

"Thank you," Sidnie replies. "It's out of control, though. It's so warm in here, I'm sure the humidity is making it worse."

Elizabeth laughs and glances at me—she likes her.

"And lastly, this is Titus Oates, Chairman of NZAI. He's not half as impressive as his name suggests."

"Unfortunately that's true," Titus says, shaking her hand, and she chuckles, because it's obviously a lie. He's like a Viking, even taller than me and Hux, with dark-blond hair, and he's extremely good looking.

"It's a nickname," Victoria advises. "His real name is Lawrence."

"Lawrence Oates—like the guy who went with Scott to the Antarctic," Sidnie states. "Of course, his nickname was Titus."

"Yeah," Victoria says, "well done."

"We also call him the Incredible Hunk," Elizabeth teases, and Sidnie giggles.

"Mack?"

I glance around and feel a jolt at the sight of a woman with short, striking red hair standing next to a good-looking younger guy.

"Hi." I see her look at Sidnie and reluctantly introduce them. "Sidnie, this is Felicity Scarlett-Rose and David Clarke. Felicity, this is Sidnie."

"Sidnie…" Felicity encourages her to add her surname.

"Just Sidnie," she says. "I'm mononymous. Like Madonna."

"Or Socrates," David suggests.

Everyone laughs, except Sidnie. Her smile fades, and even in the flashing lights, I see her skin pale. Does she know about me and Felicity? I know there have been a few pictures of us online.

She recovers quickly though, smiles, and says to Felicity, "I've seen your pictures in all the magazines."

"Pleased to meet you," Felicity says, shaking her hand, and David does the same.

"Aaron wants to know if we have five minutes for a catch up," David says to me.

"He said to go to Meeting Room Two," Titus adds.

I hesitate. I don't want to leave Sidnie alone.

"I haven't seen you here before," Felicity says to Sidnie.

"This is my first time," Sidnie admits. "I'm here with the birthday boy."

Felicity stares at her. The others look at me, eyebrows rising.

"What?" Sidnie says.

"It's your birthday?" Elizabeth asks. "Happy birthday, honey!" She raises up onto her tiptoes and kisses my cheek.

"Sorry," Sidnie says, obviously realizing her faux pas, "I forgot I wasn't supposed to mention it."

"It slipped out," I say to the others, who are all smirking. "Don't make a fuss."

"So you wanna come?" Titus asks.

"Go on," Sidnie says. "I don't mind."

SERENITY WOODS

"I'll only be five minutes," I tell her.

"It's fine."

I finish off my drink and leave it on the bar, then as I turn, bump into Felicity.

"Sorry," I say.

"It's okay." She sidesteps, staying with me as I go to walk around her. "Mack..." she murmurs, "I just wanted to say how sorry I am. You know, for what happened at your office."

I give her a cool look. "Okay."

She glances at Sidnie, who's talking with Elizabeth. "She's pretty."

"Hmm." I don't want to discuss Sidnie with her. "Are you a member here now?"

She flushes. "No. I'm here with David."

I raise an eyebrow. He's Elizabeth's Director of Computer Science, young, talented, and ambitious, and not in a good way. He's the kind of guy who'll walk all over those beneath him if it means he can get higher on the ladder. A few years ago, he came for an interview at Koru Tech before he went to Elizabeth, but despite his excellent qualifications and obvious talent, I didn't hire him because... well, I didn't like him. I sent him a letter saying he hadn't got the job, and he called my office and demanded to talk to me. When Nadine said I was unavailable, he was rude to her, and I've never forgiven him for it.

But saying anything of the sort will just make me look spiteful, so I just nod and say politely, "He's a lucky man," even though I don't mean it.

"Mack?" Titus beckons with his head.

I nod. "I'm coming." I glance back at Sidnie. "Are you sure you don't mind?"

She's chatting with Victoria again, though, and just smiles and shakes her head.

Stifling a sigh, I nod at Felicity, then follow Titus and the others across the room.

I should have just taken Sidnie to a bar for a drink, and kept her to myself.

Chapter Six

Sidnie

I watch Mack stride across the room, then realize Victoria's holding out another G&T, waiting for me to notice.

"Sorry." I take it from her, and she smiles. "He's like the sun, isn't he? Dazzling."

Next to her, Felicity, who also watched him walk away, turns back to face us. "We're all just comets shooting through his solar system, aren't we?"

Victoria gives her a warning glance.

"I'm not being a bitch," Felicity says. "I'm just stating a fact."

"I know," I reply cheerfully. "I'm guessing he dates a lot of women. I know I'm nothing special."

"He did tell you it was his birthday," she says. "He must really like you." She doesn't look jealous, just curious.

"I only met him this morning," I reply, a little embarrassed. I know this woman is his ex. Didn't he tell her when his birthday was? "It's not a big thing. Like he said, it just slipped out."

"It's all right, you haven't hurt my feelings," she says. "I knew all along he couldn't be tamed. Make the most of him while you have him." She smiles, then turns and walks off.

"I can't work out if she was being nice or not," I say to Victoria.

"A bit of both," Victoria says. "Their affair didn't end well. She went to his office and refused to leave until he explained why he hadn't called her. When he said it was over, she threw the coffee machine through Nadine's window."

"Fuck, really?"

"Yeah. You can imagine what he thought of that. He was going to have security escort her off the premises, but Nadine took her into the ladies and spent half an hour consoling her before calling her an Uber and sending her home. I think she's over him now, but it obviously stung at the time when he told her it was over."

"How long had they been dating?"

"Oh, I don't even know if I'd call it that. They hooked up a few times. I think she was convenient." She sends me an apologetic look then. "I'm so sorry, that sounds very rude."

"It's okay."

"He's single-minded. He works such long hours. When he does get time to himself, he wants something uncomplicated, that's all."

"Sex, you mean?" I ask, amused.

She gives me a wry look. "Let's just say that most of his dates are hoping it'll go further than that, but it never does." She smiles. "Until now, anyway."

"Jesus, like I said, I met him this morning. We're hardly celebrating our silver wedding anniversary. I'm not insulted. I know he just wants to have a good time, and that's okay." Briefly, I think about my secret task. Then I push it back into its box. Nope, not going to think about it.

"So who's Aaron?" I ask.

"He runs the Auckland Technology Consortium—it's a small group of the top business people, invitation only. Huxley wanted to call it Aaron's Avengers. Titus preferred The Huge Members, but they were both outvoted." She grins as I giggle.

She opens her mouth to say something else, but someone taps her on the shoulder, and she turns to greet them. I step back, to the corner of the bar, put my drink down, and pull my phone out, as I'm sure I felt it vibrate just now.

Sure enough, it's a text—from Mack. *Sorry I abandoned you. I won't be long.*

Me: *It's okay. I got to watch your butt as you walked away. I'm all good.*

Him: *LOL. My friends all think you're amazing. I don't blame them. You look stunning tonight.*

Me: *And at the end of the evening you can use my hair to mop the floor.*

Him: *I love your crazy hair. And your mouth. It was very soft.*

Me: *Aren't you supposed to be working?*

Him: *I can't stop thinking about you. I want to kiss you again.*

I warm all the way through, and it's nothing to do with the gin. Or not much.

Me: *I want to kiss you again, too. A LOT.*

Him: *Next time, I'm going to take it slower. Take my time. Kiss you until you're dizzy. Until you can't think about anything except me.*

I fan myself. *It's so hot in here. I'm supposed to be teaching you how to sext.*

Him: *I'm a quick study.*

Me: *Won't the others think you're not paying attention?*

Him: *I don't give a duck.* Immediately, he comes back: *Damn autocorrect.*

I laugh. He doesn't say anything else, and I guess he's actually having to do some business.

Sighing, I slip my phone back into my purse and pull the shoulder strap across me so it rests on my hip. I have a sip of the G&T, then a few more, and suddenly realize the glass is empty.

"Another?" Simon the bartender asks.

I blow out a breath. "No thanks, not right now." I'm feeling very merry, and it's still early evening.

Mack's still not back, and Victoria is busy talking to a group of people. I feel out of place, and a bit surreal. I'm not a businesswoman, I have no idea about business speak or financial talk, and I have no connections. I'm a copywriter for a lubrication firm who also cleans, and writes sexy stories for a sideline. I'm only here because a rich billionaire wants to fuck me, which I know is the truth, and I only agreed to come because I need the money I'm going to get from spying on him.

Actually, that's not strictly true. I want to fuck him, too. He's the most charismatic, sexy, fascinating man I've ever met, and the thought of going to bed with him is making me feel quite dizzy.

Paua of One breaks out into one of my favorite songs, but nobody cheers, all the suits seemingly oblivious to the fact that this is the most popular band in New Zealand at the moment. It only adds to my feeling of not belonging. At first I thought this place was fascinating, like going to England to see the King, but now I find it dull, full of people who only want to impress one another with their business acumen, and who seem to have no idea how to enjoy themselves.

My anxiety reaches a peak and explodes like a firework inside me. A few people are on the edge of the chessboard floor, bopping politely, but I ignore them, walk to the center facing the band, and begin to dance.

You only live once, and later I'm going to have to do something horrific that makes me quake every time I think about it. So right now I'm going to turn the dial up to eleven. And fuck them all.

*

I don't know how long I dance for—ten minutes? Fifteen? I lose track. The song changes a few times and, caught up in the music, I forget where I am, forget about everything except the beat of the music, and the thought of Mack's lips on mine.

It's only when I grow thirsty that I make my way to the edge of the dance floor. As I return to the bar, I discover that the others are already back, and they cheer as I walk up. Mack, in the process of ordering drinks, turns and smiles at me.

"You look amazing out there," Victoria says.

"Thank you." I know I must look flushed and hot, but I don't care. The beat is still pounding away, matching my pulse. I don't want to stop dancing, but I desperately need a drink. I ask the bartender for a glass of water and drink it down in one, then take the G&T that Mack's got for me.

Nobody else seems inclined to join the dance floor. "Anyway," Titus says, continuing their conversation, "I've heard that Arctic have just beaten Flyer to third place."

"They're Finnish, aren't they?" Elizabeth asks.

"Yeah," Mack says. "Based in Kajaani. It's the fastest and most efficient supercomputer in Europe."

"Wow," I say, "third place? You're talking about the Top 500, right?"

He nods.

"That's a cool LINPACK benchmark," I continue. "How many PetaFLOPS does it deliver?"

Titus, Oliver, and Elizabeth laugh out loud. Mack's eyes sparkle. "Four hundred and forty-two."

I whistle, remembering that Marise registers at just over ten. "Impressive."

Victoria leans closer to Mack and says, "How turned on are you right now?"

He just grins. I have a couple of big gulps of the G&T, and then put it down. "Come and dance with me."

The others all chuckle. "Good luck with that," Titus says with a grin.

"Mack doesn't dance," Victoria advises.

He glances at her, then looks back at me. I stand in front of him, moving a little to the music. He's still leaning on the bar, and he tips his head to the side, watching me. His planet-filled eyes glitter in the flashing lights.

I move a little closer, shimmying my shoulders, holding his gaze. He's so tall, and he smells so good. I moisten my lips with the tip of my tongue, and his gaze drops to them.

Sliding my hand into his, I take a step back.

He resists for a moment, then, to my surprise, pushes off the bar and moves forward. I let him walk right up to me and lift my arms around his neck, and he drops his hands to my hips. As I sway, he moves with me, just a little.

Closing the distance, ignoring the others, I lift up and brush my lips against his, then move back. He follows, and I lead him onto the dance floor. I don't look at the others, but out of the corner of my eye I can see them exchanging surprised looks.

The lights flash, and the beat thrums up through my feet, all the way up my body. I move my hips, and he follows, moving with me. Ooh, the guy's got rhythm, and not only that but he starts singing along with the song. It's called *Heartbeat*, and the lyrics seem to have been written for tonight. It's a duet, the male lead singer being accompanied by the female backing singer. The lead singer is young and good-looking, and he's singing about sex, about feeling his lover's heart beating as they make love.

"You're an amazing dancer," Mack says in my ear, raising his voice to make himself heard.

"You too." I'm thrilled that he can dance. He's relaxing now, getting into the rhythm, and he takes my hand and spins me around before pulling me back into his arms.

"I want to move inside you," Mack murmurs, as the lead singer goes into the chorus. "Our hearts beat as one, when I move inside you."

"When you move inside me," I repeat breathlessly, following the backing singer's vocal.

Goosebumps rise all over me. It's like a promise, or a premonition, and I can't wait for it to come true.

The music's loud, it's hot, the lights are flashing, and I know everyone's watching us. I'm drunk, but I don't care. I'm with the sexiest guy in the room, and all I can think about is getting him into bed. I haven't been this hot for a guy in years, maybe ever.

But once Mack starts dancing, he doesn't seem to want to stop. We pause for a drink, down our G&Ts quickly, and then we're back on the floor. Fast songs and slow, he doesn't let go of my hand, and we spend most of the time pinned together, his hand glued to the base of my spine while he looks into my eyes.

Time fades away. There's only the music, and Mack, and the alcohol speeding through my veins, blurring everything else into color and shadow. I don't know how much longer we dance for. Minutes? Hours? At one point the band takes a break and a DJ comes on, but we continue dancing. I'm having the time of my life. Part of me never wants to stop. But I'm in high heels, and my feet ache, and I'm tired, and so when eventually Mack says, "Want to stop for a bit?" I nod and follow him off the dance floor.

He stops at the edge and turns to face me. "Here?" he says in my ear. "Or do you want to go back to my room?"

My heart bangs on my ribs. "Your room," I say, and his eyes glitter.

Taking my hand, he leads me away, through the doors and out into the corridor. There are a lot of people around, most of them in suits or cocktail dresses, talking, laughing. Mack nods at some of them, but he doesn't stop to talk, heading away from the music, toward another set of double doors.

We go through them, and they swing shut behind us. It's quieter here, the thick carpet muffling the sound of our shoes. His hand is warm on mine as he heads to the end of the corridor, past a series of doors that I think are small offices, then turns through yet another door.

It's another corridor with a line of doors. He stops by one, touches a keycard to it, opens it, and gestures for me to precede him, and I go inside. As the door swings shut, he flicks a switch, turning on a series of discreet lamps.

It's like a hotel suite, with a sofa and chairs facing a large flat-screen TV, a desk and a leather chair against the wall, a kitchenette, and a king-size bed.

And that's all I have time to see, because seconds later he takes my face in his hands, and then he's kissing me, and everything else fades away.

This time, he doesn't hold back. He promised me, *Next time, I'm going to take it slower. Take my time. Kiss you until you're dizzy. Until you can't think about anything except me.* He seems determined to fulfill that oath.

He tilts his head to the side, and his mouth slants across mine. He brushes his tongue into my mouth, and all I can taste, see, feel, smell, is him.

With a sexy growl, he pushes me back so I meet the wall with a bump, making me gasp, and then he's kissing me again, pressing up against me from chest to thigh, making it very obvious that he has an erection. *Our hearts beat as one, when I move inside you...* Mmm, that's what I want, more than anything in the world. His hands sink into my hair, clutching at the curls, and he groans.

I slide my hands up to his neck, stroking the short hair on the back of his head with my thumbs. "I want you," I whisper as he kisses my cheek, my brow, and back down my nose.

He lifts his hands to catch mine and pins them above my head on the wall. "You look amazing tonight. Every guy in that room tonight wanted to fuck you."

My heart races. "But only you get to do it."

"Only me." He nuzzles my ear. "You smell so good." He takes my earlobe between his teeth and tugs it.

I shiver, arching my back so I can press my breasts against his chest. "Mmm... you're driving me crazy."

"Tell me what you want," he whispers, his voice husky.

"I want you to touch me." I tilt my hips, rocking them against his erection so he's arousing me. "I want to feel your hands and your mouth on me."

He trails his lips down my neck. "Where?"

"Oh... everywhere. All over me."

"Here?" Still holding my hands above my head with one hand, he strokes the other down my arm, beneath the sensitive skin of my underarm, and over my ribs to my breast.

"God... yes..."

He cups it and lightly brushes his thumb over my nipple. "You want me to touch you here?"

"Fuck... yes..."

He continues to stroke his hand down, over my hip, and down the outside of my thigh until he reaches the bottom of my dress. Then he slowly slides the material up. "What about here?"

My lips part in a sigh. "Mmm..."

Lightly, he traces his fingers over my thigh. Then he slides them up. I'm not wearing any underwear, and as his fingers find my bare flesh, his pupils dilate, and his lips curve up.

"I told you I wouldn't," I say, then catch my bottom lip between my teeth as he cups my mound.

"You did." He presses his knee between mine and nudges them apart. Then he slides his middle finger down into my folds. His mouth hovers over mine, and both of our lips part as his finger glides easily into me. "Fuck," he whispers. "You're so wet."

"It's all for you." I tilt my head back on the wall as he coats his finger with moisture then returns to my clit. Gently, he rubs in a circle.

"Tell me how it feels," he says, kissing up to my ear.

"Heavenly…" I close my eyes.

"Softer? Harder?"

"Mmm… a little harder… oh yes… just like that…"

He continues stroking me, and kisses down my neck to where my pulse beats in my throat. "I can feel your heartbeat," he murmurs, and closes his mouth over it.

I'm so turned on. I think I could come like this. "Mmm, Mack…"

He sucks, gentle at first, then harder. I laugh and try to pull free, but his hands are tight on mine. "Hey, you'll give me a hickey."

"I'm going to cover you in them so everyone knows you're mine."

"No!" I giggle and squirm to get away, but he holds me there and kisses me again.

"You're going to forget your name after I've done fucking you tonight," he says when he eventually comes up for air.

Holy shit, this guy… He moves back and, before I can gather my wits, he picks me up, then tosses me onto the bed. Ooh! I bounce and push up onto my elbows in time to see him throw his jacket over the chair before he returns and climbs on the bed on top of me.

"Sidnie," he says, the one word enough to make me melt, and then he's kissing my breasts, down my tummy, and pushing up my dress as he moves between my legs. He grazes his teeth on my thighs, taking big, gentle bites, then places soft kisses either side of my folds.

"You smell so good," he mumbles, and brushes his thumb up through the swollen skin.

I cover my face with my hands. I've definitely died and gone to heaven.

"I'm going to taste you now," he promises. "Slowly. I want you begging me to make you come."

"Mmm… Mack…"

He lowers his head and closes his mouth over my clit.

Holy fuck, that feels so good. He sucks gently, then slides his tongue through my folds, at the same time as he inserts two fingers inside me.

"You're so ready for me," he says, filling the air with the slick sound of sex as he strokes his fingers in and out of me.

"Ohhh…" I'm rapidly losing the power of speech.

"Slowly," he scolds, and withdraws his fingers. He blows lightly across my skin, and I shudder and moan. "Beg me," he says.

I shake my head. He touches my clit lightly with the pad of his finger, teasing it.

"Mack…"

"Beg me…"

"Oh God…" I tilt my head to the side, my eyelids fluttering open.

And it's then that I see it. The desk, against the wall. His laptop sits on there, open, the screensaver filling the screen with red and blue swirls. A pile of folders rests next to it. Sheets of paper are scattered across the rest of the surface.

It's as if someone has thrown a bucket of cold water over me.

I'm here to spy on him. After I have sex with him, I'm supposed to take a photo of those papers.

I don't have to. I could just have sex with him, then go home and pretend I couldn't get him to take me up to the room.

But even the thought of it fills me with shame.

I really, really like this guy. He's hot, and sexy, and funny, and gentle, and I came here completely under false pretenses. I feel about an inch high.

"Mack…" I rest a hand on his hair. He doesn't stop though, continuing to slide his fingers and tongue through my folds. Jesus, I'm going to come… "Mack!"

He stops and lifts his head. I push myself up the bed, away from him.

He blinks. "What's up?"

"I can't." Is he going to think I'm playing? Asking him to be forceful?

He stares at me, then runs a hand through his hair. The look on my face must be enough to convince him I'm not playing.

"I'm sorry." Tears rush into my eyes.

"Hey." He gets to his feet. Half of me expect him to get angry, to yell at me that I'm a prick tease, that I've been leading him on. But he just sits on the bed next to me. "It's all right. We don't have to do anything you don't want to."

I press my fingers to my lips.

He smiles and holds out his arms. "You want a hug?"

Fucking hell, this man. "Don't be nice to me," I squeak. His eyebrows rise, and I roll over and scramble off the bed.

"Sidnie? What's going on?"

"I shouldn't have come."

"I didn't think you did," he teases, getting to his feet.

"Mack—don't. I came here to spy on you."

He stares at me. "What?"

We face each other, about two feet apart. I'm shaking now.

"I was paid to come here and take photographs of your work," I say, gesturing at the desk.

He looks at it, then back at me. All of a sudden, we're both completely sober.

"By whom?" he asks.

I shake my head.

"You can't tell me, or you won't tell me?"

I just shake my head again. I'm terrified. I can't be specific as to what I'm terrified of.

The silence in the room is so loud it hurts my ears. Way off in the distance, I can hear Paua of One playing, but it no longer seems magical and exciting. I've drunk too much, and nausea sweeps over me.

"So what were you going to do?" he asks, his voice hard and flat as a sheet of iron. "Fuck me, wait for me to fall asleep, and then break into my laptop?"

"Something like that."

"Why didn't you?"

I don't reply. I just press my fingers to my lips again and hope my eyes explain.

He holds my gaze for a long time. And then eventually, he says, "I think you should go."

I swallow hard. "Will you at least let me explain?"

"Is there really anything you can say that will make this okay?"

I don't know what else to say. I'm shaking so hard.

For a moment, I glimpse disappointment and regret in his eyes. Then it disappears, leaving only a hard mask of fury.

"Get out," he says. "Before I call security."

I pick up my purse, turn, and flee the room, letting the door swing shut behind me.

Chapter Seven

Mack

"Fuuuuuuck!"

I yell the word at the top of my lungs, so loudly it makes my throat hurt.

I have no doubt that someone heard me, but at that moment I don't care. I want the whole world to know how angry I feel.

The anger inside me burns thermonuclear, and I have no idea what to do with it. I turn and look at the room, wound tight and with no way to vent it. I want to smash up the room. I want to throw my laptop, break the windows, beat the chairs on the floor until they shatter, and put my fist through the TV. I want to yell loud enough that everyone in the Chess Room can hear me, so they all know how furious I am. And how stupid I feel.

Mack Hart has just been soundly fucked by a girl, and he hasn't even taken his pants off.

I want Sidnie back here so I can vent my fury on her. She doesn't deserve to get off this lightly. I want to punish her for making me feel like this.

Ripping open the door so hard it bangs on the wall, I stalk down the corridor and out to the lobby.

Gail stands up as I approach her, and I can see by the look on her face that someone has told her about the man yelling furiously in room number ten.

"Dr. Hart," she says, cool as a cucumber, to her credit. "Can I help you?"

"Where is she?" I demand.

She doesn't ask who I mean. "She left."

I head for the elevator. I'll chase her through the whole of the CBD if I have to.

I hammer on the button, but I'm still waiting for the carriage when a voice from behind me calls, "Mack," and I turn to see Huxley enter the lobby. Someone's obviously informed him about the disturbance.

"Go away," I snap, hammering again on the button.

"Stop it." He pulls my arm. I wrench it as the carriage doors open and go to walk around him, but he steps in my way. "Mack. I'm not letting you go after her, not in this mood."

"Fuck off."

"Mack, I'm doing you a favor. Whatever's happened, it's not going to end well if you leave like this."

I stop, because I know he's right. I don't have to like it though. I stand there with my hands on my hips, breathing fast, wishing I could punch him in the face.

"Just try it," he says wryly, obviously reading it in my expression. "Come on."

"I don't want to go back to the party."

"No, I'm not planning on letting you scare off all my members. You're going back to your room."

"I want a drink."

"I think you've had enough."

"What happened to the customer's always right? I want a fucking drink." I end on a yell.

He exchanges a look with Gail. "Can you please send a bottle of Lagavulin up to Dr. Hart's room?" He puts a hand on my back then and propels me along the corridor.

I shake it off, but continue walking. He walks beside me, not saying anything.

When we get to my suite, I let myself in, and he comes in with me. I go over to the bed, sit, flop back, and cover my eyes with my hands.

Huxley doesn't say anything. I hear him moving about the room, drawing the curtains, then he comes back and stands at the foot of the bed. "I haven't seen you this drunk in a while," he says.

"It was a good party. Up until about ten minutes ago."

"I'll take that as a compliment."

There's a knock at the door, and he goes over and answers it.

"Is he okay?" It's Victoria. I give a silent groan. I don't need an audience.

"He's drunk."

"Does he need this, then?"

"Just pour him a glass, will you?"

I listen to her retrieve glasses from the cupboard above the sink, add some ice from the freezer compartment of the fridge, then splash some whisky over the top.

"You don't have to stay," I mumble.

"We'll go back down in a bit. But when I'm told that a member has caused a ruckus, I'm obliged to investigate." Huxley comes over. "Here."

I sit up, moving back against the pillows, and take the tumbler. "I was drinking gin. I probably shouldn't mix."

"I think that's the least of your problems."

I look at the whisky. It's a deep reddish-brown, and it has the distinctive Islay malt peaty smell. It's probably over twenty years old, and the bottle would have cost over a thousand dollars. Vic knows I have expensive tastes.

I think of Sidnie, and my mood sours even more.

I have a mouthful of the whisky, and sigh as it goes down smooth as silk.

"What happened?" Huxley asks, pulling the chair from the table up to the bed and sitting astride it, his arms on the back, the glass dangling from his fingers. Victoria sits on the bed beside me, also holding a glass.

"I don't want to talk about it," I snap.

"So it's your fault?" Huxley asks.

"Fuck off."

"Right. Did she… mistake your intentions?"

Is he asking if I took advantage of her? "Jesus, no, nothing like that, not that it's any of your business."

"It's my establishment, Mack. I don't care if we're friends—I have to make sure everyone on these premises feels safe."

Hurt at what he's implying, I glare at him. "Thanks for the vote of confidence." I finish off the whisky and hold the glass out to Vic. She purses her lips, then reaches over with the bottle and pours half an inch in. I put a finger under the base to keep it up, so more of the mahogany liquid sloshes over the ice.

She puts the bottle on the floor and frowns at me. "So what did she do? Or say? I've never seen you like this over a woman."

I let my head fall back onto the headboard with a thump. "I really don't want to talk about it." I bang my head again. "You should have let me go after her."

Huxley gives a short laugh. "In the mood you're in? Certainly not. When you've calmed down and you're sober, then absolutely I think you should go and apologize."

"Apologize?" Fury floods me. "You have no idea what she's done."

"No, because you won't tell us," Vic says. "But face it, Mack, you don't have a great track record with the way you treat women. You use them, then you discard them like dirty socks."

The accusation stings because it's true. She's never spoken to me like that before, though, and I stare at her, surprised and shocked.

Her expression softens. "I know you're a busy man, and you don't want the complications of a relationship, but many of the women you date are interested in more than a one-night stand, and you give no thought to their feelings. You're one of the good guys in so many ways, and you're a better man than this. Sidnie left here in floods of tears. Whatever she did, she's very upset about it. She deserves better."

I lie back, my heart thumping.

Vic and Huxley exchange a glance. Then she says, "You really like her, don't you?"

"No."

"She seemed like a lot of fun. And such crazy hair."

I think of her wild curls and feel a wave of emotion so strong that I can't speak. I slide down the pillows and cover my face with my arm.

"Mack…"

"Go away." I'm struggling to stay in control. "Please."

Huxley hesitates, then says softly, "All right."

Vic gets up and puts the bottle on the bedside table, then moves the rubbish bin next to the bed. "Just in case."

I don't say anything.

"If it was your fault, you should say you're sorry," she says. Then she walks out. Huxley follows, closing the door behind her.

I down the whisky in my glass in one, roll over, pour another couple of inches in, and roll back.

I can't work out what emotion is most powerful—anger, disappointment, or hurt. I know I'm drunk because I can't get my brain to work. *I was paid to come here and take photographs of your work.* By whom? I don't have any enemies as such. But there's a lot of money in creating the fastest supercomputer in the country. My work is valuable, and deep down I'm not shocked to know that someone is willing to pay for details of the hardware we're coming up with at Koru Tech.

I am shocked that Sidnie was the one they chose to do it.

Pulling my phone out of my pocket, I study the screen. Several messages, none from Sidnie. I open my photos and choose the one I took of the poem she dropped in my office

Obsession.

What a fucking appropriate title. This girl has burrowed her way into my brain, and I can't get her out. I doubt even a whole can of insect killer sprayed into my ear would shift her.

I touch myself as I think of you.
The nape of your neck, your clean-shaven jaw,
Your lips claiming mine the way you like to do,
Demanding, taking, sugar-sweet,
Your tongue, sliding against mine in its beautiful dance,
Your hands, stroking my skin, cupping my breasts,
Your hot mouth on my nipples,
Sucking, fingers plucking.
My fingers slide through my swollen folds,
I'm so wet for you, baby,
Aching for that feeling when you enter me,
I want you inside me,
Now,
Stretch me, fill me up, to the brim,
Ride me hard and fast…
Oh God…
I'm coming…
And it's all for you…

Cursing, I let the phone drop. I shouldn't have done that. I have a hard-on again, and it's not going away anytime soon.

Angrily, I undo my belt, unzip my fly, push down my boxers, and take myself in hand. Thinking of the way I pushed up her dress, and how I sank my tongue into her folds, I begin stroking myself, slowly at first, then more quickly as I remember how wet she was for me, and how sweet she tasted. How she moaned when I teased her clit.

Aaahhh.

I'm drunk, but I've also been keyed up all evening, and it only takes me thirty seconds to come. I fill my hand, gasping with every muscle clench, every pulse. It gives me the physical release I needed, but it's immensely unsatisfying, and nothing like how I'd hoped to end the evening, balls-deep inside her while she looked at me with those big, helpless eyes.

When I'm done, I reach over and grab a tissue, dispose of the evidence, and then flop back onto the pillows.

Fuck it.

I drink the rest of the whisky, then pour myself another glass.

At that point, my phone buzzes.

I pick it up. It's a text from Sidnie.

It just says, *I'm sorry.*

I throw it across the room. I mean to smash it against the wall, but instead it lands neatly on the carpet. This evening is doomed to be unsatisfying in every fucking way.

I drink half of the whisky in the glass.

And that's the last thing I remember.

*

At some point, I stumble to the bathroom to get rid of all the liquid I've consumed. I can hear music still playing in the distance. When I go back into the bedroom, through the slight gap in the curtains I can see the lights of the city glittering against the dark sky.

The pillow beside mine is empty, with no curly hair spread out on the pillow. No soft mouth I can kiss. No tantalizing curves I can play with in the middle of the night.

Cursing vividly and colorfully, I go back to bed and immediately fall asleep again.

*

The next time I wake, the crack in the curtains reveals that it's still dark, but a fraction lighter than it was before.

My mouth tastes like a sewer, but my head isn't too bad. I look at my watch—it's five thirty. I can't remember what time I crashed out— it wasn't super late. Around eleven? I normally only sleep for four hours. Although I had a lot to drink, I'm big and I can normally handle a good amount of alcohol. I think it was the lack of sleep over the past week that caused me to crash out for so long.

I sit up and look around. The whisky bottle is still nearly full. At some point in the night I took my tie off, but the rest of my clothes are rumpled and stained.

I get up, strip off, go into the bathroom, and set the shower running. Going back into the room, I retrieve two Panadol from my briefcase and drink them down with most of a bottle of water. Then I get in the shower and scrub myself under the hot water before turning it to cold to punish myself.

My skin tingling, I get out and dry myself, then retrieve a tee, shorts, and my running shoes from the wardrobe. I put them on, take a Sports drink with electrolytes from the fridge, slot it into a running belt, and clip it on. Finally I retrieve my phone and wallet, and add them to the belt too.

I glance at the desk, at the papers strewn across it, and my open laptop. I close it and put everything in my briefcase, telling myself it might be locking the stable door after the horse has bolted, but that I need to be more careful from now on.

Then I go out, closing the door behind me.

The place is quiet. The only person I meet is Robert, who often does the early shift on the front desk.

"Morning, Dr. Hart," he says as I go past.

"Morning, Rob." I enter the elevator, feeling his gaze on me as the doors close. No doubt Gail or Huxley left him a message about the events of last night. Huxley pays his staff to be discreet though.

The carriage sinks down, and I walk across the car park and out into the semi-darkness. It's only just after six, and the sun is just starting to appear on the lightening horizon.

I'm probably still over the limit, so I have no intention of driving yet.

Instead, I begin to run.

I go down Shortland Street, then Princes Street, heading for Albert Park. Traffic is already building up, but it's not too bad, and when I reach the park itself, I find it mainly empty, with just a few joggers like me, enjoying the peace of the early morning. The rising sun has filled the sky with a deep orange hue.

I start slow, letting my body warm up, then gradually speed up. It's hard to think while I'm running, and instead I lose myself in the physical exertion, pushing myself hard, until instinct takes over and I become like a machine, eating up the miles. I know it's not good to run after a night of drinking, but I empty the Sports drink, and I know from experience that I'll feel better doing this than just sitting down all morning.

After about forty minutes and several loops of the park, I slow as I approach the fountain, drop to my haunches, then tip back onto my butt and stretch out on the cool wet grass. My chest heaves, and I let the morning air fill my lungs.

It's only now my body's stopped that my brain finally begins to work.

Part of me doesn't want to confront what happened last night. I want to take the cowardly route, push it all to the back of my mind, and just forget about the woman I met yesterday.

But I need to think about it. Firstly, because my business is being threatened, and I'm not going to let some arsehole who can't come up with his own ideas think he can waltz in and take mine.

And secondly, because I want to understand why Sidnie agreed to do it.

It's how my brain works. Dissect and analyze. I'm not good at just accepting facts. I need to work out why something does or doesn't work.

I came here to spy on you, she said. *I was paid to come here and take photographs of your work.* But when I asked her who paid her, she wouldn't tell me. Why?

She obviously came to my office on Tuesday night looking for information. I presume she didn't find much. I have a strict policy that my staff tidy away all paperwork, lock their drawers and cabinets, and have complicated passwords on their laptops. Any confidential papers to be thrown away are shredded first, then burned. I doubt she found anything.

And then I asked her to go to Huxley's with me. My suite there is a different thing. I work there often, and although I usually still lock everything away before I leave, if I'm in the middle of something, I have been known to leave papers out until I'm done working. If Sidnie had gone through with it—if she'd slept with me and waited until I crashed out, I have no doubt she would have found something interesting amongst the papers I'd left on the desk.

So why didn't she go through with it? Why confess, when she must have known I'd throw her straight out?

I remember how she'd looked yesterday at lunchtime, when I asked her to come to the office. She was terrified. She must have thought I'd somehow caught her snooping, and that I was going to call her out on it. No wonder she'd looked so relieved when all I did was ask her out.

My insides twist at the thought that she must have said yes because she knew it would give her another opportunity to spy on me.

Was that the only reason?

The sky to the east is now a beautiful blend of rose pink and gold. It reminds me of her complexion, the pink of her blush against her golden curls.

Somehow, I don't think she's a professional spy. No, someone convinced her to collect information with the incentive obviously being money.

So why does she need money?

She's fresh out of university, and I know most students nowadays leave with loans around fifty or sixty thousand dollars. It's a hefty amount, one that can take an eternity to pay off, and is why many students end up working abroad, because wages are so much higher in Australia, the States, or the UK. Maybe the notion of paying off a good portion of that for the simple act of taking a few photos was enough to convince her.

But it doesn't sit right with me. Every kid has a student loan on leaving university. There's nothing unusual about it. And she doesn't strike me as the type of person who'd do something illegal and underhand to pay off debt she'd accumulated.

So why else would she need a significant amount of money?

It doesn't really matter. In a way, she's not the important one in this situation. It's the guy—or girl—who asked her to do it that I should be focusing on.

But Victoria's diatribe from last night is burned into my brain. *You don't have a great track record with the way you treat women. You use them, then you discard them like dirty socks... You're one of the good guys in so many ways, and you're a better man than this. Sidnie left here in floods of tears. Whatever she did, she's very upset about it. She deserves better.*

And she's right. I sleep around because I can't face commitment, and I rarely give a thought to how the woman feels when I don't call back.

I didn't give Sidnie a chance to explain, and I should have.

The sun is rising now, appearing on the horizon like a freshly cracked egg, spilling its yolk across the city. Still, I lie there for a long, long time, watching the seagulls flying above the buildings, and thinking about Sidnie, and her beautiful curly hair.

Chapter Eight

Sidnie

That morning, I call in sick at the lubrication firm. I've been throwing up all night and have one hell of a hangover. Plus I know Socrates is going to call, and that's not helping my nausea.

Concerned because, when I haven't been vomiting, I've been crying, Caro wants to stay home with me, but eventually I persuade her to go to work, insisting that I'm going to stay in bed and sleep for most of the day.

Once she and Hana have gone, though, I drag my duvet out to the sofa and curl up there with my phone.

I don't think I've ever felt this miserable, not even when Dad got his diagnosis. I was devastated then, of course, but even though he's so important to me, and losing him would be horrific, it wasn't about me. All the hurt and pain we've been going through felt indirect, as if it was light that had passed through a prism, scattering across me in bands of colorful emotions. But what happened last night was like a bolt of lightning, or a sheet of fire, burning me to a crisp in its wake. And now I just feel terrible. I let Mack down, and I've let Dad down too. It's not even as if I can console myself that my unlawful actions have been worth it. It's all been for nothing.

I watch the clock on my phone slowly move toward eight a.m. My stomach churns, and I pull the bowl I brought with me closer in case I want to vomit again. Not that there's anything left in my stomach. I'm pretty sure I turned inside out last night.

Eight o'clock arrives, and then the bastard keeps me waiting until seven minutes past before he finally calls.

"How did it go?" he asks, not even bothering with a greeting.

"Not well." I don't have the courage to say I couldn't go through with it. Instead I say, "He caught me taking photographs and threw me out."

"Fuck!" He spits the word at me.

I swallow hard. "I'm sorry. I tried."

"Did he ask you why you were doing it? What did you tell him?"

"Nothing, I swear. As soon as he caught me, he got really angry and threw me out. I didn't get a chance to tell him anything." I cross my fingers, hoping he believes me.

"Well, that's fucking brilliant," he says. "What a waste of time."

The phone slips in my sweaty hand, and I tighten my grip. "I tried."

"Not hard enough, clearly. Next time, you need to make sure they're asleep before you start nosing about."

"There won't be a next time."

"What are you talking about?"

"I'm done." My voice sounds dull, like a blunt knife. "I shouldn't have done it in the first place. And I can't do it again."

"Bullshit. Another office, another CEO. This time you'll be ready, you'll do it better."

Resentment burns in my stomach like acid. "No. I'm out. I shouldn't have agreed to do it."

"If you don't, that's it," he says harshly. "You think I'm going to give you the money out of the goodness of my heart?"

The resentment turns to anger, leaping like a flame. I push off the duvet and get to my feet. "You're a vulture, preying on the vulnerable," I yell. "Go and pick off some other fucking carcass. I'm done."

I end the call and throw the phone onto the sofa.

Then I sink onto it, my face in my hands, and bawl my eyes out.

I cry until there are no tears left. Then I cry a bit more, until my throat is raw and I'm exhausted.

I still feel terrible, but acknowledge that a seed of relief has lodged inside me at the thought of being free of him.

Holding on to that, I curl up into a ball and fall into an exhausted sleep.

*

I'm startled awake by the ringing of the front doorbell.

I push up, then scramble for my phone amongst the folds of the duvet to check the time. Eight forty-six. Blearily, I get to my feet and go over to the door. Maybe Caro's come back to check on me, and she forgot her keys again. Or perhaps it's a delivery—I know Hana has ordered some books from Amazon.

I open the door and inhale sharply.

"Morning," Mack says.

It's the first time I've seen him in civvies. He's wearing running shoes, a pair of black jeans, and an All Blacks rugby shirt—the modern sort with short sleeves that clings to the body and shows off all your muscles. Holy shit—I didn't realize his tattoo was a full sleeve. It covers his arm from the wrist all the way up to under his top. His hair is damp at the temples so he's had a shower, but he hasn't shaved, and his cheeks and jaw bear a sexy coating of dark stubble.

Despite this, he looks bright and fresh, no doubt fully rested after five seconds of sleep. Unlike myself, who looks as if she's spent all night walking up a mountain in a force ten gale.

His gaze slips down me, over my pale-pink pajamas, and then returns to my face before lifting to my hair for a moment. His eyes come back to mine, and although he doesn't smile, something in his eyes suggests he finds it amusing.

"Don't mock me," I whisper, lifting a hand to try and tuck any stray strands back into the elastic attempting to restrain them. I quickly give up and lean against the door jamb tiredly. "I've been sick all night and I haven't slept."

He studies the front of my pajama top. *Subtle, dude.* But then he says, "Are you a Hendrix fan?"

I glance down at the picture of a rising sun topped by the line from *Purple Haze* about kissing the sky. "I thought you were staring at my boobs."

I look back up. This time, even though he's still not smiling, there's definitely amusement in his eyes.

"I love his music," I blurt out. "I've got his quote on my wall, you know, 'music is my religion'?" I stop and blush. He's not here to talk about music.

He lets out a long sigh. "Have you eaten this morning?"

"God, no."

"You need to eat. Go get dressed. I'm taking you out for breakfast."

I stare at him. "What?"

"You have precisely ten minutes. If you're not ready, I'll carry you out in your pajamas." His gaze is firm. I have no doubt he means what he says.

I'm conscious that my jaw has dropped, but I can't get my brain to function. "Is this like a condemned prisoner's last meal? Are you taking me to the police station afterwards?"

He gives me an exasperated glare. "Of course not. I didn't give you a chance to explain last night, and I should have." He checks his watch. "Nine minutes and forty-five seconds."

My head spins. "Okay. Um… it's a mess in here but you can come in if you want."

He comes in, and I close the door behind him. He smells amazing— a lot better than I do, I'm sure. He walks over to an armchair and sits back, pulling out his phone, resting an ankle on the opposite knee. He's so big—he seems to fill the room with both his physical presence and his personality.

Studying his phone, not looking up, he says, "Nine minutes, thirty seconds."

"I'm going." I run down to my room and close the door.

I have the fastest shower I've ever had, pull on jeans, a mint-green tee, and my Converses, then scrape as much of my hair as I can back off my face and secure it with a strong band. A few coils spring out, but it's not too bad. There's no time for elaborate makeup, so I flick some powder across my nose, brush some mascara on my lashes, and add a bit of lip gloss.

I come back out into the living room with thirty seconds to spare.

His eyebrows rise. "You're ready."

"Of course I'm ready. I wasn't going to let you carry me out in my pajamas."

"I would have."

"I know." I pick up my purse and follow him to the front door.

The Aston sits outside, glinting in the early morning sunshine. There's no sign of Jamie at the wheel. "Are you sure you're okay to drive?" I ask.

"Huxley has mobile breathalyzers at the club," he says, waiting for me to lock the door and then walking with me to the car. "I'm fine now."

"Seriously? I still feel weird."

"I'm big. That helps."

"I'm not exactly tiny," I point out, getting in the car with him.

"You're tall, but skinny. You need some more meat on you." He eases the car out into the traffic.

I settle back into the comfortable leather seat. I have no idea what I'm doing here. My stomach's churning with nerves, and I still feel a bit nauseous.

My first thought on seeing him was that he'd come to give me a dressing down. But surely he'd have done that as soon as I opened the door? Why would he take me to breakfast to bollock me?

I didn't give you a chance to explain last night, and I should have. Is he really going to listen to what I have to say? Maybe it's not all over.

It doesn't lessen my nerves, but I do feel a flutter of hope, the first positive thing I've felt since I walked out of Huxley's last night.

"Aren't you normally at work by now?" I ask.

"Yeah. I guess I'll be a bit late today."

"When was the last time you were late to work?"

He thinks about it. "Never?" His lips quirk up.

I feel a little glow inside, but I don't comment on it. "Where are we going?" I ask.

"Princes Wharf. There's a little café that does a great vegetarian cooked breakfast."

"Okay." I'm not sure if I'll be able to eat anything, but I'm not going to argue with him.

"You got home okay last night?" he asks.

"Yes. I called for an Uber. Did you stay at Huxley's?"

He nods. "I slept until five thirty. That's unusual for me."

"How long do you usually sleep for?"

"Four hours. But I've been busy the last week or so, and I haven't slept much. So with the alcohol, I just crashed out." He stops at the traffic lights and glances over at me. "Are you feeling okay? You're very pale."

"A bit queasy." I don't add that it's mainly because I'm anxious.

We study each other for a moment. I thought he was handsome in his suit, but he looks gorgeous today. "I like the beard," I murmur.

He lifts a hand to rasp against the bristles on his cheek. "Yeah, I didn't have a razor. I'll have to call home before I go to the office."

"Where do you live?"

"In an apartment in Grafton, not far from Koru Tech."

"I bet it's a nice place."

"It's cool. It's got views over Auckland Domain, and you can see Rangitoto Island in the distance. It has a roof garden too."

"I bet that's great at night."

"It is." The lights change and he pulls away. "I don't spend a lot of time there but I—Jesus!"

He slams a foot on the brake as a battered, old car careens across the road in front of us, missing us by a whisker. The driver had obviously gone through a red light and would definitely have hit us if Mack hadn't stopped. My seatbelt locks as I'm thrust forward, although the airbag doesn't burst.

I have a brief glimpse of two terrified faces in the back seat before the car spins, skids, then hits a lamppost side on with an enormous crash.

"Oh Mack," I say, my heart racing, "there are kids in the back."

He pulls over and turns off the engine, and we get out. "Phone the police," he says, "and ask for an ambulance too."

With shaking hands, I retrieve my phone and dial 111, watching Mack run over to the car. "Police and ambulance please," I tell the person on the other end of the line, and I proceed to tell her my name and what's happened.

While I'm talking, Mack opens the driver's door and helps the driver get out past the exploded airbag. It's a woman in her thirties. She looks unhurt, but she's crying and trembling. "My kids," I hear her say as I move closer. "Are they okay?"

He goes to the back door and tugs it, but the chassis must be bent because it won't open. A young girl who was also in the back climbs over into the front seat and out the driver's door, and her mother sweeps her up into her arms, both of them crying.

Using all his strength, Mack finally wrenches open the passenger door, then ducks inside. I can hear him talking to someone, and then a minute later he emerges with a small boy, maybe a year old, clinging to him like a limpet.

"It's all right," he soothes, rubbing his back. "You're okay."

I finish the call, still shaking. Jesus, I think I'm going to throw up. I turn away, hands on my knees, then vomit into the grass on the verge.

Still carrying the boy, Mack comes over and rubs my back. "Are you all right?"

"I'm never going to drink again."

"It's the shock," he says. "Deep breaths."

Beside us, the woman comes up to make sure the boy is unharmed, and then her legs give out, and she crumples down onto the curb, the girl in her arms.

"I'm sorry," the woman says in between sobs. "Harry was crying, and I turned in the seat for just a second to see to him, and I didn't see the lights change. I'm so sorry."

Wiping my mouth on a tissue, I kneel in front of her. "It doesn't matter. The main thing is that you're all okay. Look, Harry's fine." I nod toward Mack, who's still holding the boy.

The woman wipes her nose and looks over her shoulder at the car. Her chin trembles. "My husband's going to be furious. We don't have car insurance."

I feel for her. It's not compulsory in New Zealand. Luckily she didn't damage any other cars, but it means she's going to have to pay for any work done to her car.

"Do you think it's a write-off?" she whispers.

I look at Mack. "It might be recoverable," he says, "but it'll take a bit of work."

More tears pour down her face. "Why did it have to happen at Christmas?" She puts her face in her hand and sobs. "Doug's going to kill me."

I do my best to comfort her, but she's inconsolable. I get to my feet and give Mack a helpless look as we hear the first sirens in the distance. "I wish I could do something," I say.

He nods at the police car as it approaches. "Can you explain to them what happened?"

"Sure."

He pulls out his phone and walks a few steps away, still holding the boy. Holding the phone to his ear, he says, "Ricky? It's Mack. Yeah, good thanks. Look, I wonder if you can do me a favor?"

I don't get to hear the rest of the conversation because the police car has arrived. They put down a couple of traffic cones, and one officer begins diverting the traffic, while the other comes up to us. I give a brief explanation of what happened, and she bends to speak to the woman still sitting on the ground.

Not long after that, the ambulance arrives. Nobody looks badly hurt, but the paramedics check the woman and the girl over, and then the boy as Mack returns, pocketing his phone. The boy doesn't want to let go of him, but eventually the paramedic peels him away.

"Hey, Evie," he says to the police officer. Evie? Does he know everyone in this freaking city?

"Mack!" She smiles. "You okay? Not hurt?"

"No, no. We stopped in time. Look, I've made a call to Phelps Automotive, and they're sending a tow truck to take the car back to the shop."

"I can't afford that," the woman driver says from the back of the ambulance.

"It's okay," Mack says. "I know the owner, and they have a scheme where they put aside an amount of money each month for repairs for those who can't afford it, a kind of pro bono thing. They'll fix you up and get you and the kids home."

Evie gives him a wry look—she obviously knows as well as I do that it won't be the garage who pays for the repairs. The woman driver stares at him as if he's a Christmas angel. Which, I guess, he sort of is. If angels have stubble, tattoos, and look at you as if they're thinking about kissing you all the time.

"Seriously?" the woman asks.

"Yep. They'll be here in ten minutes, and they should be able to get the work done today."

Her chin trembles again. "Thank you so much."

"No worries at all, glad I could help." He ruffles the little boy's hair. "Bye, Harry."

The boy rests his head on his mother's shoulder and gives him a shy smile.

"Want me to give a statement?" Mack asks Evie.

She shakes her head. "Ms. Beaver explained what happened and she's given us a sketch." She's very professional and doesn't smirk at my name. "But I do need you and the other driver to take a breathalyzer test."

"Sure." He blows into the machine.

My heart races for a moment, until she nods and says, "You're fine."

"Can we go, then?" he asks.

"Of course. Thanks for your help. Merry Christmas."

"Merry Christmas," I say. He nods, then puts a hand in the small of my back and guides me back to the Aston. We get in, and I sit back and blow out a long breath.

"If you're going to throw up again, please don't do it in my Aston," he teases.

SERENITY WOODS

"I'm not. I'm just a bit shaky."

He starts the engine. "You need to get some food in you." He rejoins the traffic, turns into Hobson Street, and heads for the wharf.

"That was a nice thing you did there," I say softly.

He shrugs. "It was the least I could do."

"Aw, Mack. Not many people would have done the same."

"Most people can't. There's a difference. What kind of person would it make me if I could help and choose not to?"

I don't reply, but I carry on looking at him as he turns onto the wharf and parks the car.

"What?" he says, turning off the engine and looking over at me.

"Nothing. How did you know the police officer's name?"

"She's Huxley's sister."

"Seriously?"

"Yeah. He's got four of them, so you're bound to bump into one from time to time."

"Wow, four sisters. Younger, older?"

He chuckles. "One younger, the rest older. They mother him. Elizabeth always says it's why he assumes he can charm any woman he meets."

Smiling, I unbuckle myself, and we get out.

"Over here," he says, and he leads the way across the wharf to a small café called Coffee Time. He opens the door and lets me precede him.

It's nearly nine o'clock, so the early risers have long since left, and those who come in for a coffee on the way to work have also been and gone. There are a few older couples and a younger couple who look like tourists, but otherwise it's quiet and warm.

"Hey, Mack," the Māori guy behind the bar calls.

"Morning, Jack," Mack replies, lifting a hand. He directs me to a table by the window, overlooking the harbor and the ferries to-ing and fro-ing from the downtown piers.

"Can I get you a drink?" Jack asks, appearing at the table and holding out a menu.

"Trim latte in a mug for me," Mack says, "and a veggie fry up."

"I'll have the same please," I say, too nervous to look at the menu.

Jack nods. "Coming right up." He walks off, leaving us alone.

I look around the café. Fairy lights twinkle above the counter, despite the bright sunshine. A Christmas tree sits in the corner, draped with red and gold tinsel, and hung with a set of decorations featuring kiwi birds wearing All Blacks rugby shirts similar to the one Mack's wearing. The place smells of cooked food, warm muffins, and coffee. Slowly, my stomach begins to settle.

I look back at him. He's sitting with one arm over the back of the chair next to him, watching me. His legs are outstretched, one either side of my right leg under the table. I get the feeling he's the kind of guy who's at home no matter where he is or whose company he's in.

"Do you know everyone in Auckland?" I ask.

His lips curve up. "Almost."

"How did you get the garage to come out today? We normally have to book weeks ahead to get anything done." Then I realize how stupid I sound. "Oh, of course, money."

But he shakes his head. "I've done a lot of favors for people on my way up. Phelps Automotive is part of a larger company owned by Pete Phelps. He's got garages all over the North Island. Not long after I met him at Huxley's, someone hacked into his computer and emptied his business bank accounts. He was able to get it all back on insurance, but he was terrified it would happen again. I took a look at his cyber security system and revamped it for him, free of charge. He was more than happy to help out today."

"So it's not what you know…"

"Kinda."

Jack comes back with our lattes, then disappears again. I cup the mug in my hands and sip it, hoping the coffee will ground me. "This feels surreal," I say, looking out across the water. "Last night, I didn't think I'd ever see you again. And here we are, drinking coffee."

"I can't stop thinking about you," he says.

Surprised, I look back at him. He's not smiling. He looks perfectly serious. My stomach gives a flutter, and my face warms.

"But you owe me an explanation," he continues, lifting an eyebrow.

"I know." And I take a deep breath and begin to talk.

Chapter Nine

Sidnie

"It started a few months ago," I say, speaking slowly. This isn't easy for me. "My dad hadn't been feeling well for a while. He had a pain in his pelvis, and problems peeing. He'd had it for a while, unbeknown to us. He went to the GP, who sent him to a specialist."

I stop talking as Jack returns with our breakfasts. He puts the plates before us, then goes back to fetch ketchup and mustard bottles. "Can I get you anything else?" he asks.

"No, that's great, thanks." Mack smiles at him, and he nods and goes back to the counter.

I look down at the plate. It's a great veggie breakfast—veggie sausages, mushrooms, tomatoes, spinach, a fried egg, and herb-and-chili-flecked fried potatoes. "It looks amazing," I tell him. "But I don't know if I can eat anything."

"Still feeling nauseous?" he asks.

"A bit. More because I'm… nervous."

"What about?"

I stare at him. Is he serious?

"Me?" he asks with surprise.

"Yes, Mack. You're… intimidating, even without the suit."

"I don't mean to be. I genuinely asked you here to let you explain yourself. Come on, eat something for me. The potatoes are fantastic."

I spear one and nibble at it. It's very tasty, and I realize Mack's probably right, and I need some food in my stomach. I help myself to another.

"So," he says, "your dad went to see a specialist?"

"Yes. He did an exam." I take a deep breath. "And he told him he had prostate cancer."

His brow furrows. "I'm so sorry."

I stab the egg, letting the yolk flow out over the mushrooms, and clear my throat. "There were tests, and a couple of scans. His oncologist told him that the drug that would be best for him isn't funded in New Zealand, but there's a cost-share program where the manufacturer helps pay toward the cost of the drugs."

I eat another potato, and then just like that, hunger kicks in, and my stomach rumbles. I pick up my knife, cut up one of the sausages, and tuck in properly.

"The drug is given by infusion every three weeks," I continue. "He was told it would cost around fifty thousand dollars, but a Ministry of Health directive prohibits the administration of privately funded drugs in a public hospital. So he said we would have to factor in the cost of administering it in a private clinic, which could be another hundred thousand dollars."

His eyebrows rise. It's a lot of money even by his standards.

"Yeah," I continue. "I have student loans, the same as any other graduate, and no savings—I'm working two jobs just to pay my rent. My brother's the same—he left university a year ago, but he's struggled to get a job. He's helping out at a local builder's and barely making minimum wage. My dad's a caretaker at a primary school, and Mum works at the supermarket. So there's no way we could afford that kind of money."

I was so angry at the time, frustrated and furious. But it feels as if I've used up all my emotion. Now, my words are flat and dull.

"I'm sorry to hear that," Mack says.

"We decided we weren't just going to give up. Of all the people in the world, I can't think of anyone who deserves it more than Dad." I speak fiercely. "He works so hard, and in his spare time he helps out at the local Hospice, and the SPCA shop. Anything he's ever had, he's shared or given it away. He made sure we kids never wanted for anything, even though they've never had any money."

I stop and have a big mouthful of coffee, then take a deep breath and let it out slowly. "They had a small life insurance policy that is going to pay for some of it. We've applied for a couple of grants, one of them quite big, and we're still waiting to hear back on those. They've sold their car, and they can take a three-month mortgage holiday. I set up a GoFundMe account with Dan and Kate—my brother and sister. Friends and family have been amazing. Dan and I have both done sponsored walks, and Carol and Hana and a couple of our other friends came too, so we've raised some. But we still need more."

"That must be hard," he says.

"It is. And that's why, when the opportunity arose to make some money, I grabbed it with both hands." I stop eating and have a couple of mouthfuls of coffee. I thought that was the difficult bit, but this is even harder. "Dan came to see me and said he's spoken to a friend. Eventually I discovered it wasn't a friend, it was someone who sold him weed, and… I'm not stupid… probably other drugs. He'd told this 'friend' that he needed money, and the friend told him he'd be prepared to make a generous donation in exchange for a simple task. It involved infiltrating a business and photographing important documents."

I don't look at Mack. Instead, I concentrate on the coffee in the mug. "Dan told me it wasn't something he could do—he didn't have the kind of skills that would gain him access to the office. But I did, and he asked me to do it. At first, I was disgusted with him, and I said no and walked out. But that day, Dad's pain was particularly bad, and he kept saying he wished it was all over so he wouldn't be a burden to us. I was so upset… and in the end I thought why not? I wasn't being asked to kill anyone. I wasn't hurting a *person*. Surely it wouldn't matter what I did to a big corporation."

He shifts in his chair. I don't look up at him.

"So I agreed to do it. He contacted me by phone. He called himself Socrates. I think it was a codename." I glance up then. He doesn't smile, and I look back down. "He gave me your name and the name of your company. He said he'd organize it so I would be able to clean in your office, and said I was to photograph anything I could lay my hands on."

I let out a long sigh. "I couldn't find anything, because it was all locked away. And I left thinking that was it. I cried all the way home, disappointed and relieved in equal measure. I'd seen you walking through and suddenly you weren't a faceless executive. Dodie told me you were a self-made man and that you'd built the business up yourself. I felt terrible. When you called me in the next day, I was terrified you'd spotted what I'd done on camera or something. And then you asked me out."

I look up at him, wishing I could make him understand how I feel. "I was so excited at the thought of going out with you," I whisper.

"And then I went out to the car, and he rang me, and he said it was the perfect opportunity to spy on you again that night. He said I had to do my best to get you to take me back to your suite and see if you'd left any paperwork there. He said if I didn't, he'd call you and tell you what I'd done in your office the night before."

"He blackmailed you?"

"Yes."

He gives me a puzzled look. "So surely it went according to plan? We were having sex. Why didn't you just wait for me to fall asleep, then take the photos? You don't know me, not really. You knew I asked you there for sex, so I'd have gotten what I wanted. Wouldn't it have served me right?"

He's being harsh on himself, which surprises me and touches me in equal measure.

"Can't you guess why?" I ask. His puzzled look stays, though, and I give a sad smile. "Because I liked you, Mack. I couldn't go through with it."

He blinks. Then tips his head to the side. "Liked?"

My stomach flips, but I keep my cool. "Like."

He gives a small smile. "So do you have any idea who it was?"

"No. He had a Kiwi accent. He gave me the impression he knew you. But that's about it."

"Would your brother be able to tell you anything more?"

"I've asked him. He was high when he met him. They were in a group, and there were a lot of people around. He said he can't remember. The guy gave him his phone number, and after that they only spoke by phone."

"Can you give me that number?"

I hesitate. "I don't know. If you call him, he's going to know you got the number through me or Dan. He's not a pleasant guy. I don't know what he's capable of."

"How about if I promise not to call him directly? I'd like to try and find out who this guy is who wants my work so badly."

I chew my bottom lip. Then finally I nod. I take my phone out and read him the number, and he programs it into his phone. Then he puts it away.

"All right," he says softly. "Enough about him."

"Do you believe me?"

"Yes, I believe you."

I blow out a relieved breath. "I'm so glad. And Mack... I'm so sorry, for everything. I've been terrified over the last few days, and last night... I can't tell you how awful I felt."

"Yeah, I can see that." He leans back in his chair, putting his cutlery down and picking up his mug. "I want to apologize too."

My eyebrows rise. "For what?"

"For a start, for not giving you the chance to explain yourself. I was angry and hurt, and I lashed out. And I'm sorry about that."

"I don't blame you for it."

"Well, that's kind of you, and it's more than I deserve. But it's not just that." He drops his gaze to his mug and he's quiet for a moment. I spear a couple of mushrooms and eat them while I wait for him to gather his thoughts. The sunshine falls across his face, painting his cheeks and mouth butter-yellow. I'd like to get up and kiss him and see if he tastes as warm and sweet as he looks.

I don't. But I think about it.

"Work is everything to me," he says, lifting his gaze back to mine. "It has been since I was sixteen, when I made the decision to choose computers over sprinting. I threw myself into it, and I've dedicated my life to it. I've seen the amazing things computers can do, everything from helping find vaccines for terrible diseases, to sending people into space, to solving climate problems. I know everyone thinks money must be the driving force behind people like me, and I'm not going to lie and say it isn't nice to live in luxury, and to make sure my family is comfortable. But that's not why I work. I do it because I want to help solve the world's problems, as egotistical and pretentious as that sounds."

I watch his face as he talks, mesmerized by his passion. "I understand," I say, remembering how he helped the driver of the car.

He looks back at his coffee mug. "But the thing is, when you're diverting ninety-nine percent of your time and attention to work, other things fall by the wayside. Romance is one of them."

"Okay."

"The few times I've had a relationship, the other person has made demands on me that I couldn't cope with. As I understand it—and I acknowledge that I don't have a lot of experience—a good relationship is about trust. Again, in my limited experience, when I work long hours, women don't seem to be able to trust me. They're always jealous. They constantly call me to ask me where I am and who I'm with, and act hurt because I'd rather be working than be with them. And I can't deal with that."

"Okay," I say. "Fair enough."

He frowns, then runs a hand through his hair, apparently mistaking my agreement for sarcasm. "This isn't coming out right."

"No, I understand what you're saying."

"Do you? Because I know I'm not explaining myself well."

"You told me you couldn't stop thinking about me."

"That's true."

I push my plate away, lean on the table, and study his face. "I assume you're saying that you still want me, but once you've had me, it's over."

"No! Well, yes, but not in that way."

"That clears things up."

"Give me a break, I'm trying here."

"I thought you were supposed to have an IQ of 172?"

He gives me an impatient look. "That doesn't mean anything—it doesn't give you the ability to string words together. Anyway, Stephen Hawking and Einstein both had an IQ of 160 and they were light years smarter than me."

"Mack, I'm trying to say I understand. I didn't expect anything more when I came up to your room. I knew it was only ever going to be a one-night stand. I mean, look at me, I'm hardly billionaire girlfriend material. I can't tell the difference between a Jimmy Choo and a Manilla… whatever it is."

He tries not to laugh. "Manolo Blahnik."

"Yeah, well, that proves it. You've seen my house. I clean in my spare time. I appreciate that's practically the plot for Cinderella, but I wasn't expecting to play out that scenario. I know I'm not your type."

"You're just illustrating my point. You assumed that's all I wanted, and you were right. I've never had to make promises of forever to get a woman to sleep with me. But because of what's happened before…"

"With Felicity?"

"It's happened several times, but yeah, she was the latest. Because of the way some women have reacted, I'm usually only interested in a one-night stand, and I assume that's all the other person wants too. I asked you to the party because I wanted you, and I wanted to sleep with you, and I didn't really give you a say in the matter."

"I don't know if you noticed, but you didn't have to drag me kicking and screaming," I say, amused. "I haven't had sex for a while and, the spying aside, I was hoping to get soundly screwed by a gorgeous guy."

He smiles. But he then says, "Even so, I'm sorry. You deserve better. To be wined and dined."

I gesture at the table. "Breakfasted?"

"Maybe."

"That's kind of old-fashioned."

He shrugs.

We study each other for a while.

"You wanted me?" I ask eventually. "Past tense?"

His lips curve up, just a little.

At that moment, my phone rings. I pick it up, my heart suddenly racing, but it's only Dan. I consider letting it go to voicemail, but I haven't liked doing that since Dad fell ill.

"It's Dan," I say. "Do you mind if I take it? I'll just go outside for a minute."

"Of course not." He picks up his cutlery and continues to eat his breakfast.

I get up and go out the front door onto the wharf. It's warm but breezy, and I give a silent groan at the thought that the wind is going to make a right mess of my hair.

"Hey you," I say.

"Hey." He sounds breathless. "Sid, oh my God. I don't believe it."

My heart stutters. "What's happened?"

"You did it. You're so amazing."

"I did what?"

"I don't know, whatever he asked you to do. I don't know what to say." His voice sounds hoarse with emotion.

"Dan, I don't know what you're talking about."

"The GoFundMe account. We reached the goal this morning."

My brain won't work. "What?"

"I don't know what you did. And I'm so sorry you had to do it. But I'm glad you did."

"Dan... I didn't go through with it."

"What?"

"I couldn't do it. I didn't take the photos. Well, not of anything interesting, anyway. Socrates called this morning and I told him I was out. He wasn't best pleased."

"Oh. Well. I guess he decided he had a change of heart and took pity on us. He must have decided to pay the full amount anyway."

"No. That doesn't make sense… Who did it say the donation was from?"

"It was anonymous. I just assumed it was him. Who else has that kind of money?"

Slowly, I turn and look through the café window.

Mack is leaning back, his arm on the back of the chair, sipping his coffee, watching me.

"Look," Dan says, "I'm about to go and see Dad. Do you want to come?"

"Yes. I'll be about half an hour. I'll explain then."

"Okay. It's amazing though, isn't it? He'll get the treatment, Sid, all of it."

"It is amazing. I don't know what to say."

"See you in a bit. Maybe our fortunes just took a turn for the better, eh?"

"Um, yeah. Maybe."

He ends the call.

I slide the phone back into my jeans, then slowly walk into the café and sit back in my chair.

Mack finishes off his coffee and puts down the mug. "Everything all right?"

"It was you," I whisper.

He lifts his eyebrows. "Me what?"

"The GoFundMe account met its total this morning. All of it. It was you, wasn't it?"

"I don't know what you mean. You literally told me about it five minutes ago." He lifts his mug in a toast. "Congratulations though, that's great news." His eyes gleam over the rim of the mug.

It's true—he couldn't have known about it. He didn't have time to look it up on his phone and make a payment. The only time he looked at his phone was to put Socrates' number in, and he actually showed me the screen to make sure he'd gotten it right.

We study each other for a long moment.

There's no way he could have done it. And yet he doesn't look surprised or shocked. He's not asking who could possibly afford to make a donation like that. He's not smiling, but he is looking at me with his planetary eyes that shine with a kind of private amusement at my utter bewilderment.

He organized to have the woman's car mended, and he didn't even know her. What might he do for someone he desires, someone he almost had sex with? A girl he feels guilty about sending away without giving her a chance to explain herself?

I want to help solve the world's problems, as egotistical and pretentious as that sounds.

I know it was him. I just can't prove it.

"After everything I've done," I say. "Spying on you, lying to you…"

He turns a spoon around in his fingers, not saying anything, just watching me.

"You don't know anything about me," I whisper.

"I know that you could have had sex with me last night and got the money yourself, but you didn't. Look, I'm sure whoever paid it did it for your Dad as much as for you. Cancer sucks. Nobody deserves it. And if someone is offering help, they can obviously afford it, so you should just take the money and run."

Overcome, I put my face in my hands.

"Aw," he says. "Shit." I hear his chair scrape on the tiles. He walks around the table to sit in the chair beside mine. And then he pulls me into his arms.

For a few seconds, I'm so full of emotion that my throat clamps shut and all I can do is sit there, rigid, as the realization dawns.

Dad can have his treatment. I know there's no guarantee of a happily ever after, but it's the best chance he's got.

Then the wave washes over me, and I turn and bury my face in his All Blacks shirt.

"Sorry," I squeak, trying to hold back the tears that are soaking the fabric.

"It's all right." His arms are warm around me. He lifts a hand for a second, I think to gesture to Jack or someone else behind me, and then it returns to hold me tightly.

The tsunami of emotion is brief, and then it retreats, leaving me tired and exhausted and all mixed up. Mack's leaning back in the chair, legs stretched out, looking out of the window, but as I stir, he turns and kisses my forehead before releasing me. I push back a little, wiping my face, and glancing around, embarrassed, but nobody's paying us any attention.

"All right?" he asks, caressing my hair with the hand of the arm that's still around me.

I nod. "Thank you."

"It's just a hug," he says.

"I meant for the money."

He doesn't say anything. He hasn't denied it outright. But I can see he's not going to admit to it.

There's no point in pushing him. For whatever reason, he'd rather not own up to it. Maybe he thinks doing so will make me feel more obliged to him, although his refusal to admit it won't change that.

"Are you going to go and see your dad now?" he asks.

I nod and blow my nose on a serviette. "We'll need to get a courier to transport the drug and get it made into a bag ready for infusion, to organize the clinic, that sort of thing, but we should be able to get him in this week."

"Okay. What are you doing tonight?"

"Tonight? It's my night off. I have major plans to flake out on the sofa in my pink PJs and eat ice cream out of the tub."

"Aw. Don't do that. Come to dinner with me."

I smile. "You're going to wine and dine me?"

He pulls at one of my curls. "Maybe."

He still wants me. Despite the fact that I've had no sleep and must look like Shrek's lesser-known cousin.

I lean forward and press my lips to his stubbly cheek. "You don't have to."

I wanted this guy before he paid for my father's cancer treatment. I'm hardly going to say no now. I know it's only going to be for one night. But I'm more than okay with that.

"Dinner," he says firmly. "Then we'll see."

"Okay."

He slides his hand to the back of my head and holds me there as he closes the gap between us.

He kisses me a couple of times, just pressing his lips to mine, warm and gentle, but it's enough to send fireworks exploding inside me, and from his sigh and the reluctant way he moves back, I think he feels the same.

*

I tell him I'm going to take an Uber, but he refuses, and I'm not a big enough person to not have a thrill at the thought of being dropped off at my parents' house in an Aston Martin.

He talks about light things as he drives—a biography he's reading at the moment on Neil Armstrong; the latest Bond movie; my favorite Hendrix song. I answer him shyly, my head in a whirl.

Why did he do it? I'll never be able to pay him back—not that I think he'd want me to. It's a gift, a drop in the ocean to him, although he obviously understands what it means to me.

Following my directions, he takes me south to my parents' home. As he turns onto their road, I try to see it through his eyes: the burnt-out car in the ditch just outside town, the kids playing in the street, the tagging on some of the fences. The small house in the rather dodgy neighborhood was all they could afford, but at least Dad has mowed the lawn, and he's recently repainted the fence.

"I won't ask you in," I say. "I'm sure you want the Aston to keep its wheels."

He gives a short laugh. "So I'll see you tonight. Is seven okay?"

"It's fine."

"From here or your own place?"

"Oh, back at my place, please." I clear my throat. "Are you sure about this?"

"Stop arguing with me."

I stick my tongue out at him. "You're very bossy."

"I'm used to getting my own way."

I give him a wry smile. "I bet. All right. See you later." I get out of the car, close the door carefully, then run up the path and go inside.

When I walk into the living room, I discover Mum, Dad, Kate, Dan, Kate's husband, Liam, and their seven-year-old daughter, Julia, all peering through the curtains.

"Oh my God," Kate says as I drop my purse onto the sofa. "Tell me you did not just pull up in an Aston."

I give a hesitant smile as they all turn, but it's Dad I'm looking at. He's pale and not smiling, and as I walk forward, he folds his arms.

"I told him," Dan says. "He's saying he won't accept it."

I stop walking. "What?"

"How did you get the money?" Dad whispers.

"I didn't," I say. "It was an anonymous donation."

"Sid," he warns. "Tell me the truth."

I look at Dan, who just studies his shoes. Kate clears her throat. "I'll put the kettle on."

"I'll help," Liam says, and strides out after her.

Mum comes over and gives me a kiss. "Come and sit down, love." She goes over to Dad then, and gently pushes him toward one of the armchairs. He sinks down. I can see he's fighting to keep his self-control.

Dan meets my gaze, and he looks terrified that I'm going to reveal it was his idea to contact Socrates. I still haven't forgiven him for suggesting it, but I know he only did it because he couldn't think of another option, and the idea of losing Dad is as horrific to him as it is to me.

I decide I might as well tell the truth. Well, most of it.

"I met someone last night," I say slowly. "He's the CEO of a computer technology business."

"Was that his car?"

"Yes. I was cleaning his office on Tuesday night, and I dropped something… a poem I'd written. His secretary called me and asked me if I'd come in during my lunch hour yesterday to meet him. He was really nice and handed me back the poem. We got on really well, and he asked me to go with him to a party last night. This morning, we had breakfast, and I told him that you were sick, and we were trying to raise the money. The next thing I knew, Dan was ringing to say the GoFundMe total had been met."

Dad stares at me, studying my face as if trying to see which bits are true.

"What's his name?" Mum asks.

"Dr. Mack Hart. He's twenty-eight. He's got a doctorate in computer science engineering. He's very smart, and he's very rich, and he's a bit of a philanthropist. On the way to the café this morning a woman nearly drove into his car, and she hit a lamppost and smashed hers up. He paid for a truck to come and collect the car, and he paid for the repairs. I don't think he was born with money, and he knows how hard it is not to have it, and he likes to help."

"Did you have to sleep with him to get it?" Dad asks.

My face burns. "No!" Well, it's sort of true.

His bottom lip trembles. "I can't bear to put you all under this kind of strain. I hate to think of what you had to do to get that money."

I swallow hard. "Honestly, I didn't have to do anything. It really was sheer luck. He's just a lovely guy. He didn't want anything in return."

Well, apart from getting in my knickers. But it's a small price to pay.

I wince a little as that thought goes through my head. But I push it away. I might have principles, but I'm not going to turn down the chance for one night with the most gorgeous guy I've ever met just because the thought of the money makes me feel a tad uncomfortable. He's not paying me to sleep with him—I know he'd be horrified if I thought of it like that. Getting the treatment for Dad is all that matters, and if I get one night's amazing sex out of it too, why on earth is that a bad thing?

"I'm sorry," he says, and I get up and go over to give him a hug.

"All that matters is that you can have the treatment now," I say fiercely. "You don't have to worry about anything else."

Chapter Ten

Mack

For the first time in, well, years, I'm having trouble concentrating at work.

It's the twenty-second of December, and tomorrow we'll close the offices for a few weeks so the general staff can have a well-earned break. Everyone else is winding down for Christmas, but the work never stops for me. I will be taking a couple of days off, but I'll be back in here on Monday, and the other three of my team leaders will be back on Tuesday, because we're close to making a breakthrough on the project we've been doing for Elizabeth's company, and all of us are determined to keep going until it's done.

I'm about to start writing a report on our findings, but it takes time to get my thoughts in order, which is why I'm currently sitting at my drawing board, doodling some ideas on a giant sheet of paper while my brain shuffles the information around. It's the day of the office party, and I can hear the music from the main room in the background. Not surprisingly, because they're top of the charts, it's Paua of One. It reminds me of Sidnie, and the way she shimmied her shoulders, trying to get me to dance.

Gus is lying in the puddle of sunshine by the open doors, twitching as he chases rabbits in his dreams. The late-afternoon breeze that blows in brings with it the scent of the lemon trees in the garden.

It strikes me that I'm happy. The realization surprises me, and I sit back for a moment, turning to look out at the view. I very rarely stop to smell the flowers—or lemons. Normally I'm so busy that life becomes a series of urgent moments, like beads squeezed onto a necklace with no space in between them. I like it like that, especially at Christmas, which has never been my favorite time of year. But for once, it feels good to take a minute to reflect.

Then my phone rings. Lips twisting, I pick it up and see from the screen that it's Elizabeth. I answer it and put it on speakerphone so I can continue to doodle.

"Mack Hart."

"Hey, Mack. It's Elizabeth."

"Hey you. How's it going?"

"Good. Just checking whether you've remembered it's the Huxley's Christmas lunch tomorrow."

"I had forgotten, but Nadine would have reminded me. Where is it?"

"Well that's it, they had to cancel at The Lobster Shed because there was some kind of problem with the ovens. Hux is looking for an alternative; he'll call you tomorrow morning."

"No worries."

"How's the work going?"

"I'm starting the report for you. The final results are just coming in. We're not going to get it done before Christmas, I'm sorry."

"That was your deadline, not mine," she says. "I think we can give you a few days off over the festive season."

I turn as I hear someone in the doorway, and see Jamie there, leaning against the post, holding a drink. "I've got to go," I say to Elizabeth. "See you tomorrow."

"*Kia kaha*," she says. Stay strong.

I end the call. "Hey," I say to Jamie.

"I wondered where you'd gotten to. You should come out. Join in the fun."

"I don't do fun."

He chuckles and brings the drink over. "Now I know that's not true."

I take the whiskey from him. "Thanks. Don't let me have any more though. I don't want to arrive drunk tonight."

"Fair enough. Are you staying here until seven?"

"No. Let's leave around six. I'd like to shower and change."

"Okay." He looks at the drawing board and points at my doodle of a face with curly hair. "Is that part of the research?"

"Very funny. Portraits were never my strong point."

"Doodling her on your drawing board? Man, you've got it bad."

"Fuck off," I say mildly, and he laughs.

"I'll be back at six. Enjoy yourself, you sad creature." He goes out, leaving the door open so I can hear the music.

I chuckle and get to my feet as my phone buzzes in my pocket. It's a text from Sidnie. Smiling, I take the phone over to the table by the window, sit next to where Gus is stretched out, and sip my whiskey as I read it.

Not long to go, she says. *Looking forward to tonight.*

I reply with: *Me too. Can't wait. x*

About thirty seconds later, she replies. *I keep thinking about last night. The good bits. In bed.*

My smile spreads. She wants a little dirty talk, hmm? I'm more than happy to comply.

Me: *Which bit did you enjoy most?*

Her: *All of it! The kissing…*

Her: *The touching…*

Her: *Your lips on me…*

Her: *Your tongue inside me…*

I blow out a breath. The minx is determined to get me sexed up for tonight.

Me: *Oh, so we're progressing to intermediate, are we?*

Her: *Normally I'd recommend waiting until after the first time. But it's difficult not to go dirtier with you. LOL.*

Me: *Steady on or I'll have to indulge in a little DIY before tonight.*

Her: *Ooh… really?*

Me: *Admission? I did last night, after you left. I couldn't help myself.*

Her: *Mmm. You should have done it while I was there. I'd love to watch.*

Me: *That turns you on?*

Her: *Big time. Big being the operative word…*

Me: *Thank you for that vote of confidence!*

Her: *I felt you when you pushed me up against the wall. You are not a small man.*

Me: *You definitely know how to say all the right things.*

Her: *Do you promise to take it slowly? You know, on our first time.*

Me: *I promise. The trick is to make sure there's no friction.*

Her: *How do you do that?*

Me: *With LOTS of foreplay.*

Her: *Mm. *fans self**

I chuckle. I think the sexting is backfiring on her.

I enjoy talking dirty, but you have to know your audience. Sex can be so complicated. Even if a woman enjoys the act, it doesn't mean she's comfortable going from zero to a hundred on the first date. In my experience, most women have a praise kink and enjoy compliments about their body and appreciation of what they're doing, but not all of them like cruder language and some actually find it a turn off. Which is fine—whatever floats your boat. Part of the fun is exploring each other and discovering how far you can push it.

Sidnie obviously understands all this, because she writes about exactly that—to find out what your partner likes before you jump in the deep end. But I've looked through her videos. She certainly doesn't hold back in the advanced section. Some of the things she posted actually made my eyebrows rise.

I'm not stupid—I know that what a woman fantasizes about doesn't necessarily equate to what she wants in real life. I'm sure many people daydream about threesomes, for example, but would be horrified if their partner suggested bringing someone else into the bedroom. I'm still not going straight to eleven on the dial. But even though we're starting off gently, I'm excited at the thought of being able to explore the deep end with her.

I feel a mischievous urge to ramp things up. Normally I'm not the type of guy to brag about my family jewels, but in this case I think it's warranted.

Me: *You're right, I'm not small. I'll have to ease in, very slowly.*

Her: *Oh wow.*

Me: *A half inch at a time. It won't be easy.*

Her: *Holy fuck.*

Me: *You'll have to relax. Let me slowly sink into you.*

Her: *Jesus.*

Me: *Do you think you can take it all?*

Her: *I need to lie down. I feel dizzy.*

Me: *Hehe. Regretting starting this?*

Her: *No! God no. It's just… I mean what I said. Most of what I write is from my imagination. I haven't had a huge amount of experience. Especially in the bedroom.*

My lips curve up.

Me: *I see. You need to be initiated?* I add a devil's head emoji with a chuckle.

Her: *Oh fuck, I really do.*

That makes me laugh.

"That's something I don't hear very often." It's Nadine, coming in with a mince pie on a plate, smiling.

I put the phone face-down on the table. "I'm just texting Sidnie."

She puts the mince pie in front of me. "You really like this girl, don't you?"

"I do. She's a lot of fun."

"Are you seeing her tonight?"

"I am. We're going for a drink."

"I'm glad," she says. "I've been worried about you."

I give a short laugh. She's not quite old enough to be my mother, but she tends to act like it. "What for? I'm fine."

"After Felicity, you've worked very hard. All work and no play…"

"Yeah, yeah. We've been working on Elizabeth's research, remember?"

"I know, but you seemed a bit down. It's lovely to see you smiling. Anyway, you said you didn't mind if I left a bit early. Alan's waiting in the car park, so…"

"Of course." I get to my feet and give her a hug. "Have a lovely Christmas."

"Thank you. You too."

"Enjoy your cruise."

"I will. And have a great time with Sidnie."

"Oh, I definitely will."

She laughs, waves, and leaves the room.

I sit back down and turn over my phone.

Me: *Sorry. Nadine just came in.*

Her: *I hope she didn't see this conversation!*

Me: *I read it out to her. She liked the idea of an initiation ceremony.*

Her: *LOL you're such a tease.*

I smile.

Me: *I should have asked, btw, how's your dad?*

Her: *He's okay, thank you. We've got everything organized and he's having his first treatment on the twenty-seventh.*

Me: *Not too long to wait.*

Her: *No. We've sort of canceled Christmas as none of us is in the mood for it really. But it's all good. Next year should be a better one if things go according to plan.*

Me: *I hope so. Well I suppose I should do some work. I'll see you at seven?*

Her: *Yes! I'd better go and prepare myself :-)*
Me: *That sounds intriguing.*
Her: *Like a turkey. LOL.*
Me: *That's less intriguing.*
Her: *It will be if I start talking about stuffing.*
Me: *Ha! Is that a premonition?*
Her: *Oh I think we both know how this is going to end. See you later, gorgeous*
x

I smile, stretch, and yawn, enjoying the warm sunshine. I feel surprisingly great despite last night; I think the run this morning did me good. I check the time—I have just over an hour to go before Jamie takes me home.

I could get back to work. But I can hear music and laughter from the office, and for once, I feel like being with people. This is my staff—those who've worked hard all year for me, and who deserve to feel appreciated by their boss.

Taking my glass with me, I head out of the office to join in the fun.

*

At just before seven, Jamie pulls up outside Sidnie's house. I've been home, taken Gus for a run, showered, shaved, and changed. I've chosen black trousers and a casual dark- and light-blue paisley shirt. It's too hot for a jacket. Now I feel restless and buzzy, excited to see her.

"Go get the girl," Jamie says.

I grin, get out of the car, go up to Sidnie's front door, and ring the bell.

Through the net curtains, I glimpse a scurry of movement. Then the door opens to reveal Sidnie, looking flushed and bright-eyed. She's wearing black wide-leg pants and a pretty white vest with sequins and silver spaghetti straps. Her hair is down, sparkling in places with tiny clips.

"Hey," she says. "Come in. I just need to get my purse."

"No rush." I follow her in.

Her room mates are both by the window, and they jump back as I enter.

"Don't mind them," she says, walking through the kitchen where her purse rests on the counter. "They're just being nosey."

"Fair enough," I say cheerfully.

"They want to make sure I'm safe," she says, coming back into the living room.

"We're worried it's like she's stepping into the lion's cage at the zoo," Hana says, making Caro gasp and nudge her in the ribs.

I shrug. "Sometimes a girl wants to get eaten." I hold my hand out to Sidnie.

"Oh-ho," she says, sliding her hand into mine. "Was that the right thing to say."

The girls giggle, and one whispers something to the other that makes her grin as I lead Sidnie outside. "Night," she calls to her friends before she closes the door and follows me to the car.

"You're a naughty boy," she scolds, sending me an amused glance as I open the back passenger door for her.

"I do my best." I close it, then go around to the other side and get in next to her.

"Hey, Jamie," she says.

"Evening, Sidnie." He smiles at her in the mirror, then eases the car out into the traffic.

"Are your two friends a couple?" I ask her.

"Yeah. They've been together a few years now. Hana moved in with me and Caro in our last year at university. Hana—the Korean one—is also an English major. Caro's an Early Education teacher."

"You've never fancied teaching?"

She shakes her head and pulls a face. "God, no. Not my scene at all. I've always wanted to be a writer."

"How's your dad?" I ask.

"Not too bad. Very tired. It'll be good to get him started on the treatment. We're going to have a very quiet Christmas, no guests or anything. My older sister, Kate, lives in Australia, but she's home for Christmas with her husband and daughter. It's nice to have a bit of support." She clears her throat. "Where are we going?"

"Il Pescatore. Do you know it?"

"Jeez, yes! Seriously? How did you get a table there?" She rolls her eyes. "It's all right, don't answer that."

"You haven't been?"

"Mack, of course I haven't. The starters cost more than I make in a fortnight. And now I'm nervous. I thought we were going for a veggie burger or something."

I grin. "Do you like cocktails?"

"I do."

"They serve some great ones."

"Sounds like a perfect evening," she says.

Her gaze meets mine, and a tingle runs down my spine. She's taken care over her makeup, and her eyes are dark and sultry, while her lips shine with gloss. If I were to kiss her, I know they'd be slightly sticky.

Jesus. I'm going to spend the whole evening with a fucking hard-on.

"How was your day?" she asks.

"Good. We had the office party."

"Oh, nice. Did you get to go?" she asks Jamie.

"I did. Everyone had a good time, I think."

"It was Nadine's last day," I say. "She's off for a cruise around the Pacific islands."

"How lovely."

"Yeah, she's really looking forward to it. She said the main reason she's going is so she doesn't have to cook Christmas dinner."

She laughs. "I get that. What about you two, what are you doing for Christmas?"

"We're going to our grandparents' for Christmas lunch," I reply. "Kuia—our grandmother—refuses to let us spend the day on our own."

She gives me a puzzled look. "*Our* grandmother?"

"Sorry, I thought I'd told you. Jamie's my brother. Half-brother, technically."

She stares at him. "Oh! I didn't realize. Older or younger?"

"I'm younger," Jamie says. "And better looking. But he's smarter."

She laughs, but I can tell she's curious about why he's acting as my chauffeur.

I'm holding her hand, and she looks down at my tattoo, revealed beneath my turned-up sleeve. She reaches out and traces the pattern that I told her represented my journey to New Zealand.

"You said you came here from Scotland when you were twelve," she says. "Was that with your parents?"

Jamie glances at me in the rear-view mirror, surprised, I'm sure, that I admitted even that much to her.

"With my father," I reply.

She nods. I'm sure she's curious to know more, but she doesn't push it, maybe sensing that I don't like talking about my past.

"Here you go," Jamie says, pulling over.

"Thanks."

"Just text when you want picking up."

"Will do, see you later."

We get out, and Jamie gives us a wave, then drives off.

"We could get an Uber, save him coming out," Sidnie suggests.

"He wouldn't have that. He takes his duties very seriously."

"You mentioned he has a girlfriend, right?"

I take her hand and lead her toward the restaurant. "Yeah, Emma. He lives with her in the apartment next to mine. You'd like her, she's lovely, and she adores him. They look after Gus when I'm out, which is useful."

"You're obviously very close."

"We've been through a lot together." I gesture for her to precede me through the door.

The restaurant is on the corner of two pedestrian areas, and it's always busy. It's in one of the more affluent parts of the city and mostly frequented by rich business people who want to impress clients, or wealthy couples looking for something a little different. The two walls that face the street are filled with rectangular-paned windows from floor to ceiling, and two huge sliding doors in the middle allow access to a large outdoor seated area on pleasant evenings. A row of tables lines the main restaurant, but there are also a few tables surrounded by partitions that are a little more private.

Tonight, fairy lights blink on and off throughout the place, and a huge tree stands in the corner, the tinsel twinkling and the decorations bobbing as people walk by. Carols are playing softly in the background, and the air is filled with the scent of cinnamon and orange.

"Oh," Sidnie says as we walk in. "Wow."

It's nearly Christmas, and peak time, so every table is filled, and a queue of people waits at the door. I lead Sidnie past them, and a guy in a black tux comes up to greet us.

"Dr. Hart," he says, "Good evening."

"Hey, Cesare." I gesture at the beautiful woman blushing at my side. "This is Sidnie."

"Good evening," Cesare says, giving her a little bow. "Very nice to meet you, ma'am. This way, please." He leads us past the queue of envious people and through the busy restaurant to the last remaining free table in one of the secluded areas. As we pass, every person in the room turns to look at us. I try not to smile smugly at having the most beautiful woman there all to myself.

"Goodness," Sidnie says, sliding onto the chair that Cesare holds out for her. "I feel like a rock star."

"We have a couple of Christmas parties tonight," he apologizes, as a group further down the room fills the place with laughter.

"It'll be the same all over the city," she says. "And it makes for a great atmosphere."

"Can I get you both a drink?" he asks.

"I think we're going for a cocktail," I reply, passing Sidnie the menu.

"Ooh, yes." She glances down. "I'll have a 'Getting Caught in the Rain', please."

It's a line from the old song, Escape, about liking pina colada. The cocktail contains pineapple rum, lime, mint, coconut, and soda.

"I'll have a City Summer Night please." Bourbon, blackberries, red wine, and lemon, wrapped up in an 'elegant fruity sour with a hint of smoke'.

"Of course. I'll be back to take your dinner order in a moment." He walks away.

"He's quite old for a waiter," she says, watching him go.

I chuckle. "He's the owner."

"Oh!" She looks back at me with renewed admiration at being served by the guy who owns the restaurant.

"What do you think?" I ask, looking around at the spherical lights hanging from the ceiling.

She presses her lips together, her eyes dancing. "Everyone in the room turned to look at us as the owner took us through. You certainly draw attention."

I laugh. "They weren't looking at me."

"What?"

"You look amazing tonight. Every woman here wishes she was you. And every guy is wishing he was taking you home."

"I... but..." Her cheeks flush. "Don't tease me."

"I'm not." I look at the menu. "Fancy anything?"

She looks down at hers. "Let's just say that in that shirt, you'll be lucky to make it through the evening alive."

I chuckle. "You like it?"

"I do." She doesn't elaborate, and instead blows out a long breath. "I'm too nervous to eat."

"Aw, why?"

She gives me a You-know-perfectly-well-why sort of look. "Do you think we could share a platter or something?"

"Of course. They do some great ones here."

"You order for us, then."

I smile. "Okay." I gesture to Cesare, who comes up immediately.

"We'll have the vegetarian platter to share, please," I say. "And some extra rosemary focaccia." I'm ravenous, and I could probably have eaten the platter on my own.

"Of course, Dr. Hart." He nods and leaves us alone.

"Do you come here often?" Sidnie asks. "He seems to know you."

"Huxley brought me here a few years ago, and now we often come here for business meetings."

"I can't believe you were able to get a table."

"They had a last-minute cancellation." It's true, although technically the table should have gone to the next person on their long waiting list, but we spend a lot of money here throughout the year, and Cesare was more than happy to let me have first dibs.

It's busy, and voices and laughter ring throughout the room, but it's relatively private in our little booth, and the thought that I'm finally alone with her brings goosebumps out on my arms.

"So tell me about Jamie," she says. "Is he just your chauffeur?" She looks at my face, then bites her lip. "If you want to, I mean. If I'm not intruding."

"I know it looks odd." I turn a fork around in my fingers. "I looked after him when we were young. He says he owes me for it. He's not just my chauffeur. He's more like a personal assistant. He and Nadine make sure my life runs smoothly—her in the office, him outside it, at the club, at home. Sometimes, when I'm caught up in my work, I forget about everything else. Like you said, the hyper-focus kicks in. Jamie makes sure I eat and drink, and exercise, and tries to get me to sleep, although that doesn't tend to work."

I can't explain the whole reason for our arrangement, and I know it sounds odd. But Sidnie just smiles and says, "It must be great having someone watching out for you like that."

"It is." I'm glad she understands. "You look lovely tonight, by the way."

She gives a shy smile. "Thank you."

I study her face for a moment, admiring the few freckles across her nose, the touch of pink in her cheeks, the curve of her Cupid's bow. She bears my scrutiny with downcast eyes, then eventually lifts her gaze to mine. Immediately, my temperature rises by a few degrees. Her eyes are hungry, full of desire. I think she wants me almost as much as I want her.

"I'm hoping to learn a lot from your videos," I tease.

She rolls her eyes. "I doubt I can teach you anything."

"Of course you can. Because you're an individual. We each have our own set of guidelines for dating, basic dos and don'ts, but learning to tailor-make them for each person is the hard part."

"I guess." She rubs her nose.

"Actually I think you've hit on a very important part of the process—the talking bit. Communicating needs and desires can only enhance pleasure."

"I think so. But it doesn't come naturally to many people. They're too shy, or nervous, or self-conscious to say what they really feel or like. Afraid of looking silly, or going too far. I try to remember that what comes easy to me might not come easy to everyone else."

"Talking dirty comes easy to you?"

She laughs. "Words do. But not to everyone. I've had some… personal disasters in that area, shall we say."

"Some of your partners haven't liked you doing it?"

"Not at all. I tend to scare men off."

I hold her gaze for a few seconds. "You don't scare me," I murmur.

"No," she whispers. "I can see that."

I turn my fork in my fingers. "Do Caro and Hana know about your side business?"

"Yes. But they're the only two who do. My family doesn't."

"I'm honored you told me, then."

"Kinda had to," she says. "Because of the poem."

"Oh, true."

"Although I didn't have to admit everything. I don't seem to be able to keep secrets from you."

If she told me about the real reason for being in my office, I guess she feels she can tell me anything. Oddly, I like that. "So tell me more about your book. Have you always enjoyed romance novels?"

"Since I was about fourteen, I guess. I used to read Mum's historical romances. Some of them were sweet, but some were what they call bodice rippers now, with vivid, flowery language. Lots of flaming swords being inserted into aching valleys." She giggles, which makes me smile. It's a lovely little chuckle, mischievous and naughty. "Then I got myself a Kindle and started buying online, and I read this one that made me…" She widens her eyes.

"It was explicit?"

"Oh yeah. You have no idea. Well, that was it. I read every romance I could get my hands on. I loved them. The thing is, everyone trashes them because of the sex, and obviously there are some terrible ones, but many of them have amazing storylines too."

"You don't have to justify it to me."

"Well people—not just guys, women are just as bad, if not worse—can be so damning. They call it mommy porn and smut and trashy. And… I don't know why people have to put them down just because they contain sex. What's wrong with sex?"

"Nothing at all."

"I don't think so either."

"There's a lot of shame around sex," I say. "I guess it's to do with how you were brought up, or experiences you have when you're young, I don't know. It's healthy, and it feels good, and I don't see anything wrong with having it, enjoying it, or talking about it."

She leans on the table. Her blue eyes are very light. "Me neither."

We study each other for a moment. God, I want this girl.

I clear my throat. "So how's the novel coming along?"

"Good, actually. I'm enjoying it. But I haven't told anyone, not even Caro or Hana. Only you." She smiles.

I lean on the table too, so we're only a foot apart. "I think it sounds amazing. And if you need to do any research, you know where to come." I smirk. "Pun intended."

She meets my gaze. "Noted."

Earlier, she said *Oh I think we both know how this is going to end,* and she's right. At last, I'm going to take her to bed, and give myself the best Christmas present I've had in a long, long time.

Chapter Eleven

Sidnie

Cesare arrives with our cocktails, and we sip them in silence for a moment, enjoying the mix of flavors.

It's not an awkward silence. I feel as if we have plenty to talk about. But there's an air of expectation and anticipation between us, as if it's actually Christmas Eve, and we're both waiting to unwrap a huge present under the tree.

He looks amazing tonight. The dark- and light-blue paisley shirt fits him like a dream, tight on his biceps, and showing his impressive physique. I can't believe I've got him all to myself tonight. I feel as if I'm dreaming. I'm pretty sure that no matter what I suggested, even if it was to cover him in whipped cream and lick it all off, he'd be up for it.

Hmm. There's an idea.

"Penny for them," he says, right at that moment.

I giggle, and he grins. "You don't want to know," I tell him.

"Oh, I really do."

"Let's just say it involves the removal of whipped dairy products without a spoon." I suck the straw in the cocktail, trying not to laugh as his eyes widen.

"Like that, is it?" he asks. "Is this going to be about who can turn the other on the most before we make it back to the apartment?"

"Sounds like a plan." I mean it, too. I can't imagine he wants to spend hours talking about himself, or politics, or religion, or anything deep and meaningful. I know he's only here for one thing. And I'm more than happy to give it to him.

He's leaning back now, watching me with apparent amusement. "I'm so glad I met you."

I laugh, stirring the drink. "You don't have to give me false flattery. I know I'm nothing special. And before you reply, I'm not saying that to provoke a compliment. I know I'm relatively intelligent, and I'm not bad looking. But I'm hopeless in so many ways."

His smile fades, and his expression turns curious. "You really have no idea how unusual you are, do you? I've never met anyone like you before."

His words make me tongue-tied. "That's... um... a nice thing to say."

"You said you haven't had a lot of experience," he says. "That surprises me. I would have thought guys would be lining up at your door."

"God, no. I'm too tall, for one thing. Guys like little dolls they can fit into their pocket, not Amazons who tower over them if they wear heels."

"I don't."

"Well, no, you're... what? Six two?"

"Yeah."

"So a woman couldn't tower over you unless she took a stepladder with her." I sip my drink. "I like that you're big."

He lifts his eyebrows and smiles.

"I meant your height. God, you've got a filthy mind."

He gives a short laugh, then moves back as Cesare arrives with our platter. "Thank you."

"Can I get you anything else?" the manager says.

"Another cocktail?" Mack asks me. When I nod, he says, "The same or a different one?"

"Mm, different. I'll try a Christmas Pudding Martini, please." It has syrup, sultanas, and a cinnamon stick.

"Make that two," Mack says, and Cesare goes off.

"I can't believe we're being served by the manager," I say, studying the platter.

"He likes to give the personal touch to his favorite customers."

"I've never dated a guy who's a restaurant's favorite customer. I could get used to that." I bite my lip then. I don't want to imply that I'm expecting a second date. Mack has made it quite clear he's not interested in a relationship, and I'm determined not to be another Felicity.

But he just chuckles and takes a piece of the extra focaccia. "I'm starving."

"I have a feeling you're always starving."

"You've been talking to Nadine. She reckons my father must have been an elephant."

That makes me laugh. "I like a man who has a healthy appetite."

"I've certainly got that."

"I was talking about food."

"So was I. Now who has the dirty mind?"

I chuckle and study the platter, which has pieces of toasted focaccia with rosemary butter, halloumi nuggets with spicy plum sauce, olives, hummus, tiny peppers stuffed with cream cheese, and lots of other little veggie nibbles. "This is amazing."

"Dig in," he says, and picks up a piece of quiche.

We eat for a while, talking about the food and being vegetarian, and then discussing the Christmas martini when it comes. I'm gradually starting to relax, warmed through by the pleasant atmosphere, the alcohol, the food, and the company. I guess he hasn't gotten where he is by not being able to turn on the charm, and it's evident no matter who he speaks to—my friends, his brother, his friends at Huxley's, receptionists, or waiters. He has an easy smile and a way of making you feel special when he talks to you.

I eat about a third of the platter, and he easily puts away the other two thirds. The guy eats like a horse; no wonder he moves as if he's nuclear powered.

Briefly, I wonder how energetic he is in the bedroom. I bet he can keep going for hours. What's the record for how many times a couple have had sex in one night?

"You're thinking about sex again," he says, pointing a cocktail stick holding an olive at me before eating it. "I can tell."

"How?"

"Because you're awake." He laughs and sips his drink.

I giggle. "In this instance, you were right."

"Elaborate."

"Mmm… no, I don't think so."

"It wasn't a question." He gives me a direct look.

"Ooh." I run a finger around the top of my glass and then lick it. "You're quite bossy."

"I told you, I don't make a good sub."

"Women have tried? God help them."

He gives a short laugh. "Let's just say that I much prefer to direct the action."

"I see. And what if the girl rebels?"

"Yeah, don't think I didn't see your video on brat kink."

I pull an *eek* face.

"It's a good idea to research one's…" He thinks for a moment. "I was going to say enemy, but that's the wrong word."

"Prey?"

"Hmm." He just smiles.

"So, um, what did you think? About the videos?"

He cocks his head. "Very interesting. It appeals to you?"

I stir my drink. "Honestly? It's embarrassing to admit, but I'm a bit out of my depth. Like I said, I haven't had a lot of experience. I've had huge fun reading about stuff like that, talking about it in my videos, and writing texts and other things for my readers. But I haven't tried much of it."

"Your previous partners haven't been adventurous?"

I lift the straw and suck some drips off the end. "I met my last boyfriend, Karl, at the gym, which makes him sound like he was some kind of buff bodybuilder, and he really wasn't. He was quiet and gentle, and I liked him a lot. But he was *very* vanilla. And I mean, there's nothing wrong with that. But when I tried to encourage him to… you know… be a bit more…"

"Rocky Road?"

I chuckle. "Yeah. He sort of freaked out. He said all he ever reads about is toxic masculinity, and so why would a woman want a guy to be forceful or dominant? I tried hard to explain that it's different in the bedroom, but he just couldn't see it."

"It's fair enough. It's not easy to differentiate sometimes."

"I would imagine you don't have any trouble."

He laughs and leans forward, arms on the table. "It can be a fine line to walk. The last thing most guys want to do is scare a girl, or make her feel uncomfortable. It's embarrassing and makes you feel like a heel, so I can see why guys are reluctant to jump in with both feet."

I sigh and say, "It's a shame it's all so complicated when all you want is to be screwed until your teeth rattle." I add a pout.

His lips curve up. "What did you ask your ex to do?"

"Be a bit more dominant. Take charge. Nothing weird. I'm not into violence or pain or anything involving chickens."

That makes him laugh. "Glad to hear it."

"I'd just like to be…" I sigh. "Made to feel wanted, I guess."

Mack meets my eyes and holds my gaze. We're only about six inches apart now. It's loud in the restaurant, and we're leaning forward most of the time to hear each other.

He reaches out and takes a strand of my hair, lets it curl around his finger, then winds it around a few more times.

"Ow."

"So move," he says.

I lean forward, heart racing, until we're only an inch apart.

"I want you," he says, and he closes the distance and kisses me.

It's only brief. We're in public, and it's busy, and we can hardly indulge in serious foreplay across the table.

But even a brief touch of his lips is enough to send me sparkling inside like the fairy lights around the bar.

Someone clears their throat, and we pull apart to see Cesare standing there, trying to hide a smile. "Can I interest you in a dessert?" he asks.

"Definitely," Mack says as if the guy hasn't just caught us snogging like a couple of randy teenagers. "Sidnie? Want to share a Tiramisu?"

"Ooh, yes please."

"Tiramisu for two please."

Cesare nods and smiles, then retreats.

"The food of luuurv," I murmur, thinking about my idea of covering him in whipped cream. Tiramisu would definitely be an alternative.

"You're thinking about covering me in whipped dairy products again," he says. "I can tell."

"I was, actually."

He smiles. "So," he asks softly, "are you coming back to my apartment after this?"

I study his face, his beautiful eyes, his smooth jaw. "Any woman would be crazy to say no to you."

"You're the only woman who matters to me."

"That's a nice thing to say."

"It's the truth."

Right now, I think. But I don't say it. It does make me sad though, to think that soon, maybe next week, maybe in the New Year, he'll be bringing another girl here, wining and dining her, hoping to get her into bed.

All I have is tonight, so I have to make the most of him.

Cesare brings a large dish bearing a double helping of Tiramisu with two spoons, then leaves us to it.

Mack dips a spoon into the lush creamy cake and holds it out to me. "A bit cliché," he says, "but that's what this dessert is for."

Trying not to think about how many girls he's eaten this with, I close my lips around it and let him extract the spoon from my mouth slowly.

He huffs a sigh, then also has a mouthful.

"What?" I ask, amused.

He shakes his head. Beneath the table, I can feel his knee moving where his foot is tapping on the floor. His motor's running again.

Outside, the darkening sky is suddenly lit with a flash of lightning. Mack looks out at it, lost in thought. I count, and seven seconds later thunder rumbles out to sea.

His gaze comes back to me, and he studies me for a moment before he has another spoonful of Tiramisu. "In one of your advanced videos, you talk about safe words," he says.

"Oh. Yes. I read it's a good idea. That way the guy doesn't have to worry whether no actually means no or if the girl is playing."

He turns the spoon upside down and sucks the chocolate off, then removes it and points it at the window. "Lightning," he says.

"What about it?"

He has another spoonful. "That's your safe word."

"Oh." A frisson passes through me. "Okay."

"I have a feeling you won't need it," he says. "But just in case."

I scoop up a spoonful of the dessert. "What do you mean?"

He just shakes his head and smiles. It's like being smiled at by a ravenous tiger. He has one more mouthful, then pushes the dish toward me. "Finish up," he says. "I've had enough."

I have the last bit, conscious of my heart banging on my ribs. It's a gorgeous dessert, but I'm too nervous to savor it. All I can think about is what's going to happen when we get back to his apartment.

Cesare appears beside us as I finish scraping out the dish. "Can I get you a coffee?"

Mack looks at me, but I shake my head. "No thanks," he says. "I think we're done."

"That was delicious," I tell Cesare sincerely.

"Thank you," he says in his strong Italian accent, as Mack takes out his phone and sends a text, presumably to Jamie. "It was lovely to meet Dr. Hart's beautiful lady at last."

"Oh," I say, flustered. "Mm."

Mack gives us an amused look, gets up, and takes my hand as we follow Cesare to the counter.

"I'm guessing you won't let me pay half," I say to Mack.

He just snorts, taps his Apple watch to the card reader, then slides his hand into his pocket. He extracts it and shakes Cesare's hand, who then slips whatever Mack just gave him into his own pocket and smiles. It was obviously a tip, presumably a thank you for saving the table for him. I wonder how much he gave him?

"Have a lovely evening sir, ma'am."

"Goodnight." Mack leads me out of the restaurant, past all the people waiting, out into the warm night air.

"What did he mean?" I ask, puzzled, as we walk through the pedestrian area toward the road. "It was lovely to meet your lady at last? Surely you've taken other girls there before?"

"That wouldn't be very polite."

"You didn't take Felicity there?"

"No."

"Oh."

He gives me an amused look. "I rarely saw Felicity outside of Huxley's."

"Oh. I thought you two were, like, an item."

"No," he says.

Normally I wouldn't dare mention it, but I've had two cocktails, and I'm feeling mischievous. "Victoria told me that Felicity threw a coffee machine through Nadine's window when you broke it off."

That earns me an amused look. "Yeah. She somehow talked her way into the office. I had to have stern words with the security guy for that."

"Really?"

"I like to keep my work very separate from my social life."

I think about how we sat and had lunch at the table in his office, but I don't comment on it.

"So you were the one who broke it off?" I ask.

"We hooked up a few times. It wasn't a relationship. There was nothing to break."

I suspect her heart might have been, but I don't say that. Like most men, I guess, Mack can obviously sleep with a woman a few times without involving his emotions, but I'm sure Felicity fell for him immediately. She must have been devastated to lose him if she felt strongly enough to break his office window.

We exit the pedestrian area and see the Aston waiting for us a few cars down. Mack opens the passenger door, and I slip past him into the car.

"Hey Jamie," I say as Mack goes around the other side.

"Have a nice meal?" he asks.

"Mm, it was lovely, thanks. I told Mack he should have called an Uber to save you coming out."

He chuckles. "It's fine," he says as Mack slides in and shuts the door. "I like to keep an eye on him."

I'm still intrigued by their relationship, and the way Mack hinted that he'd somehow looked after him when they were younger. I'm guessing it was connected with them coming to New Zealand. But I can tell he doesn't want to talk about it further. I guess I'll never find out the whole story.

Jamie eases the car into the traffic, and heads us back to Grafton.

I look out of the window, at the shops and houses with twinkling fairy lights and Christmas trees in the windows. Outside one larger store there's a big model of Santa dressed in shorts, a vest, and gumboots, with his sleigh being pulled by nine sheep, one of which has a big red nose.

"How old were you when you found out Santa wasn't real?" I ask Mack.

He raises his eyebrows. "What? You're kidding me?"

I chuckle. Jamie doesn't, though. He keeps his gaze on the road.

"Six, I think," Mack says.

"Aw. That's young."

"Yeah." He and Jamie exchange a look in the mirror, and then Mack looks away, out of the window. Curiouser and curiouser.

Not wanting to upset him by making him talk about his past, I resolve to keep quiet for the rest of the journey. But then Wizzard's *I Wish It Could Be Christmas Everyday* comes on the radio, and the two of them start arguing about what's the best Christmas song. Soon they've pulled me into the discussion, and we end up talking all the way back to the apartment.

"If you think anything but *Last Christmas* should get the number one slot, you're crazy," I tell them, as Jamie drives into the underground car park and parks the car.

"We'll let you win this time," Mack says, opening the door. "But only because we're being polite."

I chuckle and get out, and follow the two of them over to the elevator and into the carriage. They both touch a card to the box by the door, and Jamie hits the button for floor twenty-two, then the button for the Penthouse.

"Of course," I murmur, and Mack grins.

The two of them talk briefly about the Black Caps cricket match that's taking place over the Christmas period. Then the elevator arrives at twenty-two, and the doors slide open.

A woman is standing in the corridor, holding Gus, and she smiles as Jamie walks out. "Hey you."

"Hey." He bends and kisses her.

"Hey Mack," she says, bringing Gus into the elevator.

"Hi Em. Thanks. This is Sidnie, by the way. Sidnie, this is Emma."

We shake hands, and she gives me a big smile. "Lovely to meet you," she says. "Have a great evening."

"Thanks for looking after Gus," Mack says.

"Oh he's no trouble. I took him for a run in the park. He should crash out—I think he's knackered." She waves goodbye.

"See you tomorrow," Mack says, and the doors close.

To cover my nerves, I bend down and fuss the dog, ruffling his ears. "Aren't you gorgeous," I tell him, kissing his nose.

"I'll get jealous," Mack says.

I chuckle and straighten. "Want me to ruffle your ears?"

"Wouldn't say no." He smiles as the elevator pings, and the doors slide open. Gus immediately runs past him up the corridor to the door, obviously knowing where he's going.

"After you," Mack says, and gestures for me to precede him.

I walk slowly into the corridor, hearing the elevator doors slide closed behind me. He unlocks his apartment door, and I follow Gus in.

The hallway leads into an open-plan living room, dining room, and kitchen. The walls to the left and ahead of me consist mainly of windows, so the room is filled with the deep orange light of the setting sun. To the west is Auckland Domain, the oldest park in the city, and I can see Auckland Museum and the cricket pavilion in the distance.

"Did you know that the domain is actually the remains of the explosion crater and the surrounding tuff ring of Pukekawa volcano?" I ask him, leaving my bag on the sofa.

He bends to stroke Gus and kiss his head. "No, I didn't know that."

"It's a beautiful view." I walk to the other end of the room and pause at the edge of the main bedroom, seeing other rooms further along the corridor. In the distance, Rangitoto Island is clearly visible out to sea in the fading light.

There's also a huge bed with a light-blue duvet. I turn away as a flurry of butterflies bursts into life in my stomach.

Mack tosses his keys and wallet onto the countertop and goes through to the kitchen. "Would you like a glass of Champagne? Or something stronger?"

"Champagne would be lovely," I say, as if I drink it every day of the week.

I walk back through the apartment, taking in the furnishings. In the living room, on top of the light-gray carpet is a plush white rug with uneven gold lines spread across it like the shadows of bare trees. A sumptuous cream sofa and chairs face a ginormous flat-screen TV that's hooked up to both a PlayStation 5 and one of the latest Xboxes. An unusual, upside-down pyramid-shaped, marble table sits in the middle. There's so much space everywhere. I hadn't realized until now how cramped my and my parents' houses are.

A large dining table sits in front of the window, and there's another, smaller one outside on the covered patio. An empty glass and an iPad rest on the table, so he must have been sitting out there before he came to pick me up tonight. Mack has opened the door, and Gus is out there now, flaked out on his side on the tiles.

"It's a beautiful apartment." I stop to admire an abstract painting that's filled with what looks like ocean waves, but are all different colors. "It's not what I expected, though."

"What do you mean?" He takes a bottle out of the fridge.

"I thought you'd live in a mansion with tennis courts and swimming pools and a hundred servants."

"I have a housekeeper. Does that count?"

"It's just very understated."

He peels the wrapping off the bottle and carefully pops the cork. "That's because you're thinking of rockstar millionaires. They're the ones who have yachts and gold-plated houses and diamonds in their teeth. I'm a businessman. I like luxury, but I'm at work most of the time. When I come home, I just want somewhere comfortable and quiet."

"And a fuck-off great TV to play video games on."

"Definitely. It's my only hobby, and it's a cool way to relax, because you can't think of anything else while you're playing." He pours the Champagne into two long glasses.

"I'd love a look at the PlayStation 5. Dan's got a PlayStation 4, but it's on its last legs."

"I'll give you a game of *The Two of Us* later," he says. "It's a game for couples but I've not played it yet."

"None of your exes into gaming?"

He just smiles at me and beckons to me to come and take a glass. "Have a drink, before you pass out."

"If I do, at least there's a doctor in the house."

He snorts and hands me the glass.

"How did you know I was nervous?" I ask.

"You're breathing as if you've just finished the fifteen hundred meters. Do you want a paper bag?"

I give a short laugh and sip the Champagne. "Mmm," I say. "A lovely vintage. Is it the '69?"

He chuckles. "You want anything to eat?"

"No, thank you."

We both sip our drinks. He watches me, and suddenly I know how fish must feel in a tank in a restaurant, when a diner's choosing which one of them to have for dinner.

My heart races and my mouth has gone dry. I feel so out of my depth with both the place and the situation.

He reaches out and cups my cheek. "Sidnie... you don't have to do this. If you want to leave, that's fine. It's not a problem."

I look up into his eyes and swallow hard. "Oh that's so nice of you. Yes please, I think I'll go home."

"Really?"

I laugh at his disappointment. "No, you idiot."

His eyebrows rise. Then his eyes gleam. He moves closer to me, so I have to back up to the worktop. He stops when he's an inch away, so we're not quite touching.

"That was naughty," he murmurs, looking at my mouth.

I moisten my lips with the tip of my tongue. "Sorry, I couldn't help it. Why on earth would I want to leave? I'm nervous, but I'm not a fool."

He lifts a hand to tuck a stray strand of hair behind my ear. "Why are you nervous?"

"This is my first one-night stand. I really know how to pick 'em."

He looks surprised. "Really?"

"Really?"

"You're not into Tinder sex?"

"I have been on a few dates, but I guess I'm picky. I'm not going to sleep with just anyone."

He smiles at the compliment, lifting a hand to tuck a stray strand of hair behind my ear. "I'd never have guessed that from your website."

"I'm all talk."

"Literally."

"Well, yeah. And you… well, you've obviously done this a lot, and it's a bit intimidating, that's all."

He's still stroking my cheek, and now he brushes his thumb over my bottom lip. "I wouldn't say a lot."

"Aw, come on. Don't be modest. Gus must think there's a revolving door on the apartment."

"Not here. Didn't I say? I only moved in a month ago. I was out on the North Shore before that, but I wanted somewhere closer to work."

"Oh. I didn't realize."

"You're the first girl I've brought up here," he says.

For some reason, that really surprises me. He might have had a hundred one-nights stands, but not here. The ghosts of other women don't haunt this apartment. The thought fills me with a warm glow.

"You like that," he says, a statement, not a question.

I just nod, and his lips curve up.

He puts down his glass. Cups my face with both hands. And then he lowers his lips to mine.

Chapter Twelve

Mack

Sidnie fumbles to put her glass down, and in the end I take it out of her hand and place it on the worktop. She rests her hands on my shirt, sliding her thumb between two of the buttons so she can brush my skin.

This girl fascinates me; I love how she's so open, so warm and sexy, and yet how she also seems relatively inexperienced; it's a great conundrum. It makes me want to watch her innocent eyes widen as I do wicked things to her. How I bring everything that's obviously been in her imagination to life.

But I know she's nervous, so first things first. I press my lips across hers, from one corner to the other, before touching my tongue to her bottom lip. She sighs and opens her mouth, granting me access, and so I sweep my tongue inside, pushing her up against the counter so she can be in no doubt as to how turned on I am.

"I've been thinking about this all day," I murmur, kissing over her cheek and around to her ear. I suck the lobe and then blow warm breath across her skin, and she shivers. I know this girl loves language, and she gets turned on by talking dirty. I want to bring it to life for her. Make her fantasy a reality.

"You drive me wild," I tell her, kissing the soft skin behind her ear. "Do you know that?"

"Likewise," she whispers. She pops the buttons of my shirt through the holes, and when she reaches the bottom, pushes the two sides to reveal my bare chest. "I want to see all of you," she says, moving the shirt over my shoulders.

Obligingly, I lower my arms to let it fall, then bring them back around her.

She nuzzles my neck. "You smell amazing. And you have a fantastic body." She kisses down to where my tattoo starts at the edge of my shoulder, where the black swirls and lines follow the shape of my muscles. She traces along one of the koru shapes, then kisses across my pecs to a nipple, and teases it with the tip of her tongue.

I grunt, and she straightens and chuckles. "Sorry," she says. "I got distracted."

"Help yourself, girl. You take whatever you want from me tonight. I'm here for you." I press her against the counter, kissing her slowly, and nestle the root of my erection in her soft mound. "Tonight I'm going to worship your body. I'm going to make you come so many times you'll forget what year it is."

"Oh." She gives a helpless sigh as I plunge my tongue into her mouth and kiss her deeply. I could easily pick her up, take her into the bedroom, throw her onto the bed, and do her right now, but I don't want the evening to end, not yet. I want to draw this out for as long as I can.

"I don't care if neither of us gets any sleep," I tell her. "I want to make love to you until the sun comes up. Until you're so exhausted you can barely move."

"Oh… Mack…" She lifts her arms around me.

I hold her hips, then slide my hands up beneath her vest, over her silky-smooth skin. Tonight she's wearing a bra, and I run my thumbs over the lace and tease the tips of her nipples while I rock my hips against her.

"Mmm…" She sucks her bottom lip and hooks her left leg around me. "That feels good…"

I kiss her deeply while I continue arousing her, turned on by her soft sighs and the way she's rocking against me. She arches her back a little, pushing her breasts into my hands, so I tug her nipples a little harder, and she gasps.

"Oh," she says, circling her hips, "yes… just there…" She bites her bottom lip and her eyelids flutter closed.

Holy fuck, I think she's going to come. I kiss her, holding her hips while I press against her mound, and with that she shudders and moans, giving five or six short gasps before she eventually lets all her breath go in one long whoosh. Her eyes open, and she moistens her lips and gives me a shy smile.

"That was quick." Thrilled, I skim my hands around her waist, drawing my fingers lightly over her skin. "I haven't even gotten started."

"Me neither," she says. "It doesn't take much to get me going. Expect more where that came from."

I chuckle and nuzzle her neck. "You need a few minutes rest?"

"God, no. Rolling orgasms all the way, if you're up for it."

My head spins. "I think I've died and gone to heaven."

She laughs, takes the bottom of her vest in her hands, and pulls it over her head. "I'd say you were an angel, but I think you come from a place a lot further south."

I trace a finger over the top of her breasts where they're propped up in the pretty white bra, then slide my hands around the back and undo the catch. "Better the devil you know…" We both chuckle as I pull the straps down her arms and toss the bra away.

Her breasts are perfect, firm and high, with pinky-brown nipples that are swollen and soft from the warmth of the room. She leans her hands on the worktop, arching her spine to offer them to me as I admire them. I tease the tips with my thumbs, tipping my head to watch as they tighten into firm buds, then bend and cover one with my mouth.

Sidnie groans and drops her head back, and I feel a surge of delight as I go from one nipple to the other, licking and sucking gently as she clutches my hair and rewards me with long sighs.

Eventually I kiss up her neck, back to her mouth. "You're so fucking beautiful," I tell her fiercely, burying my hands in her crazy hair as I kiss her lips.

"I want you," she whispers, sliding her hands up my back, then scoring her nails down lightly. "I want you inside me, Mack."

"In time," I promise, undoing the buttons at the top of her pants. "You're not leaving this apartment until I've fucked you senseless."

"Oh Jesus." As I slide down the zipper, she wriggles her hips and lets the pants fall to the ground, then steps out of them. Her white lacy knickers are pretty, but I slide them down her legs, dropping to my knees to help her remove them.

Now she's completely naked. I slide my hands up her thighs. The skin of her long legs is warm and silky smooth, and when she parts her legs for me, the bare, swollen skin between them glistens.

I don't need any more encouragement; I lift her left leg over my shoulder, then slide my tongue into her folds.

Sidnie groans and drops back onto her elbows on the counter. Fuck, she's so hot, wet and ready for me. I press either side of her folds at the top to reveal the tiny swelling nestled there, cover it with my mouth, and suck. At the same time, I slip two fingers down and curve them up into her. She's surprisingly tight, despite being wet. Fucking her is going to feel amazing.

She groans, her hips rocking against my hand.

"You taste so good," I tell her, stroking rhythmically inside her. "Your beautiful body feels so good in my hands, baby. You want to come like this?"

"Ah... mmm... yes..."

"Tell me how it feels. Tell me what you like."

"Mmm... I like it... when you lick my clit... mmm... like that..."

I tease it with my tongue for a while, then cover it again with my mouth and suck. Her fingers clench in my hair.

"Too hard?" I ask.

"No... just right..."

So I do it again, alternating between licking and sucking. "You like my fingers inside you?"

"Oh God, yes..."

"You like being touched here?" I press gently on her G-spot, and her breath hitches.

"Ah... Mack..."

"Are you going to come?"

"Mmm, yes..."

I slow my fingers, then slide them out of her. "Not yet."

She groans and drops her head back. "Oh... don't tease me."

"I told you, I don't make a good sub. So, you want to come?"

"Yes..."

I kiss the inside of her thigh. "Beg me, then."

Her chest heaves, and she moans as I blow gently across her sensitive flesh.

"Please," she whispers. "I'm so hot for you. So turned on. Please let me come."

I kiss her clit. "Good girl." I slide my fingers back inside her and flick my tongue over her clit, then suck it again. She comes almost immediately, clenching hard around my fingers and pulsing on my tongue. I murmur my encouragement, stroking her butt and thigh, until she finally collapses back with a groan.

I get to my feet and pull her up, then wrap my arms around her. "That's just a starter," I murmur, as I begin to walk her back toward the bedroom.

"Wait." She picks up her glass and finishes off the Champagne. I let her put it down before I continue walking her back.

"I can taste myself," she says when I kiss her.

"Amazing, isn't it?" I slide my hand underneath her, gather some of her moisture, then touch it to her lips before I kiss her again, hungrily. She protests and laughs, but melts against me when I refuse to let her go.

"You're an animal," she says, breathless, when I eventually lift my head.

"Tell me it doesn't turn you on."

"It doesn't turn me on."

"Liar." I push her onto the bed, and she bounces and laughs.

While I remove my pants, she shifts on the mattress so she's lying across the bed, watching me with huge eyes as I push down my boxers.

"Oh wow," she says softly. "Everything about you is impressive."

"Well, there definitely won't be any friction." I take a condom out of the bedside table.

"I don't think it's polite to comment on a lady's moisture level."

That makes me laugh. I get on the bed, move over her, then lower down so I'm half lying on her. "You're no lady. I hope."

She giggles, and it turns into a sigh as I kiss her.

We kiss for a long time, as the sun finally sets behind the domain, the light fades, and the stars begin to pop out on the deep purple sky. Out in the harbor, the sea is lit with the lights of boats returning home, and the sea breeze stirs the leaves on the pohutukawa trees. But in here it's warm in the semi-darkness, as we ascend into a world of erotic promise.

"Mack," she whispers as I stroke her breasts. "I want you inside me. Please."

More than happy to comply, I reach for the condom, tear off the wrapper, roll it on, then lift up and move between her legs. She wraps them around my hips, and I press the tip of my erection into her folds before lowering down on top of her. She's breathing fast, and I'm not sure if it's just because she's aroused, or if she's nervous.

"We'll take it slowly," I tell her.

She sucks her bottom lip and nods.

"I promised you," I say, "I'll ease in. A half inch at a time."

Her eyelids lower to half-mast, and her lips curve. "I know what you're doing, you naughty boy."

"I don't know what you mean. You were tight on my fingers. I don't know if I'll fit. Do you think you can take me?" I push forward a fraction.

She inhales. "Oh…"

"I'm so hard for you right now, baby. So big." I push a little further. "Open up. Let me inside you."

"Jesus." She closes her eyes.

I withdraw a little. "Want me to stop?"

She opens her eyes again, and they're hot enough to make me burst into flames. "I think you're the eighth wonder of the world."

I laugh and slide inside her a little more. "Come on," I tease, lowering down to kiss her. "You can take it all."

I'm not completely teasing; her nervousness has made her tight, and I don't want to hurt her. But luckily the lubrication is more than making up for it, and the more I kiss her, the more she lets me inside, until eventually I'm right up to the hilt.

"Ahhh…" We both exhale, and I lift my head to look into her eyes. Hers are wide, the pupils huge.

Lifting up, I withdraw from her, stroke the tip through her folds so it strokes her clit a few times, then press it back against her entrance. This time, I watch myself disappear inside her.

"I can feel you," she whispers. "All the way up. You feel amazing."

"So do you." I kiss her. "I'm going to give you another orgasm now."

"Oh," she says helplessly. "Okay."

"You're going to lie there," I tell her, "and just take it, and there's nothing you can do about it."

Her eyelids flutter shut as I begin to move with purpose, and her lips part. As I suspected, she's close, and it only takes thirty seconds or so before she bites her lip and comes, clenching around me hard enough to make me catch my breath.

I'm sure that most women, if the guy pays attention to what they like and takes his time, can come more than once in a session, maybe once if he goes down on her, and again during sex providing he stimulates her in the right place while he thrusts. And I know some women can have multiple orgasms with brief refractory periods in between.

But this is the first time I've been with a woman who can have rolling orgasms, as she called them. Straight after her climax, she encourages me to continue thrusting by rocking her hips, and it's clear she doesn't feel oversensitive. I realize the number of orgasms she can have is only limited to how long I can keep going. Holy fuck. There's an incentive, if I ever needed one.

Thrilled, I withdraw and rotate my finger to encourage her to turn over, and she rolls onto her front before parting her thighs and looking over her shoulder at me with excited eyes. She's so fucking beautiful. I can't believe my luck.

I slide inside her again, and she shudders at this new position, pulling down a pillow and burying her face in it.

"Hard and fast, this one," I promise, and caress her breasts while I move, before eventually slipping a hand down underneath her to stimulate her clit while I thrust.

The room darkens and grows warm, and our skin soon gleams with sweat as I make love to her for as long as I can, holding on to my self-control with both hands and every ounce of willpower in my body. She comes several more times, and by the time I finally flip her onto her back and slide into her a final time, her face and neck are flushed, and her curls are in even more disarray than usual.

"I can't wait any longer, baby," I tell her.

Her face lights up, and she runs her fingers down my damp back. "Yeah, come for me. I want to watch you."

I finally let my body do what it's been desperate to do all along, and I thrust hard into her and welcome the pleasurable feelings that begin to ripple through me. To my delight, she opens her legs wide, giving herself over to me.

"Come on, honey," she whispers, "fuck me senseless, hard as you like."

I groan and increase my pace, and she fills the air with loud exclamations with each thrust that only serve to heighten the moment. I'm pounding into her so hard by now her head is almost off the edge of the bed, but she doesn't complain, she just lets it drop back and cries out, moving with me.

I come hard, heat rushing up from my balls as the pulses begin, and I thrust away, not stopping until I'm completely empty, the climax so powerful that I almost black out.

When I eventually open my eyes, it's to find her limp beneath me, breathing hard. Her breasts shine in the moonlight. The hollow at the base of her throat is glistening.

She's the most beautiful woman I've ever seen.

Chapter Thirteen

Sidnie

Mack withdraws, lifts off, and falls onto his back on the bed beside me. He covers his face with his hands.

"I think I just had an out-of-body experience," he says, his words muffled.

I roll onto my side. "I know what you mean. It's fucking hot in here. Don't billionaires have aircon?"

"I forgot to turn it on."

I blow out a long breath, then frown. "What's that noise?"

He lifts his head and listens. "It's Gus over in the doorway. He's snoring. I guess he wasn't impressed with the performance." He raises his hands and does a brilliant Maximus impression: "Are you not entertained?" Then he collapses back with a groan.

Giggling, I prop my head on a hand and feast my eyes on his body. I can tell he's a runner; he's got powerful thighs and calves, and he's toned all over. He's a truly magnificent male specimen. And I got to go to bed with him. Day-mn!

I can't believe how long he went on for. I must have had seven or eight orgasms this evening.

"The man has stamina," I say, reaching out a finger to trail down his sternum. His skin is damp and hot.

"*I* have stamina? That's strong coming from the woman who just fucked me into next week."

"Hey, you told me just to lie there and take it. I was only doing as I was told."

His lips curve up, and then we both start laughing.

"Jesus," he says, disposing of the condom, then pulling me against him. "You're incredible."

"Hey, I didn't just give myself eight orgasms, or whatever it was, I lost count. That was all you."

He shakes his head. "I've never met anyone like you. How are men not queuing around the block to get in your bed?"

"I don't know. But if you'd like to pass the word on, I'd appreciate it."

His eyes narrow at that. He doesn't like the thought of me going to bed with anyone else. Interesting.

"Have you always had multiple orgasms?" he asks.

"This is a bit embarrassing to admit, but pretty much only when I'm on my own. I discovered fairly early on that I could keep going as long as I wanted."

His intense eyes study me. "But not with your exes?"

"No, not really."

He looks puzzled at that. "Why?"

I smile and kiss his chest. "Not everyone's as patient or as interested as you, Mack."

"Patient? Everything you read says women can take forty minutes to arouse. You were, like, forty seconds."

I blush. "I don't think it's unusual."

"Most women also have to wait in between each one."

"You're obviously speaking from experience. How many women have you been with?"

"I'm not answering that."

"I'm curious."

"I'm sure you are. I don't kiss and tell."

"Mack," I say softly, "you're young, hot, rich, smart, sexy, and with a body to die for. You could have any woman you want. Why the hell aren't you married with six kids?"

"I told you before: work comes first for me. I don't have the time to devote to a relationship." His gaze is direct. I can sense something lying beneath his reluctance like a riptide, waiting to tug him under. He hasn't told me everything.

Whatever the answer, he doesn't want to talk about it. I guess I'll never know. But I've been warned, and if my heart gets broken now, it'll be my fault.

I kiss his chest. "Fair enough."

He sighs and looks out at the view. "I need to take Gus out one more time. You want to come up with me, see the garden?"

Surprised, I nod, happy to draw out this moment as long as I can. "Sure."

We get up, and Mack tugs on his trousers and shirt but leaves it unbuttoned. Not sure whether we'll see anyone up there, I put on my underwear and pull on my clothes. He fetches Gus, and then leads me out of the apartment, through another door, and up a set of stairs, Gus scampering beside us.

My jaw drops as we emerge into the warm summer night. The garden covers the whole rooftop. Half of it is lawn, big enough for Gus to have a short run and a sniff around. There's a sheltered outdoor sofa and chairs overlooking the city, trimmed bushes and small trees in large round pots, flower beds, and a glass barrier around the whole thing that makes it look as if you could just walk right off the edge.

"Can anyone in the block use this?" I ask.

"No, just me, and we had stairs built from Jamie's apartment too." Holding my hand, he walks me across to the barrier, and we stand there looking at the view. The twinkling lights of the city spread out before us, reflecting off the water in the harbor. I can't see Rangitoto now because it's dark, and the city lights mean the stars are barely visible, but the moon hangs bright in the sky above us like a Christmas bauble, and it's still a magnificent view.

Mack starts humming, and I realize it's the song *Heartbeat*. "I can't get it out of my head since we danced to it," he says, turning me toward him. Holding my right hand, he slips his right onto my hip, and I rest mine on his shoulder.

We move slowly as he continues singing, his deep voice reverberating through me. I'm afraid to breathe in case I break the spell. It's a magical moment, dancing in this man's arms in the warm summer breeze, under the light of the nearly full moon. My body is still humming from our lovemaking, and I feel deliciously relaxed. But I also feel sad.

I don't have the time to devote to a relationship. His message was quite clear. This is a one-off, and I'm not to expect a follow-up call. He told me himself he has ADHD, and it sounds as if he loses interest in girls at light speed. When he did let himself get involved with Felicity, it ended badly because she obviously didn't understand that his work is everything to him, and any relationship will clearly come second. I'm sure he's going to be very careful to keep any future liaisons to a minimum, so the girl doesn't get the wrong message.

His open shirt flutters in the breeze, revealing his light-brown skin and the sprinkling of hairs across his chest. Unable to resist, I lean forward and kiss just beneath the dip at the base of his throat. His breath hitches as he inhales, and then he lowers his head to kiss me.

He does so slowly, and we gradually stop moving, my arms rising around his neck, his tightening around me. His lips move across mine, and it's like a long, slow, gentle goodbye.

When he eventually lifts his head, I force a smile onto my face. "I'd better get going," I say, moving back and dropping my arms.

His eyebrows rise. "What? You don't have to go." He catches my hand as I turn to walk back to the stairs. "Stay the night. I'll get Jamie to take you back in the morning."

"No. I'm sure you're super busy before Christmas. I need to sleep and then shower and change in the morning before I go to work." I smile. "But thank you."

He meets my eyes. Does he know why I'm going? Does he understand I'm already so crazy about him that if I stay, leaving him will definitely break my heart? Having an IQ of 172 doesn't mean he's an expert at reading emotions or understanding women.

But I'm determined not to make a fuss. I will not be another Felicity.

I turn away and walk toward the stairs. Gus runs past me, and when I pause at the top and look over my shoulder, Mack is following, his hands in his pockets.

We go down the stairs and along the corridor to his apartment. "I just need to get my purse," I say, "then I'll call a cab." I see the look on his face and add, "I do it all the time. It's perfectly safe."

His jaw knots. "You're not going in an Uber at this time of night."

I give him a direct look. "Excuse me?"

He glares at me.

"We're not in the bedroom now." I pick up my purse. "Thank you for a lovely evening. I had a wonderful time." I take out my phone and dial for an Uber, hoping he can't see my shaking hand. "There, all done."

I give Gus a last stroke, then walk to the door and go out. When I turn, he's leaning against the door jamb, hands in his pockets.

"Don't go," he says. He looks puzzled, as if he's not sure why he said that.

I move closer to him, reach up, and kiss him. "Thank you," I whisper, looking him in the eyes. I hope he knows that I mean for the evening, and for everything he's done for my family.

He doesn't say anything.

"See you later, alligator." I move back and look at him expectantly. "You're supposed to finish the rhyme."

He doesn't. He just continues to study me with that slightly puzzled look. I remember then that he told me, *I'm used to getting my own way.* It occurs to me it might be the first time in a while that someone has stood up to him.

"Text me when you get home," he says. "Please."

I go into the elevator and press the button, and give him a nod as the doors close.

The Uber arrives only a couple of minutes after I exit into the warm night. I get in, and soon we're weaving through the busy city. There must be plenty of Christmas parties happening tonight, and the streets are filled with people in suits and glittery dresses, some with Santa hats or reindeer antlers or flashing earrings, all celebrating the festive season in their own way.

When the car pulls up outside my house, I thank the driver and get out, then send Mack a text. *Don't get your knickers in a twist, I'm home.*

He comes back immediately. *Don't mention knickers. I'm already having trouble getting you out of my head.*

I smile, but it also makes me sad. It's been less than fifteen minutes, and he's trying to forget me.

Night, I text. Then I slide my phone into my purse and go inside. Caro and Hana are in their room and there's no light under the door, so I go straight through to my room. I'm tired, and more than ready to crash out.

After going to the bathroom and changing into my pajamas, I check the phone again as I climb into bed. The screen remains blank—no more messages.

Disappointment settles over me like a big gray blanket. But as I lie there, I make myself think about how wonderful the evening was. I think about the way Mack kissed me, and his beautiful eyes as he made love to me. And I remember the way we danced on the rooftop, with the moon hanging above us in the sky.

I don't regret it, I'm glad it happened, and I'm not going to be sad about it.

Keep telling yourself that, Sid, and you might begin to believe it.
I turn out the light and pull the duvet over my head.

*

The next morning, I open the curtains to discover it's raining.

"Seems appropriate," I mumble. I can hear someone in the shower—probably Hana, so I go into the kitchen.

"Morning." Caro's there eating toast. On the table are a pair of dirty socks, a bill from the electricity company, two plates with the remains of their dinner last night, and an empty wine bottle containing a candle. The wax has dripped all down the side and over half the table.

Thinking about Mack's housekeeper with some envy, I pick up the plates, put them in the sink, and run cold water over them.

"Sorry," Caro says, "I meant to do that."

"It's okay." I throw her a smile. For the first time, though, I think that maybe it might be nice to have my own place. I'm sure Caro and Hana would rather live on their own, too. But what could I possibly afford to rent on my own? Only a room in another house, and that would leave Caro and Hana short here, too.

"How did it go?" Caro asks, waggling her eyebrows.

I open the fridge. The bag of bread only contains a crust, and there's no butter. I close the fridge again, then flick the kettle on for a cup of tea.

"We don't have any milk," she says.

I flick it off again, then come and sit at the table, resolving to treat myself to a coffee and a breakfast bun on the way to work. I can't afford it, but I don't care. "It was wonderful," I admit, bringing my legs up and wrapping my arms around my knees. "He took me to Il Pescatore."

"The Italian? Holy shit. The meals there are, like, fifty bucks each."

"I know. It was absolutely packed, and the manager himself showed us to a table right in the middle. We shared a platter and a tiramisu, and I had two cocktails."

"Then what?"

"He took me back to his apartment." I press my lips together.

Her eyes widen. "And…" I just smile, and she grins. "Really?" She leans forward on the table, eager for details. "What was he like?"

In the past, I might have been excited to boast about the sexy guy who made me come eight times before thrusting me into next Tuesday. But for some reason, I don't want to talk about Mack now. It feels too private, not something I want to share and let others paw through as if they're at a charity shop going through the belongings of someone who's recently died.

Instead, I say, "He was lovely. I had a great time, and I'm really glad I went. But that's it, I'm afraid."

"What? Seriously?"

"Yeah. He's a busy guy, and he told me he doesn't have time for a relationship. But that's okay. It was just like a Tinder hookup, right? You can't expect to find Mr. Right on the first go. I mean Dr. Right." I give a small, sad smile.

"Aw," she says. "You really like him, don't you?"

"He's amazing. But I knew I'd never be the sort of girl who'd be able to hold his attention."

Hana comes into the kitchen, wrapped in a robe, her hair hanging wet around her face. "Hey you! How did it go?"

"Yeah, good. I'll let Caro give you the details. I need to have a shower." I smile at them both, then leave the room and head for the bathroom.

I try not to think about Mack as I shower, but it's impossible. My head is full of memories. As I slide my hands over my soapy skin, I remember his hands doing the same. The way his eyes lit up as he gave me orgasm after orgasm, directing me from one position to the next with sheer enjoyment. I had such a fantastic time. But there's a lot more to a relationship than great sex.

*

It's 23rd December, and the last day at work, so there's a pleasant party atmosphere. Like most companies in New Zealand, Lubricanz will close for two weeks over Christmas, which means I can go with Dad when he has his treatment. Christmas is going to be a bit of a damp squib this year. But that's okay; at least we know his treatment will begin on Tuesday.

The building where I work is situated on an industrial estate, and consists of a cluster of factory buildings, warehouses, and an office block. At eleven, I stop for a pleasant morning tea that's been organized for the staff, choose a mince pie and a piece of Christmas cake, and take them and a coffee back to my desk.

Today I'm working on an advert for car magazines about their new MaxEngine oil additive. I sit at my desk and get to work, checking the details one of the engineers has provided, and trying to wrestle them into smooth copy.

"The primary benefit is friction reduction within the boundary lubrication regime, where metal-to-metal contact causes component wear. This protection is crucial to the ring zone, turbocharger and camshaft lobe areas in engines, and the pump, cylinder rods and valves in hydraulics."

I try not to think about the connection between lubrication and a certain young billionaire who screwed me senseless last night.

The phone on my desk rings. I look up, startled, lost in the world of cars, and pick it up.

"It's me," Charlie, the receptionist says. "Can you come out here for a sec?"

"Sure." I hang up and finish off my coffee, then leave the room I share with the marketing director and head through the building to reception.

I can't help but compare it to Koru Tech's swish building as I walk to the front desk. This place is very practical—all painted in white with black trim with the Lubricanz logo on the wall, two black plastic chairs for waiting visitors, a water cooler, and a couple of car magazines on the table. The only splash of color comes from a beautiful bouquet of red roses resting on the counter.

"These are lovely," I say to Charlie, "you lucky thing. Nobody's ever sent me flowers."

She smiles. "Until now. They're for you."

My eyebrows rise, and my heart bangs. "What?"

"There's a card on them."

With a shaking hand, I remove it and open the envelope. It contains a card with a printed photograph of a Cocker Spaniel wearing a tea towel on its head like a shepherd in a Nativity scene. A hand belonging to someone who's just out of shot holds a plastic gold star above the dog's head.

I laugh and turn it over. The handwriting says 'Merry Christmas. M. x'

My heart swelling, I look at the bouquet of roses. They're all buds that are just beginning to open, and they smell divine.

"There are two dozen," Charlie states. "I counted them."

"Wow." I pick the cellophane-covered bouquet up gently. It has a huge red bow around the bottom. The stems are wrapped neatly in a special wet cloth covered with more cellophane to keep them fresh.

"I'm guessing they're from someone special," Charlie teases.

"Yeah," I murmur. "He's special all right."

I walk back to my office, stopping every ten feet as someone comes over to admire the flowers and laugh at the photo of Gus in the tea towel. "They're from a friend," I tell them, not sure how else to describe him.

Back at my desk, I stand the flowers carefully on a spare chair, then take out my phone. I nibble my bottom lip as I wonder what message to send.

It was a beautiful thought, but it's not as if he's asked me out again. He enjoyed himself, and he's polite enough to want to say thank you. That's all the flowers were for.

Me: *I've just got the flowers. They're absolutely beautiful. Thank you so much.*

Him: *I'm glad you like them. <3*

Ooh, a heart!

Me: *And the photo of Gus! Please give him a kiss from me.*

Him: *Hey, I'll be keeping any kisses you're giving out to myself.*

My lips curve up. I think for a moment about what to say next. I don't want to say anything that makes him think I'm like Felicity.

Me: *How's work today, busy?*

Him: *Always. I'm finishing off a report on our latest research for Elizabeth.*

Me: *The Elizabeth I met at Huxley's?*

Him: *Yeah. We're working on a project together. I'd hoped to get it done by Christmas but it's taken longer than I thought.*

Me: *What's it about?*

Him: *Stuff I won't bore you with.*

Okay, he doesn't want to talk about it. Fair enough. I change the subject.

Me: *I saw that you spoke at the International Conference on Supercomputing.*

Him: *Where did you see that?!*

Me: *Wikipedia! The font—or fount—of all knowledge :-)*

Him: *Oh, LOL. Yeah. That was pretty cool. It was virtual, so I was able to do it here in the office.*

The mention of his office makes me think about his 'secret' suite. He doesn't know I was in there. How can I ask him about it?

Me: *You obviously work long hours. Do you ever look up and realize the sun is coming up?*

Him: *Many times! I often work till three or four am. I've got a bed in the office, so sometimes I crash there if I can't be bothered to go back to the apartment.*

I smile, but it fades slowly. I keep forgetting he's a billionaire genius who works all hours under the sun.

Time to end it, Sid.

Me: *Well I'd better get back to work. Thanks again for the flowers. They really are beautiful.*

Him: *Beautiful flowers for a beautiful girl. x*

I bite my lip, put my phone down, and turn back to my computer.

It was a wonderful thing for him to say. But it's time to move on.

Chapter Fourteen

Mack

At eleven, I have a meeting with the other three members of my senior management team: Eoin, Cherry, and Kai.

Eoin—confusingly pronounced Owen—is a smart Kiwi guy with ginger hair in his early thirties that I met through Huxley when we were at university. He's a top-rate computer science engineer, very smart, and fairly high on the spectrum, which means he can struggle a little socially because of his brusque and direct manner. That has proven invaluable to me though, as he's not afraid to point out any weaknesses in my work, and I need someone like that working with me to keep me on track.

Cherry, who hates her name because she says it makes her sound like a porn star, was born in Australia but has lived here for the last ten years. When I met her, she was working for MediTechNZ, but Elizabeth told me unselfishly that she thought Cherry was wasted there and had the knowledge and skill to flourish at Koru Tech. When I offered her a job, she jumped at the chance, and less than a year later I promoted her to head one of my teams because she impressed me so much. She's also in her thirties and a great computer engineer, although her main skill lies in the collation and bringing together of information. Where we sometimes get lost in the minutiae, she's able to get us to step back and look at the big picture.

Kai is Japanese, and I've also known him since university. He was the guy who worked with me to develop the computer processor we sold to Intel, and he's the main one who created Marise with me. Communication is important to me—I like to connect with other smart people and share what I know, especially to the youngsters coming up in the industry. But Kai is much quieter than me and doesn't enjoy public speaking, so he prefers to work in the background and let me be the face of the company.

The three of them each head a team of computer science engineers, and everyone's been working super hard to finalize the MediTechNZ project.

"Our teams are analyzing the final results as they come in," Cherry states at the meeting. "Everyone's prepared to work through Christmas until it's done."

I doodle on my pad, tempted, but eventually lean back with a sigh. "As much as I'd love to do that, we've all been working over twelve-hour days for months, and we all have families. Elizabeth is happy for us to take a break, and I think she's right. Everyone needs it, and they'll come back refreshed and ready to double and triple check everything before we submit the work."

"You're taking time off?" Eoin asks. "I don't believe you. You'll send us home and then sneak back in."

"Nope. I'm off tomorrow to the Bay of Islands with my family. I'll be back first thing Monday morning."

"You're having a whole weekend off?" Cherry grins. "I think we should call the Guinness Book of Records."

"Yeah, yeah. I plan to eat a whole tray of roast potatoes, drink half a bottle of whiskey, and then pass out in front of the TV for forty-eight hours."

They all chuckle. I smile at Kai. "Are you going to spend some time with Sakura?" He's been dating her for a couple of months now.

"Yeah," he says. "Actually I have something to tell you. We're getting married!"

It's such a shock that we all stare at him. He grins and gives a shy shrug.

"You don't hang around," I comment before I can think better of it.

He gives me a look. "We've been dating for a year."

"What? Jesus, really?"

"We met last Christmas."

I'm stunned. Was it really a year ago?

I get up out of my chair and walk around the table to him. "I didn't mean to be rude—I've lost track of time, that's all. Congratulations—it's amazing news. I'm so pleased for you."

He laughs, gets up, and we exchange a long hug before he breaks away to hug the other two.

"When's the big day?" Cherry asks.

"July. Sakura wants a winter wedding, so we're going to Queenstown. You'll all be getting invites, of course."

"Will it be a traditional-style Japanese wedding?" Eoin wants to know.

"We're both Christians so we want it in a church, but we liked the idea of having some traditional customs. She's going to wear a wedding kimono for the ceremony."

"It sounds amazing," Cherry says dreamily. "I can't wait."

We all smile at each other. "Well, that's as good a place as any to stop," I say, closing my laptop. "So, back here on Monday. Final results by end of the day Tuesday. Draft analysis… let's say Thursday lunchtime? That's the twenty-ninth. Let's aim to get it to Elizabeth by close of business Friday, and that gives us one day's leeway. But I'd like to get it done and dusted this year."

They all nod, tidy up their things, and we make our way out of the board room.

When I get to my office, I discover that Kai has followed me in. I put down my laptop and turn to face him. "You should have told me," I scold.

He shrugs. "I've been meaning to for a while, but… well, I know you're against marriage."

I frown. "Not for other people."

"You see it as a ball and chain around your ankle. You don't think a girl exists who will treat you like a homing pigeon, letting you fly free with the knowledge that you'll come home when you're ready."

I don't say anything, because he's right.

"Sakura knows how important my work is to me," he continues. "She has her own life here—her family and her job. She doesn't expect us to be joined at the hip."

His voice is a tad defensive. I'm not surprised. In the past, the four of us have joked that we'll still be working here twelve hours a day when we're a hundred, going around the office on our Zimmer frames. We've all struggled with partners who've been upset that we'd rather be at work than at home with them. Cherry has been dating her present boyfriend for a few months, but I've already heard her having one argument with him when I walked past her office. Eoin is gay, and I suspect he has the same problem because he broke up with his last partner six months ago, and I don't think he's dated much since.

I wonder if things will change for Kai when he's tied the knot. Maybe Sakura will show her true colors when she's wearing the ring. It'll all begin then—the calls after hours asking where he is, the arguments, the accusations that he can't love her as much as he loves his job.

Kai gives me a twisted smile. "She loves me, Mack, and because of that, she's happy that I'm doing what I love. She doesn't want to change me."

I'm cynical, but I'm not going to say that to him. "I'm really pleased for you."

"You should try it," he says.

I give a short laugh. "No thanks."

"We all have to grow up sometime," he says.

I meet his gaze, and we study each other for a moment. When we were at university, the two of us worked incredibly hard, but we also played hard, with Huxley and several others, and none of us were ever short of girlfriends. It was a good life, and I enjoyed it, but his words make me feel as if he thinks I'm still acting like a frat boy, whereas he's moved on.

It stings. But I guess that's because he's right.

His expression softens. "I want you to be my best man."

My eyes widen. "What about your brother?"

"I love him dearly, but I only see him twice a year. He'll understand. Will you do it?"

That genuinely chokes me up. "Of course," I say, my voice hoarse.

We exchange a big hug, both swallowing hard, then break apart with a laugh. "Catch you later," Kai says, and he leaves the room.

I watch him go, then wander over to the sliding doors. Gus gets up from his bed and runs past me to chase butterflies on the lawn. I watch him, battling with an unusual emotion, something I don't feel often: envy. I'm envious of his happiness, but mostly of his belief that he's found the perfect woman, and that everything's going to be all right.

Despite my drive to get the project finished, I've been looking forward to going up to the Bay of Islands to see my family. Now, though, I feel irritated and resentful, and I hate myself for it. I wish I hadn't agreed to go. If I could stay, I could lose myself in the work, and then I wouldn't be plagued with thoughts of Kai's honest but cruel words.

Briefly, I think about Sidnie. I could text her, or even call her. I'd love to hear the sound of her husky, sexy voice.

We all have to grow up sometime.

Do I want to? I like my life. I love my work. It's everything to me, and it fills my world. There's no space for anything else. I don't want to have to consider someone else's feelings. To have responsibilities outside of the office.

I look down at Gus, who's resting his muzzle on his paws, watching me. His eyes say *Frat boy.*

"You can talk," I tell him grouchily. Back in November, I let him mate with Elizabeth's miniature poodle because she wanted Spoodle puppies, but after Christmas he'll be going to the vet to be neutered. "You won't be laughing when the vet cuts off your family jewels."

He comes over and puts his head on my lap. I laugh and kiss his head. "Sorry, dude. You won't know a thing about it, I swear."

I sigh. This isn't getting the report written. Turning away from the view, I go back to my desk, open my laptop, and get to work.

*

Just before one, Jamie comes in to tell me it's time to leave for lunch with my colleagues from Huxley's.

"Do you know where it is?" I ask as we walk through the offices.

"Slow down," he complains. "I can never keep up with you." I adjust my pace, and he blows out a breath. "At Il Pescatore."

I stop walking and look up at the ceiling. He gives me a curious look. "I thought you liked it there."

I start walking again. "I do."

"Is this to do with Sidnie?"

"No, not at all. Well, a little bit. Yes. Stop interrogating me."

He grins. "Did she like the flowers?"

"She did. And the photo of Gus." I smile as I think of her opening the card.

"You're smiling again."

"No I'm not."

Still arguing, we go over to the car and get in, and Jamie heads for the Italian restaurant.

"What time do you want to head off tomorrow?" he asks.

"Four-ish?"

"Is that Mack o'clock? Do you mean seven p.m. or do you really want to go at four?"

"I really want to go at four. Drag me out by the hair if you have to."

"Oh, I will. Emma would like to get there for dinner."

I smile. He has never berated me once for being late or making him wait, but that's his subtle way of saying he's ready for a vacation. "Fair enough. You know you could drive up with her tonight?"

"No, I'm good." He says it firmly, and I don't argue.

A few minutes later, he pulls up outside the restaurant. I unbuckle my seatbelt, then sit there for a moment.

"Did you know that Kai is getting married?" I ask.

"No! Hey that's great news."

I nod and look out at the shoppers walking past with their bags full of Christmas presents and food. "He said we all have to grow up sometime."

Jamie doesn't reply, and when I look back at him, his lips twist in a wry smile. "Ouch," he says.

"Not everyone thinks you can only be complete with a relationship," I say gruffly. "Why does everyone assume their way is the only way? It's the same with religion, politics, and now marriage. Why do people always have to proselytize?"

"I guess when they think they have the recipe for happiness, they like to pass it on."

"I'm not unhappy."

"Okay."

"I'm not."

"Are you trying to convince me or yourself?" He sighs. "Don't glare at me. I've never told you how to live your life. All I will say is that Sidnie makes you smile, and that has to be a good thing."

I scratch at a mark on the Aston's dash. Then I open the door.

"Text me when you're done," he says.

"Yeah, thanks." I get out, close the door, and head for the restaurant.

It's a few minutes after one p.m., and Titus, Oliver, Elizabeth, and Victoria are already there. They all cheer as I walk up, and I grin and take the remaining chair at the round table as I say, "Afternoon."

"So glad you came." Elizabeth leans over and kisses my cheek.

"I'm surprised Jamie could pry you out of the office," Huxley comments.

"Don't tell me you're working through Christmas," Victoria scolds.

"No. I'm off to the Bay tomorrow."

"Wonders will never cease." She grins.

I roll my eyes and smile as Cesare comes up. "Afternoon, Dr. Hart," he says, beaming.

"Hey. Merry Christmas."

"And to you, sir. Can I get you a drink?"

"What's everyone else having?"

"Champagne," Elizabeth and Victoria say together, and laugh.

I grin. "Champagne sounds good."

He nods. "Are you all ready to order?"

I haven't had a chance to look at the menu, but I know I want his famous Carbonara that has enough garlic and pepper in it to make your head explode. We give our orders, and he notes them all down.

"Thank you," he says. He smiles at me. "And may I say how lovely it was to meet your beautiful lady yesterday."

Everyone stares at me. "Cheers," I say to him wryly. He glances around, pulls an *eek* face, and hastily withdraws.

"Oh..." Victoria's eyes dance. "So you did apologize?"

"For what?" Titus looks intrigued. "What happened?"

"Nothing," I growl. "We had dinner, that's all."

"I knew you liked her," Elizabeth says softly.

"Mack and Sidnie, sitting in a tree," Huxley sings. "K-I-S-S-I—"

"Fuck off, Hux."

They all laugh, and then thankfully Titus turns the subject to business.

I listen, but for once my mind isn't on the conversation. We're not at the same table that I sat at with Sidnie, but I can easily picture her here, her blue eyes sparkling, her sexy, husky voice sending shivers down my back.

We all have to grow up sometime.

A waiter pours some Champagne into my glass, and I have a sip, thinking about Sidnie drinking it in my apartment. How I pushed her up against the countertop, and went down on her right there and then. How sweet she tasted.

Surreptitiously, I take my phone out of my pocket and turn it on. I bring up my texts. Then I send her a message.

Me: *Hey. How's your afternoon going?*

Her: *Oh, hi! Good thanks. I can't stop looking at the roses. They're gorgeous.*

Me: *So glad you liked them.*

Her: *What are you up to?*

Me: *Having lunch with the gang from Huxley's. At Il Pescatore, funnily enough.*

Her: *Oh I envy you. That was such a lovely place.*

Me: *What are you doing right now?*

Her: *Having a sandwich. Not quite so impressive. And daydreaming.*

Me: *What about?*

Her: *You really have to ask?*

Me: *Tiramisu?*

Her: *Ha! Maybe. I'm disappointed I didn't get around to the whipped dairy products fantasy.*

"Are you texting her now?" Elizabeth asks.

I turn the phone face down. "No."

"You're smiling," Victoria comments.

"Jesus. I smile all the time."

"You really don't."

"Will you lot shut up? It's an important message from the office."

Elizabeth giggles and the others grin, but she doesn't press it, and instead asks about their plans for the New Year.

I turn the phone over again, holding it on my thigh. So Sidnie is still interested in talking dirty? Well two can play at that game.

Me: *Me too. Although I'd prefer it if I was doing the licking.*

There's a pause, and I can imagine her sitting there, lips curving up. I hope she's pleased I contacted her.

Her: *Oh no. This is my fantasy. I'm definitely doing the licking. I think I'd start with your chest.*

Me: *Really?*

Her: *Mm. I'd take a spoonful of the cream and smear it all across your nipples.*

Holy shit. This isn't the easiest conversation to have at the dinner table. But I'm not going to be the one to back out.

Me: *Okay. Then what?*

Her: *Very, very slowly, using the tip of my tongue, I'd lick it off each nipple.*

Me: **fans self* Okay, you win.*

Her: *Oh I'm not done yet. I'd take another spoonful and trail it down your stomach and follow that beautiful line of hair that goes beneath your belt.*

Me: *Am I still wearing trousers in this fantasy?*

Her: *Actually, no. I wouldn't want to get cream on them.*

Me: *God forbid.*

Her: *So you're naked now. Well, I think it would be better if we were both naked. Or would you prefer me in sexy underwear?*

Me: *At this point you could be wearing a boiler suit and I'd still be turned on.*

Her: *LOL. I'd kiss all the way down your stomach, licking the cream off as I went. And then I'd get another spoonful…*

Me: *Maybe we should stop there.*

Her: *And I'd smear it all over your cock.*

I blink.

Me: *Jesus.*

Her: *Then I'd cover it with my mouth and start sucking.*

Me: *Sidnie, have mercy.*

Her: *I want you in my mouth, Mack. Deep in my throat. I want to suck you till you come, until you fill my mouth with your silky fluid, and drink you dry.*

There's a brief pause. Then she texts again.

Her: *By the way, we're moving to Intermediate. Did I mention that?*

Conscious that the table has gone quiet, without moving my head, I glance up. They're all watching me with amusement. Presumably one of them asked me something. I didn't even hear them.

Slowly, I lean forward and put my head on the table.

"Aw," Elizabeth says as the others all laugh, and she pats me on the back. "Poor Mack. Is she driving you insane?"

I sit back, and blow out a helpless breath. "I think my head's going to explode."

Victoria smiles; she knows how unusual this is for me. "When are you seeing her again?" she asks.

"I wasn't planning to." I glance down at the last text she sent and quickly type, *Later, Minx,* send it, and put the phone back in my pocket. "But I think she has other plans."

"She bringing you to your knees?" Elizabeth asks, amused.

"Or the other way around?" Huxley says with a grin.

"Hey," Victoria says, as she sees the look on my face. "That's not how we talk about each other's partners."

Huxley's eyebrows rise. "Oh…" He looks at my face and his expression softens. "I didn't realize. I'm sorry, that was very rude. I went for the cheap laugh."

Confused by how I felt when he said that, and Victoria's reply, I just say, "Don't worry about it." I smile at Cesare as he arrives with a couple of the meals, and I change the subject, asking Titus for his opinion on an article I read on AI in this month's IEEE Transactions on Pattern Analysis and Machine Intelligence.

We don't talk about it again. It's only when the meal's done and we're on our way out that Huxley mentions it.

"Mack," he murmurs while the others wait, "I want to apologize again. I hope you know I'd never purposely offend you. I was brought up to respect women, and I'm ashamed of myself for what I said."

"Bro, come on. I know you were joking."

"Yeah, but I feel about an inch high. Sidnie is a lovely girl and you obviously like her a lot. She didn't deserve that. If someone were to say that about Joanna…"

I glance at Elizabeth at the mention of the only girl that Huxley has ever cared about. She meets my gaze, then looks at the ground.

I smile. "You're one of the good guys, and life's too short to take offense where none is meant. Seriously, don't worry about it." I clap him on the back, and we walk toward the cars. "Merry Christmas."

He hesitates, then just smiles and says, "Merry Christmas." He crosses the road and walks away, hands in his pockets. I know it's going to bother him for some time.

I look at the others, who are talking amongst themselves as they wait. They give me rueful smiles as I walk up.

"He fell on his sword," Titus says, "but we were all to blame. I'm sorry, Mack."

"Jesus, it was nothing. Don't worry about it."

"Are you going to call her?" Victoria asks.

"Yeah, maybe when I get back from the Bay."

"I hope you have a great Christmas." Elizabeth stands on her tiptoes and kisses my cheek. "See you soon."

"I'm planning to have the report to you by the end of next week," I tell her.

She nods and goes over to her car.

"See you later," I tell Titus and Victoria. "Have a great Christmas."

"You too." They go over to their car, as they're both heading back to the club.

I open the door of the Aston and slide in. "Hey," I say to Jamie.

"Have a good time?"

I nod and pull out my phone. "Yeah. For several reasons." Smiling, I pull up my texts, and start talking to Sidnie again.

Chapter Fifteen

Mack

Christmas Eve

"You want another veggie fritter, Mack?"

I blow out a breath and flop back in my deckchair. "No thanks. I'm absolutely stuffed."

"You haven't actually managed to fill him up?" Koro, my grandfather, sounds most amused. "I didn't think it was possible."

"You leave him alone," Kuia, my grandmother, scolds, coming over to kiss the top of my head. "He has a big brain, and it takes a lot of calories to fuel it."

"Big head," Jamie says, and grins.

I give a lazy smile, too content to bicker.

It's around eight p.m. on Christmas Eve, and I'm at Matauri Bay, sitting on the deck with my family, looking out over the Pacific and the Cavalli Islands. The memorial to the Greenpeace flagship, Rainbow Warrior, sunk by the French while on its way to protest against a French nuclear test in 1985, is just to the north on the hill. The sun is setting, and the color of the sky matches the fruit in the bowl on our table—strawberry, mandarin, and blueberry.

Koro grew up just down from here, living in a tiny house with six brothers and sisters and not a penny to his name. He worked his balls off and ended up running his own building firm, and made enough money to give his own kids a comfortable life, but the house he owned with Kuia was still tiny. When I made my first million, I bought this piece of land for them, and Koro built this house, full of light and space, with four large bedrooms to house the many guests who come and go. Tonight, there are about fifteen of us here—my grandparents, their two daughters and their families, Jamie, Emma, and me. Jamie isn't related by blood to them, but my father adopted him when he brought us to New Zealand, and they've always treated him like their grandson.

"Come for a swim," Anna, my fourteen-year-old cousin, pleads. Her sister, who's twelve, picks up my hand and tugs it.

"I'll sink," I groan. "Give me half an hour for my dinner to go down."

"It'll be dark then," Anna complains.

"Leave him alone." Their mother, my aunt Aroha, shoos them away. "You've been bothering him and Jamie all afternoon."

"Give me half an hour," I call after them, "and I'll give you a game of cards."

They cheer and run away, down to the sea.

"Sorry," Aroha apologizes, coming to collect my plate. "They're so pleased to see you both. They've talked about nothing else for days."

"I'll clean up," I tell her, starting to get up, but she pushes me back down.

"Have a rest," she says. "We all know how hard you work."

I sink back into my chair, a little embarrassed. "It's not like I work down a mine," I mumble.

"Don't worry about him," Jamie says. "He just sits there all day playing Solitaire."

They all chuckle. I give a good-natured smile.

"Anyway," he continues, giving me an impish look, "did he tell you he has a girlfriend?"

Everyone's eyes widen. "Oooh," Aroha and my other aunt, Manaia, say together.

"Mack!" scolds my grandmother. "You never said!"

"Thanks," I say to my brother. "This is exactly what I need."

He just grins, and Emma, sitting beside him with her head on his shoulder, giggles.

"Come on then, spill the beans," Aroha says.

"Nope." I have a swig of beer.

"Her name's Sidnie," Jamie says. "She's twenty-two. She's got an English degree."

"What does she look like?" my grandmother wants to know.

"She's tall, slim, and she's got this crazy, blonde, curly hair," Emma says. "She's very beautiful."

"Nice," Aroha's husband adds.

"She's not my girlfriend," I say wryly. "We've been on one date."

"Two dates," Jamie says.

"All right, two dates. But that's all."

"He was texting her the whole way up here," Jamie says.

"What are we, fourteen?" I complain. "Will you shut up?"

"She makes him smile," Jamie comments, and everyone says, "Aw...!"

I roll my eyes and have another swig of beer.

"What's she doing this Christmas?" Koro asks.

"Not much I think." I sigh. "Her father has prostate cancer, would you believe?"

Immediately, everyone's eyes fill with pity. "Oh no," Koro says. "What are the odds of that?"

"One in sixty-four."

His lips curve up, and everyone else grins.

"What?"

"It was a rhetorical question," Koro says. "Trust you to have the exact answer."

"It's basic probability. One in eight times one in eight." He raises an eyebrow, and I give up. "Anyway, he has his first treatment on Tuesday. She told me they'd canceled Christmas this year."

"You should have brought her up here," Koro says.

"Wouldn't she be looking after her father?" Kuia asks.

"She has an older sister who's staying with them at the moment."

"Then why don't you call her?"

I frown. "I don't think so."

"Seriously," Aroha says, "all joking aside, you should. It sounds as if she's having a tough time. It would do her good to have a day or two away. You know what this place is like. It's very healing."

It's true. There's something about the ocean that has the power to heal.

I pick at the label on the beer bottle. "It's too late now."

"Then get her up tomorrow."

"She wouldn't want to spend Christmas Day with strangers."

"A stranger is just a friend you haven't met yet," Aroha points out.

"I bet she'd like to spend it with you." Koro smiles.

"Why don't you phone her?" Jamie suggests. "Sound her out? She might say she wants to be with her dad anyway. But I bet she'd appreciate a call."

"All right, I'll call her, but just because I was going to ring anyway." Glaring as they all grin, I get to my feet, pick up my phone, and head away from the house, along the sand.

I've been out in the sun all afternoon, and as I'm only wearing swim shorts, the sea breeze is pleasantly cool on my skin. My toes sink into the sand as I walk along the water's edge, scrolling down to Sidnie's name. I pull up the contact, then hesitate. Jamie's right and going away from home might be the last thing she wants to do. Then again, she might enjoy a night away.

Just one night. But what implications does it have? One more date. Asking her here, to a place that's very special to me? To meet my family? That's not something you do with a girl you have no intention of seeing again.

But do I really think I won't see her again?

We all have to grow up sometime.

I press the call button and hold the phone up to my ear.

I'm a great public speaker. I've talked to members of Parliament at the Beehive; I've given lectures at universities; I've spoken at an international conference to over a thousand people.

But I'm nervous calling this gorgeous twenty-two-year-old. Why am I nervous?

"Hello?"

"Hey. It's me. Mack," I add, just in case my name didn't come up on her screen.

She gives that gorgeous giggle. "You think I didn't recognize your voice?"

"I said it without thinking. I'm nervous."

"Why?"

"Because I'm calling you."

"Aw. If it's any consolation, my heart leapt through the roof when I saw your name."

I smile, looking down at where the waves are washing over my feet. "How are you doing?"

"Not too bad. Just watching a movie with the folks."

"How's your dad?"

"It's a good day for him. He's been telling jokes. Excited about Tuesday."

"That's good."

"What are you up to?"

"Standing with my feet in the Pacific, talking to you."

"Sounds idyllic."

"Yeah, kinda."

"Better than South Auckland." She laughs.

I glance over my shoulder toward the house. They're all watching me, although they quickly look away, trying to disguise it. Lips twisting, I look back at the sea.

"I've got something to ask you," I say.

"Oh?"

"It's just an idea, and feel free to say no. But I was wondering whether you'd like to come up to Matauri Bay tomorrow. Spend the day here, or the afternoon at least. And stay the night with me."

She's quiet for a moment. I look up at the stars just beginning to pop out on the darkening sky.

"Of course," I say when I can't bear the silence any longer, "I'm sure you want to stay with your dad right now."

"It's not that," she says quickly. "I mean, I do, but Kate's here, and he's sleeping a lot of the time anyway. Mack, you must understand why I'm hesitant? And why I didn't stay the night at your apartment?"

"Yes, of course. And the last thing I want you to feel is obliged."

"Obliged?"

"Sid, I wasn't born with money. I know how life can be a struggle without it. And I know how difficult it is to accept money when you don't have it. I'd hate for you to feel as if you have to spend time with me as a kind of payment." I stop then. Jesus. Why not call her a prostitute and have done with it?

"Mack," she says softly, "that's not it at all. Although thank you for finally admitting that you were the one who paid the money. That makes me feel a lot better."

I study my feet again.

"The reason I didn't stay the night... and why I'm hesitant to join you..." She sighs. "I don't know how to explain to you what you're like. You must know how people react to you. Felicity compared you to the sun. She said you were dazzling, and that we're all just comets shooting through your solar system."

156

I cover my face with a hand. "Ah, shit."

"Don't blame her, I know what she means. The first time I saw you, striding through your offices, I just thought, wow. You blew me away. Not just your looks—I mean, you're gorgeous—but there's something about you, something magnetic… mesmerizing. It took every ounce of willpower I own to walk away from your apartment. I guess I'm saying I could easily fall for you, if I haven't already. And I know coming up there, spending time with you would be amazing, but it would make it so much harder to walk away."

I pick up a stone and skim it across the top of the water, then slide my hand into the pocket of my shorts. "What if I don't want you to?"

"Do you mean that?"

"Sid, I can't stop thinking about you. Everyone's commenting on it. My family, the guys yesterday… I nearly passed out at the dinner table."

She giggles. "That was a pretty saucy conversation."

"It was, over my Carbonara. I don't know what you've done to me, if it's witchcraft or something. But I'm obsessed."

"You're saying you keep thinking about sex?"

"No. Well, yes. All the time. That can't be a shock when you're texting about covering me in whipped cream and then sucking me dry. But I mean that's not all. I just…" I don't know how to explain myself. I've never done this before. "I miss you," I say simply.

"Oh…" I can hear the smile in her voice. "I miss you too."

"So, will you come up here?"

"Surely your family won't want a stranger intruding?"

"There'll be a lot of people around tomorrow. Probably thirty or so. Nobody will even notice you. It'll just be barbecues and swimming and drinking and then falling asleep in the shade."

"It sounds amazing."

I laugh. "Yeah."

"Have you brought your laptop?"

"Uh, yeah, but I haven't opened it since I got here. I'll check my emails before I go to bed. But I've promised myself no work till I get back on Monday morning."

"So if I say yes, what will happen?"

"I'll pick you up, say, three-ish? Give you time to have lunch with your folks? And then we'll fly up."

"Can you get a flight this late?"

"Sidnie, darling, I have my own plane. And a helicopter, but we can't talk so much in that."

"You have your own plane?"

"Yeah. You can have a glass of champagne on the way."

"Oh my God. I'm totally coming."

My lips curve up. "It's not that good."

"Mack! You've got sex on the brain."

"And you haven't?"

"Might have." She giggles again. "So we'll get to move to Intermediate level, then? Is that possible in the house with all your family around us?"

"We won't stay here—there's a lot of family and not many rooms. I'm in a tent tonight."

"Seriously?"

I grin. "Yeah. Single guy has to kip on the sand. But I won't subject you to that."

"Squeezing into a one-man tent with you might be fun."

I fantasize about it for a moment, then discard it. "No, I'll book us into a hotel nearby. I want you in a bed. And I want walls around us for when I make you scream."

"Ooh, Mack."

"Sidnie, you have to learn that if you tease me, there will be consequences."

"You're going to make me pay?"

"Big time."

"Mm. Now who's the tease?"

I smile. "Three p.m. at your folks' house?"

"Three p.m."

I pause and look up at the moon. "I can't believe it's Christmas Eve."

"I know. I haven't been feeling Christmassy at all, but now I feel as if someone's given me a ginormous parcel with a big red bow, and I can't open it until the morning. I'm so excited."

I chuckle. "You can unwrap me tomorrow."

"Oh, you can count on that."

"Merry Christmas, Sid."

"Merry Christmas, Mack."

I end the call.

Smiling, I turn and walk back to the others. They all look up expectantly as I approach.

"She's coming tomorrow at three," I say.

They all cheer, and I laugh and sit back in my deckchair. "You have to promise not to overwhelm her," I tell them.

"We won't." Aroha grins. "You're smiling."

I scowl. "No I'm not."

She reaches over to squeeze my knee. "She's obviously good for you."

"Yeah, yeah." I get up again. "I'm going to play cards with my cousins." I go inside, where the two girls and the other kids are setting up a game around the table.

Just like Sidnie, I feel as if tomorrow is a glittering present Santa's left under the tree. I can't wait to see what lies beneath the shiny paper.

*

I pull up outside Sidnie's parents' house on Christmas Day just before three. Just me today—I left Jamie in Matauri Bay.

As I put the handbrake on, the front door opens, and Sidnie comes out. She looks amazing in an above-the-knee bright orange beach dress, but she doesn't have a bag. I lower the window as she comes up to the car, hoping she hasn't changed her mind.

"Everything all right?" I ask.

She bends down and leans on the sill. "I'm so sorry. Mum and Dad have asked if you'd come in for a second."

"Oh. Sure." I unbuckle myself.

"They want to ask you about your prospects," she says, straightening as I open the door. I give her a wry look as I get out. "Not really," she adds. "But they do want to say thank you."

I lock the car, then hesitate. "That's not necessary."

"I know. I told them it'll be embarrassing for you. But they think it's the least they can do. And they want to meet the guy who has their girl all a-quiver."

I move a bit closer to her and hold her hand. "I make you all a-quiver?" I bend my head to kiss her.

She lets me, then moves back and scolds, "They're watching us. Didn't you see the curtains twitch?"

I laugh and let her lead me up the path and into the house.

We enter a small hallway, and then go through a door into the living room. Wow, it's tiny. Six people are standing there, all looking at me eagerly.

"Everyone, this is Mack. Mack, this is my sister, Kate." She indicates a slightly older version of herself without the wild hair.

"Hello, Mack." Kate shakes my hand, looking at me with big eyes. "Wow, you're gorgeous."

"Jesus." Sidnie glares at her as I try not to laugh. "Your husband is standing right here. This is Liam."

I shake hands with a guy around the same age as me, with a brown beard and kind blue eyes who looks unbothered that his wife has just complimented me in front of him.

"Hey, Mack," he says, "good to meet you."

"This is Julia," Sidnie states, putting her hands on the shoulders of a young girl, maybe seven or eight years old.

"You're an All Blacks fan," I state, smiling at her rugby top.

"I got it for Christmas," she says, and blushes.

Sidnie smiles. "And this is my brother, Dan."

Unfortunately Dan has inherited the curly hair, although his is light brown, and he crops it very short. He's obviously the middle kid. I smile, although I'm not sure what to make of him. I know he's the one who connected Sidnie with the so-called Socrates. Sidnie said it was at a nightclub, and I have a sneaky feeling Socrates is a drug dealer, which doesn't bode well for Dan.

"Pleased to meet you," Dan says.

"This is my mum, Jane." Sidnie indicates a woman in her early fifties. She's the origin of the curly hair, although hers is now gray, and she pulls it back tightly into a ponytail. She's still attractive, and her eyes sparkle as she shakes my hand. "It's so good to meet you," she says. "We've heard a lot about you."

"No we haven't," Kate says. "Sid won't tell us anything."

I grin. Sidnie rolls her eyes and turns to the last man in the room. "Mack, this is my dad, Craig," she says unnecessarily.

Craig is mid-fifties with a receding hairline. He looks tired, and his T-shirt hangs on him, suggesting he's lost weight. But his smile is bright, and when I shake his hand, he rests the other one on top of it and keeps it there.

"I'm so pleased to meet you," he says.

"Likewise."

"You're so young. Much younger than I thought."

I smile. "Thank you."

He's still holding my hand. Looking into my eyes, he swallows hard. "I don't know how to say thank you."

"You just have, and you're very welcome."

He finally releases my hand, but I can see he's choked up. Jane moves closer to him and rubs his arm, while sending me a rueful smile.

"You're going through a very tough time," I tell them. "I understand how you feel. My dad also had prostate cancer." I feel Sidnie's gaze on me, but I don't look at her.

"I'm sorry," Jane says. "Is he... okay?"

"Unfortunately it was many years ago, and it wasn't discovered until it was too late. He died. It's partly why I try to help others in the same situation—because I know what it feels like. It's appalling that so many drugs aren't funded in this country when you can just cross the Ditch and they have them all." It is frustrating that many of the drugs we can't get here are available in Australia.

"That's right," Jane says, "that's how we feel."

"It was such a shock to be told the best drug for me wasn't funded," Craig says. "The oncologist said we should try to find the money, but it's a huge responsibility to put on my family. I was all for just saying screw it, I'm done, but they wanted to try and raise the money, and then I'm the cruel one for refusing to fight, you know?"

"It's tough all ways round," I say, as Jane's face reddens. "Most men are raised to believe it's their responsibility to provide for the family, and I'm sure it doesn't come easy to make the conscious decision to put them in debt."

"I won't have to now," he says. "Thanks to you."

"I'm glad I could help." My throat tightens at his obvious gratitude.

"Anyway, we should be off," Sidnie announces, sliding her hand into mine.

"It was so nice to meet you," Jane says.

"Good luck with the treatment," I reply. "I hope it goes well."

I wave goodbye, and we head out into the hallway. I pick up Sidnie's bag, scolding her as she tries to take it from me, then say, "Christ, what have you got in here? Lead-lined shorts?"

"Ha-ha. Mum made me bring a large tin of Cadbury's Roses for everyone."

"Sidnie, we have so much food we'll be eating until March."

"I know, but we're big on manners."

I unlock the car, put her bag in the back, and we get in. I start the Aston and pull away, and drive to the end of the road.

Checking to make sure there's nothing behind me, I stop at the Give Way sign, leave the car idling, and turn to face her.

"Hello," she says.

"Hi."

She tucks a curl behind her ear. It immediately springs free.

"Thank you," she says, "for coming in. It meant a lot to them."

"It's fine. It was nice to put faces to names."

"You're wonderful."

I chuckle. "Because I said hi to your folks?"

She just gives me a helpless look.

"Come here," I murmur, and I slide a hand to the back of her head and hold her there while I lean forward and kiss her.

Her lips are warm and sweet, and I kiss her several times before pulling away reluctantly. "Hold that thought."

Chapter Sixteen

Sidnie

It's only a short trip to the airport. Mack parks the Aston, and then we walk over to the terminal. It's the first time I've ever been able to walk past the queues of passengers waiting restlessly for delayed flights. Instead Mack speaks to a flight attendant at a separate desk, and then we go onto the tarmac to a small plane. A guy in a smart navy suit is waiting by the steps, and he smiles as we walk up.

"Will, this is Sidnie," Mack says. "Sidnie, this is Will Ferrers, our flight attendant."

"Pleased to meet you, ma'am," Will says. "Welcome on board."

And so begins my first journey in a private jet. The interior is all cream and light gray, and the eight chairs are tan leather. Mack and I sit opposite each other across a table, and we buckle ourselves in as the pilot announces that we're prepared for takeoff and will be landing at the Bay of Islands airport just after 1.15 p.m.

Will checks our seatbelts, does a brief safety talk, then takes his seat toward the back of the plane as it goes down the runway. Just a few minutes later we're up in the sky, surrounded by fluffy white clouds.

Will releases himself from his belt then comes up and asks, "Can I get you a drink?"

"Champagne?" Mack asks me. I nod, trying to act as if I do this all the time.

"And anything to eat?"

"No thanks," Mack says when I shake my head. "We'll be eating tonight."

Will goes off, and soon we hear the popping of a cork.

"Doesn't he mind working on Christmas Day?" I murmur.

"He knows he's on call over the weekend. Don't worry, I make it worth his while."

Wondering how big a bonus he pays him, I smile as Will brings our glasses over, then returns to the back of the plane.

Mack holds up his glass, and I tap mine to it. "Cheers," he says.

"Cheers." I sip the Champagne, studying him over the rim of my glass. He's wearing navy cargo pants and a short-sleeved white shirt. I can't imagine he was wearing that on the beach, which means he changed to come and see me. He's obviously been out in the sun because his light-brown skin bears a sun-kissed glow that wasn't there before. He looks young, healthy, and gorgeous.

"Don't look at me like that," he says wryly.

"Like what?"

"Like you want me as a trimming for your Christmas dinner."

"I feel another joke about stuffing coming on."

He chuckles. "How are you?" he asks softly. "Really, I mean?"

"Okay. Dad wasn't as good today. He was in quite a bit of pain. Mum cried this morning."

"Aw."

"Dinner was a bit of a sorry affair; none of us ate much. Dad will probably spend most of the evening dozing."

"Your mum didn't mind you going?"

"No. I asked her and Kate if they would rather I stay, but they both told me to go." I don't add that Kate's reaction was, "Sid, he's loaded. Jesus, of course you have to go!"

I know he's worried I feel obligated because of what he did, and that makes me sad. I don't want either of us to think about his money when we're together.

Still, there's something I have to say about that before I close the subject. "Mack, you've admitted you paid for the treatment. That obviously means you knew about my dad before you took me to breakfast. How did you find out? Was it the FBI?"

"In New Zealand? No, Sid, I doubt you have an FBI file."

"Then how? Please. I'm curious. I don't blame you for finding out, in fact I'm glad you did. I won't tell anyone."

"Okay. I Googled you."

"What?" I hadn't expected it to be that simple.

He sighs. "I like to think I'm a good judge of character. When I calmed down, it occurred to me that I couldn't imagine you wanting the money just to pay off your student loan. There had to be another reason you'd need a large amount of money quickly. I Googled you, discovered the names of your parents and siblings, Googled them, and found the GoFundMe account. It wasn't rocket science."

I can't imagine where on Google he'd find out the names of my family. "How did you... Oh, never mind." I keep forgetting he's a computer genius. It wouldn't surprise me if he opened the Internet, reached in, and just took the information out. At least I know now.

There's one more thing I've been meaning to ask him. "Have you looked into Socrates' phone number?" I ask.

He nods. "It's a burner SIM. He probably switches it out as soon as he's called you. No way of tracking who it belongs to."

"That's a shame." I feel a stab of guilt, wishing he could have found him.

"Forget about him," he says firmly. "I'm not devoting a single second of my time to him."

I nod. "I'm sorry to hear about your dad," I say, changing the subject. I was surprised he revealed that to my family, but I could see my father getting choked up, and I know Mack was trying to reach out to him. "How old were you when he died?"

"Twenty. Only two months before I sold to Intel."

"Just before you got your money. That sucks."

"Yeah, well, even if I'd had the money I do now, I don't know that it would have made any difference. But I can't help but blame myself that I wasn't able to help."

"It was hardly your fault."

"I know. It's not a rational thought." He sips his Champagne, studying me. "You look lovely today."

He wants to change the subject. I'm happy to be paid compliments. "Thank you."

"I hope you've brought your togs."

"I'm wearing my bikini under my dress."

He inhales, then blows out a long breath, and I giggle.

"Have you been to Matauri Bay before?" he asks.

We talk for a while about the Northland, and it seems like no time at all before the pilot is announcing he's beginning the descent, Will clears our glasses and buckles himself in, and the plane lands.

We say goodbye to Will, and Mack thanks the pilot, and then we head out into the hot sub-tropical weather.

Jamie's waiting for us in a silver Ford Everest. "Koro's car," Mack says as we walk toward it.

SERENITY WOODS

"Oh, Jamie won't have been able to have a drink on Christmas Day," I say, feeling guilty.

"He doesn't drink," Mack says. "Never has."

It's too late for me to ask why, as Mack's opening the door for me, and I get into the car. "Hey Jamie!"

"Hey Sidnie. So cool you could join us."

"I'm really touched to be asked," I reply, buckling myself in.

"Couldn't not," he says. "Mack was moping."

"Shut up." Mack gets in beside me.

I laugh. "Me too." I lean over and kiss his cheek. Before I can move back, he slips a hand to the back of my neck, holds me there, and kisses me again, long and lovingly.

When he eventually lets me go, I press my lips together and look at Jamie, who's pulling out of the car park. He glances in the rear-view mirror and smiles.

"So how many people are there today?" I ask as we pass kiwi fruit and mandarin orchards, and stalls that would normally be selling plantains, cherries, and strawberries if it wasn't Christmas Day.

"I dunno," Mack says. "Thirty? Thirty-five?"

"More than that," Jamie says. "Another ten or so arrived this afternoon."

"Wow," I say nervously. "I don't know that many people in total."

"We have a big extended family," Mack says. "Lots of aunts, uncles, and cousins. Don't worry, nobody will even notice you're there, I'm sure."

Yeah, *right.* Jamie drives along the road that follows the beach, then finally slows and turns onto a drive beside a large house just across the road from the sand. Lots of people are sitting on the deck, talking, eating, and drinking, their paper hats from the crackers fluttering in the breeze, and some of the kids are wearing headbands with reindeer ears. More are playing rugby on the beach or splashing around in the sea. A big Christmas tree stands in the window, and another one leans at an angle on the beach, trailing tinsel on the sand. Loud music floats along the beach on the summer air. A typical Kiwi Christmas.

As I get out of the car, Gus bounds up to me, and I bend and fuss him. Then I have to stop, as everyone wants to come up and say hello.

I must shake hands with fifty or sixty people, and I rapidly lose track of their names. Eventually we come to the end, and Jamie's girlfriend, Emma, says, "I'm so sorry, that must have been a bit overwhelming,

166

come and sit with me." I follow her to the table and take a seat beside her, not far from Koro and Kuia—Mack's grandparents.

Koro is in his seventies, a quiet, tall Māori guy who gave Mack a big hug when he walked up to him. Kuia is a typical grandmother—plump, cheery, and obviously the matriarch of the family, bossing everyone around and filling the air with her hearty laughs.

Mack vanished a couple of minutes ago, and I look around for him, but can't see him anywhere. Shrugging, I accept a glass of wine from one of his aunts with a smile. "He said nobody would even notice I'm here," I say, sipping the wine.

"He was fibbing," Emma states. "Everyone was excited to meet you."

"Why? I'm hardly anything special."

"Because you're the first girl he's ever brought up here," Kuia says.

"Oh." That surprises me. "He never brought Felicity here?"

"Who?" Kuia asks.

Jamie snorts. "Noooo. He was never serious about her."

My heart leaps. He's serious about me? We've only had two dates; we've only slept together once.

"That's better." Mack comes out of the house, rests his hand on the back of my chair, and leans past me to help himself to a mince pie from the plate in the middle of the table. Ooh, he's taken off his shirt and changed into swim shorts. His torso and legs are bare. He smells divine.

He eats half the mince pie in one go and looks down at me. "Fancy a swim?"

"Sure. I should put some lotion on first or I'll burn to a crisp." I reach into my bag and extract the bottle, then stand and follow him to one side of the deck in the shade. He goes over to pick up two beach towels, and I peel my beach dress up and toss it over the back of a nearby chair.

He turns back, and his eyes nearly fall out of his head. "Whoa."

"What?" I ask innocently. "It's just a bikini."

"You've got to warn me when you're going to do that."

Smirking, I squirt some lotion on my hands and rub it over my arms, chest, and face.

"Give it here," he says, and he pours some onto his hands, rubs them together, then moves behind me. Placing his hands either side of my neck, he draws the lotion over my shoulders, then down my back, slowly smoothing it in.

I glance over at the table. They're all watching us and grinning.

"I think you've rubbed it in enough," I say.

"Mm, I missed a bit." He chuckles, brushes his hands down my arms, then slides his hands around my waist. I lean back against his warm chest and look over my shoulder at him, and he lowers his head and kisses me.

Then he lets me go, takes my hand, and says, "Come on! The sea's waiting," and we run down the sand to the water, Gus bounding at our heels.

It's warm in the shallows, cooler further out. Mack runs and dives in headfirst, Gus right next to him. I follow a bit more sedately before I lower myself down and push out. It's glorious, a mix of sensations, with the sun hot on my face, and the cold water swirling over my skin.

Mack surfaces right next to me, showering me with droplets, then pulls me into his arms and kisses me, his mouth slanting across mine, sending my heart racing.

"Everyone's watching," I scold, lifting my arms around his neck.

"Don't give a fuck." He kisses me again. "I missed you."

"Mm. I missed you too." I let him spin me around in the water, happier than I have been in a long time.

"Stop that you two." Jamie dives into the water nearby, splashing us and Gus, and Emma laughs as she swims up.

"Shoulders wars," she yells, pulling two pool noodles with her.

"Oh no." I squeal as Mack dives under the water, swims beneath me, then lifts up so I'm on his shoulders.

Emma tosses me a noodle, then shrieks as Jamie lifts her, too. "No bashing, only poking," she advises.

"Sounds like my kind of game," Mack says, and I giggle.

We proceed to battle, with much yelling and numerous overbalancings and falling into the sea. Gus swims to the shore and leaps around barking at us. By the time we stop, I'm exhausted and completely soaked.

Mack takes my hand and pulls me to shore, then picks up one of the beach towels he left there and wraps me in it. "Come here," he says, and he pulls me into his arms and rubs my back. His wet hair has turned spiky, and his light-brown skin glistens with water droplets.

He's the very epitome of health and beauty. Such a contrast to my father, who's so tired and weak and pale.

I lean against him, and he tightens his arms. "You okay?"

"A bit tired."

He kisses the top of my head. "You need something to eat and drink."

"Mm." I turn my head and kiss his chest. "I am quite hungry."

"Come on." With his arm still around me, he leads me up to the house.

I quickly change into another beach dress, this one a pretty light blue, and attempt to tame my hair with a butterfly clip. Then I rejoin the others, letting Mack guide me to a seat and pour me a glass of wine.

Apparently some of his cousins have been out on the boat, fishing, and it arrives back laden with snapper, mussels, crabs, and even a huge kingfish that they set to cleaning down on the rocks.

Koro fires up the barbecue, and Aroha chops some of the mussels and mixes them with a batter to make fritters. I don't eat seafood, but the wonderful smell of cooked food still makes my stomach rumble. I offer to help, but Kuia and her daughters wave me away, so I sit and chat with Mack, Jamie, Emma, and some of their cousins until dinner's ready. It's not long before the table is loaded with heaps of steaming fish, mussel fritters, orange kumara or sweet potato that's been baked in foil, vegetable kebabs, barbecued corn on the cob, and several large salads.

When she discovers that I'm also vegetarian, Kuia cuts open the baked kumara and mashes the inside with butter and cheese, then takes the grilled vegetables off the skewers and piles them on top, adds a barbecued corn on the cob, a couple of large mushrooms that have been stuffed with a breadcrumb and Parmesan mixture and then grilled, and two slices of homemade cheesy bread smothered in butter.

I eat until I can't eat any more, feeling a lot better once I have some food in my stomach. Emma plies me with wine, and by the time the sky begins to darken, I feel content and chilled.

Someone lights citronella candles all around the deck, and one of Mack's cousins produces a guitar and proceeds to strum some carols and Christmas songs that everyone sings to.

There's a swing seat just in front of the house, and Mack and I end up on that, with Jamie and Emma sitting opposite us, Gus at our feet, and a few others of our own age scattered around. I curl up next to

Mack, and look up at him to see him staring off into the distance, lost in thought.

"Are you calculating Pi to a thousand decimal places or something?" I ask, and Emma chuckles.

He brings his gaze back to me and lowers his mouth to my ear. "No. Just thinking about a plan of action."

"Oh?"

"For tonight."

Ooh, he means when we get to the hotel. A shiver runs down my spine. How exciting.

I'm just about to ask for more details when his younger cousins bound up and try to persuade him to get up and boogie with them. He insists, "You know I don't dance."

"You danced with me," I point out, and the girls' eyes widen.

"If you danced with your girlfriend, you can dance with us," one of them insists.

But Kuia shoos them away, saying, "Stop bothering him. He's having a well-earned rest," and they sigh and go off to play on the sand with Gus.

It leaves me with a little buzz in my stomach, though. Am I his girlfriend? He didn't argue.

The sky darkens, and everyone grows merry as wine and beer and whiskey flows. Someone lights up a joint, which doesn't surprise me as marijuana grows in abundance all over the Northland. When it gets to Mack, he takes it but passes it to me.

"You're not smoking?" I ask, shaking my head, not wanting to if he isn't.

"Nah." He passes it to someone else. "It makes me fuzzy."

"Alcohol doesn't?" After having a few beers, he brought out a bottle of whiskey that must have been rare and expensive, judging by the oohs and aahs from the guys. One of the cousins is pouring it out now.

"Alcohol speeds me up." Sure enough, his foot is tapping, and his knee is bouncing rapidly. He's radiating energy. I'm surprised he's not glowing. He meets my gaze, and it's like I've stuck a fork in an electric socket, sending a delicious shock all the way through me. He's thinking about having sex again. With me. Ooh.

"Here you go," the guy says, coming up and handing Mack a tumbler of the amber liquid, and me another glass of wine. It's my third, or is it my fourth? I feel very merry and relaxed and excited too about going back to the hotel with him.

"Are you watching the All Blacks at the weekend?" Jamie asks Mack.

"The Lions match in London? Yeah, probably." Mack's pulled on a T-shirt to combat the evening chill, and he's sitting now with his legs stretched out, rocking us a little with his bare feet. He has a swig of his whiskey.

"They were talking about that rear tackle the Aussie prop made," Jamie continues. "They said it was a… um…" He clicks his fingers, trying to remember the word.

"Reach around?" I suggest.

Mack coughs into his whiskey, Emma giggles, and the others burst out laughing.

"Sorry." I press my fingers to my lips. "Did I say that out loud?"

Mack wipes his mouth on the back of his hand and gives me a wry look. "Don't do that."

"I said sorry," I say cheekily.

His eyelids drop to half-mast, and then he slides a hand into my hair to hold my head and kisses me. I blush as everyone cheers.

He lifts his head, ignoring the others, and murmurs to me, "We'll finish these drinks, then head off, I think." His eyes glitter in the candlelight.

"Okay," I say into his ear. "I'm very tired. I'm looking forward to a good night's sleep."

He's getting the hang of my sense of humor now, though, because he just smirks.

It takes us another half an hour to finish our drinks, collect our stuff, and say goodbye. Everyone comes to give us a hug and kiss. Koro and Kuia are the last, and they give me a kiss and then Mack a big hug.

"You take care now," Koro says fiercely. "Don't be a stranger. And don't work too hard."

"I won't," Mack promises, giving my hand a squeeze down by our sides.

"You keep him busy," Kuia tells me, "keep him out of the office."

"I'll do my best," I promise with a smile.

"It was lovely to meet you," she says. "I've never seen him smile so much. You're obviously good for him."

Mack rolls his eyes and puts Gus in the back of the car, then gets in, and I laugh and slide into the back beside him.

Jamie and Emma are with us, and they're also going to be staying at the hotel. Jamie starts the car, and we all wave as he reverses out, then heads up the road.

"Jesus," Mack says, "I'm sorry about that. I didn't expect them to be quite so interested in you."

"It's fine. I had a lovely time. And it's a wonderful house and location."

"I can't imagine waking up every morning with that view," Emma says. "Not that ours is bad!"

"Do you think you'll always live in the city?" I ask Mack.

"I don't know. I used to think so, but..." He trails off and looks out of the window.

Jamie glances at him in the rear-view mirror, then smiles at me, before looking back at the road.

"Have you got a busy week ahead?" Emma asks Mack.

"Yeah. We need to finalize a project by Friday, so it's all systems go when we get back to the office."

"What are you working on?" I ask.

"A new microprocessor."

Once again, Jamie glances at him and frowns. I have a feeling Mack isn't telling me something. I know he's working with Elizabeth, and he told me she owns MediTechNZ. Is it something medical? I think about the invitation in his rubbish bin, and his nomination for the MacDiarmid Award. Clearly it's some kind of secret project, and he doesn't know me well enough yet to reveal it.

Well, that's okay. We've only been on a couple of dates, even though he invited me to his family home. And I haven't forgotten that I was sent to spy on him. He's been exceptionally forgiving. I'm not going to complain if he doesn't quite feel ready to divulge all his business secrets yet.

Chapter Seventeen

Sidnie

It turns out to be a thirty-minute drive to a hotel near Paihia in the Bay of Islands. I hadn't expected we'd go that far, but when Jamie pulls up out the front, I can see why Mack decided to come here. It's small but exclusive, the units overlooking a selection of hot pools, and then beyond them the Bay, the ocean sparkling in the moonlight.

"I'm amazed you got two rooms," I say as we retrieve our bags. "I thought everywhere was booked at this time of year."

"Mack knows the owner," Jamie says. "He was able to shuffle some bookings around and make space."

"And Gus is welcome here?"

"Yeah, Mack will make it worth his while."

Money certainly does seem to solve most problems.

"I'll check us in," Mack says, walking across to the receptionist, and Jamie goes with him.

I stand with Emma and our bags, holding Gus's leash. Emma smiles at me. "It was good of you to come."

"I can't believe he asked me," I say softly, looking across at him. He's signing the check-in document. Oh, he's a leftie! I didn't know that.

"He seems completely captivated by you," she says. "I've never seen him like this."

"Oh." My face warms. "How long have you known him?"

"Jamie and I have been dating three years now."

"Have you met many of his girlfriends?" I smile as her lips twist. "It's okay, I know there have probably been a lot."

"No, quite the opposite. I mean, I'm not saying he's been a saint. Have you met the others at Huxley's?"

"Huxley himself, yes, and Victoria, Elizabeth, and Titus."

"What about Kai?"

"No, who's he?"

"One of the directors at Koru Tech. They all went to the University of Auckland together. Mack, Kai, and Titus did computer engineering; Huxley and Victoria did a business degree; Elizabeth did chemistry, I think. But they all met at some party and clicked. They're all geniuses in their own way, and they all worked hard and played hard. I think for a few years it was all sex and drugs and rock'n'roll, you know? Alongside the work, of course. They all work incredibly hard, but especially Mack. The guy's a force of nature."

"Tell me about it." We watch the two of them walk back to us, carrying the key cards to the rooms.

"I see you're a leftie," I say as we wait for the elevator. "Trust you to have deviant behavior."

Jamie and Emma laugh. Mack's eyes gleam, and as the door opens and I walk past him, he smacks my butt.

"Ow."

"Then behave."

I settle Gus beside me, and then my eyes meet Mack's as the doors close and the elevator rises. Jamie's busy nuzzling Emma's neck as he whispers to her. I poke my tongue out at Mack. He lifts an eyebrow. I can see the energy fizzing away inside him. I think I'm about to get soundly screwed.

Ooh.

The doors ping and open, and we walk along the corridor to the two rooms that are next to each other.

"See you at breakfast?" Jamie asks.

"Yeah, how about eight a.m.?" Mack suggests.

"Sounds good. Goodnight."

We all wave, then disappear into our rooms.

The room is huge, and the front wall is all glass, looking out at the view of the Pacific. There's a king-size bed covered in a plush white duvet, a sofa and chairs, and a kitchenette, and a beautiful bathroom through a side door all decked out in white marble.

"It's gorgeous," I say, putting my bag down. "Thank you so much for this, Mack."

"I'm just glad you came." He puts his bag and Gus's bed down, then walks over to me and pulls me into his arms. "At last," he murmurs, "I have you to myself."

I put my arms around his neck. "I'm all yours."

"That might be the nicest thing anyone's ever said to me."

We both chuckle, then he lowers his lips to mine and we exchange a leisurely kiss.

When he eventually moves back, I run my hands through my hair and wince. "I might take a quick shower. My hair's full of sand and all sticky from the sea."

"Sure—or would you prefer a bath? It's big enough for both of us."

"Ooh, that would be nice. First, though, do you mind if I ring home? I just want to check they're all okay."

"Of course. Look, I'll set the bath running, then take Gus out for a last quick walk. By the time I come back the bath should be done."

"Okay."

He puts the plug in the bath and turns the taps on, then grabs Gus's lead. He gives me a quick kiss, then leaves, the door closing slowly behind him.

I retrieve my phone and go onto the balcony as I call my parents' house. I watch Mack and Gus exit the front of the hotel and cross the path to the grassy verge above the beach. Mack strides out, as usual, Gus having to jog to keep up with him.

"Hello?" It's Kate.

"It's only me."

"What are you calling for? I thought you'd be partying the night away."

"Just wanted to check up on everyone."

"Aw," she says, and I can tell she's smiling. "We're all right. We've just finished watching a movie, and we're having supper now. Dad perked up a bit after his sleep and said he was hungry. They're cheerful enough."

"And are you and Liam okay?"

"We're fine, Sid. Stop worrying."

"Okay."

"Go and enjoy yourself. You deserve it." She hesitates. "I'm sorry it's been such a strain on you. It's not fair. I feel guilty that I haven't been able to help."

I trail a toe through the dusting of sand on the tiles. It's true that it's been a tough couple of months with repeated visits to GPs and specialists, as well as all the stress with the money. But it's not her fault. Liam is Australian and has a big family over there, and she now has a job there, so it's not as if she can just drop everything to come over to New Zealand whenever she feels like it. I'm lucky she's here at all.

"It's fine," I say. "We managed."

"Well, anyway, I'm glad to be able to help while I'm here. Are you having a good time?"

"Oh yeah. We spent the afternoon at the beach, and now we're in a hotel in Paihia. It's gorgeous, right on the seafront."

"I guess there are some benefits to going with a billionaire," she teases.

I examine my fingernails. "It's not about his money."

She sighs. "I'm sorry."

"I know he paid for Dad's treatment, but I don't want it to be about that. He doesn't want me to feel obliged to go out with him, you know? And I don't want to think about his money. It's just crass."

"Yeah, I shouldn't have mentioned it."

"I like him, Kate. He's smart and funny and hot, and I think he'd make me feel like a million dollars even if he didn't have a cent to his name."

"Aw, you're so sweet. Well, go and have a great evening. You're coming back tomorrow, right?"

"Yeah, mid-morning I think."

"We'll see you then. Take care."

"You too."

"Have a great time with him. If you can still walk tomorrow, I'll know you didn't give a hundred percent."

"Kate! Jeez. Love to everyone." I end the call, rolling my eyes.

Below me, Mack and Gus are making their way back. Mack looks up, sees me, and blows me a kiss. I do the same, warming through, then go back inside to make sure the bath isn't running over.

It's half full, so I turn off the taps. There aren't any bath salts or anything, which seems strange, but there's a container of shower gel, so I pump a couple of handfuls of that into the water and swoosh it about a bit to make a few bubbles.

The front door opens, and I go back into the living room to see Mack come in with a wagging Gus. "Nighttime biscuit, then bed," Mack informs him, pulling a packet out of his bag and producing a doggy biscuit. Gus sits, then takes it back to his bed, turns around half a dozen times, and finally settles down to crunch happily.

"It smells great out there." Mack pours some cold water into a bowl and puts it on the tiles for Gus. "Jasmine all along the front of the hotel, lemons on the trees, and the salt from the sea. It smells like freedom." He chuckles. "You want a drink? I thought I'd call room service."

"Mm, yes please."

"G&T?"

"Ooh yes."

"Want anything to eat? I might get a sandwich."

"You've got hollow legs. I'm fine, thank you."

He makes the call, and I go into the bathroom and start taking off my jewelry. A few moments later, he comes in, goes over to the bath, and presses a button on the side. A loud hum begins, and then jets start shooting bubbles through the water.

"Oh! I didn't realize it was a spa bath." I'm excited. I've never been in one before.

I go into the living room to plug in my phone, and he follows me, then pulls me into his arms again. "I've been thinking about this all day," he murmurs, sliding his hands down over my hips and kissing up my jaw to my ear.

"I'm all sandy," I whisper.

"You smell of summer." He nuzzles my ear, then bends and picks me up.

I squeal. "You'll drop me!"

"What do you weigh? A hundred and twenty pounds?" he scoffs.

"I'm five foot ten—if I weighed a hundred and twenty pounds you'd miss me if I turned sideways. I weigh distinctly more than that."

"Good job I'm six two then." He turns, sits on the bed, and lies back so I'm on top.

I kiss him, and he sinks his hands into my hair, then laughs as his fingers get caught in the sticky curls. "I see what you mean."

"I know. It's disgusting, sorry. It's like seaweed."

"It's not like seaweed. It's beautiful." He kisses me. "You're beautiful." He looks into my eyes for a long moment, and my heart bangs on my ribs. He opens his mouth to say something, but at that moment there's a knock on the door, and Gus barks. "Room service," he says. "Can you hold Gus?"

I lift off him and pick up Gus's lead, and Mack goes to the door to let the guy bring in the tray with our drinks and his sandwiches. We don't normally tip in New Zealand, but I spot Mack giving him a folded note, and the guy says, "Oh, thank you, sir," before heading out.

"These look good," Mack says. "Mind if I eat in the bath?"

I laugh. "Not at all. The idea of having the G&T in there is quite—oh!" I stop at the entrance to the bathroom and clap a hand over my mouth.

He follows me with the tray and stares, then starts laughing.

"I didn't know it was a spa bath," I say meekly. "I put some shower gel in."

The bath is filled with bubbles. There are so many that they're spilling out onto the floor and floating in the air.

"At least it's a wet room," he says. He picks up the lighter and lights the candles on the shelf above the bath, then turns off the lights. The candles make the bubbles glitter and sparkle. "It looks very Christmassy, like a grotto."

"I'm so sorry," I say, guilty at having almost flooded the place.

He puts the tray on the marble step by the bath, then pulls me against him, still chuckling. "Come here," he murmurs, and he kisses me, while down at my thighs he begins to catch the material of my dress up in his fingers. When he's gathered it all, he lifts it up my body, draws it over my head, and tosses the garment into the bedroom.

I do the same with his T-shirt, and then he takes off his shorts, while I remove my underwear. Now we're both naked, and my pulse picks up as he slides his arms around my waist, and we're skin against skin. He gives me a long, luscious kiss, then moves back and gestures at the bath. "After you."

"How ingenious putting the tap in the middle," I say, sitting on the edge and swinging my legs over. "Very thoughtful." I lower myself down to the right, laughing as the bubbles almost engulf me.

Mack gets in the left-hand side and sinks down. The water is now three-quarters of the way up the bath, hot and bubbling. It's heavenly.

He leans over the edge to collect the drinks and passes me mine, and we clink glasses before leaning back and taking a sip. The cool alcohol is a welcome contrast to the heat of the bath, and I hold the glass to my face as he reaches over again to fetch the plate.

He offers it to me. Actually, the sandwiches look yummy, and I give in and take one. I nibble mine, while he eats half in one go.

"This is fun," he says, amused.

"I've never spent a Christmas Day like it."

"Me neither."

"Thank you so much for asking me to spend the day with you. I've had such a lovely time."

"I'm glad. My family thought you were wonderful. Mind you, I'm not surprised." He leans over for another sandwich.

I finish mine, then have another sip of the G&T. "I don't know what I've done to deserve you. I feel like Cinderella."

"I wonder whether she knew not to put foam in a spa bath?" I poke my tongue out at him, and he chuckles. "Want another sandwich?"

"No, thanks. You have a big appetite."

"I do." He smirks.

I lean back with my drink. He's lying back too, with his legs wide apart around mine. I slide my right foot up his thigh, stopping just short of exploring with my toes.

"Careful," he says. "Or I'll drop the soap and have to find it again."

"I'm banking on it."

He gives a short laugh and reaches for the last sandwich. "Don't look at me like that," he says to Gus, who's standing on the marble step, staring at him. "You've had your biscuit."

"Aw, Daddy. It's Christmas," I say, and he sighs, eats three-quarters of it, then offers the last bit to the spaniel. Gus eats it, although I'm sure he'd rather have had some meat in it.

I scoop up some bubbles and put them on Gus's head. He chases them about for a while, then finally gets bored and wanders out back to his bed

"Look, I'm Santa," Mack says, piling bubbles on his head, then adding a beard.

I giggle, put down my drink, and pick up a small handful. "You need a mustache." I lean forward and place a thin line of the bubbles above his top lip.

Before I can stop him, he slides an arm around me and kisses me. When I move back, I'm now wearing the beard and most of the bubbly hair, and we both laugh.

I return to my end of the bath, and we sit there for a while, sipping our drinks. I can feel my pulse gradually speeding up. The promise of great sex hangs in the air between us like the bubbles that are sparkling in the candlelight. Mack's leaning back, resting his arms on the edge of the bath. He has impressive, defined biceps—I'm guessing he does weights as part of his workout. His dark tattoo glistens on his light-brown skin. He has a five o'clock shadow, and although I love that he's usually clean shaven, I like that hint of manly stubble.

"You've caught the sun," he says.

I touch a hand to my nose. I put lotion on it, but it's still a bit pink. "You could even say it glows."

He chuckles.

I have a mouthful of G&T. I feel relaxed and content and excited and turned on, all rolled into one. His eyelids have slipped to half-mast, and his eyes have that lazy look to them that tells me he's thinking something naughty.

"Tell me what you want to do to me," I say softly.

His lips curve up, and he caresses me with his gaze. "I want to make love to you for as long as I can. All night, if possible."

The thought thrills me, but, feeling naughty, I shake my head. "No. Tell me what you really want. We're at intermediate now, remember?"

"Define intermediate."

"More explicit language. More intimate details."

He cocks his head. "Like... I've been thinking about fucking you senseless all day?"

I inhale. "Yeah, that'll do it."

"I haven't been able to stop thinking about you. About being inside you." His eyes glitter. "I want to make you come over and over again, until you can't take it anymore. Until you're so exhausted from being pleasured that you're begging me to stop."

I exhale in a rush, resting my cheek on my glass. "Mmmm..."

He finishes off his drink and leans over to put the glass on the tray. Then he lies back again and beckons me toward him.

I finish my drink too, put the glass on the tray, and move up the bath. He twirls a finger, and I turn so my back is to his chest, and he pulls me back into his arms. The hot water swirls around us, and clouds of bubbles float up into the air.

"That's all true," he murmurs, tightening his arms around me as he kisses my neck. "But I do want to make love to you. Slowly. Taking my time. I want to make the most of you. I feel so lucky to have you here, in my arms. I'm going to worship your body tonight, Sidnie. You don't have to do anything. I want to make you feel like a queen. I want to love you until all you can think about is me. Until I fill your mind, your body, even your soul."

I lean my head back on his shoulder and close my eyes as he brushes his hands down over my belly and thighs. "Mmm."

"Can I wash your hair?"

I smile. "If you like."

So he proceeds to wash it, soaking it first, then reaching for the shampoo and pouring a little into his hand. He rubs his hands together, then slides his fingers into my curls and gently massages it in.

He takes a long time to do this, sliding his fingers over my scalp slowly, making sure to massage from my hairline all the way over the top of my head and then down the back to the nape. By the time he's done, I'm tingling all over, caught up in a haze of lazy arousal.

He picks up one of the empty glasses, fills it with fresh water from the tap, and rinses off the suds, keeping a hand on my forehead to stop the water going in my eyes. Time and again he does it, until the curls are completely clean.

"Conditioner?" he asks.

"Please."

He smooths some creamy conditioner down the hair, then tells me to sit up. "I'm going to wash your back," he says.

Sighing, I sit forward and wrap my arms around my knees. He gets a small amount of shower gel, then proceeds to rub his hands over my back. He does it very slowly, using his fingers to draw circles and other shapes. Then he brings them down my arms, pulling me back so he can reach my hands, then washing the sensitive skin beneath my arms all the way up to my shoulders.

I expect him to move to my breasts then, but he doesn't. Instead he gets some more gel and asks me to lift my knee to my chest, and he washes my leg, leaning forward to massage my foot and slide his fingers between my toes, making me giggle. Smiling, he does the other leg, then washes my knees and up my thighs.

Next he combs through my hair as best as he can with his fingers as he uses the glass to rinse off the conditioner.

By this time, I'm so turned on I'm almost shivering with desire. My whole body feels as if it's humming. My breasts, nipples, and between my legs are aching for his touch. And finally, it seems as if he's ready to pay them some attention.

Chapter Eighteen

Sidnie

"So," Mack murmurs, tipping a little more gel onto his hands and rubbing them together. "Intermediate, eh?"

"Well, normally I'd suggest waiting a few more dates," I say, moving my hands through the bubbles, "but I think you're a star pupil."

He slides his arms under mine. "Oh you do, do you?"

"Mm. Definitely top of the class. I—ooh..." I lose my train of thought as he smooths his hands over my breasts.

"Go on." He kisses my neck as he brushes his thumbs across my slippery nipples.

"I was just saying... that I... think maybe you could... possibly... I can't remember what I was going to say." I sigh and close my eyes.

Chuckling, he teases the tips with the pads of his fingers, then takes them between his forefingers and thumbs and tugs them gently.

The water swirls across my skin, just at the level of my breasts, enhancing the sensations he's arousing. He lifts a hand, tucks it under my chin, and turns my face up to look at him, then presses his lips to mine before sliding his hand back down.

"You have amazing breasts," he murmurs, kissing me slowly from one corner of my mouth to the other. "They fit in my hands perfectly, like they were made for me." He cups them to show me, then continues teasing my nipples.

"I think maybe I was made for you," I say, sighing.

"It's a nice thought." He kisses my chin, my cheekbone, over my closed eyelids, and back down my nose to my mouth. When I part my lips, he touches his tongue to mine, then slides it into my mouth.

I give a little moan and arch my back, pushing my breasts into his hands. But he tuts and stops stroking them.

"Slowly," he scolds.

"You're making me ache."

"Good. Don't worry, you'll get plenty of chances to come this evening. But when I'm ready, okay?"

"You think you're the boss of me?" I say breathlessly.

He kisses down my neck, then fastens his mouth on the place where my pulse beats, and sucks—probably not hard enough to leave a mark, but enough to make me groan.

"Oh, I'm definitely the boss of you," he states. Leaving my breasts, he slides his hands down my body, over my stomach, to my hips and then my thighs. He strokes down the outside of my legs to my knees, then ever so slowly up the inside to the top. Lightly, he brushes his fingers between my legs, and I shudder.

"Now, my little wordsmith," he says, "it's your turn to tell me what you want me to do to you."

"Mmm... make me come..."

"I need a lot more detail than that. What do you want me to do?" Beneath the water, he draws his hands over my thighs to the outside, then back to the inside.

My face is warm now from both the heat of the water and his teasing. "Touch me," I whisper.

"Where, Sidnie? Here?" He strokes down to my knees.

"Higher."

He brings them up to the middle of my thighs, circling his fingers on the sensitive skin. "Here?"

"Higher."

He strokes right up to the top of my thighs, to the crease where my legs meet my body. "Here?" He trails a finger over my mound, then parts his fingers in a V shape and slips them down either side.

"Mmm."

He lifts me up a little so I'm on his lap, sending the water swirling around us. The sensation is almost enough to make me come on its own. He parts my legs and brings them over his. Now, when he strokes back to the top of my thighs, I'm lying open and exposed to his touch.

"You want me to touch you here?" He places a finger just down from my entrance and draws it up lightly over my swollen skin.

"Mmm. Yes."

"How about... here?" He presses more firmly, sliding his finger into my folds.

I suck my bottom lip. "Yes..."

"I think you're the wettest thing in the bath. Look." He takes my hand and, with his on top, slides it down over my body. As my fingers glide down, I can feel my slippery moisture and my swollen folds. He's right—I'm very turned on.

He moves his hand up and down, forcing me to arouse myself. My swollen clit throbs under my touch.

"Show me how you make yourself come," he whispers in my ear.

I can't do that... can I? I look up into his beautiful eyes. They're wide, gleaming. His breathing has quickened, and I can feel his erection pressing against my back. He's turned on at the thought of me pleasuring myself.

The G&T is working, and I discover I'm brave enough to try it.

"All right." I begin to circle my finger over my clit. "I'll show you."

"Good girl."

Ohhh... does he know how much that turns me on? My sigh turns into a moan, and I lie back and relax as much as I can, even though I'm conscious of him watching me as I touch myself. He continues to stroke my body, bringing his hands up to cup my breasts and play with my nipples, then occasionally sliding his right hand back over my mine so he can follow the movement of my fingers.

Wanting to get him hot under the metaphorical collar, I slip my fingers down through my folds and insert two fingers up to the middle knuckle. "Aaahhh... that feels good."

He exhales with a kind of grumpy sigh, and I hide a smile. Sliding my fingers out, I shift a little to get the angle right, tilt up my hips, and slide my middle finger a little further down, with his hand still on top of mine. Gently, I tease the muscle there with the tip of my finger, just a bit.

"Ooh," I murmur, looking up at him with innocent eyes. "So tight."

His lips curve up, and his eyelids lower a fraction more. "You remember what I told you about teasing me? There are always consequences."

I bat my eyelids. "Are you going to spank me, Daddy?"

He gives a short laugh, crushes his lips to mine, and plunges his tongue into my mouth. Pushing my hand away, he cups my mound and slides his fingers down into me, as if he's hungry for me, for my pleasure. With his other hand he plucks at my nipple, and I've been on the edge so long it's enough to send me tumbling over. I grab the sides of the bath as I come, my hips jerking with each powerful pulse, and I gasp several long moans against his lips, my whole body shuddering as he guides me all the way through my orgasm.

I blink as I return to earth, and find myself looking up into his amused eyes.

"You're so fucking hot," he says. "Jesus, I'm crazy about you."

Delighted at his words, I turn in the bath, push up onto my knees, then carefully move astride him. It's a gorgeous, wide bath, and I'm just able to fit on his lap.

"Mm," I say, cupping his face. "And I'm bonkers about you, too."

He laughs, but he can't reply because I'm too busy kissing him. His jaw rasps against the soft skin of my hands, so fucking masculine I'm sure it could also make me come again. I tease his tongue with mine, and slide my hands up the short hair on the back of his head, feeling it prickle my skin.

Lifting up, I move my hips until I feel the tip of his erection pressing against my entrance. I push down, and just feel him enter me before he grips hold of my hips.

"Condom," he says, his voice husky.

"Oh." I pause and look into his eyes. "Well, I'm on the pill if you want to leave it." He hesitates, though. "I'm clean," I say. "Are you?"

"Yes." Still he waits, and I can see thoughts passing behind his eyes.

Is he worried I'm not telling the truth? That maybe I'm trying to trap him by getting pregnant? Maybe, because of what I did, spying on him, he has a lingering doubt that I might lie to him. It makes me sad, but the last thing I want is for him to worry about it.

"It's okay." I go to lift up. "We'll wait until we're out of the bath."

But he holds me there, then brings me back down. When he's just inside me, he says, "Go on, you do it so I don't hurt you."

Touched that he agreed and that he's still thinking about me, I lower myself onto him. He needn't have worried. I'm so aroused from all the foreplay and my orgasm that I slide onto him in one move.

"Aaahhh…" He closes his eyes for a moment. "Jesus."

"Is that nice, baby?" I kiss his lips lightly, holding his face in my hands. "Do you like being inside me?"

"Yeah…"

"Without barriers, just skin on skin." I rock my hips, reveling in the feel of him sliding inside me. "Oh, you feel good."

He palms my breasts and begins teasing my nipples again. "Too much?" he murmurs.

I shake my head. "Just right," I say, bending to kiss him.

He sighs, and we kiss like that for ages, me moving slowly on top of him, with his hands skating over my wet skin, up my back, over my breasts, up my thighs, and returning to my back.

"I like riding you like this," I tell him, nibbling his bottom lip. "Come for me."

He opens his eyes and gives me an amused look. "Already?"

"I don't care. I want to watch you."

"I'm not done yet, girl. Come on. Time to get out."

"Aw."

"I want you on the bed. I've been dreaming about ten different positions since the last time we slept together. I want to try as many of them as I can while I still have the strength."

Giggling, I lift off him, then get out of the bath. He follows, and we reach for the big, fluffy towels and wrap ourselves in them, kissing as much as we can in between. He grabs another couple of towels, then steers me into the bedroom, where Gus is curled up in his basket, filling the air with soft snores.

"Sorry about that," Mack says. "It's not the most romantic of backgrounds."

"I don't know. It makes me think of bed anyway. It's better than Barry White."

He laughs, unfolds the two spare towels, and rolls them out onto the bed. Then he turns to me and removes mine. "Turn around," he says.

I do as he says, and he covers my hair and towel dries it gently. When most of the moisture has gone, he dries the rest of me, and then I do him, removing the drips from his arms, back, chest, and legs.

He tosses the towels back in the bathroom, and pulls me into his arms. "Your skin is all pink," he murmurs, brushing his hands down over my breasts.

"The water was hot. Oh, and all the sex, too."

He chuckles and kisses me. I sigh and lift my arms around his neck, but we've only kissed for a minute when he moves me back to the bed and says, "On you get."

I climb on and lie back, and he gets on with me. He leans over me, looking down with heat-filled eyes.

"I'm going to taste you now," he says.

"Oh. Mm. Okay." I shiver. His eyes are so intense.

"But first I'm going to kiss you all over." He starts by kissing up my nose and over my brows. "I'm going to brand every single inch of your skin, so every part of you belongs to me."

I close my eyes, my lips parting at his words. It's a provocative thing to say when I don't even know what this is. Are we dating? Am I his girlfriend? Everything he does implies I am. It's just that we haven't discussed it yet. Not that I care right now.

"Relax," he murmurs, kissing my ear, then down my neck. "Just let me worship you. But I don't want you to come." He stops, and I open my eyes to see him staring into them. "Not until I'm ready," he states.

"I can't promise anything," I admit.

"If you do, there'll be a price to pay." He lifts my hand, takes each fingertip in his mouth, and sucks.

I give him a helpless look. How am I supposed to last through this?

"Do you know how many erogenous zones there are?" he asks, kissing my palm, my inner wrist, and down my arm.

"A hundred and fifty?"

He laughs. "It wouldn't surprise me if you have that many."

He kisses down over my breasts, but doesn't spend long there, traveling around to my ribs, then down over my tummy and hips. Then he moves and kisses my feet, dipping his tongue between my toes, kissing up my instep, the inside of my ankle, and all the way up the sensitive skin of my thigh. It feels as if every inch of skin is an erogenous zone. Every piece of me is tingling by the time he kisses back up to my lips.

"Turn over," he says.

I roll onto my front, and he proceeds to kiss all over my neck, my back, the backs of my legs, and my bottom, nibbling the muscles there before sliding his tongue down between my cheeks.

"Ooh, Mack!"

He laughs and lifts up. "Turn over."

I shift onto my back again, and this time he pays attention to my breasts, lovingly sucking each nipple for a while before finally moving off. He stretches out beside me, tucks a pillow under his head, then beckons. "Here," he says, tapping his lips.

I don't need telling twice. I lift up, straddle him, and move until I feel his hot breath on my thighs. Then, leaning on the headboard, I close my eyes as he swipes his tongue right up my core.

SERENITY WOODS

"Ohhh…" The sensation is amazing, and I shudder as his hands find my breasts and toy with my nipples while he licks and sucks.

Already turned on and buzzing, it takes less than thirty seconds before I come again, clutching hold of the headboard as he hooks his arms over my thighs and holds me there until I'm done.

"I'm sorry," I gasp, as I lift up and fall onto my back, my chest heaving. "That was so amazing. I couldn't hold on."

"You're a freak of nature." He rises and leans over me. "I love it. I'm having the time of my life."

Warmth spreads through me as he lifts my legs around his hips and presses the tip of his erection into me. Then he lowers down and presses his lips to mine. "Ready for me, baby?"

"Yeah."

"You want me inside you?"

"Mm, yeah…"

He brushes his tongue against mine. "You gonna take all of me?"

"I'll try."

Keeping his lips above mine, our breaths mingling, he eases his hips forward and slowly slides inside me.

"Ohhh…" I sigh. "Mm. That feels so good."

He nibbles my bottom lip. "You like the feel of me inside you?"

"Mm. Yeah. You fit me so perfectly." I watch his face as I clench my inner muscles.

His eyes close briefly in lazy appreciation. "Ah. You're so tight."

Continuing to murmur in my ear, he gives leisurely thrusts, taking his time to build up our pleasure. Soon I'm in a hazy spiral of bliss, as if I'm drunk, the world fading away around me, so there's only the man who's making love to me, because despite his declared intention to fuck me senseless, this is lovemaking, pure and simple, far too slow and sweet to be anything else.

It doesn't take long for me to feel the flickers of an orgasm, the first small waves of pleasure deep inside. He obviously notices somehow, because he slows down his pace and lifts his head as I come, watching me as I clench around him, sighing with each beautiful pulse.

When I open my eyes, he kisses me, and I flop back onto the pillows and stretch my arms above me, reveling in the last ripples of ecstasy.

I then run my hands down his back, feeling the muscles move as he continues to thrust. "Mack?"

"Mm?" He kisses me again.

188

"Can I be on top?"

"Whatever the lady wants." He rolls, bringing me with him.

He props his head on the pillows, and I get comfortable astride him. Then I bend over him and touch my lips to his.

"I want to make you come," I tell him, running the tip of my tongue over his lips. "Will you do that for me?"

He gives a long sigh. "If you insist."

"I do. I think it's time I took charge. I want to watch you come inside me."

He catches my hands in his and pulls them above his head. It lifts me up so my breasts are level with his head. "When I'm ready," he says, and then he covers a nipple with his mouth and sucks.

I groan, beginning to rock my hips. I might have known he'd still direct the action. Jesus, he's going to make me come again if he carries on like this. Kate will be happy—I'm going to have trouble walking tomorrow.

It takes a while for me to reach that point again, but Mack seems in no hurry. He strokes my breasts, my ribs, my back, then returns to stroking my breasts again, licking and sucking all the while. I can't believe how long he can hold on. I didn't tell him last time, but part of the reason I've not tended to have multiple orgasms with previous partners is that it's only taken a minute or less of penetration for them to finish, and most guys don't have any interest in carrying on after that.

But Mack goes on forever, arousing me slowly, until I'm hot and tingling and teetering on the edge. It's warm in the room, even with the aircon on, and my face is hot so I know I must be flushed. Our skin is damp and glistening in the moonlight.

"You look so fucking sexy right now," he murmurs, holding my hips and pushing up with each thrust so he's stimulating my clit as he moves. "You were made for sex. With me."

The way he adds that at the end is enough to send me tumbling over the edge, and I come again, tightening around him, and leaning on his chest as I gasp at the intense pulses deep inside me. God, it's almost too much, and I know the clenches must be hard because he grunts and his fingers tighten on my hips.

When I'm done, I sit there for a moment, drawing air deep into my lungs, hot and sticky, all my nerve endings tingling with pleasure. He waits for me, and when I'm finally done, he wraps a strand of my hair around his hand and pulls me down for a kiss.

"Now can I watch you come?" I ask, giving him an exasperated look.

His lips curve up. "Go for it."

So I do, rocking my hips on top of him, and driving him in and out of me at a faster pace. I move his hands above his head, and he gives a lazy smile, stretches out under me, and closes his eyes.

I bend and touch my tongue to each of his nipples in turn, tracing around the edge before flicking the tip, and he exhales, his breaths coming more quickly, one hand lowering to slide into my hair. He clenches his hand and groans, suggesting that now he's given himself permission to come, he's not far. Mm. Pushing up, watching him concentrate on the feelings deep inside him, I continue to move, and he meets each thrust of my hips with one of his own.

"Tell me how it feels," I whisper.

His lips curve up a little, and his eyes open a fraction. "Amazing."

"How far are you?"

His eyelids lower again. "Close."

I slow down a little, and he groans.

"I'm gonna fuck you real slow," I say. "Make you wait."

He opens his eyes and gives me an exasperated look. "I could just throw you on the bed and fuck you."

"You could, but you won't. You're going to let me have my own way just this once. I'll take you all the way, don't worry. I'm not going anywhere until you've come inside me."

He groans again, lowering his hands to hold me, but I put them above his head again, then lower down until I can brush his lips with mine.

"Tell me when you're gonna come, Mack." I kiss him, then delve my tongue into his mouth briefly. "Tell me when you're going to fill me up."

"Jesus, Sid..."

"Come on, let me take you all the way. Can you feel my pussy clenching around you?"

He opens his eyes and looks into mine as I tighten my muscles around him.

"I can feel your cock all the way inside me," I whisper, kissing him again. "It feels so fucking good. You're so big, baby, stretching me, filling me up."

He blinks slowly, his eyes turning hazy.

I kiss him again. "Mm… Can you feel it coming?"

"Yeah…"

"Are you going to come for me, baby?"

"Fuck, yes…" His face creases with pleasure, and I watch with delight as he climaxes. I ride him through it, slowly, feeling every jerk of his hips, every shudder he gives, and he's so beautiful, so gorgeous, I can't believe I'm here, making love with him, it's so amazing, I wish it never had to stop.

But of course it does, and eventually his breath leaves him in a whoosh, and his chest heaves as he tries to get more oxygen in his lungs. I cuddle up to him and nuzzle his neck, and he tightens his arms around me, holding me there.

"Now tell me that wasn't what the doctor ordered," I say smugly.

Chapter Nineteen

Mack

Eventually, Sidnie moves off me and stretches out beside me with a sigh. I reach over and get her a tissue from the box on the bedside table. She gives me a shy look before using it.

"That's a first for me," I say, moving up behind her as she reaches over to throw the tissue away. I pull her back into my arms so we're spooning, and she nestles back against me with a sigh.

"And me," she says. "Did it feel different?"

"Mm. More sensitive." But it wasn't just that. When she first told me she was on the pill, and that we didn't have to use a condom, my first emotion was wariness, because guys are told from a young age that wearing one means we stay in control, and it doesn't come easily for me to give that up.

But then something strange happened—I realized I trusted her. If she was brave enough to tell me why she'd originally come to my office, I'm sure she wasn't then going to lie to me about being on the pill.

I kiss her hair, and she sighs. "I'm so tired."

"I'm not surprised. All those orgasms must use up some energy."

"Mmm. I guess."

I nuzzle her neck. "You have a very dirty mouth."

"Oh, I'm sorry, do you want me to stop?"

I chuckle and nip her ear.

"Ow! Mm." She wiggles her bottom against my groin.

"Don't do that or we'll be starting all over again."

She giggles, then goes quiet. After a few minutes, her breathing levels out, and I realize she's fallen asleep.

I'm tired too, but my brain's racing, and I know it'll take a while for it to quieten. I don't stress about it, though. I'm quite content lying there, with Sidnie warm and soft in my arms and Gus snoring lightly in his bed, while I look out through the gap in the curtains at the Christmas moon hanging over the ocean.

I have a busy week ahead of me, and thoughts about the tasks I need to do mingle with memories of our lovemaking and the emotions she stirred up inside me. It's a pleasant blend, and with some surprise I realize I'm happy. Exceptionally so.

I'd never have wished for this. I didn't think I needed it in my life. But now she's here, I can't ever imagine wanting to let her go.

"Merry Christmas," I whisper, kissing her shoulder.

Then I fall asleep.

*

To my surprise, when I wake up it's light. It's rare for me to sleep all night, but I guess the alcohol and all the exercise wore me out.

Sidnie is lying on her tummy, her head facing me, her arms snuggled up to her chest. She's still asleep, her cheeks pink, her curls tumbling across the pillow. I lift my head—at some point in the night, Gus jumped up onto the bed, and he's asleep too, curled up between us.

I think he's as crazy about her as I am.

I roll onto my back and look up at the ceiling. I need to be careful. I don't know her that well yet. It's possible that as soon as she realizes how I feel about her, she'll turn into Felicity, and start making demands I can't deal with. I don't think she will—she's an entirely different fish from Felicity—but I can't tell.

Gus stirs, stretches, and yawns, sees I'm awake, and pads up the bed to give me a kiss.

"Morning, dude," I murmur, ruffling his ears and kissing his nose. "You want to go for a run?" As quietly as I can, I get up and open my case, looking for a fresh pair of shorts and a top.

"Hello, you two."

I turn to see Sidnie smiling at us.

"Sorry, did I wake you?" I walk over to the bed and bend to give her a kiss.

She returns it sleepily, then shakes her head as I straighten. "No, I was already rousing. Are you going out?"

"I thought I'd take Gus out for a run."

She sits up. "Can I join you? If you'd rather go alone that's fine, I don't mind."

My eyebrows lift in surprise. "Do you run?"

"Mm, most mornings. I doubt I'm as fast as you though." She chuckles.

"Then sure. Come on. It's a beautiful morning."

"Are you wearing running shoes?"

"Normally I would, but I'll go barefoot on the sand."

"Okay." She finds a T-shirt and shorts in her bag, and after a brief visit to the bathroom, the two of us and Gus head out to the elevator and go down into the lobby. We head over the road, stop for Gus to have a pee on the grass, then descend onto the beach.

"What an amazing morning," she says.

The sun is just appearing above the horizon, flooding the Pacific with golden light. The sky is coral and amber, still dark blue to the west, but there's not a cloud in the sky.

We walk down to the water's edge, while Sidnie fixes her hair back with an elastic. The shallows, not yet warmed by the sun, are cool on my feet. There's hardly any wind and thus few waves, and the water rolls elegantly up the sand before drawing back and leaving it dark gold and glistening.

Following the water line, we walk for a few minutes to warm up, then start jogging. I start slowly, then set a medium pace as I realize she can easily keep up with me. Gus runs alongside us, bounding in and out of the sea.

We run for about twenty minutes, then stop to catch our breath and play catch with Gus, throwing sticks into the sea for him to swim out and fetch before we start heading back.

"You want to race?" I ask her, feeling the need to pick up the pace now I've warmed up.

She laughs. "Absolutely not. Go on, spread your wings. I'll catch you up."

I stop and pull her into my arms, then kiss her, holding her head with one hand. Her curls flutter around us, and she laughs, then sighs and melts against me, returning the kiss with enthusiasm. When I finally move back, her eyes sparkle in the sunlight.

"Go on," she whispers.

I turn and head back up the beach, gradually increasing my pace as I find my stride. It's a glorious run, the wet sand springy beneath my feet, the sea breeze cooling my hot skin, and as I draw the salty air deep into my lungs and my muscles grow loose, I feel exhilarated. My race was the hundred meters, but I also competed in the two hundred, four hundred, and fifteen hundred meters as a kid, and I'm still fairly fast at all of them. By the time I slow as I approach the hotel, I feel full of energy again, as if the rising sun has filled me with its light.

I stand there, hands on hips, catching my breath as I wait for Gus and Sidnie to catch up with me. When she arrives she's red-faced, and she bends over at the waist, her breaths coming in gasps.

"Fuck me, you're fast," she says. "I knew you'd won that trophy, but I didn't realize just how fast you were."

"Well, not as fast as I could be, but yeah, not bad."

"What did you run the hundred meters in?"

"When I was sixteen my PB was 10.75. The national record for under seventeens was 10.73 so I didn't quite break it, but I was close. I'm faster now, but the New Zealand men's record is 10.08 and I'm nowhere near that."

"Who holds the New Zealand record?" she asks as we start walking back to the hotel.

"Eddie Osei-Nketia. His father held it before him for twenty-eight years. His name's Augustine."

She laughs and bends to fondle the spaniel's ears. "Gus?"

"Yeah."

"I like it."

We cross the road and go back into the hotel. "Gus is dripping all over the floor," she says as we go up in the elevator.

"Yeah, I'd better give the cleaner a tip when we go."

She grins. "It must be nearly seven, right? We're meeting Jamie and Emma at eight?"

"Yeah. I might rinse Gus off in the bath and then put the hair dryer on him."

"I'll help."

We spend a fun fifteen minutes washing and drying Gus, by the end of which we're both completely soaked, and then I give him a biscuit and let him collapse in his bed while we strip off and get in the shower together.

"Are you sore after last night?" I murmur as I wash her back with shower gel.

SERENITY WOODS

"Tender," she admits. "Unsurprisingly considering the workout I got."

I chuckle and turn her in my arms to face me. "I'm sorry about that."

"No, you're not."

"I'm not sorry for all the sex. But I am sorry if I hurt you."

"You didn't hurt me," she whispers, kissing me. "You're incredibly gentle considering you're such a big guy."

"You know how to say all the right things."

She laughs as she smooths her hands across my chest and shoulders. "I meant in height and breadth, but yeah, that too." She sighs then, slides her arms around me, and rests her cheek on my chest. I kiss the top of her wet curls, enjoying the feel of her wet skin against me.

"You okay?" I ask.

"Mm. Dad has his treatment tomorrow. I want to be there, but… I kinda don't want this to end, you know?"

"Yeah." I stroke her back, resting my lips on her hair.

"You're busy too, aren't you?" she asks. "You have to finish your project for Elizabeth."

"Mm."

"Your new microprocessor."

I might not know her well, but I've been with her enough to pick up on the slight tease in her voice. She knows I was lying. I feel a twinge of guilt, wondering if she'll mention it.

But she lifts her head, kisses me, and says, "I hope your week goes well and you finish your project in time. I'm sure you will."

"I'm not going to have much free time," I warn. "Any, in fact."

"I know." Her blue eyes are wide and open as I look from one to the other.

There's a long pause.

I might as well just say it. "But I don't want you to see anyone else."

Her lips curve up. She's fucking beautiful when she smiles.

"I won't if you don't," she says.

"Don't be smug," I scold. "It's not an attractive quality."

She laughs and kisses me. "Come on. Let's go and have some breakfast before you fade away."

*

We meet Jamie and Emma in the restaurant, and Jamie and I have a full cooked breakfast while the girls have cereal and fruit.

I'm pleased that Emma and Sidnie seem to get along so well. Emma has been really good for Jamie, and I can see he also likes the four of us spending time together.

We take our time eating, chatting about movies and music and books, and it's with some reluctance that we finally agree to retrieve our bags and check out. Gus has been snoozing in our room, but he perks up when we return. We take him and our bags out to the car, and Jamie drives us to the airport.

Soon we're on the plane returning to Auckland. Sidnie is fairly quiet, lost in thought as she looks out of the window. I'm sure she's thinking about her father. It's going to be a difficult few days for her. I feel a twinge of disappointment that I'm not going to be around much to help her through it. It surprises me. I'm not family, and I'm not her husband, or partner, or boyfriend. Am I? I don't think two dates counts as going steady. And yet I told her I didn't want her to see anyone else.

I didn't think I wanted a relationship. And yet now, the thought of not being with her makes me feel bereft.

I'm so shit at all this. How do people negotiate these treacherous waters every day? How do they balance their relationships and careers? I know most people don't work quite as many hours as me, but some must do. How do they make it work?

Maybe they don't. The divorce rate is one in three, when it comes to it.

I think about my mother, the memories floating through my brain like rain clouds over a beautiful summer sky. Freud would have a lot to say about her influence on the way I am. But I can't blame everything on her. I've been gone a long time, and at some point you have to take responsibility for the way you live your life.

Is it a good enough reason not to enter into a relationship because you're worried it won't be successful? I'm many things, but I like to think I'm not a coward.

Sidnie told me, *I'm saying I could easily fall for you, if I haven't already. And I know coming up there, spending time with you would be amazing, but it would make it so much harder to walk away.* She understands. I told her then, *What if I don't want you to?* At the time, all I knew was that I wanted to be with her, and that hasn't changed.

We all have to grow up sometime. Kai's words have really stuck with me.

"Are you doing Chinese algebra in your head?" Sidnie asks.

I look around to discover them all watching me, smiling.

"Why Chinese algebra?" I ask. "Is that harder than ordinary algebra?"

"All algebra is like Chinese to me," she says. "It must be amazing to have your brain."

"It must be amazing to have your boobs. Sorry, did I say that out loud?"

She and Emma giggle, and Jamie grins. I put my arm around Sidnie and kiss her temple. Stop worrying, I scold myself. You're not your mother. And neither is Sidnie. Just take it a day at a time.

*

We take Sidnie home, and after she's given Gus a hundred kisses goodbye, I walk her up the path to her front door.

"Thank you for such a lovely time," she says. "Especially for all the hot sex."

I chuckle. "You're welcome. Good luck tomorrow. I hope the treatment goes well."

"Thanks." She blows out a breath. "I'm nervous, but it's a good thing. It means hopefully he can start getting better afterward."

I take her hands in mine. "If I don't call," I tell her, "it's because I'm knee-deep in reports, and no other reason."

"I know." She smiles. "Don't worry. Maybe we can catch up next week, when you're done?"

Her face is like the sun, blindingly beautiful. Her summer-sky eyes are clear and hold no resentment or frustration. Kai's words about marriage fly through my mind like the birds soaring above us: *You see it as a ball and chain around your ankle. You don't think a girl exists who will treat you like a homing pigeon, letting you fly free with the knowledge that you'll come home when you're ready.*

She lifts up on tiptoes and kisses me, just once. Then she moves back.

"I get one kiss," I say, "Gus gets a hundred. How's that fair?"

"His ears are softer than yours."

"Fair enough. I'll speak to you soon," I tell her firmly.

"Okay." She waves to Jamie and Emma in the car, gives me one last smile, and goes inside.

I return to the car, feeling a mixture of emotions: sad, wistful, hopeful, and energetic all at once. I'm excited about finishing the project, and I can already feel the hyper-focus ready to kick in. As much as I've enjoyed Christmas, I love my work, and I'm ready to throw myself back into it.

And when I'm done, hopefully Sidnie will be waiting, like the pot of gold at the end of the rainbow.

*

Jamie drops me and Gus at the office, then heads home with Emma.

Even over the holidays, some of the staff is here. I chat for a while with Matiu, our head of security. He's married, but his kids are grown up and his house is full of grandchildren, so after a noisy Christmas Day, he was more than happy to escape on Boxing Day. He lets me into the building, and Gus and I walk through the empty offices, enjoying the peace and quiet.

There will be a few staff keeping an eye on Marise, making sure she runs smoothly at all times. My team will be in tomorrow first thing, and they'll be working all hours to get the project finished. Today, though, it's just me.

I go into my office, open the sliding doors, and let Gus out. The garden is fenced so he can't escape, not that he'd want to. He likes sniffing about and spends most of his time asleep on the deck.

Leaving him there, I walk back through the offices and down to Marise's room. I open the door and go inside.

The machine hall is over an acre in size, brightly lit, with a spotless, white-tiled floor. Marise gives the room a blue glow. Her monolithic black cabinets hold over 160,000 computer processing units. These must be kept under thirty degrees Celsius, and without cooling they'd quickly rise to over a hundred degrees in a matter of seconds, which would be like having a hundred household electric heaters operating within a meter-square space. She therefore has a large water-based liquid cooling unit that fills the air with a dull roar. A complicated secondary pipe system carries the cooled water close to the CPUs, then as the temperature rises, sends it to heat exchangers to be cooled back down. Inside the processors are twenty miles of Infiniband double data rate cabling to connect the thousands of nodes. She's a thing of beauty, and my pride and joy.

This hall is kept spotless to avoid contamination to the computer. Visitors and those who work here wear white coats, and touching the machine is forbidden.

Today, though, I rest a light hand on the nearest cabinet. Her roar is deafening—if I was to spend more than fifteen minutes in here, I'd need ear plugs. But at least nobody will be able to hear me talking to myself.

"You'll always be my first love," I say. "But I hope you'll understand that there's someone else in my life now."

She continues to roar, but to me it's as if she's singing. She's like Sidnie—beautiful, elegant, and I'm utterly obsessed with her.

I rub my thumb over one of the screws holding the cabinet together. Then I turn, leave the hall, and go back to my office.

It's time to get to work.

Chapter Twenty

Sidnie

It proves to be a relatively quiet week.

On Tuesday, we visit the private clinic where Dad is finally given the drug he needs, and he's told to return in three weeks for the next dose. We take him home and spend the next few days keeping a close eye on him, as some of the side effects of the drug can be severe.

I don't have to work at Lubricanz, but I do a couple of cleaning jobs to keep Dodie happy. Other than that, I go out for lunch with Caro and Hana one day, and do some shopping for Mum. But with plenty of spare time on my hands, I finally get stuck into writing my book.

I don't know whether it's because I've had such inspiration lately, or if it's because I can escape from the real world into my fiction, but the words come easily, and I find myself writing several thousand words a day. I have a battered old laptop, and sometimes I sit in Dad's bedroom, or next to him on the sofa, and write while he dozes in front of the TV. Occasionally I go in the garden and sit under the umbrella, and let the warmth of the summer sun and the smell of the lemon trees waft over me as the words flow.

Not surprisingly, the hero of my romance novel is tall, dark, and gorgeous. I decide to make him a billionaire, and smart, too. Basically, it's a biography of a rather handsome nerd that I know, but I'm having too much fun to change him. My heroine falls head over heels with him quickly, and then it's time to write the first love scene. I have a whale of a time directing them in the bedroom, then have to go inside for a cold shower afterward.

I tell Mack about it when he texts me. I hadn't expected to hear from him at all, but he messages me often, usually at erratic times— five a.m. or eleven thirty p.m., or when he's running in his gym, or when Nadine forces him to stop for five minutes and eat lunch. The texts are short and sweet, distracted and occasionally filled with baffling information. Our conversations tend to go like this:

Him: *Today we discussed the quasi-opportunistic distributed execution of demanding parallel computing software in grids.*

Me: *Are you speaking English?*

Him: *Sorry. Forgot who I was talking to!*

Me: *Me >* And I include a picture of Homer Simpson.

Him: *LOL. You're more like Marge with the hair.*

Me: *I'm going to dye it blue now.*

Him: *Noooo! I love that you're naturally blonde. (I checked.)*

Me: *Cheeky!*

Then he disappears for four hours before returning with a photo of Gus with a bird sitting on his head.

Once he sent me a selfie with the caption: *This is to prove I'm working. Do you think I need some sleep?* The photo shows him with two days' worth of stubble, ruffled hair, and dark shadows under his eyes, although the sexy smile is still the same.

I save it as wallpaper on my phone, then send him one back that I take in the mirror wearing just my bra and knickers and a pout.

Him: *Whoa. That's a much better selfie than mine.*

Me: *Glad you like it!*

Him: *I'm going to show the team.*

Me: *Don't you dare!*

Him: *I won't. This one's all for me. Think I need to take some personal time.*

I sigh at the thought of him doing a little DIY while he's looking at the photo.

Me: *Miss you.*

Him: *Miss you too. Not long now.*

I can't remember when he said he'd be finished—I think he wanted to get the report to Elizabeth before the end of the year, which is Saturday.

Therefore, when the doorbell goes on Friday around six p.m., I'm not even thinking about him when I go to answer it.

I open the door, and there he is, leaning against the wall of the porch, hands in the pockets of his black jeans, smiling.

"Mack!" Exultant, I throw my arms around his neck, and he laughs and hugs me.

"Mmm, I missed you." He buries his face in my neck and inhales. "I'd forgotten how amazing you smell."

I'm so pleased to see him that my throat tightens and tears prick my eyes. I hadn't realized until that moment how afraid I was that he'd change his mind over the days we were apart and decide he wouldn't want to see me again.

"Hey." He moves back and holds my face in his hands. "Is everything okay? How's your dad?"

I rub my nose, trying to control my emotions. "He's good. Very tired, and he's been nauseous, and had a few headaches. But not too bad."

He strokes his thumbs over my cheeks, then bends and kisses me. I sigh and lean against him, and we exchange the sweetest kiss I've ever had, bathed in the warm early evening sun.

When he eventually moves back, I give a short laugh and take a slow, shaky breath. "How's the project going?"

"Done," he says. "I've just had a meeting with Elizabeth to officially hand it over."

"Oh Mack, I'm so pleased for you." My heart skips a beat. Does that mean he's free now?

But he says, "I'm so tired. I'm going to take tonight to crash. I wondered if you're free tomorrow?"

"Definitely," I say, my heart swelling.

"I don't suppose you play tennis?"

"Oh! Yes, actually. I did quite well at school. I haven't played much this year, but I still have my gear and racket."

"Well, Huxley has organized a one-day tournament for tomorrow. It's for charity, all proceeds going to Cancer Research. I forgot that he'd roped me in some time ago—I was supposed to be partnering Victoria in the mixed doubles, but she's sprained her wrist. So I wondered if you'd like to be my partner?"

Delight fills me at the thought of not only partnering him, but also raising money for the charity currently closest to my heart. "I'd love to."

"Cool." He grins. "There's a party afterward at the club we can go to if you want."

"Okay. I'll bring a dress as well."

He nods. "Well, before I go, can I come in? I have something for your folks."

"Oh." I chew my bottom lip, knowing Mum would prefer to tidy up before seeing him. But hell, she'll have to deal with it. "Of course." I wave to Jamie in the car. "He's welcome to come too."

"Nah, I won't stay long." He comes in, and I notice then that he's carrying a backpack. "In here?" he asks, gesturing at the living room, and when I nod, he goes in.

"Oh!" I hear Mum say, and I go in to see Mum, Liam, Kate, and Julia all getting to their feet, flustered.

"Please," he says, "don't get up. I'm sorry to disturb you all, but I just called by to see Sidnie, and I wanted to see how you were doing." He directs it at Dad, who's sitting in his chair with his feet up.

"I'm good, thank you," Dad says. "It's been a tough few days for Sid. I'm glad you came to see her."

Mum pats down her hair. "Can I get you a drink?"

"No, thank you," Mack says, "I won't keep you long. I just wanted to drop off a few Christmas presents." He grins, lowers onto the sofa, and unzips the backpack.

As puzzled as the others, I watch as he takes out a bottle in a beautiful silver display case that makes it look as if the bottle is suspended in mid-air. "Sidnie told me you drank whiskey," he says to Dad. "I know you're not supposed to drink while you're on your medication, but I thought this could be something to look forward to when your treatment is finished. I'm sure Liam won't mind sharing it with you." He smiles at my brother-in-law, then hands it over to Dad. "Sid said you liked Glenfiddich. This is my favorite—it's a thirty-year-old. I hope you like it."

Dad's jaw drops as he turns the case in his hands. Mum usually only buys whatever's on special at the liquor store, which is usually a cheap blend. "It's wonderful," he says. He nods and swallows. "Thank you so much."

"You're welcome." Mack clears his throat. "For the ladies in the house, something to treat yourself with." He struggles to remove a large box from his backpack, and in the end I have to hold it so he can wiggle the box out. He hands it to Mum. "It's from the Treats to Tempt You chocolate shop in Doubtless Bay," he says.

"I know it," she replies, jaw dropping. "They do specialist chocolates."

"Yeah. I know the owner—Tasha. Sidnie said you really like cherries, so I asked Tasha to make up a special box. The bottom layer is all cherry-filled chocolates. The rest are assorted flavors."

She glances at me, her eyes sparkling, then smiles and bends to kiss his cheek. "Thank you so much, they're wonderful."

Finally, he looks at Julia, delves in a hand, and brings out a rugby ball. He spins it on his hand, catches it—smart bastard—and hands it out to her.

Shyly, she comes forward and takes it, then stares at it as she realizes there are signatures all over it. She lifts her gaze to his, and her jaw drops.

"Yeah," he says, "I know someone who works at Eden Park. The All Blacks were there on Tuesday, and he asked them to sign the ball for you. They're all on there, I think." He points to a couple of the signatures and reads out the names.

"Thank you," Julia says, her eyes like saucers.

"Yes, thank you," Kate murmurs. "That's so thoughtful of you."

He shrugs, smiles, and gets to his feet. "Well I'd better go. I've slept, like, six hours in five days. I'm dead on my feet. *Kia kaha*." He directs the words at Dad—it means stay strong. He waves and heads for the door.

I glance at my family and silently mouth *Oh My God!* then follow him outside.

"Mack," I say as he pauses on the porch, "they were incredibly generous presents. Thank you so much. Everyone was feeling a bit low, and that's really cheered them up. That whiskey! It must be worth a fortune."

"Fifteen hundred dollars. Don't tell him." He moves closer to me, putting his hands on my hips. "Aren't you going to ask what your present is?" he murmurs, touching his lips to mine.

"Is it really great sex?" I say huskily. "I'm crossing my fingers."

He chuckles, pulls something out of his back pocket, and gives it to me. It's a long narrow black box. I open it and stare. It's a pen—a beautiful one, with a black barrel and an off-white cap.

"It's a Montblanc," he says. I know they're one of the most expensive pens you can buy. "It's a Jimi Hendrix special."

"Oh my God, really?"

He runs a finger along it. "The engraved pattern on the cap is inspired by one of his guitar straps, and the pattern on the barrel resembles a WAH pedal. The clip looks like the vibrato bar of an electric guitar."

"Is it silver?"

"Platinum."

"Holy fuck. It's beautiful." I'm incredibly touched by the symbolism of it, that it reflects our conversation about Hendrix when I wore the T-shirt with his lyrics on it. He remembered. How wonderful.

"I guess jewelry would probably have been more romantic," he says, surprisingly awkwardly for a guy who has so much self-confidence. "But I know you're writing a book, and I thought you could use it to sign a copy for me when it's printed." He smiles.

I rest my hand over my heart, taken aback. "I don't know what to say. It's the most thoughtful, beautiful gift I've ever had."

"You wouldn't rather have had the great sex?"

"Well, if it's still on offer..."

We both laugh.

I look up into his eyes. "Thank you. For everything."

He bends his head and kisses me. Then he straightens again. "I'll pick you up tomorrow morning, ten-thirty. The tournament starts at eleven."

"Okay," I say happily. "See you then."

He waves and returns to the car, getting in beside Jamie, and the car pulls away.

I look at the pen, which I know would probably have cost over a thousand dollars. The pen itself, and the presents he gave my family, are wonderful. But the best gift was his compliment: *I know you're writing a book, and I thought you could use it to sign a copy for me when it's printed.* He didn't make fun of my dream, and he has faith that I'll finish it and publish it. That in itself is priceless.

Sliding it into my pocket, I smile and go back inside.

*

The next day, I open the door at ten thirty, just before he knocks on it.

"Morning." I inhale as I see him standing there. He's wearing a white polo shirt with blue trim and white tennis shorts that reveal his gorgeous muscular brown legs.

"Wow," he says, staring at me.

I look down. I'm wearing a white tennis dress. It's very short, especially with my long legs, and only just covers the white Lycra shorts I've got on underneath.

He sighs with a touch of exasperation. "How am I supposed to play with this kind of distraction?"

"You'll manage, I'm sure," I say wryly, coming out with my bag and racket, and closing the door behind me.

He puts an arm around me as we walk to the car, then kisses me before he opens the car door. "Hello," he murmurs.

"Hi." I love the way he makes my pulse race just with one look from those gorgeous eyes.

He lets me get in before closing the door and walking around the other side.

I lean over and give Gus a stroke in the back before turning and buckling myself in.

"Morning, Jamie," I say.

"Hey, Sidnie!" He smiles at me in the rear-view mirror.

Mack gets in the other side, closes the door, and also buckles himself in.

"How are you feeling?" I ask Mack as Jamie pulls away.

"Better. I slept all night without waking. I think Gus thought I'd died. I woke up to find him poking me with his paw and staring at me."

I chuckle. "So you're all ready for the day?"

"Yep. Raring to go."

"So tell me a bit about the tournament."

"Huxley does it each year. It's at Redwood's Sports Club. You pay to enter, and he invites business people from all over the city to come and watch, all proceeds to charity."

"Ah. I hadn't realized it was quite so high profile."

"It's a big event. There's an impressive lunch halfway through and an awards ceremony at the end."

"How many rounds?"

"Eight couples, so seven rounds, and there are four courts, which means there's no downtime, so that's cool."

"Who else is playing?"

"Hux and Elizabeth—they'll be easy to beat because she's only two foot tall."

I giggle. "Titus?"

"Yep, I think he's partnering Chrissie, one of Huxley's other sisters. Not sure who else is playing. They'll all be club members. It should be fun."

"Are you playing, Jamie?" I ask.

He shakes his head. "I don't know one end of a racket from the other. I'll be watching, and Gus-sitting." He glances at his brother in the mirror. "You should be warned, Mack is very competitive."

"What a shock." I grin at him. "Are you going to throw a tantrum if we lose a game?"

"We won't lose," he says. "We're gonna win the tournament."

I feel the first flutter of alarm. "I've never played at club level. And I'm a bit out of practice."

"Maybe, but you're playing with me, and I just know we're going to make a great team." His eyes gleam. He's nuclear-powered today, sparks practically flying from his fingers and the tips of his hair. Mmm. I just hope he has enough energy left for the end of the day. I'm in the mood for some fantastic sex.

His lips curve up. "Stop it," he murmurs.

"How come you can read my thoughts?" I complain, poking him with the end of my racket.

"It's not difficult." His eyes take on that lazy look that I know means he's thinking about sex.

"Get a room, you two," Jamie says with amusement.

I giggle. "It's his fault."

"Yeah, right." Mack pulls me up against him and kisses me. Mmm. I like nuclear-powered Mack.

I'm excited for the day. I love playing tennis, and I have a feeling the single-sex doubles we used to play at school are going to be nothing like playing with Mack. I just hope I don't let him down.

When we get to the sports club, we find it already bustling with both players and visitors. I haven't been here before, and I soon realize it's not like the sports ground I go to that lets everyone in. This is an exclusive establishment that requires an expensive membership. Today anyone can watch the tournament, but the place still reeks of money.

Jamie takes Gus around the outside to find Emma, and Mack walks me through a large wood-paneled and carpeted foyer that smells of beeswax and out the other side to a large function room. One side faces the courts, and the sliding doors have been pulled back to let the morning sunshine pour in. This is where the players are congregating, mixing with some of the guests. Waiters are handing out soft drinks and snacks. As I pass a couple of clusters of people, I hear conversation about stocks and shares and takeovers being discussed. Obviously, as well as raising money for charity, everyone sees this as a chance to catch up on business.

Mack walks up to where Huxley, Elizabeth, Titus, a young woman who must be Huxley's sister Chrissie, and Victoria are standing talking. They're all in tennis gear, apart from Victoria, whose wrist is in a brace. The others greet me warmly, and Elizabeth kisses me on the cheek.

"So glad you could make it," she says.

"I'm looking forward to it."

"You realize you're partnering the most competitive man in Christendom," Victoria says, amused.

"So I've heard. I keep telling him I haven't played much since high school."

"Don't listen to her," Mack says. "She's going to be amazing."

He turns away as someone speaks to him, so he misses the amused look they all exchange, but I don't. I blush, and Elizabeth winks at me.

There's no time to talk, though, because Huxley steps up to the mic and calls for everyone's attention. I'm not surprised he runs a business club. He's a striking guy, tall and good-looking, and very charismatic. He seems more outgoing than Mack, clearly knowing everyone present and taking time to speak to everyone at some point.

"Okay," he says, "we're about ready to start. Let me run through the rules for anyone who's not been here before. There are eight couples, so there'll be seven rounds, four before lunch and three after, fifteen minutes each, with five minutes in between to change courts and have refreshments if needed. The couple who wins the most games gets a point. And no ads."

Normally in tennis you have to win by two points, but I know that no ads means no advantage. That means sudden death after deuce, so you only have to win by one point. It speeds things up and eliminates the problems of games going on for too long.

"Mixed doubles rules," he states, "pretty much the same as ordinary doubles, except that on the deciding point in a game, the server must serve to the player of the same gender on the opposing team. And now, a quick note on etiquette. This tournament is for charity and supposed to be fun. So those of us with the stronger physique, take care when facing the gentler sex. Basically, I'm asking Elizabeth to take pity on us poor defenseless males."

She grins, and everyone laughs.

"The match list is on the board," he continues, "and all the umpires will have a copy, but you've all been sent a link to the online version that will be updated after each match, so use that if you can. Best of luck, and may the best couple win."

Everyone cheers and starts heading outside.

I go over to the board and look at the list of matches. Mack and I are couple C. Our first match is against Rawiri Wihongi and Ngaire Jones on court four. Match three is against Titus and Chrissie. Match five is versus Huxley and Elizabeth.

And our last match is against Felicity Scarlett-Rose and David Clarke.

"Fuck," I say out loud.

Mack moves up behind me and puts a hand on my hip as he reads the list. "What's up?"

"Look at the last match."

He reads it and gives a short laugh. "That'll be fun."

I spin my racket in my hand. "Okay, now I really want to win."

He meets my eyes, his own lighting with enthusiasm. "That's my girl."

"Come on. We've got battle to do."

Chapter Twenty-One

Mack

I can tell Sidnie is nervous, mainly because lots of people are watching. But as we walk onto the court, all I feel is energized. I just know she's going to be great. She's fast—okay, not as fast as me—but she can run, she's tall, and she's determined.

We don't get off to a great start, though. We lose the toss, and Rawiri opts to serve first, so I choose to receive. He's not a particularly big guy, but I've played against him a couple of times, and he's great at the net, so I know it's going to be a challenge. Sure enough, his first serve is hard and fast, and I just manage to return it, but it clips the net and bounces over the line. He then serves to Sidnie's backhand, and she just manages to hit it, but it rattles the net. I return his next serve, but it's not low enough; Ngaire volleys with a backhand, Sidnie returns it, and Rawiri slams it down between us. He finishes with an ace, and now we're one game down.

I half-expect Sidnie to look downcast, but as we change ends, she moves close to me and murmurs, "She's got a weak backhand. Concentrate on that."

I nod. "Okay."

We split and go to our starting positions, and it's my turn to serve.

Rawiri has obviously forgotten I'm a lefty, and completely misses my hooking serve. So I start with an ace, and that's enough to perk Sidnie and me up. Ngaire returns my serve, but my heavy topspin forehand goes across court to her backhand, and Sidnie was right— she gets her racket to it, but the return is weak enough to allow me to reach the net and slam it down the middle between them. Rawiri manages to return my next serve, but Sidnie's fast and volleys it back, Ngaire only just gets it back over the net, and I spin it enough to fool Rawiri and he hits it out of court. My last serve is a good one, and

Ngaire only just gets it back; Sidnie then volleys straight at her, and Ngaire squeals and misses it completely.

Now we're starting to find our feet, and I can see Sidnie's confidence growing. We win the next game easily, and then it's her turn to serve. She aces against Ngaire on the first shot and gives me the most beautiful smile as she walks to the other side. We're 40-15 up when the umpire calls time, which means the match is ours.

"Congratulations," Rawiri says, shaking hands as the crowd cheers. "Good game."

"Excellent serving," Ngaire tells her.

"You're so great at the net," Sidnie replies, "I nearly didn't return some of those volleys."

Smiling, I sling my arm around her, and we pick up our bags and start walking to the next court.

"Have I told you how hot you look in that dress?" I murmur, nuzzling her ear as we walk.

"Hot being the operative word," she says, wiping her brow with the sweat band she wears on her wrist. "I'm melting."

"Did you put lotion on? I'm happy to rub some in for you."

"My breasts are covered, in case you haven't noticed."

I laugh and kiss her temple. "I don't know why you were worried. You're a talented player."

"I'm lucky to have Usain Bolt as a partner. You're so fast, Mack. I don't know how you covered the ground on that last shot."

Talking about the game, we get to the court, have a few swallows of one of the energy drinks offered by the club, and then it's time for match two.

Starting to find our stride, we win the match easily, barely dropping a point.

After that, it's off to play Titus and Chrissie.

This match is much more difficult. Titus is even taller than me, built like a brick shithouse, and with the muscles of a Viking. Chrissie is smaller than Sidnie, but she's fast and great at the net, and the four of us are a good match. Every point goes to fifteen-all, thirty-all, and deuce, and if it wasn't for the no-ads rule, I'm sure every game would have taken us forever to complete.

When the umpire blows the whistle, it's one game all and thirty-all on the third, so we get to finish the tiebreaker. Luckily, I'm serving, as Sidnie opted to open the match by serving after we won the toss.

Remembering Huxley's rules on etiquette, I've tailored my serves to the women players on the court, and I don't want to change that now. Instead of using force, I aim for clever placement, made easier by being a leftie. I serve down the middle to Chrissie's backhand, and she hits it into the net to make it forty-thirty. The last serve to Titus is more difficult. I serve the first at light speed, but it bounces a fraction over the tramline.

"Out," the umpire calls.

"Lucky bastard," I call to Titus, who grins, and the crowd chuckles, easing the tension a little.

Sidnie blows me a kiss. Lips curving up, I serve, Titus returns as I run into the net, I volley over, Chrissie volleys neatly back, and it's a low, sneaky ball. But Sidnie somehow manages to scoop it up for a wonderful high lob over their heads. Titus runs back, manages to get to it, smacks it hard—and it sails just over the outside tramlines.

"Match to Dr. Hart and Ms. Beaver," the umpire declares.

Sidnie and I high five, then laugh and hug before circling the net to shake hands with Titus and Chrissie.

"So close," I say, clapping Titus on the arm.

"We were outplayed," he admits. "You two make a good team."

"Yeah." I put my arm around Sidnie. "We do."

She grins and lifts her face to receive my kiss as we walk off the court.

We win the next match easily, and then it's time for lunch. Just sandwiches and cake, nothing too heavy to slow us down at the net, but I still make Sidnie shake her head with how many sandwiches I manage to put away.

"Have you checked the table?" Elizabeth asks as we join her and Huxley on our way for match five. "You're neck and neck with Felicity and David—you're the only two couples who haven't lost a match yet."

"Plenty of time to crash and burn," I say cheerfully, unzipping my racket cover as we arrive.

Sidnie chuckles and joins me on the court, waving to where Jamie and Emma are sitting in the shade with Gus. The umpire tosses the coin, and we win and choose to serve. It's hot now, the sun high in the sky. We've both reapplied lotion, and we're both wearing hats with peaks to keep the sun out of our eyes.

"Anything I should know about these two?" Sidnie asks me as we walk back to our places, and Huxley and Elizabeth walk to theirs.

"I know I joked about Elizabeth's height, but she's an excellent volley player. She's easy to lob, though, so Hux plays at the baseline. It's about placement with these two—making him run, then lobbing the other side, or volleying to her backhand. Don't worry, we've got this."

I turn out to be right. They make us work for it, and catch us out a few times with some sneaky moves, but we're all over them, and they know it. We go two games up, and in the third, sensing defeat, Huxley and Elizabeth turn it into a comedy match.

"We need to distract them," Huxley tells her. "Get your kit off."

"I'm not getting my boobs out just so you can win a match," she protests.

"I'll take mine off then," he says, and starts undoing the tie on his shorts.

She rolls her eyes. "If you do that, I'm going to call for new balls."

The crowd laughs and cheers, thoroughly enjoying the show.

The two of them play the fool in the final game, including cheating, with Elizabeth telling me, "All's fair in love, business, and tennis, Mack, I keep telling you."

We join in to make it fun, and I manage to hit a ball from under one leg, while Sidnie tries to put Elizabeth off her serve with a comedy dance, making her laugh.

But it makes no difference. Just a few points later, the match is ours, to much cheering from the crowd, who thoroughly enjoyed the spectacle.

Then it's on to match six, which is against a couple who plays on the club's team.

Sidnie checks her phone as we walk to the next court. "Felicity and David won, too. We're still equal on points." She huffs in frustration. "Dammit. You just know it's going to come down to the last match."

"Of course it is. It was written in the fucking stars. But first things first. This couple we're about to play is pretty good and play regularly for the club. It's going to be a tricky match, so stay on your toes."

I hold out my hand, and she slides hers into it.

"We make quite a good team, don't we?" she asks. Her face is pink, and her curls peek out from beneath the hat despite her attempts to restrain them with an elastic band. She looks amazing in her tennis dress, with her gorgeous long legs.

"We're fantastic," I tell her. "In more ways than one."

Leaving her with that, I go up to the umpire for the toss. We win and choose to serve, and Sidnie and I take our places.

As I expected, it turns out to be a hard-fought match. On the first game they're a hair's breadth from winning forty-love, but we fight back to bring it to deuce, only to lose it on the final point. By game two, Sidnie and I are fully warmed up and playing well, and we win it relatively easily.

The third game is harder. Sidnie's serving, it's very hot, and I think she's getting tired. We get to deuce just before the umpire blows the whistle, and then she's serving for the match. She sends the first serve out. Her nerves get to her, and the second serve isn't a strong one. The woman gives a sound forehand that sends it whistling to Sidnie's backhand. Sidnie hits it, but it bounces out of the tramlines.

"Fuck it." She bends at the waist, hands on her hips, breathing hard, then straightens as I walk up to her. "I'm so sorry."

"Don't worry about it."

"I lost us this," she says, obviously disappointed with herself.

"They played well, Sid. Don't be so hard on yourself." I lift her chin and kiss her.

"Aren't you mad at me?" she whispers. "I thought you were the most competitive man in Christendom."

"Felicity and David also lost. We're equal on points—the only two couples to have lost one game. So we still have a chance. But even so, why would I be mad? You're playing so well. Your volleying is stunningly good. And your serves are the fastest I've seen out of all the women today."

She tucks her hair behind her ear. "Thank you."

"Come on. Let's have a drink and get ready for the last match."

I can't lie and say I don't want to win. I don't really care about the tournament—I am competitive, but it's a charity match, and as long as everyone has fun, I'm happy to have played well and won a few games.

I do want to beat Clarke. I've never forgiven him for being rude to Nadine, and I know he won't have forgiven me for not giving him a job. I don't think the fact that he's dating Felicity is a coincidence. She's rich and stunning, and I bet he thought I'd be jealous when I found out they were dating.

Spoiler: I'm not.

Somehow I can't imagine Sidnie throwing my coffee machine through a window, even if we broke up.

The thought keeps a smile on my face all the way to the next court.

*

Sidnie

Fuck, I'm nervous. Why does the whole tournament have to depend on the last match?

I honestly didn't think we'd do as well as we have. It's obvious to me that I'm the weak link in our team, but I imagine that's normal in mixed doubles. Mack's serves are fast as bullets, and he's like lightning on the court, covering space in half the time it takes me to run around. No doubt he could improve his technique if he played a lot more, but for a nerd who spends most of his days with his head stuck in computers, he's pretty damn good.

I'm doing okay, but I'm hot and getting tired. I used to go to the gym regularly, but I haven't been for a few months. I do run most mornings, but I can tell I haven't been doing weights, and my arms and shoulders are aching.

Still, I've made it this far, and Mack's compliments were nice enough to keep my chin up and give me hope that I can at least hold my own.

There are four matches taking place, but everyone knows this is going to decide the winner, and the majority of spectators have gravitated over here, and are taking their places in the stands under the shade. Mack grabs a couple of energy drinks from the cooler and brings one over to me, and I drink half of it, hoping it'll perk me up.

"Have you played them before?" I ask, watching David and Felicity removing the covers from their rackets and walking over to the umpire.

"No." Mack finishes his drink and tosses the can in the recycling bin. "We'll have to make it up as we go along." He grins then—he's enjoying it. "Come on, sexy. Let's do this."

We join them by the umpire, who tosses a coin. David calls heads—and it's tails. We choose to serve.

"May the best couple win," Felicity says.

"At least the game's a bit more even now you've partnered with a real woman." David glances toward the stand and laughs before he walks away. Felicity stares at Mack, then drops her gaze and follows him.

I frown. Was David talking about her? That doesn't make sense.

Then I follow his gaze to the stand and realize what he meant. He was referring to Mack's previous tennis partner, who's sitting there with her sprained wrist. It was a disparaging remark about her being a transgender woman.

My jaw drops. "He was talking about Victoria?"

Mack has stiffened, and he doesn't say anything as we walk across the court.

"You okay?" I ask cautiously.

He looks at me then, and his eyes are filled with fury. "I'm going to crush that motherfucker," he snaps. He points his racket at me. "And you're going to help me."

Delight fills me. "Absolutely. Just tell me what you want me to do."

His lips curve up, and he slides a hand to the nape of my neck and kisses me then, hard, ignoring the crowd, who immediately give a huge cheer. When we break apart, his expression is filled with determination. "You serve," he says. "Show the fucker that women can play as well as men."

I nod, because it'll also mean he gets to serve in the important third game. "Let's do it."

We take our places, and the game begins.

Immediately, I know it's going to be tough. David's not quite as tall as Mack, but he's muscular, and he's obviously played before. He returns my serve easily, and he's into the net immediately, providing a wall through which it's difficult to direct the ball.

Felicity is almost as tall as me, and she's also a great volley player. The four of us are well matched, which isn't surprising considering we've both only lost one game. We go fifteen-all, and then thirty-all.

Considering I'm so tired, though, I serve better than I have all day, maybe buoyed up by Mack's compliments. On my next serve to David, I catch him on the backhand, and he clips the net on the return, sending the ball spinning out of the court.

"Fuck it!" he yells, clearly furious as he stalks to his next position.

I glance at Mack, who winks at me. I hide a smile and walk to the other side, and serve against Felicity. It's an ace, and it wins us the game.

The crowd claps, and we change ends. David's muttering to himself. I glance at Felicity. The two of them aren't talking, and she's quiet, but she looks determined.

We take our places, David to serve, and the crowd falls quiet.

David serves toward the middle line, and I think he's forgotten Mack's a leftie, because he returns it with a solid forehand, slicing it across the court, just out of David's reach. Love-fifteen.

Now David's serving to me. Keyed up, I manage to return it, and the four of us exchange a flurry of volleys. But a well-placed spin by Felicity sends the ball straight down the middle, and Mack and I both miss it. Fifteen-all.

"Shit." He blows out a breath.

"Sorry," I murmur as we walk back from the net together.

He just rests a hand in the middle of my back for a moment before he parts to go back to receive the serve.

This time David has remembered he's playing a leftie. He sends it to Mack's backhand. Mack returns it and sends it spinning across the court, but it's too high, and Felicity slams it down on the ground just out of my reach. Thirty-fifteen.

I clip the edge of David's serve to me, and it flies off into the crowd. Forty-fifteen.

David serves to Mack. He returns with a solid backhand. Felicity counters with an incredible volley that cuts right across me, completely wrong-footing me, and losing us the game. It's now one-all.

I retrieve my energy drink and have a few swallows before returning to the net. At least Mack's serving. But I can see the other two are as determined as we are.

Mack misses his first serve. On the second, David returns it, then runs in to the net. I volley it back straight at him, a tad too high. He smacks the ball with a volley that shoots toward me at a million miles an hour. It hits me on my upper left arm with a loud thwack that makes me squeal.

"Jesus." Mack runs over to me. My dress is sleeveless, so it's easy to see the scarlet mark the ball has left on my skin.

In professional mixed doubles it's common for the men to play on the fact that the women are usually the weaker players, but it certainly doesn't follow Huxley's rules of etiquette.

Still, it's not an illegal move, and I shrug off Mack's hand and say, "Don't worry about it," even though it's stinging like hell. But all it's done is make me even more determined to win.

Mack hesitates, but when I walk back to my position, he strides off to the baseline. I see Felicity look at him, but his gaze is fixed on David, who's not bothering to hide his smile.

It's love-fifteen. Mack serves to Felicity. She just gets to it, but hits it into the net. Fifteen-all.

He misses his first serve. Hits the second to David's backhand. David returns it easily, but I'm waiting and slam it down at Felicity's feet. She squeals and swings but misses it. Thirty-fifteen.

The tension is rising on the court. The spectators are excited, watching with bated breath. Mack bounces the ball a few times, and I'm sure he must be talking to himself silently, psyching himself up. He serves—and misses. Serves again, and David returns. I volley. Felicity volleys back immediately. David lobs Mack, but he's fucking fast, and he's back in time to return it with a solid backhand that takes David by surprise. He tries to volley it but misses. Forty-fifteen.

"Aaaargh!" David screams his frustration. Felicity glares at him, but he doesn't notice.

Mack walks toward me, and I face away so they won't see whatever tactic he wants to share.

"You've got the best legs in the whole tournament," he murmurs.

"Apart from you," I counter, and we both laugh, which I'm sure enrages David.

Mack walks back to the baseline, absolutely buzzing with energy, and he throws the ball up around his back and then catches it, causing the crowd to cheer and David to glare.

He bounces it a few times, and the crowd falls quiet. He tosses it high.

Then he serves an ace.

"Wooooo!" I yell, run over to him, and throw my arms around him, and he laughs and hugs me.

"Game Dr. Hart and Ms. Beaver," the umpire states.

"No," David yells. "It was out. The ball was out."

We break apart as the cheers of the crowd die down.

"It was out," he repeats furiously. "Way over the line. You've got to be fucking kidding me."

"The ball was in," the umpire states. "Game over, Mr. Clarke."

Mack gives David an amused look, then goes over to put the cover on his racket.

"No!" David smashes his racket on the ground.

"Dude." Mack's smile fades. "You lost. Show a bit of sportsmanship."

"Fuck off." David grabs his bag and ruined racket and walks away, leaving Felicity standing there, looking horror stricken.

"I'm sorry," she mutters before picking up her own bag and following him off.

Mack purses his lips and approaches the umpire. "I'm sorry about that. Are you sure the ball was in?"

"Absolutely," he replies through his microphone so everyone can hear. "Not a doubt in my mind. The game is yours."

At the same time, several people sitting in the stands near the baseline yell, "It was definitely in!"

Mack nods, and the crowd cheers and whistles again.

He comes over to me, puts his arms around me, and lifts me up. "Champions!" he says, and laughs. And then he lowers me down and crushes his lips to mine. "You're amazing," he says when we finally break apart. "Do you have any idea how crazy I am about you?"

But there's no time for me to reply, because Victoria, Jamie, Emma, and some of the others who've made their way over from their matches come up to congratulate us, and I'm lost in a whirl of happy exultation that's only increased by the memory of Mack's words as they continue to swirl in my head throughout the rest of the afternoon.

Chapter Twenty-Two

Sidnie

We eventually make it back to the function room, where everyone continues to congratulate us. A waiter comes up with a tray of glasses of champagne, and Mack and I toast each other with a smile before joining in with the cheers as Huxley urges everyone to raise their glasses to us.

Then it's time for the awards ceremony. It's only as Huxley takes the mic and starts talking about how successful the day has been and how much money we've raised that I look around and realize I can't see David and Felicity.

"They've left," Mack murmurs when I ask him where they are. "Talk about bad sportsmanship."

But there's no time to talk about it because Huxley is entertaining the crowd by awarding certificates and gifts like cans of tennis balls or T-shirts for best lob and best drop shot, and fun things like best dressed player. Titus gets the award for the largest tennis bag. Chrissie gets the one for fanciest shoes. He gives Elizabeth the award for the best victory dance because apparently she moonwalked after they won a match, and she promptly repeats it and makes everyone laugh. I get best hair, which makes me roll my eyes and poke my tongue out at him. Mack gets 'player who ate the most at lunch', which makes me giggle and him grin. Elizabeth then goes up and gives Huxley the award for best trash talker, which makes us all cheer.

Then it's the trophies for the top three places. In third place are Rawiri and Ngaire, and they go up to get their trophy to lots of cheering and whistles.

"Second place goes to David and Felicity," Huxley says. "Unfortunately they've left, so I'll have to pass it on to them later."

Everyone claps politely, but I can see people muttering about David's performance at the last match. He didn't do himself any favors there. What an idiot, considering there were a lot of his business colleagues here.

"And first place goes to Mack and Sidnie," Huxley announces with a smile.

Mack takes my hand and leads me through the crowd and up to Huxley, who presents us with the trophy of a tennis ball on a small plinth and a magnum of Champagne. We lift the trophy in the air together and laugh, then rejoin the crowd with everyone cheering and clapping us on the back.

"Thank you all so much for making the day so successful," Huxley adds. "And don't forget, it's the New Year's Eve Party tonight at the club from seven p.m. I hope to see you there!"

"Well done you two," Elizabeth says as we walk up to her and the others.

"It was great fun," I reply, smiling as Mack gives me the trophy to hold.

"How's your arm?" he asks, turning me so he can inspect where the ball hit.

"It's okay." I'm lying—it hurts like hell, but there's no point in making a fuss. Mack frowns as he examines it, though, because it's already starting to turn purple and green.

"How did you get that?" Chrissie asks.

"David smacked it at her from about six feet away," Mack states.

Huxley, who joins us in time to overhear the comment, says, "Seriously?"

"It's fine," I say, seeing Elizabeth frown and remembering that David works for her.

But Huxley and Mack exchange a glance that tells me they're not going to forget David's behavior today.

We stay for one more glass of Champagne, and by then everyone's starting to get ready to leave. Huxley and Victoria have to get back to the club ready for the evening, and most of the players announce they need some downtime before the party.

We grab our bags and, still holding our trophy, I wave goodbye and follow Mack out of the sports club and over to where Jamie's standing talking to Emma by the car, Gus lying by his feet. We all get in, and Jamie drives us back to the apartment.

"Quite a day for you guys," Emma says as we all go up in the elevator. "I bet you're knackered."

"At least we have a few hours before the party," Mack says. "Are you two sure you don't want to come?"

"No, thank you." Emma exchanges a glance with Jamie, who gives her a small smile.

"What's going on?" Mack asks.

Jamie hesitates and looks at his girlfriend, who nods, her eyes dancing. "We weren't going to say anything," he says. "It's still early. But… Emma's pregnant."

"And feeling very sick," she admits with a laugh, "so I'm going to bed early tonight!"

Mack's eyebrows shoot up, and he pulls his brother into a bearhug while I throw my arms around Emma. "Oh, congratulations!" I say to her. "How far along are you?"

"Only eight weeks, so it's a bit too soon to announce it really. But we couldn't keep it a secret from you guys."

"I can't believe it." Mack moves back to study his brother's face. "It's fantastic news. I'm so pleased for you."

"Thank you." Jamie's face is flushed, and he's obviously pleased at Mack's reaction. "We don't mind saying that it wasn't planned, but we're really happy about it. And I've asked her to marry me, and she's said yes."

That leads to more cheers and hugs. "We only want a small do," Emma says, "I'm not into the big white wedding, and I don't have a lot of family. We might even have it on the beach up north."

"That sounds amazing," I say. "Oh, what fun."

"We can all talk more about it later," Emma says. "Right now I'm sure you two need a rest!"

"And you," I tell her, "I'm sorry you're feeling so sick."

"Throwing up three times a day," she says cheerfully. "See you later."

They walk out of the elevator into their apartment, and we go up to the top floor and head toward Mack's. Gus runs in before him, sniffs around, then immediately gets in his bed, exhausted from all the day's excitement.

We put our bags down, and Mack stretches, then goes into the kitchen and takes out a bottle of water from the fridge. He drinks half of it, then glances over at me mid-drink and slowly lowers the bottle. He wipes his mouth and raises an eyebrow. "What?"

I shake my head. Honestly, this guy. He's still in his tennis whites, although he's taken off his shoes and socks now, so he's barefoot. He's all sun-kissed and glowing, his normally neat hair ruffled. I know he's going to be warm and sweaty beneath his top.

Maybe it's the fact that I'm still buzzing from our win, or because of what happened on the court with David and Felicity, or it could be the two glasses of Champagne I had on a nearly empty stomach, but I feel *hot as*, so turned on that I could easily push him onto the floor and do him then and there.

He screws the top back on the water bottle, leaves it on the counter, and comes over to where I'm leaning on the countertop. "Seriously," he says, amused. "All that exercise, and you're still thinking about sex?"

I grab a handful of his top and pull him toward me. "I want you," I tell him, my lips brushing his. "Right now."

He laughs and kisses me, then gently pushes me away. "Let me have a shower first. I'm all hot and sweaty."

"Are you trying to turn me on?"

He chuckles, trying to catch my hands, but I manage to get one beneath his top and slip it up his back. Oh, man, he's right—my fingers slide over his hot, damp skin. Wow, that's so erotic I almost come on the spot.

"Sidnie," he scolds, pulling my hand out, "I'm disgusting, please, let me have a shower."

"No way." I lean forward, press my lips to his neck where the V of his top reveals his skin, and lick the hollow at the base of his throat.

"Jesus." He growls. "Stop it."

Wanting to fire him up, I push him, but he's like a fucking monolith, and he doesn't move. So I shove him harder with both hands, forcing him to step back. He pushes me in return, not hard—just in play—but it makes me stumble. My pulse races, and before I can think better of it, I draw back my hand and give him a sound slap around the face. It's not hard, there's no anger behind it, but it makes a crack that startles both of us.

Oops.

His eyes blaze. Before I can react, he puts a hand on my collarbone, just below my throat, and pushes me up against the wall with a move that knocks the breath from my body. I look up at him, and my heart pounds.

He holds me there, looking thoughtful for a few seconds. His eyes are wide, intense.

Then he cocks his head. "You want to play. Okay, we'll play. But you're going to regret being sassy with me."

Feeling brave, I taunt, "You're all talk."

He looks at me for a moment. His eyes are lazy. Amused. "Would you like to repeat that?"

I shiver. He suddenly seems a lot taller and bigger than me. I feel as if I've poked a tiger through the bars of his cage with a stick, and now I've realized the cage door is open. Holy fuck. I'm not brave enough to say it again.

"I thought not," he says. Slowly, he lowers his lips to just above mine. He waits a second, then brushes his lips up my jaw to my ear, and warms it with his breath. "You wanted to rile me up? Well, it worked."

I inhale, my heart hammering.

"Now I'm in the mood to fuck you within an inch of your life." His eyes gleam. "And I'm going to make you come over and over again, until you beg for mercy."

"W-what about the safe word?" I whisper.

"I told you that if you teased me, there'd be consequences." His voice is low and husky. "Safe words aren't going to work today. I'm going to keep fucking you until I'm ready to stop, understand me? I'm going to do whatever I want to you. And you just get to lie there and take it."

My chest heaves. I can't tell whether he's serious.

His lips curve up, just a fraction.

Then he pulls me away from the wall and starts walking me backward. I assume he's taking me to the bedroom, but to my surprise he directs me through the living room, then out through the doors onto the patio.

He drags one of the chairs away from the table with one hand, then pushes me so my butt is resting against the table.

My eyes widen, and I glance over my shoulder to the apartment block opposite. "Mack! People can see us."

"I don't give a fuck." He slides his hand up my tennis dress, hooks his fingers in the elastic at the waist of my Lycra shorts, and pulls them down in one swift movement, as if he's whisking away a tablecloth beneath plates and glasses in a magic show. I squeal, but he pushes me back onto the table, then lifts my legs to pull off my shoes and the shorts. Before I can complain, he slides his hand up my thigh, slips his fingers beneath the elastic of my knickers, and moves his fingers down into me.

His eyes gleam. "Sidnie," he says, amused, "you're wet already. Am I turning you on?"

"Jesus." Embarrassed, I try to push his hand away, but it's like trying to move a steel bar fixed into a wall with concrete.

"You're such a dirty girl," he says, kissing my jaw.

"Fuck off." The words leave my mouth before I get a chance to vet them.

He slides a hand into my hair and pulls my head back so I'm looking right into his eyes. "Say that again. I fucking dare you."

My lips part. Heart pounding, I can only watch as he pushes down his shorts to release his erection, tugs aside my knickers, and slides the tip of his erection down through my folds. No foreplay then. Wow, he's really going for it.

Still gripping my hair, he pulls me onto my back on the table, holds my hip with a hand, and thrusts forward, burying himself deep inside me.

I arch my back and cry out, "Aaahhh…"

He leans over me and begins to give long, slow thrusts, almost pulling out each time before sliding back in right to the hilt. I daren't look around because I'm convinced someone must be able to see us. Instead, I close my eyes to shut out the world. Immediately, though, he demands, "Open," and I look up at him. My pulse is racing, and even though I'm trying to stay in control, he's not making it easy.

He kisses me then, forcefully, insisting, not asking that I open my mouth, and he plunges his tongue inside, kissing me deeply while he thrusts hard. Ah, no, I can already feel the first twinges of an orgasm way off in the distance.

He lifts his head and gives a smug laugh. "Already? Wow, go on then. Squeeze your pussy around me, honey. You're so fucking tight. Come on."

I let my head drop back and squeeze my eyes shut. Think about something else, I urge myself… But it's impossible. He's too insistent, too sexy, and at that moment he changes the angle, grinding against me with each thrust, hitting me at exactly the right spot. And he knows it, the bastard—he knows exactly what he's doing.

"Sidnie…" he warns me as I bite my bottom lip, "do as you're told."

The orgasm hits me, and I groan as I'm overcome by five or six powerful clenches around him.

He stops moving, waiting until I've finished, giving a minute rocking of his hips to see me through it. When I'm done, I open my eyes and glare up at him.

He withdraws. "Good girl."

Groaning, I flop back on the table, but he grabs my hands and pulls me up. "No rest for the wicked," he says, and he turns me around.

"Ah… Mack…" But I already know there's no point in protesting.

He yanks down my knickers and removes them, then puts a hand between my shoulder blades and pushes me onto my elbows on the table. After separating my legs with a knee, he moves my feet apart, slides his erection beneath me, and with one smooth thrust, he buries himself balls deep again.

"Aaahhh…" My hands clench into fists, and I rest my forehead on them. "Fuck."

"Are you regretting your little outburst yet?" He starts moving inside me again.

I know this is all play. I'm sure if I were to say the safe word, he'd stop. But I don't want to. I'm so turned on, I'm turning molten inside. This guy… Every time I think of him coolly scoring that last ace on the court, it nearly gives me an orgasm.

He thrusts away, setting up a steady pace, and I stifle a groan. How long can he keep going? I need to show him he's not as in control as he thinks… but I have no idea how to do that when I'm face down on the table being screwed soundly from behind.

He's pulled the skirt of my dress up over my hips, and I know he's admiring my butt as he caresses it with a hand. He slows and withdraws, and I feel his fingers move down into me, gathering my moisture. Once again, he enters me. Then he slides his fingers down the base of my spine… over my tailbone… and down between the cheeks of my bottom…

"Oh fuck." I cover my face with my hands.

He spreads the lubrication he gathered there, then licks his fingers and adds some more. I can't stifle a groan, and I feel him give a short

SERENITY WOODS

laugh. Then he slips his thumb down and presses against the tight muscle. Gently, he pushes the tip of his thumb inside.

I clench and groan, and he bends forward over me. "Time for orgasm number two." He removes his thumb, licks it, then replaces it inside me.

"Oh Jesus." I moan as he starts thrusting again, continuing to tease me with his thumb, and there's no hope for me at all. In less than thirty seconds pleasure begins to sweep over me, and he grunts and thrusts harder, riding me all the way through my climax, and leaving me gasping and shuddering on the table.

He withdraws, pulls me up, and then lifts me, wrapping my legs around his waist. I give up all pretense of fighting him and crush my lips to his, and continue to kiss him as he carries me through to the kitchen.

Once we're there, he lowers my feet to the floor and strips off my dress and underwear. Then he lifts me onto the countertop and, without a pause, pulls me to the edge and slides inside me again.

"Tell me how badly you want me to fuck you," he demands as he begins to thrust.

"So badly," I murmur as he kisses me. "Oh God, I want you so much…"

I've never been screwed like it. He takes me in so many different positions I lose count, in every room in the house, making me come over and over again, fast, slow, and everything in between, with his mouth, his fingers, and during penetration, until I'm well into double figures.

By the time we get to the bedroom, I'm exhausted and aching, completely molten inside, and desperately feeling the need to right the balance of power between us.

"Mack," I whisper as he lowers my feet to the floor. I lift up and brush my lips against his. "Can I taste you?"

He hesitates. Ooh, he's thinking about it.

"Please sir," I whisper. "Dr. Hart. Let me taste you."

He gives a wry smile, but I can see I've got him. Without being told, I sink to my knees, push down his shorts and boxer-briefs, and close my hand around him. Then, looking up at him, I lower my lips and take him in my mouth.

"Aaahhh…" He slides his hand into my hair and clenches his fingers. "Jesus, that feels good."

I remove my mouth and lick all the way up his shaft. "Fuck my mouth," I whisper. "Hard as you like. I won't break."

He closes his eyes and tips back his head, giving a helpless sigh. Hiding a smile, I take him in my mouth again and suck him as I stroke up and down with my hand.

Ohhh... now I've got him—I can tell by the way he holds my head and moves his hips. I take him as deep as possible, and he groans, pushing that little bit further, forcing me to take him. Fuck, that's so hot, and I can see he's losing it. It takes less than thirty seconds before I feel him tensing. I'm surprised he's lasted that long after the length of time he's been screwing me—the man's a freak of nature.

"Sidnie..." He whispers. "I'm gonna come..."

I think he's warning me in case I don't want him to come in my mouth, but I just look up at him and take him deeper, and that's it—he groans and comes, filling my mouth. I take it all, still looking up at him, and he watches through hazy eyes as I deliberately and slowly swallow.

"Oh... fucking hell." He gives a short laugh, lets his head drop back, and gives a long sigh.

I lick my lips, feeling slightly smug. Two can play at that game.

Unfortunately, it turns out to be a severe case of hubris, because he's not done yet.

Chapter Twenty-Three

Mack

I look at Sidnie, my heart still racing from my climax, only to catch a glimpse of smugness on her face before she wipes it away. Oh-ho, so she thinks she's got me, does she?

Her eyes light with alarm as she realizes she hasn't been quick enough to hide it. I whip off my top, then push my shorts and underwear off, and she laughs and turns away to scamper across the bed, but she's forgotten that I can cover a hundred meters in just over ten seconds, and I catch her easily and flip her onto her back.

I lean over her, pinning her hands above her head and straddling her, holding her down.

"You think that's it?" I slide a hand over her breasts, then drop it between us and circle a thumb over her clit. She jerks and moans.

"Have mercy," she says, her chest heaving. Jesus, she looks amazing, her face and chest flushed pink, her hair in disarray, naked and stretched out beneath me. "You told me I'd beg for mercy, and I am. Seriously, I'm exhausted."

"Like I care about that." I sit back, looking down at her bare, swollen pussy that's pink and glistening from all her orgasms. Fuck, she's beautiful. I stroke her clit, occasionally dipping my fingers down into her, keeping my touch light, because I don't want to make her sore. "I think you've got one more orgasm in you," I say softly.

"Ah, Mack, no..." She closes her eyes and groans.

I relent for a moment, and instead take myself in hand and start arousing myself. "What?" I ask as she lifts her head and stares. "You think you're the only one who can have multiple orgasms?"

"I... but... oh..." Speechless, she watches as I grow hard again. "Oh dear."

I give a short laugh and move between her legs. "Maybe next time you'll think twice about being cheeky to me?"

She looks up into my eyes, and they're so full of admiration and helplessness that it makes me melt. "Yes sir," she whispers, giving me a mischievous little smile.

I stop and just look at her for a moment, caught up in my feelings for her. It's been an amazing day, and it's all down to her.

"Good girl," I murmur, and she sighs.

Gently, I press the tip of my erection into her and slide inside. Her eyes flutter shut again, and she gives a soft moan.

"We're gonna go slow," I tell her. "Because we're going to come together, okay?"

Her eyes open at that, curious and interested.

"It's going to take communication and coordination," I say, "but we've already proven we can do that, right?"

She nods, her lips parting as I release her hands. She lowers them and rests them on my chest, fanning them out admiringly over my pecs.

"I need you to tell me where you are," I say. "Out of ten. I'm at three right now."

"Five," she says immediately. "I'm way ahead of you, boy."

I chuckle and lift up a little so I'm not grinding against her. "Then I have some catching up to do."

So I thrust for a while, not touching her anywhere else, just enjoying the sensation of being inside her, being enveloped in her velvet heat, and concentrating on my own pleasure. "Four," I murmur as my pulse begins to speed up, then, "Five," not long after.

She pulls me down to kiss her and wraps her legs around my waist.

"Fuck," I say, "six and a half," and she giggles and opens her mouth as I thrust my tongue inside.

Jesus, she's so hot, moving with me as if she was made for me. "Six," she whispers as I caress her breasts, and then, "Seven..." as I lower my mouth to her nipples and suck.

I can't help it; even though I climaxed only minutes ago, she's too sexy and too beautiful for me to last much longer. I'm soon at seven, and then we say, "Eight," at exactly the same time and give brief smiles before I frown and pick up the pace. This time I move up an inch so I'm arousing her as I move, and she groans and drops her hands back over her head.

"Nine," she says before too long, "careful."

"I'm there with you, honey." I feel the first twinges of my climax deep inside and look into her eyes. "Are you ready?"

She nods, eyes sparkling, and I push up onto my hands and thrust hard.

Despite our best efforts, she comes a few seconds before me, but by that point we don't care, and we lock together as our bodies clench and pulse, hot skin sliding over hot skin, lost in the beauty and the bliss of it, the ultimate pleasure that two people can experience together.

We're just floating down to earth when Gus jumps on the bed and pads over to lick my shoulder.

We both burst out laughing, and I push him away. "Not now, dude."

Sidnie giggles and puts a hand on him as he flops at the bottom of the bed. "I think we must have woken him up."

"That was you." I withdraw and collapse onto my back with a groan. "I think they might have heard you in Wellington."

"Oh jeez. What's a girl to do when she's been fucked into next Tuesday?"

I give a short laugh, then blow out a long breath.

She yawns. "I'm so fucking tired."

"Me too." I look over at the sun streaming through the open window, the net curtains billowing in the breeze. "What a perfect summer day."

She's quiet for a moment. Then she yawns again and says, "You have nice legs."

I chuckle, then close my eyes.

Within a minute, all three of us are asleep.

*

I wake about an hour later.

The sun is a little lower, but still hot and bright. I'm on my back, naked and on top of the duvet, the summer breeze brushing over me like a silk scarf.

I turn my head. Gus has snuck up the bed next to Sidnie and curled up to her back. She's lying on her side facing me, still asleep.

Rolling onto my side, I prop my head on a hand and study her.

The bright sexual flush has faded from her skin, but she's still sun-kissed, her nose a bit pink. Her curls tumble across the pillow like cotton candy, golden and fluffy. Her skin is smooth and unblemished, although she has a mole just above her left nipple that I've already kissed a few times.

The bruise on her left arm where David hit her with the ball is a livid purple and green. I glare at it, filled with a sense of protectiveness I hadn't thought to feel. He hurt my woman. Part of me wants to destroy him for that.

My woman. I smile at my own words.

I think about Jamie, getting married, and with a baby on the way. I'm so pleased for him. He had a tough start, and it's no less than he deserves.

I admit to feeling a tad… what? Wistful? Puzzled? Envious? Of both Jamie and Kai. They seem so confident in their love. So sure it's all going to work out.

Do I want what they have? Love? Marriage? Children? I've honestly never considered it before. My work has always been the most important thing in my life, and women interfered with that, to the point where I was convinced I would never be able to mix the two.

But now?

Sidnie let me work this week. She didn't complain. Or badger me with calls or texts, not until I messaged her first. And when she did text back, she always made me smile. The only time I've seen her sad was at the Bay, when she was tired and thinking about her father, and she's done nothing but enrich my life a hundredfold. She's happy and positive, like a sunrise, full of beauty and promise.

At that moment, she stirs and opens her eyes.

She looks at me, blinks, then smiles. "Hello, you."

"Hey, sleepy."

"What's the time?"

"Five thirty."

"In the afternoon, right?"

I laugh. "Yeah. We haven't slept that much."

"Have you been awake long?"

"Only a few minutes."

She sighs.

I reach out a hand and gently touch the bruise on her arm. "Is it sore?"

"Tender."

I reach over and kiss it. Then I bend and kiss her mouth.

She narrows her eyes at me as I move back. "You're a very naughty boy."

"You're the one who riled me up. I told you there'd be consequences."

She pokes her tongue out at me, and I chuckle.

"You want something to eat?" I ask.

"Will there be food tonight?"

"Oh yeah, but I'm hungry now."

"Of course you are," she says, amused. "Sure, I could eat."

"Stay there. I'll get it."

I go into the kitchen, take out some hummus, veggies, cheese, and a bag of Kettle Chips, pile a load of it onto a plate, and bring it back into the bedroom with two cans of diet soda.

"Mm, that looks great." She sits up against the pillows, draping the duvet over her, and we eat from the same plate, dipping the chips, cheese, and veggie sticks in the hummus.

As we eat, I rest my hand on the duvet, palm up, and she slides hers into it.

"I'm so glad we won the tournament," she says.

"Yeah, me too."

"I'm so sorry that David insulted Victoria. That was a horrible thing to say."

"She's heard it all before. But it still got to me."

"It must have been hard for her."

"It has," I say with feeling.

"What was she like at school?" She gives me an apologetic look then. "If you don't mind talking about it. I don't mean to pry."

"No, it's okay. When I first came to New Zealand, they put me in Year Seven for a couple of months, then moved me up into Year Eight because I found the work too easy. It was tough—everyone had already formed friendship groups, and I was a year younger than most of the guys. But then I met Huxley. His parents were rich, and he had a PlayStation, and I didn't. We got talking about gaming, and he invited me around to his house to play it. He knew Kai—he's always known everyone—and he introduced us, saying he knew we'd get on. Which we did, of course."

"Kai who formed Koru Tech with you?"

"Yeah. With Eoin and Cherry." I lift her fingers and kiss them. "Anyway, one day Hux and I were walking through the school, and we went around the back of a building and saw a group of guys pushing another boy around. You know what kids are like, it happens a lot, but Hux surprised me by walking right up and pushing one of them over. I ran in to join him, and the two of us were already tall, so the other kids ran off. The boy thanked us and then got upset. Hux—all of twelve but already putting people at ease—asked do you like gaming? And the boy said yeah, and we got talking about one of the games we'd been playing, and I think then he realized that we didn't care that he was different. And that was it. He became one of our closest friends."

Her eyes are wide. "That was Victoria?"

"Yeah. She was sixteen when she told us she identified as female. I think it took her a month to pluck up the courage to tell us. Hux's first words were, 'About fucking time,' and I said, 'What a shock,' and then we started talking about the rugby, and that was that. Many years later, she told us she loved us for that."

"Aw," Sid says.

"She was nervous about announcing it at school, but again, most people had guessed anyway, and I think it was easier than she'd expected. The school was surprisingly supportive and helped where they could. When she went to university, she went as a woman, and I don't think half the people there realized. She had tough times, of course. It was far from easy for her. But she had sex reassignment surgery at twenty-one, just after she graduated, and from the moment she came home, she was so happy, it was amazing. I completely forget about it now, and I think she does half the time, too. But when arseholes like David mention it, it brings back the times when I had to watch her being unhappy and bullied, and it just makes me mad."

It's her turn to kiss my hand. "I'm glad we beat David," she says. "You didn't like him even before we played, did you? Why so? Because of Felicity?"

"What do you mean?"

"I wondered if it bothered you that he's dating her."

"Why would it bother me?"

She gives me an impatient look. "Because she's your ex?"

"She's not my ex."

It's her turn to look confused. "What do you mean?"

I shrug. "We had sex, like, four or five times. That doesn't constitute a relationship. Not in my book, anyway."

"Mack, we've had sex three times," she points out. Luckily, she's amused rather than annoyed at what she obviously sees as a male faux pas.

I raise an eyebrow. "I can count, Sid. But when we have sex, we burn with the energy of a thousand suns. It wouldn't matter if I'd had sex with Felicity a million times, it would never compare to our three."

Her face pinks—she likes that.

"Besides," I add, "I wasn't in love with her."

She lifts her gaze to mine. I return it for a moment. Then I let my lips curve up a tiny bit.

Her eyes widen. "Are you saying..." She stops, as if she can't bear to say it in case the magic disappears.

"That I'm in love with you? I think so. I haven't been in love before. But if I were, I think it would feel like this."

She gives me a beautiful smile that warms me right through. "I think I'm in love with you too," she whispers.

I reach out and tuck a strand of hair behind her ear. Then I grab her and roll onto my back, bringing her with me. She squeals and laughs, and then we exchange a long, lingering kiss.

"We're going to have so much sex," she says. "Maybe you should start eating steak to build up your stamina."

I slide my hands up from her butt to her ribs, then underneath her to cup her breasts. "My dick's going to be an inch shorter if you keep up like this."

She giggles, then kisses me again, long and lazy, the sun lying across us like a warm yellow blanket.

On the bedside table, my phone buzzes.

She lifts her head, sighs, and reaches over to get it, glancing at the screen as she gives it to me. "Talk of the devil," she says, lifting off me.

I look at the screen—it says Felicity. I frown. She hasn't phoned me for a long time.

"Want me to go out?" Sidnie asks.

"No, of course not." I answer the call and put it on speakerphone as I sit back against the pillows. "Hello?"

"Mack? It's Felicity."

"Hey. You're on speakerphone, by the way, and Sidnie's in the room."

"That's okay," she says, "I'm glad she's there. I wanted to apologize to you both for what happened on the court today."

Sidnie and I exchange a look of surprise. "Okay," I say. "But you didn't actually do anything. It's David who should apologize."

"I think we both know that's not going to happen. He's an arsehole, Mack. I... broke up with him." She clears her throat.

"Oh, I'm sorry," Sidnie calls out. I send her an amused look. She shrugs and lifts up a palm as if to say, *I felt like I had to sympathize.*

"It was awful what he said about Victoria," Felicity continues. "I know what she means to you, and I'm so sorry. And for his behavior when we lost. I was so embarrassed."

"Don't worry about it," I say softly.

"All right. Well, I just wanted to say sorry. And Happy New Year."

"Happy New Year to you, too."

"And I hope you win the award, Mack. You deserve it."

I go still. Sidnie's eyebrows rise.

"Who the fuck told you about that?" I snap.

"Ah... shit. Never mind. Forget I said anything."

"Felicity—"

She hangs up.

I glare at the phone, then toss it onto the bed.

"What award?" Sidnie asks.

"It's nothing. Some stupid thing Elizabeth was involved in." My stomach churns. Fucking Elizabeth. I told her to drop it. Why the hell would she tell Felicity? Then it occurs to me—maybe she didn't. Maybe she told David, who then told Felicity. That would make more sense, even though it still makes me mad.

Sidnie studies me for a moment while I fume inwardly. Eventually, she taps my phone and checks the time, then says, "You still want to go to the party this evening?"

"Yeah," I say. "Now I do."

"What do you mean?"

I inhale deeply, let it out slowly, then smile. "Why don't we have a shower, and then we can get ready?"

I wait for her to counter with a question or quiz me about the award. But instead she says, "Come on, then. But no touching of the erogenous zones in the shower." She draws a circle around the middle of her body. "Any more orgasms and you won't be able to do anything with me for a fortnight."

I chuckle, get up, and pull her to her feet. "Your whole body is one big erogenous zone. I'd better not touch you at all."

Loving her for not plying me with questions, I take her into the bathroom, and we shower together under a lukewarm spray. I wash her gently with the shower gel, using my hands to smooth it over her skin, but taking care not to touch anywhere too sensitive. It still makes her sigh, though, and eventually she folds her arms close to her body and leans on my chest, pressing her lips to my wet skin. I put my arms around her and stroke her back, and we stay there like that for a while, letting the water run over us.

I try to put David-fucking-Clarke to the back of my mind, and just enjoy being with her. Resentment continues to burn in my stomach, though, and I know it's not going to go away until I have it out with Elizabeth.

Eventually we turn off the shower and dry ourselves, and then it's time to get dressed. Sidnie's brought a pretty nude-colored vest with bands of sequins across it, and she's matching it with some black trousers and a pair of extremely sexy high-heeled sandals.

"I finally get to wear them without worrying about being taller than the guy," she says as she puts them on.

"If you're trying to avoid more orgasms, it's not working," I tell her, and she giggles as she goes off to do her hair and makeup and ring her folks before we go out.

I choose a wine-colored dress shirt with pink paisley trim around the buttons, cuffs, and the inside of the collar, and pair it with black trousers and Oxford shoes. Then, while I wait for her to finish getting ready, I take Gus down to Jamie, as he texted me to say they're staying in for the night and they'd love to have him, to save him being on his own.

"Wow," Sidnie says when I walk back into the apartment. She comes into the living room, slotting in her final earring as she studies me with admiration. "You look hot."

"Thank you." I put my hands on her hips and nuzzle her neck. "You smell divine."

"So do you."

"Are you sure you want to go out? Or shall we just stay in and make out all evening?"

She chuckles and pushes me away. "No, I think we should go. I know you have Things To Do." She gives a wry smile.

She knows I'm still seething away inside about Felicity's comment. Oh, this girl already knows me so well.

"How's your dad?" I ask her as we head to the door.

"He's okay. Still feeling nauseous, but he's coping."

"He doesn't mind you not being there?"

"Nah. Kate said they've played a few board games, but he'll probably go to bed around eight. Mum might as well, she's tired out. Kate and Liam are going to watch a movie with Julia, but I doubt they'll stay up until midnight. It's all good." She sighs as we go out, and I close the door behind us. "I can't believe it's New Year's Eve. I wonder what next year will bring?"

"Good things, I hope." I take her hand and lead her toward the elevator. "If nothing else, I've got you, so it's already going to have a fantastic start."

Chapter Twenty-Four

Sidnie

Jamie drives us to Huxley's, and tells us to text him when we're ready to be picked up. Once again, I suggest we get an Uber, but both of them discount it.

At some point, I need to ask Mack about what happened in Scotland with Jamie and their parents, because I'm sure that's the reason for their closeness now. Will he tell me? It's so early in our relationship, and there's no law that says he has to tell me his life story. But he's told me he's in love with me. He's made it clear he wants to continue to see me. So at some point, he's going to have to open up a little. I'm in no rush, but I'm not going to give my heart to a guy all the time he has secrets.

As we get out of the Aston and head toward Huxley's, my stomach flips with nerves. Something's going down tonight, and I'm not referring to what might happen when we get back to the apartment. Mack's angry about Felicity mentioning the award, not with her, I think, but with Elizabeth for some reason. I tried asking him, but he changed the subject. And I'm not supposed to know about the MacDiarmid Award, so I can't quiz him on it.

I think about the invitation that he ripped up and put in the wastepaper bin, puzzled as to why he's angry about the nomination. I would have thought he'd have relished the opportunity to receive an award. Most people would. But then Mack's not most people. That's one thing I've learned about him, anyway.

There are a lot of people around, making their way into the club; more it seems than for the last party we came to here. Mack says hello to a lot of them and introduces me, and I soon get lost in a sea of names and faces. He holds my hand tightly, though, keeping me by his side, which I like.

When we get to the lobby, I go to walk down to the Chess Room, but he pulls me to the left, toward the corridor to the offices. "I just need to pick something up," he says.

I glance up at him, conscious that his posture has changed; he's tense, walking fast, looking through the glass part of each door as he goes. Sure enough, as we pass one, he stops, then walks backward to the door. Without waiting, he opens it and goes in, releasing my hand.

I stop in the doorway awkwardly, seeing Elizabeth there at the table in conversation with a couple of guys. I don't think it's a formal business meeting as none of them have laptops or paperwork—it looks as if they're catching up before the party that evening. She's wearing a pretty silver top with gray trousers, and she's propped her feet in their black sandals up on the table.

"I need to talk to you," Mack says.

She raises an eyebrow. "I'm in the middle of something."

"Now," he snaps.

She studies his face, then slowly takes her feet off the table, looks at the guys, and gives them an apologetic smile. "Can I get back to you?"

"Sure." They get up and frown at him before they leave the room. I let them pass, then hover in the doorway, not sure whether to stay or not.

"Okay," she says, amused, "you got my attention. You want to sit?"

He ignores the offer and stays standing. "Felicity called me. She said she hopes I get the award. What the fuck?"

Elizabeth's mouth opens, but nothing comes out. Eventually she closes it and frowns.

"You told her?" Mack says.

"No."

"Are you lying to me?" he demands.

She gets to her feet. "No. Jesus, calm down."

"I told you to withdraw the nomination."

"I'm not going to do that," she says mildly. Wow, she's brave. He's glaring at her, his hands on his hips, radiating anger. Jeez, I hope I'm never the focus of that. Mind you, even though he's furious, he's still the most gorgeous guy I've ever seen.

"Why?" he queries. "You know how I feel about this."

"It's not about you, Mack. Don't you think the work deserves some acclaim?"

"It's… like…" He's so annoyed he can't get the words out. He waves a hand in the air. "Archeology. The answer is buried beneath the soil and all I have to do is dig it up. I'm not inventing anything that isn't already there."

"Bollocks."

"Elizabeth—"

"I'm not fucking withdrawing it, Mack. Deal with it."

"This is not what I want," he yells.

"I don't care," she yells back.

I edge out of the door, desperate to be anywhere else, but half wanting to see what happens.

"Why did you tell Felicity?" he shouts at her. "Of all people."

"I didn't."

"Well someone fucking told her. So I'm guessing you told David."

"I haven't told anyone."

"Don't lie to me!"

"I'm not fucking lying!"

"Oh no," I say, and I cover my mouth with a hand.

Mack turns his glare on me. "What?"

I stare at him, horrified. My heart shudders to a stop as I put two and two together and make fifteen. Holy fucking hell.

Elizabeth looks from me to him, then back again.

He blinks, and his expression softens a little. "What's the matter?"

I lower my hand and clear my throat. I'm actually shaking. "Um… when I was in your office that night, cleaning, I found the invitation with the nomination in your rubbish bin. I took a photo of it and sent it to Socrates. It's pretty much the only thing I found. But… Mack… that means…" I can't bring myself to say it.

He stares at me. Then he gives a humorless laugh and runs both hands through his hair.

"What?" Elizabeth says.

He puts his hands back on his hips and blows out a breath. "Dan—Sidnie's brother—told a guy at a nightclub that he was desperate for money, and this guy—who called himself Socrates—said he'd lend it to him if he did some work for him, namely, spying on me to find out about the new research. Dan told him he had no way of getting close to me, but that his sister did. He told Sidnie, and she agreed to look for information if this Socrates got her into the office."

Elizabeth glances at me. "And you're still dating her?"

I blush scarlet.

But Mack says, "She agreed to do it because her dad has cancer—prostate cancer, Elizabeth."

"Oh, Jesus." She folds her arms and stares at her feet.

"They couldn't afford the private treatment—it was over a hundred thousand dollars."

She closes her eyes. I frown. There's something about her reaction that's more than just regret.

"She admitted everything before we slept together," he continues. "And I believed her. I still do. And that means that David is Socrates."

"He actually mentioned the word the night of the Christmas party," I murmur. "When I said I was mononymous, like Madonna, he said, 'Or Socrates.' I just didn't think…" I stop speaking as Mack glares at me. Oh fuck. I've really screwed up.

He turns his laser-like stare back to Elizabeth. "Can you tell me honestly you're not behind this?"

"What do you mean?"

"You didn't ask David to spy on me?"

She stares at him. "Why would I do that? You were doing the research for me. I'd already paid you for it."

"Because if David had the technology, he could do future research in house, and it wouldn't cost you anything. And he'd be the one getting nominated for awards and gaining all the glory."

She goes completely white. "I've known you for ten years," she whispers. "Do you honestly think I'd do that to you?"

"All's fair in love, business, and tennis. Your words, Elizabeth."

She swallows hard. "I didn't do it. I wouldn't. I swear." She sits and puts her head in her hands. "I don't believe this. That fucking arsehole."

He looks at her for a moment, then he turns his glare on me.

I'm still shaking. I'm terrified—not of him, although he is intimidating when he's furious. But I feel like I started all this, and it's my fault. He's just told me he's in love with me, and then this happens.

"I'm so, so sorry, sir," I squeak. Wait, sir? Why did I say that? It just came out. Fuck, now he's going to think I'm being sassy.

His eyebrows rise.

"Shit, I don't know why I said that," I add hastily.

He looks across at Elizabeth, who has sat up and is watching our exchange. She's still pale, but her lips curve up.

SERENITY WOODS

"You two are going to be the death of me," he says. He looks back at me. My eyes fill with tears, and I press my fingers to my lips.

He sighs, pulls me toward him, and kisses my forehead. "He's a nasty piece of work, and it's not your fault."

"You're not angry with me?" I ask in a small voice.

He slides a finger under my chin and lifts it so he can look into my eyes. "Well, I can't promise there won't be punishment when we get home."

"Jesus," Elizabeth says, "I'm dying over here and you two are getting it on."

He gives a short laugh and moves back. "You stay here," he tells me firmly as I try to gather my wits. "I've got a score to settle." He strides out of the room.

I let out a shaky breath and sink onto the nearest chair. "Should I go after him?"

"I'll sort it." She's already on her phone, and she holds it to her ear. "Hux? Mack's on the warpath, looking for David Clarke. It turns out he's been trying to steal Mack's work at Koru Tech, and he tried to rope Sidnie into his scheme." She listens for a moment. "Seriously, the most I've ever seen him. Can you and Titus find them? Text me when you know something. All right." She hangs up.

"Thank God." I cover my face with my hands for a moment. "I really thought it was all over then." My throat tightens. I'd come so close to losing him—again. "He was so mad. I can't believe you yelled at him."

"His bark is worse than his bite," she says. "I've known him since I was eighteen, and we've argued a few times over the years. Besides, he can't ditch me, I know where the bodies are buried." She smiles. "You know they were all in a band, right—Mack, Hux, and Titus?"

I give a shaky laugh. "No."

"They were terrible. They thought they were Nickelback. Mack dyed his hair blond, and it was all sticking up." She illustrates it with a gesture from her head upward.

"I wish I'd seen that."

"Give me your phone number. If I can find a photo, I'll text it to you."

I do, and take hers, too, pleased to be involved with his friends.

She sighs then, tips her head back, and runs her hands through her hair. "Jesus, David. I can't believe it. I trusted that bastard. I'm so sorry, Sidnie. I feel responsible."

"Of course not, it wasn't your fault. I'm just shocked he'd do something so underhanded for some research."

"Well it's not just any research," she says, lowering her hands.

"What do you mean?"

She tips her head to the side. "You know what Mack's been working on?"

"No. He sort of sidestepped the question when I asked."

She smiles. "It's a cure for cancer. Specifically, prostate cancer."

I stare at her as my mind grinds to a halt. "*What?*"

"Well, not a cure. He gets cross when I say that. He's been working with MediTech to develop a mathematical model to represent the interactions between some tumors and common immunotherapies. This can't be done by hand—we need a powerful computer to crunch the enormous amount of raw data. Marise can do millions of simulations to predict tumor responses to treatments, drastically reducing the amount of time it takes to carry out the research. He's just given us the report. Starting Monday, I'll set the wheels in motion to put it into practice."

My head is spinning. "Why didn't he tell me?"

She takes a pen out of her top pocket and plays with it. "Probably because of your father. He wouldn't want to give you false hope in case the research didn't produce the expected results. But it has. We'll be running drug trials very shortly. I suspect he's going to ask to get your father on them."

I sit back, shaking my head. I'm trembling again. Oh my God…

"No wonder he forgave you for spying on him," she says. "He gets very angry about the cost of unfunded drugs in this country. If anything was going to convince him to forgive you, it was telling him about your dad."

"Is he for real?" I whisper. "I can't believe he's so…" I want to say magnificent, but I'm too embarrassed.

She smiles. "Yes, he's for real. He's an old-fashioned philanthropist. He genuinely wants to help people and fight the system. He's laser-focused on his goals and he works incredibly hard. He's not perfect though, just so you know."

I give a short laugh. "I'm sure."

"You know he's a year younger than the rest of us? They put him up a year at high school and he went to university at seventeen."

"Yes, he did tell me."

"I think a combination of that, and the fact that he's possibly on the spectrum, just a little, means he's sort of... I don't know, boyish, you know? Huxley's the same, in a way, and Titus, they're all as bad as each other. They think because women like having sex with them that they're all grown up, but none of them has a clue about relationships really. Mack's going to fuck up from time to time, but it's only because he doesn't know what he's doing."

I smile. I really like Elizabeth. She's such a nice person, managing to be beautiful and feminine and gentle and kind, and yet smart and easily able to hold her own amongst all these confident men. "So you nominated him for the award because of that research?" I ask.

She nods. "The MacDiarmid Medal. It's run by the Royal Society, and it's a prestigious award for outstanding scientific research. He'd absolutely walk it. But he's very cross that I nominated him, as you saw. He wants me to withdraw it."

"Will you?"

She laughs. "No. He deserves to win. But he won't go to the awards dinner. I don't even know if he'll accept the award if he does win. He might return it, and that would be a shame. The work deserves the publicity. It's not all about him. But he feels under the spotlight, and he's not comfortable there."

"When's the award dinner?"

"Next Friday." She clicks her pen on and off. "You know about his father, right?"

"I know his dad died from prostate cancer."

"Yeah, because he couldn't get the drugs. My grandfather was the same, only it was bowel cancer in his case. It's why we've both been so focused on this. It was very late when Mack's dad was diagnosed—he died within six months of the diagnosis. Mack was at university. He was devastated."

I lean forward on the table. "You know his mother was Scottish?"

"Yeah."

"He came to New Zealand when he was twelve, didn't he?"

"Yeah."

"Do you know what happened in Scotland?"

She plays with her pen, maybe deciding how much she should reveal. "You should really ask him."

"I will. I don't want to get you into any more trouble. But I just feel it would help me to understand him."

She sighs. "I know his father went to the UK on vacation when he was young. He met Mack's mother, and they had a brief fling. I'm not sure but I suspect she asked him to stay in Scotland with her, but he said he couldn't leave New Zealand forever. He returned here. She then discovered she was pregnant with Mack, but never told him. After she'd had Mack, she then hooked up with another guy and had Jamie. As far as I understand it, there were a few more guys after that."

I frown. "What happened then?"

"All I know is that Mack found his father online and wrote to him. Shortly afterward, his father and his grandfather—I think you've met him—landed in the UK, took Mack and Jamie away, and brought them back to New Zealand."

My eyes widen. "With their mother's permission?"

"I believe so. It went through the courts anyway, and she didn't contest it. I don't know any more than that, sorry. Hux or Victoria might, I'm not sure, but I doubt they'd tell you. Those three have always been pretty tight."

My mind is whirling again. Something must have happened in Scotland to make Mack track down his father. Did he ask him to come and get him? And why did his mother—Iona, I'm guessing—let him go?

"I've never seen him like this with anyone else," she says, smiling. "I've always thought that he doesn't trust women. So it says something about how crazy he is about you."

I blush.

"You really like him, don't you?" she asks.

I just smile back. Then, curiously, I ask, "I know I'm being nosy, but did you two ever have a thing?"

"Me and Mack? God, no. He's far too intense for me. I like my men much more relaxed and affable."

"Like Huxley?"

She gives me a wry look.

"Maybe I'm wrong," I say. "Are you dating anyone?"

She sighs. "No. I have terrible taste in men, I'm afraid."

"Huxley seems nice."

She flicks her pen through her fingers and gives me a mischievous look. "He asks me out every month, without fail. Has done since we first met."

I laugh. "Really?"

"Yep. He sends me flowers or some other gift and a note that asks for a date. He's persistent, I'll give him that."

"But you haven't said yes?"

She shakes her head.

"Why not? He's pretty gorgeous."

"He only wants me because he can't have me. He's a tomcat, always has been. Can't keep it in his pants. I'm not going to be one more notch on his bedpost." Her eyes flash.

Then she glances at her phone as it buzzes. "Talk of the devil," I say and grin.

Lips twisting, she reads a text, then gets to her feet. "Someone's told Mack that David's just coming up in the elevator. He's heading for the lobby. Come on."

He told me to stay here, but I'm worried about what he's going to do, so I follow her out of the meeting room and along the corridor.

As we walk through the double doors into the lobby, I immediately see David coming out of the elevator. He's with another couple of guys, and they're all laughing at some private joke. The lobby's fairly busy, people handing in coats at reception, Ed the bouncer checking badges and making sure nobody's sneaking in who shouldn't be there.

At that moment, the doors leading down to the Chess Room fly open, and Mack strides through—Huxley, Titus, and Victoria hot on his heels. He stalks across the lobby, right up to David, who turns at the last minute, just in time to see his life flash before his eyes. Mack pushes him with both hands, not dissimilar to the way I pushed him in his apartment, but a hell of a lot harder so that David stumbles back and bangs into the wall. Mack follows it up by putting his forearm across David's throat and pinning him there.

"You motherfucker," he barks, loud enough for everyone to hear.

Ed the bouncer scurries across the lobby, but Huxley puts out a hand and stops him. The two of them and Titus stand a few feet away. David's companions look at the scuffle, alarmed, but clearly not wanting to get involved. Everyone else in the lobby turns to watch with wide eyes.

"Get the fuck off me," David snaps, trying to push him away. But Mack is taller and heavier, and eventually David realizes the only way to break free will be an all-out fight, and he doesn't appear to have the stomach for that.

"Hey," one of David's friends says, "what's going on?"

"He's been trying to steal my research," Mack announces. "And he's been taking advantage of vulnerable people, trying to pay them to spy on me." He glares at him. "You dare to go after my girl? I ought to smash your fucking teeth down your throat."

Victoria glances over at me and winks, and my face fills with heat. My girl? I like that.

"She wasn't your girl at the time," David points out.

"Shut the fuck up." Mack bangs him against the wall once more before dropping his arm and taking a step back.

David, obviously embarrassed to be shown up in front of his friends, and conscious of everyone's eyes on him, smooths back his hair. "She dropped her knickers pretty quick for you. Who knows, maybe she'll do the same for me if I ask nicely."

"Ouch," I say, wincing.

Elizabeth groans. "That's fucking done it."

She's right. Mack gives the guy a sound left hook that meets David's nose with a loud crack, and blood sprays over them both.

"Owwww!" David doubles over, holding his hands to his face, while blood trickles through his fingers. "You've broken my fucking dose!"

Titus puts an arm around Mack, hauling him back. He pushes him away, but doesn't attempt to hit him again. His expression is exultant though—he enjoyed doing that.

Elizabeth pushes through the crowd and marches up to David. "That's the least of your problems," she announces. "I trusted you. I took you on even though others—including Mack—warned me against you. And you reward me by doing this?" Even in her heels, she's much shorter than all the guys around her, but with her flashing eyes and firm voice, she's an imposing figure despite that. "You're fired," she snaps. "And don't think you'll be getting a reference, either."

"And you're banned from the club, too," Huxley states. "It's been an expensive evening for you, dude. Go on. Fuck off out of here."

One of David's friends pulls his shirt. "Come on. Let's go."

Someone stuffs some kitchen towel into his hands. He holds it to his nose, lets himself be led into the elevator, and the doors close.

There's a collective exhalation amongst the crowd, and then everyone starts talking at once.

Ignoring them, I slip through the crowd up to Mack and stare at his blood-spattered shirt. "Wow."

He accepts some kitchen towel from the receptionist and wipes his hand. "Hello," he says to me.

"Well, aren't you the knight in shining... dress shirt?"

"Nobody speaks about my girl like that," he states.

"The man's a weasel," Huxley says. "He deserved everything he got."

"Besides," I add, "I didn't drop my knickers immediately. It took me twenty-four whole hours."

That breaks the tension, and everyone laughs.

"Jesus," Victoria says to Mack, "look at the state of you."

He looks down at his shirt. "Oh. Yeah."

"I think maybe I should take you home," I tell him. "Clean you up a bit."

"Good idea," Huxley says. "Although it'd be good to see the New Year in with you both."

"We'll come back," Mack replies, taking my hand and leading me toward the elevator. He stops there and hesitates, looking back. "Sorry."

"The fucker got what was coming to him," Elizabeth states. "Fuck him."

He nods, we walk into the carriage, he presses the button for the ground floor, and the doors close.

I look up at him as the carriage descends. He's buzzing again. I'm sure he could run the whole of Auckland on his energy. Jesus. I'm absolutely crazy about this guy.

He blows on his knuckles, glances down at me, and raises an eyebrow. "Seriously?" he says. "After all your orgasms this afternoon, you're still thinking about sex?"

I just give him a helpless look. What's a girl to do?

Chapter Twenty-Five

Mack

Luckily, David's gone by the time we leave the building. I text Jamie, and then Sidnie takes the kitchen towel and attempts to clean my hand while we wait for him to turn up.

I look down at her as she gently wipes the blood off my skin. Now I feel calmer, it seems almost funny to think I hit David. I've been into a few scuffles in the past, usually aiding Huxley when he's bitten off more than he can chew helping out some damsel in distress, but it's always bravado, pushing and shoving and fronting up, with no blood being spilled. But when David said that line about Sidnie, I finally understood what people mean when they say they see red. I didn't know she was in the room, but the thought that the comment would get back to her sent me over the edge. I had no control over myself at that point. All I wanted was to crush him.

Her cheeks are a little pink now. She knows I'm watching her.

Bending my head, I brush my lips along her cheekbone. She lifts her face, and I kiss her.

"You're a naughty boy," she says when I eventually lift my head.

I shrug. "And you love me for it."

She smiles, then looks over as Jamie pulls up in the Aston. "Come on. Let's get you home."

We get in the car, and Jamie looks over his shoulder, startled. "Jesus! What happened?"

"Mack got prehistoric," she says.

"I was fighting for your honor," I protest.

"That's more than I ever did."

I laugh. "That's from a movie, isn't it?"

"Groucho Marx in *Duck Soup*." She kisses my knuckles. "What am I going to do with you?"

"Would you like some suggestions?"

"What the hell's going on?" Jamie demands.

We tell him as he drives us back to the apartment. I can see Jamie's genuinely shocked by the whole story.

"I feel terrible," Sidnie mumbles when I mention the bit where she spied on me.

"We all do crazy things when our family is in need," I say, exchanging a look with Jamie in the rear-view mirror. He nods then, and I know he understands what I'm referring to.

Sidnie doesn't say much, even when we get back and take the elevator up.

"Are you going out again later?" Jamie asks.

"Not sure yet," I reply. "Can I text you?"

"Of course. I'll keep Gus for now. Let me know if you want him."

When the elevator arrives, he goes down to his apartment, and I let us into mine.

It's close to sunset now, and the place is filled with a deep rose-gold light. I toss my keys and wallet onto the kitchen counter, toe off my shoes, and start unbuttoning my shirt as I walk through to the bathroom. After dumping my shirt into the laundry basket, I run some hot water into the sink and start washing the blood off my hand. "Ouch." My knuckles are tender, bruised from clashing with David's face. The memory of the moment makes me smile.

I look up then, and in the reflection of the mirror, see Sidnie leaning against the door jamb, watching me. She's taken off her sandals, and when I look down I see her sexy pink-painted toenails peeking out from beneath her trousers.

I meet her gaze for a moment. She seems thoughtful. I can't tell what she's thinking. I return to cleaning my hand, then take a towel and dry it carefully.

She pushes off the doorframe and goes into the bedroom, and I follow her in. She sits on the bed, cross-legged, while I go into the walk-in wardrobe and hunt for a new shirt. I pull out another dress shirt—this one black with silver patterns that I think she'll like.

I hang it on the door frame. Then I sit on the bed beside her, flop back, and look up at her.

She picks up my left hand and kisses my sore knuckles. "Southpaw."

"Yeah. Look, I'm sorry."

"What for?"

"Acting like a caveman."

"I was teasing you."

"Yeah, but you were right. I know you can stand up for yourself. You don't need me racing in to save you."

She kisses my hand again. "What you did wasn't just about me. And it wasn't just about him trying to steal your research. It was to do with what he said about Victoria. And it was for betraying Elizabeth. You're very protective of your women."

"You make it sound like I have a harem."

"If the cap fits." She smiles. "I asked Elizabeth if you two had ever been an item."

"Elizabeth? She's far too short for me."

"She said you were too intense for her."

I chuckle. "Yeah, probably."

"She also said she knows where the bodies are buried."

"That's true."

"She mentioned something about a band. And your hair…"

I groan. "It seemed like a good idea at the time."

She giggles. Then she says, "If I tell you something, you promise not to be angry with her?"

"Okay…"

"She told me about your research."

I meet her eyes. "Ah."

"Why didn't you tell me, Mack?"

"I hadn't finished. I didn't want to give you false hope."

"That's what she said you'd say."

"My part's done now. Her team will start running trials very soon. Depending on how his current treatment goes, I'd like to get your father on it."

She kisses my hand again. "Thank you." She studies my knuckles. "She also told me a little about you coming to New Zealand."

I close my eyes and sigh.

"Can you tell me the rest?" she asks.

"What did she say?"

She summarizes what Elizabeth told her. "She said she didn't know any more than that. But…" She takes a deep breath. "I've got one final admission to make."

I meet her eyes, then slowly sit up. "Okay."

"In your office, well, in Nadine's office, she'd put something in the rubbish bin. I'm ashamed to say I took it out and opened it. It was a birthday card addressed to you from someone called Iona."

I study my hands.

"I'm guessing that was your mum?" Sidnie asks.

I nod.

"That's it," she says. "I've told you everything now. And I'm so sorry for what I did, with the award and the card. I really regret it. But the thing is, Elizabeth doesn't know why you won't go to the awards dinner. She thinks it might be something to do with your dad, but some instinct tells me it's about your mum. Am I right?"

I lean forward, my elbows on my knees. I was always going to have to tell her at some point. It might as well be now.

"Yeah," I say in a low voice. "As Elizabeth told you, my mother fell pregnant with me by mistake, after she hooked up with my dad when he was over there on his big OE." Most Kiwis have an Overseas Experience when they're in their late teens or early twenties. "She fell for him big time, but it was just a fling for him. He had no intention of staying in Scotland. She was very angry with him for that. When she fell pregnant, she wanted to terminate the pregnancy, but she was Catholic, and her parents were very old school and forbade her from doing it."

"Thank God," Sidnie says.

"There were times when I was young that I wished she had," I say in a harsh voice. "She resented me—hated me, even. And she did everything she could to make my life a misery. As early as I can remember, so we're talking, what, three, four years old? She would lock me in a cupboard for hours if I made any small transgression."

Sidnie pales. "Jesus."

"She'd send me to bed without dinner. When I started school, she'd never give me any lunch or money to buy any. She showed me no love at all, no affection. She beat me regularly, with her hands, a wooden spoon, an umbrella, whatever she had to hand. When it was my birthday, she never bought me anything. She'd lock me up and say it served me right for thinking I was special that day."

"That's why you don't like birthdays," she whispers.

I nod. "And if I came home from school and said I'd won an award for spelling or maths or something, she'd beat me and say it was wrong to boast and I was an evil child."

"Oh Mack, I'm so sorry. Is that why you won't accept the award?"

"I can't stand up in front of people and admit I've done something I'm proud of, Sid. I just can't. I hear her voice every day, even now."

Sidnie's eyes glisten, but I'm too far down the road to stop.

"She went out with several guys after Dad left, and eventually she got pregnant again, with Jamie. The guy was out of the picture by the time she had him. She'd put on her headphones, take drugs, and leave Jamie crying for hours. Once he was weaned, I used to sneak in and carry him out, and feed him mashed bits of food I could find."

"What about her parents, did they know what she was doing?"

"They knew. They just didn't care. They had five other children, who all had several kids. I was just one of fifteen grandchildren, too many lives to look after and not enough money to go around. My grandfather died a year after Jamie was born. My grandmother lost her marbles after that. Not that she had that many to begin with. She went into a home, and my mother never visited, as far as I know."

I flop back on the bed again and look up at the ceiling. "When Jamie was five, Mum met a new guy. Jock, he was called. It would be funny if it wasn't so fucking sad. He moved in with us. He was obnoxious— loud, often drunk, and abusive. I was nine by then. Getting smart. Sometimes he'd smack me around, but mostly I knew how to keep out of his way. But Jamie was just a kid. Noisy, wanting attention, wanting affection. Jock was so cruel to him. I'd do my best to protect him— trying to keep him quiet and out of sight, but of course when you're in the same house you can't do that all the time. So Jock would beat him. He was often covered in bruises."

"Didn't the authorities notice?" Sidnie asks, horrified. "Didn't the school?"

"We lived in the roughest part of Glasgow. Every other kid there went to school with bruises. I hope it's better now. But back then, the stories about foster care were horrific. It made you get clever at hiding the bruises, even at that age. But it got worse."

"Oh no. How?"

I cover my face with my hands for a moment, then let my arms fall back tiredly. "Jock starting abusing Jamie sexually."

"Oh Mack, no."

"He tried it with me, but I fought him hard enough to make it too much effort for him. But Jamie was only seven at that point. Too tiny, too thin and small and weak, to put up any resistance. I tried to stop it, but Jock would lock the bedroom door. I thought about telling the police or the school, but I was worried they'd separate us and put us in different homes. Seriously, Sid, some of the stories… I thought we'd be out of the frying pan and into the fire."

"So what happened?"

"I was getting pretty good with computers by then—I used them at school and at the local library. I knew Dad's name—she'd told me that much. So I started looking for him. It took a while. Do you know how many Tipene Harts there are in New Zealand? There's one in practically every town, and I didn't know where he came from. I had a Facebook account, and I messaged every one of them that came up. Some of them got back to me, some didn't. Most of those that did said they'd never been to the UK. And then one day, I found him."

"Oh my God."

"Yeah. Now, I think how lucky I was that he either didn't reply or tell me to fuck off. What guy wants to know he's fathered a kid twelve years ago after a quick fuck with someone who didn't mean anything? But he messaged me back and said that yes, he'd been with Iona McManus when he was in Scotland twelve years ago, and that probably meant he was my father."

"That's amazing."

"I told him everything. About Jock, and Jamie, and how terrible it was there. I told him I hated her, because I did. I still do." My voice is flat. "Every year, she sends me a birthday card. I told Nadine several years ago to throw them in the bin, which is what she does now. I don't want anything to do with that bitch."

Sidnie lifts my hand and kisses my knuckles. "I'm so sorry."

I sigh, trying to let go of the hatred, because I know it's not good for me. "I told him what Jock was doing to Jamie. I mean, Jesus, Jamie wasn't even my dad's kid, but he was appalled. He asked me if we had passports. I said we had, because Jock and Mum had taken us to France for a couple of days, mainly to buy cheap wine. Dad then went quiet for a couple of days, and I thought I'd blown it, and that I wouldn't hear from him again. And then, out of the blue, there was a knock on the door, and there he was, with Koro. The two of them had gone around the family and scraped together all their savings for two tickets to Scotland."

"I can't imagine how you must have felt."

"Yeah, it was pretty amazing. Mum screamed when she saw him and tried to shut the door on them, but Dad forced his way in. He came into the living room, and I saw him and I knew immediately it was him. I jumped up and threw myself into his arms, and he gave me the biggest hug."

I stop for a moment, covering my face as my voice turns husky with emotion, then run my hands through my hair. "Jamie came into the room, and Koro picked him up and hugged him, even though obviously he wasn't related to him in any way. And Dad said, 'We want to take the boys.' Jock yelled, 'You can't do that.' He didn't want to let us go because he got child payment for the two of us. So Koro got out an envelope, and he said, 'There's a thousand dollars in here. It's all we can afford. Take it and give us the boys. Or we'll do it through the courts and it'll cost you a fortune.' A thousand dollars is five hundred pounds—that's nothing, really. But Jock snatched up the money and said, 'Good riddance.'"

"What about your mother?" Sidnie asks, appalled.

"She walked into her bedroom and closed the door. She didn't even say goodbye."

Sidnie pressed her fingers to her lips, her eyes glistening. "That's awful."

"Yeah. Now, I understand that she must have had severe mental problems. But even so, the little boy inside me can't forgive her."

"So you just got on a plane and came here?"

"Yep. Once we were here, Dad and Koro did it all legally, and Dad got custody of both of us. It was tougher with Jamie because of course he wasn't his son. They eventually tracked down his father, though, who wasn't interested in him at all, and both he and Mum just signed everything they sent. It was a headache for Dad at the time, and there must have been moments when he regretted doing it, I'm sure. But I never saw it in him or his family. They took us in immediately, and they showered us both with love and affection."

"And so that's why Jamie does what he does?"

"Yeah. He always says he owes me everything. He missed me terribly when I went to uni. When I graduated, and after Dad died, I got the money from Intel, and I offered to pay for Jamie to go to university too, but he said he didn't want to be away from me again. I was in the process of starting Koru Tech, and he announced he was going to be there for me and do whatever I needed. I just laughed at the time, but he stuck to his words. He looked after everything—getting an apartment, driving me around, getting my groceries, organizing a housekeeper, whatever needed doing, so that I could focus on the work. I barely saw the light of day for several years. You know what I'm like—I get obsessed, and I was twice as bad then as I am now. He made sure I ate and exercised and forced me to keep to a routine. He fielded calls and meetings with Nadine and acted like a bouncer so I wasn't constantly interrupted. I don't know what I'd have done without him."

Sidnie looks out of the window for a moment. The sky is now purple, the same color as the bruise on her arm. I study her face—her straight nose, pale skin, her Cupid's bow, her crazy hair. She's so fucking beautiful. How did I end up with a girl as gorgeous as this, both inside and out?

"Elizabeth said you don't trust women," she says, turning her gaze back to me. "Do you think that's right?"

"Maybe it was." I take her hand and kiss it.

"I can't believe you trust me," she whispers. "After what I did, taking photos of your research, that's so close to your heart. Do you really forgive me for it?"

"You did it for your father. I'd have done the same, if someone had offered me the money when my dad was sick. Of course I forgive you."

She leans over me then. "Dr. Mack Hart. You just make me melt, you know that?"

I chuckle. "You find it incredible that someone could forgive you?" I stroke a finger across one of her eyebrows. "You're like the essence of summer and sunshine, sweetheart. Bright and warm and full of joy. I don't believe you could knowingly be dishonest or deceitful. You were the worst spy in the history of spy-dom."

"I was, a bit." She kisses me. Lifts her head to look at me. Then kisses me again, longer this time.

When she eventually moves back again, I give a long sigh. I'm tired—it's been a hell of a day. "Do you really want to go to the party tonight?"

She smiles. "Not really."

"What do you say we stay indoors? Get Gus up here, order some Uber Eats, play a bit of PlayStation, then watch a movie until midnight?"

"I think that sounds like the best night ever."

I laugh. "Come on, then."

We get up and take off our party outfit. She's brought a fresh shirt and jeans with her for tomorrow but nothing comfortable, so I lend her one of my T-shirts to lounge around in, enjoying the way it hangs on her smaller frame, and the fact that it leaves her legs bare.

I go down to Jamie's and fetch Gus, and tell Jamie that we're in for the night. We exchange a hug and wish each other Happy New Year. Then I go back up to the apartment, and Sid and I dial for takeout after deciding on Thai food.

It doesn't take long to come, and we dish it up into bowls, take it into the living room, and watch a movie while we eat. The sun sinks into the ocean, and the sky slowly darkens, the stars popping out on the velvety blackness.

When the movie finishes, we take Gus for a walk up in the garden, then come back and decide to watch another movie, full from the dinner and content to stretch out and just be together. When that one finally comes to an end, we pick up the PlayStation controllers and spend the rest of the time as we wait for midnight playing *The Two of Us* together, fighting giant wasps and flying planes through tunnels to escape. It's the first time I've played a game with a girlfriend, and it's a whole different experience. It's only when we're halfway through that I realize why.

Sidnie is mine. I don't mean she belongs to me—I'm not that much of a Neanderthal—but she is my girl. I told her, *I don't want you to see anyone else*, and she said, *I won't if you don't*. But that's the closest we've come to explaining how we feel, apart from all the sex. We haven't talked about where we go from here.

A few weeks ago, I know I made her feel as if I was only interested in a one-night stand. I was, I freely admit it. I feel embarrassed about that now, but it's how I felt at the time. I couldn't envisage ever meeting a girl who made me feel as if I'd give everything up for her.

Like she said, we've only slept together three times. But she already means so much more to me than any other woman I've met.

I've said I'm in love with her. Does she understand what that means?

I pause the game and put down the controller.

"Oh," she says, "I was enjoying that!"

I study the controller for a second. Then I look at her and say, "Are we going steady?"

Her eyebrows rise, and her lips curve up. "Um… I guess. Is that what you want?"

"Yeah."

"All right," she says, and grins.

"Move in with me," I say.

Her eyes widen, and she laughs. "What? We've been dating, like, two weeks."

"Don't make fun of me. I haven't done this before. I don't know if there's an official length of time you're supposed to wait. There's no fucking manual I can go by. All I can do is say what I feel. And I don't want you to leave."

She looks into my eyes, and she smiles as she cups my face with a hand and brushes her thumb across my lips.

"Well?" I ask.

She hesitates. "I might need to go home sometimes, to help Mum out."

"Of course."

"And… I'd want to keep seeing Caro and Hana."

"Sidnie, you'll be free to do as you please, I'm not going to cuff you to the bed." I purse my lips. "Although that's not a bad idea…"

She giggles and kisses me. I throw the controller down, grab her, and pull her onto my lap. She laughs, wraps her arms around me, and we exchange a long, luscious kiss.

"I don't want to come home and find you're not here," I mumble when she eventually lifts her head.

"You're really very sweet sometimes," she murmurs. "The answer's yes."

Joy floods me. "What a great way to start the New Year."

She checks her phone. "Talking of which… it's nearly midnight. So now I'm going to give you a kiss that lasts a whole year." She chuckles, gets settled astride me, takes my face in her hands, and lowers her lips to mine.

And I'm more than content to let her.

Chapter Twenty-Six

Sidnie

The next day—New Year's Day—Mack phones Kai and tells him he's not going to work, then reluctantly admits he's spending the day with me.

I hear Kai laugh from across the room.

"Yeah, yeah," Mack says, "take the piss all you want." He hangs up.

"It's New Year's Day," I say, amused. "Do both of you normally work then?"

"We normally work every day of the year, even Christmas Day. But I sense things are going to be changing." He grabs me, starts kissing me, and walks me back to the bedroom. "Time for some serious sex."

"Lightning."

"Don't care."

I giggle and let him toss me onto the bed, where he lies on top of me and then proceeds to kiss the living daylights out of me.

It turns out to be one of the best days of my life. We make love slowly, in the morning sunshine, then eventually force ourselves to get up, and Mack takes me to the house I share with Caro and Hana so I can pick up some of my things. They're both super excited for me, although sad to think I might be moving out, but I promise them I'll see them often for girlie nights, especially when Mack's working on a project.

We go back to his apartment, change into running gear, and take Gus for a run in the park. It's the start of a new year, and everything seems brighter and shinier than usual—even the birds sound happier, dancing about in the trees.

Afterward, we shower together and change, and then we join Jamie and Emma for a lunch she's prepared, and spend a pleasant hour with them eating and chatting and just getting to know each other a little better.

In the afternoon, Mack seems tired—I think he's still getting over his frantic week. So we lie on the bed for a read, and after about fifteen minutes, I look over and see that he's dozed off.

I study him for a while. It's strange to be able to observe him without him being constantly on the move. He looks younger asleep, nearer my own age, as if he's an ordinary guy taking time to doze in the afternoon with his girl. You'd never know he's a billionaire genius with a nuclear core for a heart that gives him all this incredible energy, the closest to Iron Man you can get in real life.

I kinda like dating a superhero.

I lie back then, looking out of the window and thinking about Elizabeth nominating him for the MacDiarmid award. *The work deserves the publicity. It's not all about him. But he feels under the spotlight, and he's not comfortable there.*

I reach over for my phone, bring up Safari, and Google it.

'The MacDiarmid Medal is awarded annually to a person or team who, while in New Zealand, has undertaken outstanding scientific research that demonstrates the potential for application to human benefit, such as in the areas of health, environment and technology.'

Lowering the phone, I think about it for a while. And slowly, an idea begins to form.

Looking at Mack, making sure he's still asleep, I send Elizabeth a text.

Almost immediately, she comes back. *Shit, why didn't I think of that? I'll get onto it. Thanks, Sidnie!*

"Who was that?" Mack's woken up, and he heard the buzz of the text arriving.

"Kate," I say, turning my phone off and tossing it aside. "Just saying Dad's feeling better today." I move closer to him and kiss him. "Hello."

"Hello." He yawns, stretches, then pulls me on top of him. "I kind of like being lazy," he murmurs, kissing me.

"I get the feeling it's a new adjective for you."

"Yeah. I can see why it's so attractive to people."

I chuckle and let him kiss me for as long as he wants. Inside, though, I feel a seed of hope and excitement that maybe I've helped Elizabeth, and in doing so, I'm going to help Mack get the recognition he deserves. I might not be able to completely remove the spotlight, but maybe I can help Elizabeth change its focus.

*

I exchange a few more texts with Elizabeth throughout the week. Mack goes back to work Monday—his interest in being lazy didn't extend to more than one day—and it's easier to communicate with her when he's not there. I'm kept busy—I visit my folks most days, helping out, especially when Kate, Liam, and Julia return to Australia on the third. Wednesday, I go out for a drink with Caro and Hana, and update them on everything that's been happening.

Lubricanz is still closed for the holidays, so I don't have to worry about work until next week. I do some cleaning for Dodie on Tuesday and Thursday, because even though Mack has asked me to move in with him—and he's a billionaire—I have student loans and I'm still paying for the room with Caro and Hana, and I'm not comfortable asking him for money, so I need to work.

But during the day when I'm not doing anything else, I open my laptop, sit out on the patio at the table, and work on my book. I meet Mack's housekeeper, Alison, when she comes in to clean and do the washing and buy groceries, and at first that's a bit weird. But she's in her forties, friendly and mumsy, and she fusses around me, getting me drinks and lunch, which is kinda nice. We chat sometimes, but she mainly leaves me to work, and eventually I get used to having her come in, and feel less awkward about it.

With more free time to write, I'm able to get really stuck in. Words flow from my fingertips, and I can stretch my legs with the longer format, and really get invested in the characters. Sometimes I ramble a bit—an editor is going to fill the page with red lines, I'm sure—but I really enjoy writing it, and I'm pleased with how it's coming along.

To my surprise, as I know he used to work until at least ten most nights, Mack is home by seven every evening. Sometimes we have takeout, or a dish that Alison prepares, but a couple of times I cook for us, just stir fries with noodles or pasta with veggies, and we eat it while watching a movie, the height of domesticity, which seems to make both of us incredibly happy.

Then, on Thursday, when we're sitting together on the sofa, watching the TV, Mack's phone rings.

"It's Hux," he says, answers it, and puts it on speakerphone. "Hey. What's up?"

"Hey guys," Huxley says, obviously guessing I'm there. "Vic and I hadn't heard from you, so we wondered if you were coming tomorrow?"

Mack frowns. "Coming where?"

"To the club. The Twelfth Night Party?"

"Is there one?"

"Jesus. You didn't get the email? I told Vic her mailout screwed up. Yeah, we're having a do. I'm not sure about numbers now if nobody got the fucking memo. Can you come? Help me out?"

Mack looks at me and rolls his eyes. I smile and say loudly, "Yeah we'll be there, Hux, don't worry."

"Cool, sweet as. Seven thirty p.m. Sorry about the late notice. See you then."

"See ya." Mack ends the call and props his feet back on the coffee table. "Unusual for Vic to fuck up the email."

"Yeah." I curl up beside him, heart hammering. Part one of the plan is in motion. I should be able to get him there. Keeping him there, though, is another matter…

"You okay?" he says. "You look nervous."

"I'm fine." I need to distract him. "I keep meaning to ask, do you think Huxley and Elizabeth will ever get together?"

He laughs. "Not in this lifetime."

"I'm serious. Elizabeth told me he asks her out once a month without fail."

"Yeah. He does it to wind her up."

"Every month? Seems like a very long-winded joke."

"I guess."

"They flirt all the time."

"Yeah. There's a kind of merry war betwixt them."

I chuckle. "Much Ado about Nothing? You think they're like Benedick and Beatrice?"

"Kinda."

"You know they end up together, right?"

"I think that ship has long sailed."

"He doesn't like her?"

"Eh… He's crazy about her. But you know he has a daughter, right?"

My eyebrows rise. "No! Really? How old?"

"She's eight. Her name's Joanna."

I'm stunned. "So he was only, what, twenty when he had her?"

He nods. "He got a girl pregnant at university. Brandy, her name was. Well, is. She lives not far away, in Herne Bay." He names an affluent suburb in Auckland.

"Jesus. Wow. What happened? I'm guessing they're not an item."

"No. They were never a couple—it was a one-night stand, I think, and neither of them seemed interested in it being anything more. He didn't tell us much about it at the time. He's very private despite being the most gregarious guy I know. But he's stood by her all these years. He bought them a house, and he pays for Joanna to go to a private school. He has Joanna every other weekend, and he always goes to parents' evenings and dance recitals and stuff like that. He's a great dad."

I'm really surprised. I think about Elizabeth, and the way her expression changed when she talked about him. "So... what happened with Elizabeth?"

"They'd just met, in their second year. She really liked him, I could tell. They were flirting a lot. She was hoping he'd ask her out. And then he goes and gets another girl pregnant. Elizabeth was really shocked and quite upset, I think. That was pretty much the end of it, from what I remember anyway. We were all working every hour under the sun by that point. Then the baby was born, and Hux was off helping out where he could. Elizabeth pushed him to the back of her mind and concentrated on work."

"But he did ask her out?"

"Yeah, a while after Joanna was born. She said no, and continues to, and they both date other people."

"But nothing long term?"

"No, they're both too focused on their careers at the moment, I think. They like each other, but there's this barrier between them they can't break down. It's a strange relationship. Too much water under the bridge, you know? They're the best of friends now, and I guess they don't want to spoil that."

I curl up next to him as he puts the movie back on, and rest my head on his shoulder. It makes me sad to think of Elizabeth and Huxley seeing other people, even though deep down they obviously have feelings for one another.

Life has a strange way of bringing people together, though. You never know what's around the corner.

※

The next evening, Jamie drops us off at the club just after seven thirty.

I've already told him the reason for us being there. Emma's catching an Uber and she'll arrive in a few minutes, once we've gone up. Everyone else should be here, because Huxley told them all it starts at seven. I cross my fingers that everything goes according to plan.

"See you later," Mack says, waving to Jamie. Jamie drives off, disappearing around the corner, where I know he's going to find a parking space so he can run back.

I hold Mack's hand as we walk into the club and go through to the elevator. He's been quiet today, and I wonder whether it's because he knows it was the afternoon of the Royal Society Awards Dinner. I haven't mentioned it, though, and neither has he.

He's wearing the black dress shirt with the silver patterns that he didn't get to wear on New Year's Eve. I've chosen a simple black dress and my high-heeled sandals. I've taken extra care over my hair and makeup, enough for him to comment on it as we left, but I don't think it's made him suspicious.

"You okay?" I ask, reaching up to kiss him as the elevator rises.

"Yeah. I'm just not really in the mood for this." He slides an arm around my waist. "I'm beginning to enjoy our evenings at home."

"Want me to buy you some slippers and a pipe?"

He chuckles and kisses me. "I can think of worse things."

The doors slide open, and we go into the lobby. The only people there are Gail on reception and Ed, standing by the door.

"Wow, it's quiet," Mack says, waving to Gail. "I guess Vic really did screw up the emails."

"Evening, Dr. Hart. They're all in the Chess Room," she calls.

"Thanks. Evening, Ed."

"Evening, Dr. Hart." Ed opens the door for us, and we walk through, and along the corridor.

"I can't hear any music," Mack says. "What the fuck's going on?" He walks up to the double doors, pushes one open, and walks inside.

Immediately he stops as there's an enormous cheer. The Chess Room is filled with people, who all whoop and let off streamers and party poppers as they see him.

He stares for a second. All his friends are here—Elizabeth, Huxley, Titus, Victoria, Kai, Cherry, Eoin, and many more from both Koru Tech and the club, all smiling and cheering as they look at him.

Shit, I think, this was a mistake. I didn't know they were going to do this.

Unsurprisingly, Mack backs away, meets the door with a bump, then turns and strides out of the room.

The cheering dies down, and I hear Elizabeth say, "Fuck."

"Don't worry," I call out. "I'll get him back." I turn, go through the doors, and run along the corridor, eventually catching up with him in the lobby.

He's already at the elevator—damn his fast legs—and banging on the button to call the carriage.

"Mack," I say, "wait."

He glares at me. "Did you know about this?"

"Yes. It's not what you think, I swear."

"It's not to do with the fucking award?"

"Well, yes, but not in the way you—Mack!" I yell at him as the doors slide open and he goes to enter the carriage. He stops, but only because Jamie and Emma are there, looking surprised as they see him.

"What the fuck?" he says.

I give Jamie a helpless look. "Don't let him in."

"Come on," Jamie says, walking out, straight toward Mack so he has to take a few steps back. "You're not going."

"Get out of my way."

"Sweetheart." I tug on his hand. "Wait, please."

He stops, but his chest is rising and falling quickly, and I can see panic in his eyes.

"Hey." I move up close to him and cup his face with a hand. "Look at me."

He's glancing around the room, like a wild animal looking for a means of escape, but eventually, as I wait, his gaze meets mine.

"Do you trust me?" I whisper.

He blinks a few times. Then, finally, he nods.

"All right," I say. "So believe me. It's not what you think, okay?"

"I'm not going in there," he states. "Not until you tell me what's going on."

I'd hoped to let Elizabeth make the announcement, but I realize that I won't even get him in the room unless I tell him. "She changed the nomination," I say. "To include your team. Kai, Cherry, and Eoin. The award goes to all of you, Mack, to the company, in recognition of the amazing work you've all done. Don't you think your colleagues deserve that?"

He blinks a few more times. "We won?"

"Your *team* won. The spotlight's not on you. Not as much, anyway." I stroke his face. "You lead the team, sweetheart, you're always going to be the focus of any attention. And when you've achieved something amazing, it *is* okay to stand up and tell the world, and to be rewarded for it. Your mother was wrong. It's not something to be ashamed of, and it's not arrogant."

He swallows, then looks down at his feet, sliding his hands into his pockets.

"You can trust me," I say. "And you can trust all these wonderful women who are just crazy about you now. Victoria, Nadine, Emma, all your family who worship you, and Elizabeth. She wants to say thank you for what you've done. Do it for her. Do it for me."

He lifts his gaze then to meet mine. "For the team."

"For the team."

He blows out a long, shaky breath, then finally nods.

Jamie grins and puts a hand in the middle of Mack's back. "Come on, dude."

Mack grips hold of my hand tightly. "I'm not doing it without you," he says.

"It's okay. I'm right here." I walk with him back through the door that Ed's holding with a smile, and along the corridor. "It's all right. I'm not going anywhere," I tell him, and then Jamie opens the doors to the Chess Room.

We walk in, and this time the greeting is more subdued, presumably under Huxley's direction. But everyone's still smiling, and they all clap as we cross the floor to where Huxley and Elizabeth are waiting on the stage at the front. Besides them, Cherry, Eoin, and Kai are sitting in three of the four chairs that have been placed there. They all grin as we walk up.

"Thank God for that," Huxley says wryly.

Mack runs a hand through his hair, looking more boyish than ever as I lead him onto the stage toward the fourth chair. He sits, then grabs me and pulls me down onto his knee, making everyone cheer. I put my arms around his neck, happy to stay there if it means he stays, too.

"We're glad you could make it," Huxley says. "Sorry about the ruse. It's Elizabeth's fault." He gestures to her to come forward and take the mic. She walks up, then has to spend a few seconds lowering it. Huxley snickers, and she glares at him as everyone laughs.

"Hey everyone," she says, "thanks for coming tonight. You all know why we're here. The Royal Society Awards Dinner took place earlier today. I put forward the team at Koru Tech for their research into prostate cancer as a nomination for the MacDiarmid Medal. Well…" She glances over her shoulder at the team sitting on the stage. "I'm sorry to say that they didn't win."

I blink. Fuck. What? She'd told me they were a shoe-in. All around us, everyone's exchanging glances, clearly puzzled. Huxley looks alarmed.

"But…" Elizabeth smiles. "The reason for this is because, at the last minute, the organizers of the awards changed my nomination."

To the surprise of all of us, she steps back out of the way of the white screen behind us. Victoria presses the button on a remote control, and a video begins playing of a woman standing in front of the Royal Society logo.

She introduces herself as Aroha Johnson, the president of the Royal Society Te Apārangi.

"The Rutherford Medal is the most prestigious award instituted by Royal Society Te Apārangi with the support of the Government," she says.

Mack inhales, and his jaw drops. He's obviously heard of the medal.

"It recognizes preeminent research, scholarship or innovation," Johnson continues. "In addition, exceptional contributions may be taken into account to the promotion, encouragement and improvement of public awareness, knowledge and understanding of research; education; and the management of societies and institutions. Not only has the team at Koru Tech been involved in the groundbreaking research into the treatment of prostate cancer, but they have also contributed on many occasions to the education of others about the creation of supercomputer Marise and her use in the research."

Tears prick my eyes. I know the others have occasionally done talks at schools and universities. But she really means Mack.

"We have voted unanimously to award the team at Koru Tech the Rutherford Medal," she says. "It comes with prize money of a hundred thousand dollars."

We all gasp. Obviously it's a drop in the ocean to the billionaires in the room, but it's still a significant amount of money, and it's a wonderful acknowledgement of the value of their research. I know Mack will plow the money back into the business, so it can only help with their future work.

"Ms. Tremblay explained your reluctance to attend the dinner and receive an award," Johnson says, "and while we are disappointed not to be able to give you this in person, we are more than happy for her to award it on our behalf. Congratulations to you all, and, from all of us in New Zealand, thank you for your contribution."

The video stops. Everyone breaks out in a huge cheer, and Elizabeth turns and smiles at the team. They all get to their feet, and one by one they go forward to accept their certificate and medal.

Mack is last. He walks up, gripping my hand tightly, refusing to let me go.

I take the certificate for him, and Elizabeth hands him the medal.

"Congratulations," she whispers, and tugs at his shirt until he bends so she can kiss him on the cheek.

"Speech," Huxley calls, and several others echo the word.

Mack turns to his team. "Would any of you like to say something?"

They all shake their heads. "You speak for us," Kai says.

He sighs and turns back to the mic. "For once," he says, his voice ringing out through the room, "I'm speechless."

"It's a fucking miracle," Huxley says, and everyone, including Mack, laughs.

"I honestly don't know what to say," he continues. He clears his throat. "I suppose I should thank a few people. First, of course, my amazing team, Eoin, Cherry, and Kai, and all the members of their teams who have worked tirelessly to get the research completed."

Everyone cheers, and they all give little bows and laugh.

"Wow," Mack says, flustered, "I can't think. Thank you to the Royal Society too, of course—it's such an honor, and I'm incredibly touched that Koru Tech won. To Huxley, Titus, and Victoria for all your support over the years—I wouldn't be here without you."

They all wave, and Victoria presses her fingers to her mouth, obviously emotional.

"To Jamie and Emma," he says, "my brother and his wife-to-be, who've made sure I eat and shower," he grins as everyone laughs, "and who have given me the time and space to devote to the work. And, of course, to Elizabeth." He holds out an arm, and she comes up and gives him a hug. "You know how important you are to me," he says quietly, and she wipes her face as tears trickle down.

"And finally," he says, and to my surprise, he turns to me, "to Sidnie. She's the one who convinced me to come back here. I haven't known her for long, but she's taught me more about love and acceptance of other people—and of yourself—in the past few weeks, than I've learned in a lifetime." He kisses me briefly, then puts his arm around me as he turns back to the mic. "She understands how important it is for any successful person to have a team around them. In that sense, there's no such thing as an individual achievement. We all owe our success to our friends and family who are there to give their support. So thank you to everyone who has helped me in any small way to get where I have. I appreciate and honor you all."

He kisses the medal and holds it up.

Everyone cheers, and then they all start crowding around, wanting to see the medal and to congratulate him and the others. Now it's all done, he's happy and laughing, although he still doesn't let go of my hand. We make our way down to the floor and move slowly through the throng, Mack accepting hugs and kisses and cheers, as gradually the lights dim and music starts up. Eventually he gets to the bar.

"I need a drink," he says to Simon, the bartender, who grins and pours him a whiskey. He orders me a G&T, too, and when we get them, we touch the glasses together before having a good few mouthfuls.

"It was Sidnie's idea," Elizabeth says, appearing before us. "To nominate the team."

Mack looks at me and shakes his head. "I should have guessed."

"Thank you," she says, and hugs me. "I'm glad you got him here."

I hug her back. "My pleasure."

He looks at the medal in his hand. "I still can't believe it."

"The Rutherford, Mack," she says. "That wasn't my doing. They did that all by themselves."

He looks at it as if he can't believe it, and I can see he's getting choked up.

"Want me to get a chain put on it so you can wear it around your neck?" I ask.

That makes them both laugh. He puts an arm around me and pulls me tightly against him. "What would I do without you?" he murmurs, pressing his lips to my brow.

I slip my arms around his waist, and I stay there for a long time, while his friends come up to laugh and joke with him, and the lights swirl across the dance floor in rainbow-colored beams.

Epilogue

Mack

February 14th - Five weeks later

"The whole day?" Sidnie's delighted. "You're kidding me."

"Nope." I grin as she throws her arms around me, and fall back onto the bed with her in my arms. "It's Valentine's Day," I say. "The last place I want to be is at the office."

I don't feel guilty about having a day off. January was a busy month, and February is turning out to be the same. Or maybe it's just how life is for me now. My days are filled with work—a new project at the moment for Titus, as well as further research for Elizabeth—and I'm also in the first stages of developing a brand-new microprocessor, something I'm keeping very quiet for now. But for the first time in my life, I'm beginning to keep a balance between my work and home life.

That's not to say I'm working a nine-to-five day—I think Sidnie and I have both accepted that will never happen. I'm usually at the office by seven a.m., and I'm rarely home before seven in the evening. But seven p.m. is better than ten p.m. or midnight, and I haven't worked through or stayed at the office since Sidnie moved in with me.

Why would I, when I can come home and see the girl who's turned my life around? Even when I'm at work, we're still in touch through the day. She's gone back to work at the lubrication factory, but she texts me regularly—often with dirty texts that make me blink in the middle of meetings—and we usually have a half-hour phone call around lunchtime that I look forward to all morning.

In the past, I've watched romcom movies and read love poetry with a kind of baffled skepticism, convinced that romance and love is a fantasy created by the manufacturers of greeting cards and Valentine's Day gifts.

But here I am, on Valentine's Day, lying in bed with my gorgeous girlfriend, about to give her my gift.

"Hold on," I say as she sits astride me and rocks her hips against mine. "I've got something for you."

"I know you have." She rocks again, arousing me, and I give her a mock glare as I start to get a hard-on.

"Not that. Well, yes, that, but later. Get off." I roll over and then get up. "Here." I retrieve the parcel and card I'd hidden under the bed. Gus leaps up and snuffles the present, and I push him away. "It's not for you."

She laughs, moves back against the pillows, her legs crossed, and takes the parcel, which is about four inches square. "Ooh, thank you." She waves the card at me and her eyes sparkle. "Did you follow the rules?" '

"You tell me."

She opens the envelope and takes out the card. Then she starts giggling. I grin. She told me that we both had to find the dirtiest cards we could. Mine says 'My tongue can do way more than just lick an envelope.'

"I'll prove it in a minute," I tell her.

She giggles, then opens it and smiles. I've written 'we heart you', and signed it Mack and Gus. "Thank you," she says, bending to kiss Gus's head, and then she leans forward and kisses me, too.

"Open the present," I say.

"Your card first," she replies, and digs it out from under her pillow.

I open the envelope and pull out the card, then start laughing. There's a picture of an iced donut, and it says, 'I want you to glaze my hole.'

"Seriously?"

"It made me laugh," she says, pulling the parcel toward her. "It was either that or one that said, 'Out of seven billion faces, I want to sit only on yours.' That came a close second."

"Trust you to win the competition."

She chuckles and tears off the paper to reveal the box, then takes off the lid. Her face lights up. "Oh, Mack."

It's a silver charm bracelet, bearing six tiny charms—an open notebook, a closed hardback book, a typewriter, a fountain pen, a pen in an inkpot, and the last one I had specially made—a little silver disc with the name Sidnie Beecham—the pen name she's chosen, which was her mother's maiden name. She's finished her book and it's currently with an editor, and she's hoping to publish it by the end of the month. She's already set up her website and social media pages, and she's so excited to get the book out there.

I asked to read it, which surprised her. She balked at first, saying she was too embarrassed because some of it was autobiographical, but I persisted, and in the end she caved. I smiled many times when I read it, recognizing myself occasionally in the billionaire who swept the office girl off her feet, but overall I thought it was an excellent read considering it was her first novel, and I can't wait to see what readers think of it.

"It's wonderful," she says breathlessly, "Oh Mack, I love it." She takes it out and puts it on, then holds up her arm so the light catches it. Then she turns and throws her arms around me. "Thank you so much."

"I'm glad you like it."

"I do, it's amazing, so thoughtful and personal. You're the best boyfriend ever."

I grin and kiss her. "So that means I'm getting some later?"

"You were always getting some regardless of what gift you got me." She laughs, reaches over the bed, and retrieves two parcels. "Here you go."

"Two?"

"That one first."

I open the smaller present. It's a candle in a jar that says, 'Thanks for the orgasms.'

I laugh. "You're welcome."

She giggles and pushes the other present over to me. It's about the size of an A4 piece of paper, and it feels like a picture in a frame. I tear off the paper and study it. It looks like a sound wave, the kind made by a piece of music. There's no text on it explaining what it is.

"Here," she says, and she turns the picture over. On the back is a QR code.

Giving her a puzzled look, I reach for my phone and scan it. A voice recording pops up, and I press play.

Sidnie's voice begins singing *Heartbeat*, the song by Paua of One that we danced to on that first evening. "Our hearts beat as one when you move inside me," she sings.

My jaw drops, and I turn the picture back over. The sound wave has been created by Sidnie singing the song. "Oh, it's fantastic," I say, genuinely stunned by the originality of the gift. "I love it."

She flushes with pleasure. "I'm so glad!"

I put my arms around her and pull her back onto the bed, then give her a long, luscious kiss. Beside us, Gus is playing with the paper, ripping it into a thousand tiny pieces and eating half of it, but he's happy and quiet, so I let him and concentrate on the softness of her mouth and the feel of her silky skin against me.

"I'm crazy about you," I tell her when she eventually comes up for air.

"And I'm absolutely bonkers about you."

I roll her onto her back and begin kissing her neck, over her breasts, and down her tummy. Gradually, I disappear beneath the duvet. "Happy Valentine's Day," I tell her, my voice muffled, and she sighs.

To think I nearly went to work today. I'm such an idiot.

*

Much later, around ten a.m., we're making ourselves coffee and toast in the kitchen when the doorbell rings.

Sidnie looks up. "Oh, is that Jamie?" He's the only person who ever rings our doorbell.

"Probably." I wipe my hands. "I'll get it."

My pulse picks up speed as I walk through the apartment and open the door.

He's standing there, grinning, holding a large cardboard box.

"Ready?" he says.

"Did Elizabeth do it?"

"Yep. Exactly how you wanted."

I inhale deeply and blow out the breath, then take the box from him. "Thanks."

"I'll leave everything else out here," he says, gesturing at the other items he's put on the floor.

"Okay. Thanks for doing this, Jamie. I really appreciate it."

"You're welcome. Best of luck." He waves and goes back into the elevator.

My mouth has suddenly gone dry. Carefully, I bring the box into the apartment and close the door.

"Was it Jamie?" Sidnie calls.

"Yeah. Can you come in here?" I go into the living room and gently place the box on the floor.

She walks in, seeing the box as Gus runs up to it, tail wagging. "Oh! What's that?"

"Your Valentine's Day present." I gesture at it, my heart pounding.

She stares at me, taken aback. "Another one?"

"The real one. The other one was a stopgap."

Frowning, she comes forward and drops to her knees on the floor, while I perch on the arm of the chair. Gus is very excited by this point, and I chuckle and pull him away. "Careful," I tell her. "It's very delicate."

The box is made of firm cardboard and has holes cut in the sides. As she goes to open the top, it moves, just a little.

"Oh!" She jumps back and laughs, and then her eyes light up. Suddenly excited, she opens the flaps and reveals a tiny bundle of curly ginger fur with two big brown eyes.

"Oh my God!" She claps a hand over her mouth and looks up at me, then back at the puppy.

"It's one of Elizabeth's Spoodles," I explain. "He's Gus's baby."

She keeps her hand there, and her eyes glass over. "He's beautiful!" she squeaks. "Is... is he mine?"

I smile. "Yes, he's yours. You can call him whatever you want—he doesn't have a name yet."

She sniffs. "How old is he?"

"Nine weeks. I've got all the stuff for him—collar and bed and that kind of thing. Jamie's left it outside."

"Oh, Mack." She finally lowers her hand and picks the puppy up out of the box. "He's so beautiful."

The puppy snuffles and tries to bite her finger, and she laughs and hugs it. Then she shows him to Gus as I finally let him free. "Look, Gus, it's your little boy! Isn't he gorgeous?"

My throat tightens as I see her genuine delight. I can remember getting Gus and feeling like that. She told me she's always wanted a dog but had never been able to have one. I'm thrilled that she finally gets to have the experience.

And it's at that moment that she spots it, tied to the puppy's collar.

She frowns. Turns it to look at it. Stares at it. Then lifts her gaze to me.

Heart hammering, I lower onto one knee. "Sidnie Beecham," I say, and smile, "will you marry me?"

She blinks.

Then she bursts into tears.

"Not quite the reaction I expected," I say, a little nervously, sitting on the carpet next to her.

Still holding the puppy, she puts an arm around me and buries her face in my neck. I rub her back, smiling as Gus bends down with his backside in the air, tail wagging furiously, wanting to play. I stroke the puppy's ears, which are long with curly strawberry-blond hair. He's soft as silk and incredibly beautiful. Carefully, I untie the ring from his collar.

"Hey," I say eventually, when it looks as if her tears are finally drying up. "Are you okay?"

She wipes her face and nods.

I hold up the ring. "You haven't answered me yet."

She stares at it with wide eyes. "Is it a real diamond?"

"Of course it's a real diamond. Did you think I'd get you a fake one?"

"It's enormous."

"It's eight-point-seven carats." It also has tinier ones set in the side of the ring. It cost me three hundred thousand dollars, but I don't think I'll tell her that because she might faint.

She looks up at me with her big blue eyes, fringed with wet lashes. "You really want to marry me?"

"I do. Hence the ring."

"But we've only been living together for a month."

"That's true. Like I said, there's no rulebook. Is there an official length of time I need to wait?"

She gives me a wry look. "No, but… how can you be sure?"

I give her an exasperated look. Then I realize she's genuinely bemused. Even after everything I've said to her over the past few weeks, and all the amazing sex we've had, she honestly doesn't comprehend how I feel.

I lift her left hand to my lips and kiss her fingers. Time to put aside the jokes and teasing, and speak from my heart.

"I've never felt about anyone the way I feel about you. I'm madly in love with you, Sidnie. I think I fell in love with you the moment I walked past you in the building, when you were wearing your cleaning coveralls, with your crazy hair. That feeling has only intensified. You make me a better person. You've changed me so much for the better. You've enriched my life. I can't imagine ever being without you. I love you. And I want you to be my wife. I want you to wear my ring so every other guy who looks at you knows you belong to me. And yeah, I know that sounds prehistoric, but I don't care. You're mine, and I want to stand next to you in church, or on the beach, or anywhere else you'd rather do it, and, in front of our friends and family, promise to love you forever."

I stop, a little embarrassed at my outburst.

"Oh," she squeaks.

"Is that a yes?" I ask helplessly.

She smiles then, the most beautiful smile I've seen her give. "It's a yes."

Relief washes over me like a tsunami, so strong it takes my breath away. With a shaking hand, I push the ring onto her finger, where it catches the sunshine streaming through the window and glitters.

Then she lifts her face to me, and I kiss her, while the puppy wriggles between us, biting her hair and tugging it until we break apart with a laugh.

*

We take him up to the garden to explore, then carry him back down, and I collect all the stuff Jamie left and bring it inside. We put the tiny bed next to Gus's, and find a box to put the toys in that Elizabeth has kindly bought for him.

Finally, we sit back on the rug in the middle of the living room and watch him trying to bite Gus's tail as he runs around.

"Have you thought of a name yet?" I ask.

Sidnie nods. "Eddie."

"Oh…" I laugh. Eddie Osei-Nketia, Gus Nketia's son. "That's brilliant."

"It suits him, too. Doesn't it, Eddie?" She pulls him away from Gus and redirects him to chew the ears of a toy in the shape of a rabbit.

I smile and lean on the sofa, propping my head on my hand. "Jamie and Emma have said they'll happily look after him if you need to go out at all."

"Really? I was wondering what to do with him when I go to work."

I take a deep breath and sit up. "Actually, I wanted to talk to you about that. It's entirely up to you. I know you don't mind your job, and it's possible you might prefer to have your own money—I get that, absolutely. But I was wondering whether you'd like to give it up and write full time instead? I know it's probably going to take a while to make decent money from it, but the more you can write, presumably the quicker that will happen. And until then, if you don't mind being a kept woman..." I give her a mischievous smile.

Her jaw has dropped again. "Are you serious?"

"Yeah. I thought I could give you an allowance. Like, fifty bucks a week or something."

Her lips twist, and she pushes me.

"You'd have to complete certain tasks to earn that," I add.

"Tasks?"

"Sexual favors."

"Obviously."

I laugh and pull her into my arms. "Seriously, though, it'll probably be easier if we have a joint account. You can spend what you like then."

"Fucking hell, stop it. My brain's going to explode."

I chuckle and kiss her hair. "It's just an idea. I want you to have everything. I'm so impressed that you've written a book, and I want you to have the opportunity to write as much as you want and make a real go of it. The best thing about being wealthy is that it provides the chance to fulfil your dreams. I'd give that opportunity to everyone if I could. There's nothing worse than desperately wanting to do something and not having the money. Unfortunately I can't give it to everyone. But I can help you. So what do you think?"

"I think it sounds amazing," she whispers.

"But it's just an idea. I don't want you to think I'm looking for you to give up everything for me. I mean, that would be nice," I tease, "but..."

She kisses me. "I'd love the chance to write full time. I can't believe I'm this lucky, that's all."

I hold the toy rabbit while Eddie tugs its ear. "I was thinking, too, that I know I work long hours, and that might make the days long for you. So I thought that maybe you might like to come to work with me sometimes? We could put a desk in my office for you. Eddie and Gus would be able to play in the garden. We'd be able to have lunch together. Jamie will run you home when you've had enough." I purse my lips as she gives me a bemused look. "It's just an idea," I add awkwardly.

She cups my face with a hand and strokes my bristles—I haven't shaved yet today—with a thumb. "You're the most generous man I've ever met," she whispers. "I don't know what I've done to deserve you."

"Well, the sex is pretty good."

She smiles. "Apart from that."

"I told you, Sid. You've taught me so much. You've exorcized my ghosts, and you've made me a better man. I was cynical and suspicious of anyone who said love like this existed. I didn't believe in soul mates."

"Do you think that's what we are?"

I bend my head and kiss her. "Yes," I murmur. "Without a shadow of a doubt."

She lifts a hand to look at the ring that sparkles on her finger. "And you really want to marry me?"

"I do."

She lowers her hand and looks up into my eyes. "On one condition."

"What's that?"

"That you never stop talking dirty to me." Her eyes twinkle.

My lips slowly curve up, and then I grab her and tip her back onto the floor. She squeals and giggles, and then wraps her arms around my neck as I give her a long kiss.

Eddie tugs her hair, but she just laughs and continues to kiss me, and we stay there like that on the rug for a long time, while the dogs play around us, and her diamond ring sparkles in the February sun.

Newsletter

If you'd like to be informed when my next book is available,
you can sign up for my mailing list on my website,
http://www.serenitywoodsromance.com

About the Author

USA Today bestselling author Serenity Woods writes sexy contemporary romances, most of which are set in the sub-tropical Northland of New Zealand, where she lives with her wonderful husband.

Website: http://www.serenitywoodsromance.com
Facebook: http://www.facebook.com/serenitywoodsromance

Printed in Dunstable, United Kingdom